Anita Frank was born in Shropshire and studied English and American History at the University of East Anglia. She lives in Berkshire with her husband and three children and is now a full-time carer for her disabled son. This is her first novel.

THE
LOST ONES

Anita Frank

ONE PLACE. MANY STORIES

HQ
An imprint of HarperCollins*Publishers* Ltd
1 London Bridge Street
London SE1 9GF

This edition 2019

1

First published in Great Britain by
HQ, an imprint of HarperCollins*Publishers* Ltd 2019

ISBN:
HB: 9780008341220
TPB: 9780008341213

MIX
Paper from
responsible sources
FSC
www.fsc.org   FSC™ C007454

This book is produced from independently certified FSC™ paper to ensure responsible forest management.

For more information visit: www.harpercollins.co.uk/green

This book is set in 10.6/15.5 pt. Sabon

Printed and bound in Great Britain by
CPI Group (UK) Ltd, Croydon, CR0 4YY

For Rebecca

Chapter One

Sunday, 6th May 1917

The brass plaque, polished so it shone like burnished gold, was mounted pride of place on the chantry wall – a new, if unwelcome, addition to the village church. Our boxed family pew was situated directly opposite, and rather than crick my neck to observe the vicar intoning from his elevated position in the pulpit, I found myself captivated by the ornate inscription.

IN MEMORY

ROBERT RICHARDSON

2ND LIEUT, 3RD MILITIA BN, BERKSHIRE REGT
BELOVED ONLY SON OF MR AND MRS HENRY RICHARDSON
KILLED IN ACTUAL FIGHTING IN FRANCE, 2ND JULY 1916
AGED 18 YEARS

DUTY NOBLY DONE

I closed my eyes for a moment as I recalled the blissful summer of 1914: all baking heat and leisurely pleasures; a cricket match on the village green. I remembered a willowy school boy: a muss of ruffled blond hair, cheeks dimpled by an irrepressible grin, a streak of red down the thigh of his white flannels, a powerful run up, a perfect windmill arm, the satisfying clatter of stumps, a smatter of applause. They never found his body. His parents had been forced to settle for the plaque rather than a grave. He was just eighteen years old, a school-boy officer fresh from the fields of Eton.

As I read and re-read the words, my fingers strayed to the gold locket that hung against my black coat. It no longer gleamed, dulled as it was by too much caressing. I finally managed to tear my eyes away, but my gaze only strayed as far as the front pew, settling on the poor boy's parents. They sat shoulder to shoulder, rigid with grief. Mrs Richardson, once a charismatic, vibrant woman, had been greatly reduced by her son's death. Her plump and rosy cheeks were now sunk into hollows, giving her a cadaverous appearance, while her finely appointed mourning clothes sagged over her diminishing frame. I had no doubt she was aware of another mother, sitting just a few rows back. Mrs Whittaker's broad shoulders shook with misery, for her anguish was still fresh and raw. We three cast sombre shadows, stagnant pools of grief amidst the amassed congregation.

I returned my focus to the vicar's monotonous monologue purporting to the value of sacrifice, but it wasn't long before I found myself shifting irritably on the unforgiving pew. My experiences nursing in France with the Voluntary Aid Detachment had exposed faith as a fallacy. I had seen too much barbaric waste to still believe we were being guided by a higher purpose. The vicar's words now did little to change my opinion. Not for the first time that morning, I wished I hadn't come, but my parents had made it very clear that my weekly attendance at the Sunday service was an issue of duty, if not belief. My presence, it seemed, was not a matter for discussion.

I let out a soft sigh as I fidgeted again, my impatience and discomfort rising. The respectful attention the congregation afforded the vicar's words annoyed me. Apart from Old Man Withers, who at ninety-one was forgiven for nodding off during services, my fellow parishioners were focused on the pulpit. I was the only one in this aged church who had seen first-hand the unmitigated destruction of life. Perhaps it was a kindness to allow them their naivety, their conviction in the righteousness of this conflict. Let them be dedicated to their Holy War, to their God's will, but I could no longer share that dedication.

It appeared I was not the only member of the congregation struggling to endure the service. I spotted our young housemaid, Annie Burrows, crushed into the end of a pew occupied by our few remaining servants. Whilst the housekeeper, Mrs Scrivens, and our butler, Brown, along with a couple of maids, gave the vicar their rapt attention, Annie had become distracted by Mrs Whittaker's muted sobs. She wore a strange expression on her face as she watched the broken-hearted mother, one I was unable to decipher. She must have felt the weight of my scrutiny, for she twisted in her seat and locked gazes with me. Caught spying, I felt my cheeks blaze as I looked away.

It was, of course, a widely accepted opinion that there was something very odd about Annie Burrows. When I had returned from France, broken and debilitated by Gerald's death, her surprising presence at Haverton Hall had been one of very few things to elicit my interest. I learned that Mrs Burrows had approached my mother just a few months after I had left, in the autumn of 1914. Emaciated by the cancer that was devouring her, she had come seeking employment for her thirteen-year-old daughter. My mother had agreed at once – given the extent of our debt to their family it was, she told me later, the very least we could do.

It had not been a popular appointment amongst the rest of the staff, that I did know. Even Mrs Scrivens had asked my mother in no uncertain terms to reconsider. Annie had quirks of character that others found perturbing – peculiar distraction, incessant whispering, suspicious furtiveness. My mother, determined to honour her obligation, was unmoved by the housekeeper's appeal. As the war progressed and the household staff steadily depleted, Mrs Scrivens had little choice but to promote Annie to upstairs work, to which she applied herself with quiet diligence. Over time, the housekeeper's opinion improved, and Annie learnt to subdue some of her more unusual behaviours. Yet I still found there was something strangely unnerving about the young maid, an otherworldliness to her that I could never quite put my finger on.

Behind me someone attempted to stifle a coughing fit. The vicar finally drew his dreary sermon to a close, casting a stern look over his flock. Upstairs the ancient organ wheezed into life, and we rose as a single body, apparently rallied by words of faith. I opened the leather-bound hymn book, my gloved fingers fumbling through the flimsy pages until I had found the one required: 'God Is Working His Purpose Out'. I snorted.

Around me, voices blended – my own did not join them. I sensed rather than saw my mother's disapproving frown. I sneaked a glance down the aisle. Annie Burrows was staring into the open pages of her hymnal. She too was silent.

We remained standing to accept the vicar's parting blessing, before shuffling from our pews, filtering out into the aisle, queueing for the arched doorway to the rear. There was a murmur of polite conversation as neighbour greeted neighbour, but I chose to fix my eyes on the uneven flags beneath my feet.

When at last we reached the vicar, I hung back while Mother stepped forward to proffer her thanks and my father made some intelligent observations on the sermon. I skirted round them and ducked out into the porch, pressing through the mingling crowd, until I managed to free myself from the throng. I sidled down the path, averting my eyes from the freshly domed grave of Private Tom Whittaker, who had clung onto life long enough to make it home. A wreath of white roses had been laid upon the heaped earth and the tips of their petals were now beginning to brown and curl. I fought to quash a sense of envy that at least his family would be able to set fresh flowers down whenever they wished. A strip of ocean kept me from Gerald's graveside. It grieved me to think of his resting place languishing unadorned.

I hurried on, eager to leave the post-service conviviality behind me. Chippings crunched beneath my feet as I moved through the silent congregation of lichen-covered headstones, their platitudes faded, their inhabitants forgotten. I was not the only one to have disengaged from the churchgoers: Annie was crouched before a modest headstone lying in the shadow of the cemetery wall. I knew whose it was, for I had stood beside it myself a decade ago, paying my respects to her father.

Jim Burrows had died saving my little sister Lydia from the devastating fire that had engulfed Haverton Hall all those years ago. It had been deemed miraculous that he had succeeded in finding her when all other attempts had failed, lowering her to safety from an upstairs window before succumbing to the flames. In the end though, his sacrifice proved to be in vain: her smoke-charred lungs were so badly damaged she died a few weeks later, but we were always grateful for the precious extra time that his bravery had granted us. However devastating those days had been, as we watched her suffer each painful breath, they had afforded us the opportunity to hold her, kiss her, cherish her – to say our final goodbyes. Annie's father had been there one minute and gone the next, with barely a body left to bury. How much more difficult it must have been for Annie and her mother to come to terms with such abrupt loss. I often wondered about their regrets, the things they might have said, if they had had but a chance. Instead, all they had was a gravestone. I looked away as I passed by, affording Annie her privacy. It seemed we both sought comfort from the dead.

I broke off from the path and headed to the far side of the church. Our Marcham family mausoleum was Grecian in design, a mini-pantheon. Truth be told, it was far too grand for the size of the graveyard, towering disproportionately over the humble headstones that surrounded it. Its stone walls were weathered, blackened by rain and frost, and the paint was beginning to flake from the wrought iron gates that barred the door. I had seen those gates opened twice in my life: once when I was eight to witness my grandfather being laid to rest, and two years later, when poor Lydia had been entombed.

It had been built for my grandmother. I had never known her, but a magnificent portrait hung pride of place on the staircase and as a child I had been quite captivated by her magical radiance. Thinking of her now, it struck me how tragedy had stalked my family. She too had died well before her time, when my father was still a boy. My grandfather would never speak of her accident, but I remember the yearning sadness that dulled his eyes on those rare occasions her name was mentioned and how his grip would slacken on his ever-present Dublin pipe as she entered his thoughts. I never quizzed him, but I did summon the courage to ask my father about her, late one evening when he had come up to the nursery to bid me goodnight.

A keen horsewoman, she had been thrilled when my grandfather had presented her with a new hunter, but tragedy had struck on their very first outing. Skittish in unfamiliar countryside, the horse bolted and in a moment of madness, before my grandmother could regain its head, it took on an impossible fence. They tumbled to the ground together in a horrifying mêlée of flailing limbs and terrifying screams as my grandfather looked helplessly on. He carried her back to the hall as grooms tried to catch the traumatised horse, still stumbling about the field. In her last agony-laden hours, my grandmother made him promise not to punish the animal, a promise that was forgotten as the final breath slipped from her parted lips.

My father vividly recalled the harrowing cry that had sounded through the house, a feral keen of mourning. He remembered too the rage and the fury; my grandfather rampaging through the Hall, retrieving his shotgun from the gun room and his ominous journey to the stable block. My father had raced after him, fearful of the impending catastrophe, as the grooms cowered from my grandfather's path. Only Jim Burrows, then little more than a boy himself, had stood his ground, blockading the horse's stall.

No one knows what passed between them that day, but when at last my grandfather emerged, the gun broken over his arm, the cartridges in his hand, he was ashen. The hunter wasn't destroyed, but he was swiftly sold. From that moment on, my grandfather demonstrated an almost deferential respect for the young groom, and they could often be found in quiet conversation, despite their disparity in both age and position.

I always thought it strangely fitting it was Jim Burrows that plunged into the flames that night to save Lydia, though tragedy would result for both our families. It was as if the fates of the Marchams and the Burrows were inextricably entwined. And now some would say I owed Annie Burrows *my* life, but I chose not to dwell on that.

A large yew tree grew to the front of the mausoleum, below which stood a simple bench. The seat planks were split with age and still greasy from the overnight shower, but I drew my coat around me and sat down anyway, impervious to the damp. Perhaps it was macabre of me, but I always found great solace here, sitting in quiet contemplation of those who had passed: my grandmother, my grandfather, Lydia, and now Gerald.

My fingers were drawn once more to my locket. I fumbled with the intricate clasp, until it fell open into its two hinged ovals. I had no interest in the image captured in the right-hand side, a representation of myself I no longer recognised – youthful, optimistic . . . happy. Instead, I focused my attention on the pale photograph contained in the left. It was a studio portrait, at first glance stiff and formal, but if you looked closely, as I always did, you could see in the eyes a glint of humour, bright enough to shine through the shadow cast by the peaked officer's cap, and the neat moustache failed to conceal an upward curl of the mouth that hinted at suppressed laughter. I felt the familiar ache in my chest and snapped the locket shut, wiping at the warm trickle in my nose.

'I saw her come this way. She has taken to sitting under the yew tree when she's here.'

'And how has she been?'

I jumped to my feet. The pompous tones of Dr Mayhew had

every inch of my body preparing for flight. I had the advantage – whilst I could hear their approach, neither he nor my mother could yet see me. My pulse quickened as I darted out of sight down the far side of the mausoleum, pressing my body against the cold stone, the long, wet grass licking at my stockinged ankles. Closing my eyes, I held my breath. The rim of my hat butted against the stone.

'Oh!' Close now, my mother sounded perplexed. 'I'm sure I saw her come this way.'

'Perhaps she's made her way round the church to the front. No matter. I think I should come and see her again though.'

'Oh yes, I do wish you would, Doctor. She's still not at all herself, you know. I am so afraid she might do something silly again, indeed' – her tone lowered – 'I have good reason to suspect it.'

'Now that would be a very worrying development.' His voice was grave, and I could just picture him rocking on his heels, his fingers interlocked behind his back, his chest puffed out with characteristic self-importance. 'I had hoped after all this time we were beginning to see some signs of improvement. Look,' he let out a long, exasperated sigh, 'I'll pop by and see her. Perhaps we can talk more then.'

I waited in my hiding place, suspicious they might be faking silence as a lure – I'd been caught out by that trick before, but I was more cautious now. Minutes passed. My toes began to ache from the penetrating cold. At last I opened my eyes.

Annie Burrows stood not more than a few feet in front of me. Her eyes were the most extraordinary shade of blue – violet almost, a peculiar, unnatural shade – set too close to the narrow bridge of her nose, giving the impression she was cross-eyed, though closer inspection revealed this was not the case. Unsettling, all the same.

'They've gone.'

She paused, waiting to see her words register, before turning and walking away across the grass. Bewildered, I withdrew from the shadow of the mausoleum to watch the young maid disappear through the lychgate. A single magpie flew out from the branches of the yew and landed on the path before me, its sleek black plumage glinting in the weak morning light that was only now beginning to penetrate the cloud. He strutted on his spindly legs, his head tilted as he fixed me with his calculating eye.

'One for sorrow,' I murmured as I dropped down upon the bench succumbing to a wave of desperate misery that quite threatened to overwhelm me. 'Oh, Gerald.' His name escaped me as a mournful whisper. I sought comfort from a happy memory: a warm July day before the war, a picnic. I could recall the moment in clear detail: the burbling brook, a tartan blanket, bitter ginger ale – tangy relief to our parched throats – and the brush of Gerald's arm against mine as we bathed in the sunshine. It had been a perfect afternoon. I could even hear our laughter, hear his voice. Every tiny facet of the day was crystal-line, everything, that is, but Gerald's face. That precious part of the picture proved frustratingly elusive. When I tried to focus on it, I found it clouded – blurred and vague. My heart ached.

What I had always feared was coming to pass: I was beginning to forget him.

Chapter Two

For a long while after Gerald's death, I feared I had surrendered my sanity to grief – in the early days, I had certainly surrendered my will to live. For the first day or so after it happened, Matron, a stern Welsh woman with a reputation for brooking no nonsense, had been surprisingly indulgent and understanding. I lay immobile in my bed, unable to eat, unable to sleep, unable, even, to weep. My fellow VAD nurses spoke in hushed almost reverential whispers as they moved around our tent, eager not to disturb me. Their sympathy was as tangible as their relief that the tragedy had not been theirs.

When I showed no signs of improvement, Matron had suggested a trip home might sort me out, but as my stupor spread from a few days into a week, her tone became more strident, her patience wearing thin, until a sojourn at home was not a suggestion but an order. The girls packed my things for me. I think we all understood I would not be coming back.

I can't remember much of the journey from the continent, I had lost all interest in life by then. I do remember standing at the ship's rail as she rolled across the churning grey Channel. I remember holding onto the rain-soaked railing and thinking how slippery it was beneath my freezing fingers. I rested my booted foot on the bottom rung, staring at the heaving waves as they crashed against the hull. My head dropped towards my chest as I strained to hear the siren's call enticing me from beneath the surging waves, the spray spitting in my face with contemptuous disregard for my suffering.

The ship listed and I stumbled sideways. An officer caught my arm and steadied me, his face half concealed by a bandage. He shouted over the roar of the waves that it might be best if we go back in, and I offered no resistance as he took my elbow and guided me through the iron door. He said something to a nurse inside, something I couldn't hear, and she came to me as he disappeared down the stairs, his heavy boots clanking against the steel grated steps to the lower deck. Her face softened when she saw my blank expression. She led me back to my quarters and put me to bed, tucking the blankets about me so tightly I could barely breathe. Perhaps she thought they might hinder any further attempts at wandering.

My mother met me off the boat when it docked. Our elderly chauffeur had driven her down, all the way to Portsmouth – goodness knows where they got the petrol. I remember being startled by the juxtaposition of our shining motorcar next to the unloading detritus of war: the gravely wounded on stretchers, the shattered bodies and blood-soaked bandages. The same nurse escorted me off, her arm firm around my back as she helped me down the gangplank, one faltering step after another.

She said something to my mother as she handed me over, but her words escaped me – lost amongst the shouts and the moans, the slamming of ambulance doors and the whine of engines. I was becoming accustomed by that time to people discussing me as if I wasn't there. It was to continue for weeks after I returned – Dr Mayhew shut away with my parents. I was too numb to feel any resentment. I would get better eventually, everyone assured me in cheery voices dripping with insincerity and trimmed with doubt. I was not to be left alone, Dr Mayhew had advised. Close supervision was required for someone plunging to such perilous depths. Home, he warned, might not be a suitable environment. Options had been discussed.

And then my dear sister Madeleine had arrived, bringing quiet compassion, sympathy and understanding. Gradually, the edges of the yawning cavity left by Gerald's death began to contract. The emptiness receded, little by little, though it never vanished. I was at least able to rise from my bed, eat, think and occasionally I even managed a wan smile, just for a moment, until I remembered again. It was, Madeleine assured me, the beginning of my recovery and I was to force myself towards it, like an exhausted mountaineer with the pinnacle in sight, because the alternative was too awful to consider.

It was proving to be a long and arduous climb. There were still some who anticipated my fall.

I was late to rise, following yet another disturbed night, but I found I could get away with being a lie-abed these days. I had few pressures on my time, and Mother went to great lengths to ensure I wasn't taxed in any way.

Having availed myself of the pitcher and basin on the washstand, I dressed without fuss, drifting towards the draped windows as I fastened my locket about my neck. Once done, I reached up and thrust apart the heavy curtains, blinking against the sunlight that flooded the room.

Annie Burrows appeared below me, carrying a pail of ash towards the flowerbeds, her ginger hair vibrant in the morning sun. The cinders would be scattered to enrich the soil, but it was not the performance of this daily chore that drew my attention – it was Annie's extraordinary behaviour.

She was talking to herself in a most animated manner, gesticulating with her free hand before breaking into smiles – in an odd way she looked almost radiant. With anyone else, it might have been amusing – charming even – to see them so caught up in their own little world, but with Annie, the whole display was rather eerie.

She stopped. Her head shot round to fire at me a scowl so targeted I recoiled into the curtain folds, taken aback by the animus it appeared to contain. My heart beat faster and it felt like an age before I had the courage to peek out from behind the jacquard screen. She was gone; the garden was quite empty. Only my discomfort remained.

I had by this time missed breakfast, but I knew Mother would be taking tea in the morning room, and I resolved to join her there – a cup of tea would be just the ticket to restore my equanimity and set me up for the day.

As I started to make my way across the hall I caught sight of my reflection in the foxed glass of the mirror hanging above the fireplace and I drew up short. I backtracked to stand before it, my fingers straying to the pale blue cardigan I had donned – it looked incongruous against the heavy black of my dress.

The reintroduction of colour to my clothing was a very recent concession to my parents. They had, in truth, become embarrassed by my funereal attire. In their eyes my bereavement lacked legitimacy – Gerald and I had not been officially engaged, there had merely been an understanding between us. It seemed a sparkling ring and an announcement in *The*

Times were needed to validate my grief – as it was, they considered eight months shrouded in deep mourning quite long enough.

I had been a melancholic shadow in the house for so long that I found it curious to catch sight of myself now sporting this dash of the unfamiliar. I was a dull duckling learning to embrace its decorative adult feathers – soon I would be transformed beyond all recognition.

I moved away from the mirror and walked on. Gerald was gone. A piece of clothing changed only how I looked, not how I felt – I would learn to skirt the gloom in colourful attire, just as I was learning to indulge my suffering in private.

The morning-room door opened as I approached, and Annie emerged with a large wooden tray hanging from her hand, which knocked against her calf as she closed the door behind her. She started when she saw me, belatedly curtsying before stepping to the side to allow me to pass. She revealed no hint of our earlier episode. I paid her little heed as I reached for the door handle.

'Dr Mayhew.'

I jerked my fingers back from the ribbed brass as if it had burnt me.

Her gaze climbed to my face. 'He's in there, with your mother, miss.'

I was grateful for, if surprised by, the warning. Dr Mayhew had grown impatient of my grief – in his eyes it had morphed into something else, something that did not deserve sympathy or delicacy. In his opinion, I was showing signs of hysteria – that peculiarly female affliction he found so intolerable and which required a firm hand, cold baths and country retreats – a euphemism, I soon learnt, for asylums catering to the more genteel lady. He would have had me suitably incarcerated on my return from France, but Madeleine intervened on my behalf, persuading my parents that time was all I really needed. In the end, my parents relented, but Dr Mayhew continued to prowl in the wings, unconvinced by my paper-thin performance of improvement, constantly critiquing, whittling away my parents' confidence, ever hopeful of vindication.

I contemplated the best course of action. If I returned to my room I would be doing little more than delaying the inevitable: I would either receive a summons, or – even worse – they would come and find me. I looked at Annie.

'Come and get me in five minutes,' I instructed, 'say there's a telephone call for me. You can say it's my sister.'

I couldn't tell whether she was regarding me with compassion or contempt and to my irritation I felt myself flush. She dipped her head in assent, and with a strategy in place, I reached again for the door handle.

Dr Mayhew stood up the moment I entered, the dainty cup and saucer with its pattern of entwined pink roses looking faintly absurd in his meaty grasp. He had been the village doctor for as long as I could remember, but I had never taken to the man. He had the habit of walking into a room and demanding its deference – such pomposity did not sit well with me and never had. He had not aged well, it had to be said. Flabby jowls folded over the starched collar of his shirt, and the red thread veins in his cheeks and a bulbous, purple-mottled nose confirmed popular suspicions he was rather too fond of his drink. His hair, once thick and black, was now thin and grey, a few lank strands draped over his sharply domed head, though his thick mutton chops still flourished and seemed to offer some balance to his generous girth.

'Here she is, the young lady herself. How is our patient this morning?'

I smiled, but only because it was expected of me. It grated that he still saw fit to refer to me in this way, as if I was ill and always would be. I was not ill. I was grieving.

'I am quite well, thank you, Doctor,' I said, greeting my mother before attending to the tea things laid out upon the sideboard.

'No more nightmares?'

I put down the teapot, pushing away the images that had plagued my sleep. 'None at all.'

'So, the medication is working then?'

I thought of the untouched bottle of pills tucked away in my dressing table drawer. I turned back to face him, my teacup in hand. 'It appears so.' I smiled over the rim and took a deep gulp of the lukewarm liquid.

His studied me, inscrutable. I knew I mustn't flinch – an inadvertent tremor of my hand, a quiver in my voice, any nervous darting of the eyes and he would have me locked up before the day was out. I took another sip of tea, and with a steady hand, rested my cup back into the saucer.

Mother hadn't moved from her chair. She was staring into the fire, her lips pursed. She was finally roused by the quiet tap at the door and Annie bobbing into the room.

'Mrs Brightwell is on the telephone for you, miss.'

She held my gaze for a beat longer than necessary, leaving me to suspect she resented her part in the duplicity, but I was unconcerned. I had achieved my aim: my escape was secured.

'Oh! Madeleine? I'd better come straight away.' I contrived a look of polite – if not sincere – disappointment and took a final, hasty gulp of tea. 'Goodbye, Dr Mayhew.'

I didn't shut the door fully behind me. I indicated my gratitude to Annie with a curt nod which she acknowledged before returning to her legitimate chores. I, however, loitered.

'How is she really?' Dr Mayhew asked.

'She was caught at the lake again, the other evening.'

I hadn't realised my mother knew.

'With intent?'

'Annie saw her going and followed her down. She brought her back before she had the chance to . . .' She didn't need to finish – we all knew what happened last time.

'Well, I must say, that is most disappointing to hear. I thought she was making better progress – she's seemed a little more collected of late.' He let the dread sink into my poor mother before making a half-hearted attempt to reassure her. 'Well now, we shouldn't leap to the worst of conclusions every time. Perhaps it was nothing more than an innocent walk that took her that way – it is a beautiful spot after all, and nothing did happen – but we must also . . .' He left a meaningful pause. 'As you well know, my dear Mrs Marcham, there are a lot of women mourning in this country today. The majority will no doubt overcome their grief in time, but the added trauma of what Stella went through – it might be she never recovers from it.'

'Then what should we do, Doctor? God knows I can't lose another daughter.'

'The medication should help – if she takes it.'

'She says she is, but if she's not?'

'Then maybe we should revisit the idea of a short break away.'

I recoiled from the doorway, a bile of fury rising up inside me. I would never agree to it. I would not be incarcerated simply for feeling a natural human emotion.

The concept was insane – but I most certainly was not.

Chapter Three

I slammed my bedroom door and retrieved my secret stash of cigarettes from underneath the wardrobe. Kneeling on the grate of my fireplace, I tapped one from the packet, dangling it from my bottom lip as I rasped a match across the rough strip on the matchbox. I held the flame to its tip and drew in, a deep shuddering breath, before blowing the smoke up the chimney. Mother didn't know I smoked and would certainly not approve. It was a habit I had picked up early on in my VAD career, while serving at the 1st General in London. Another nurse had advised it after a horrendous shift. She promised me it calmed the nerves.

I leant against the blue Delft tiling of the fire's surround, with their quaint images of windmills and fishermen, and felt my tension begin to ease. I closed my eyes, fatigue dampening my fury.

I was alarmed to hear a gentle knock at the door, but I reasoned it would not be my mother or Dr Mayhew. Annie cracked it open, a linen basket balanced on her narrow hip.

'I have a few things to put away, miss.'

I took another drag on my cigarette before gesturing her in. I held the smoke in my mouth then let it slip like silk into my lungs. Stubbing the butt out on the charred stone of the grate, I scrabbled to my feet, batting the air with my hand to dissipate the lingering taint. Annie began filling the drawers of the tallboy.

I drifted towards the window intending to lift the sash for some fresh air, but I saw Dr Mayhew below, engaged in parting pleasantries with my mother, so I left the window shut. I had no desire to draw attention to myself.

'I take it you're not an admirer of Dr Mayhew either,' I said with idle curiosity.

'Not really, miss.'

'Any particular reason?' I turned my back on the window, resting my bottom on the sill.

'He's always pegged me as a troublemaker.'

'Oh?' I was only mildly interested and made no effort to press her when she didn't respond. She carried on placing the folded clothing within the drawers as if I'd never spoken. The carriage clock on the mantelpiece chimed the hour.

'Mother knows about you finding me the other evening.' I left the unspoken accusation suspended in the air, a gossamer thread connecting us. I had not requested her confidence, but I had rather taken it for granted she would remain mum.

She made no attempt to face me. 'Mrs Scrivens caught me going back to my room. She thought I had been engaged in some . . . assignation. I had no choice but to tell her.'

'I wasn't going to do anything silly.' I recalled curling my toes over the rough edge of the jetty and the inviting oblivion awaiting me below the dark surface. 'I just . . .' I turned to rest my forehead against the cool glass, flimsy under the pressure. I watched Dr Mayhew's car pull away. What was the point? How could I make anyone understand that somehow on the jetty I still felt close to Gerald? It was the one place where I didn't feel the terror of him slipping away. Standing there, if I closed my eyes and focused, I could almost feel the warmth of that late August sunshine on my cheeks and sense his solid presence beside me. I could almost hear those magical words 'marry me' and feel that explosion of joy again. Who could blame me for searching out a crumb of happiness amongst this feast of misery?

Annie shunted the drawer to. 'Dr Mayhew . . . There are things he doesn't understand.'

'He seems to understand very little about grief.' I made no attempt to conceal my bitterness.

'Which is something we both know all too well, miss.'

I looked at her. I could only speculate as to what damage might lie beneath her carefully crafted façade. She had lost everyone dear to her. Jim Burrows had died to save his master's daughter, condemning his own child to a life without the love and security of a father. How had that made her feel? Less valued? And then her poor mother, left to bear the burden alone – it was a tribute to her they had remained free of the workhouse. I could only imagine what deprivations they had been forced to endure. Perhaps, then, it was not so surprising Annie was odd and aloof – her world had been ripped apart at such a tender age and for what? Lydia had died anyway. Sometimes I wondered how she could bear to be around us. Perhaps she couldn't.

She dipped a curtsy and made to leave, but before she could close the door behind her my mother appeared, sweeping in as Annie slipped out. Feeling petulant, I turned away.

'Have you been smoking in here?'

'I don't smoke, Mother.'

'Don't treat me like a fool, Stella!'

She bustled over to my nightstand and pulled open the

shallow top drawer, its brass handle rattling with the violence of her action. She began rifling through the contents.

'What are you doing?'

'Where are they? The pills Dr Mayhew gave you?'

'Why do you want them?'

She held out her hand. 'Give them to me, Stella.'

With rising ire, I yanked open a drawer in my dressing table. I snatched out the small brown bottle and slammed it into her palm.

'There!'

She held it between her forefinger and thumb and raised it to eye level. 'Untouched,' she observed.

'I don't want his pills, Mother. I don't need them.'

'These pills are to help you.'

'These pills, Mother, are to sedate me. I can't be any trouble if I'm not capable of functioning.'

'They are to help you cope.'

'I won't take them. I simply won't. I don't want to be numb. I want to feel – I need to feel.'

'Sometimes we feel too much.'

'That is better than feeling nothing at all! You can't just wave a magic wand and make me forget everything – make me better. You heard Mayhew. I might never recover.'

'Oh!' Mother threw up her hands in disgust. 'Listening at doors now are we, Stella? Is that what you have been reduced to?'

'With the two of you conspiring to put me away, I will indeed listen at doors. At least then I know what you're planning.'

'Oh, Stella.' She collapsed on the end of my bed, her shoulders sagging as the fight deserted her. She tapped the bottle, the pills rattling against the glass like a maraca. 'I don't want you to be "put away", Stella, but neither do I want to lose you. I've already buried Lydia, I cannot bear to give up another child.' Her face creased with pain, and she suddenly looked so aged and worn that I was rather shocked. It was like coming across an old doll, fondly remembered as young and beautiful, but finding it had become ragged and chipped from too much play. Pain numbed her eyes as she looked at me. 'I do understand what you are going through. I know you think I don't. But I do know loss, Stella, I know the pain it brings.'

Of course, she knew loss, I could never deny that, though I resented her belief that Lydia's death affected her most of all. She would tearfully declare that she had lost a *part* of herself, whereas, in her view at least, Madeleine and I had only lost a companion. But Lydia was so much more than that. She was our constant shadow, our extra limb, she was our clown when we were in the doldrums and our willing scapegoat whenever were in trouble, always confident her angelic sweetness would deffuse our parents' anger. She was our sister and if not a physical part of ourselves, she was a precious, irreplaceable feature of our very existence and even now we carried her in our hearts, always.

I had never quite forgiven my mother for withdrawing from us the way she did, wallowing in her own grief whilst almost ignoring ours. But with the loss of Gerald, I had perhaps come to understand her more, her apparent selfishness, for I was convinced no one else could possibly be suffering as I was. My grief for Gerald was not indulgent, it was all-consuming, and its intensity seemed to validate the love I had always felt for him. He was my future, but when he died, that very future was taken from me. I now had to consider that Lydia's death might have left my mother feeling the same way.

'I'm not going to do anything silly again,' I said at last.

'Promise me?'

I forced a smile and sat down beside her, our shoulders brushing. I took the bottle from her hand and tossed it into the grate. It clattered onto the tiles of the hearth. 'I refuse to take the pills, but I promise, I won't do anything to hurt myself. I couldn't do that to you.'

She nodded, her innate dignity struggling with overwhelming emotion. She took my hand.

'Good,' she said, issuing a gentle squeeze before relinquishing her hold as she stood up. She patted my shoulder and took her leave, but she paused in the doorway.

'It will ease, Stella – your sadness. You will learn to live with it. We all learn to carry on in the end.'

I sat quietly once she had gone. It was my fault, of course, that she lived on her nerves, so readily entertaining her worst fears, her greatest nightmare. I had to acknowledge my culpability.

I had not been home a week when Annie Burrows dragged me from the lake. I'd managed to escape my mother's watchful eye and I knew exactly what I wanted to do with the precious moments her distraction had afforded me. I walked out, setting a steady but unhurried pace, straight to the lake, striding with intent down the wooden jetty, my footsteps echoing on the boards, the water gently lapping below. I paused for a moment when I reached the end, briefly allowing myself the succour of my most cherished memory, before I stepped out into thin air. The freezing cold of the dark waters as they closed over my head was shocking. Yet as I sank lower, threads of pondweed tickling my legs as my skirts billowed about my waist, I made a conscious decision not to struggle, not to kick towards the silvery light diffused across the surface now far above my head. In that moment, I experienced peace the like of which I hadn't felt for weeks. I relaxed into the lake's watery embrace, which was no longer frigid and frightening, but warm and consoling. I was not afraid. I think I was relieved.

Swallowed by my watery tomb, I did not hear the splash of Annie Burrows leaping into the lake beside me. It wasn't until I felt urgent fingers clutch at my waterlogged clothing that I realised I was no longer alone. As I was hauled round her face appeared before me, glowing like a moon in the midnight sky. I fought against her, trying to prise myself loose from her iron grip, lashing out with my feet, bubbles rippling from my mouth, but she was surprisingly strong and stubborn. She wrapped her arm around my chest, ignoring my clawing fingers, and powered herself upwards with such force we both exploded through the glassy surface, instinctively gasping for air. I cried in fury as she dragged me towards the edge, our boots slipping in the silty bottom. She grunted with effort as she wrenched me up onto the bank. I sobbed with frustration as we lay on our backs, exhausted and soaked to the skin, our hair streaked across our faces, breathless, staring at the leaden sky above us.

She spat out sour water and wiped her mouth on the back of her hand, her chest still heaving. People came running towards us, shouting in alarm: my mother, my father, Mrs Scrivens, Brown, a gardener. Mother was wailing. We were both hoisted to our feet. Someone began pulling at my wet things; a jacket was draped around my shoulders. Amidst the flurry and fuss,

Annie stumbled towards me, thrusting her dripping face into mine the second before she was tugged away.

The young maid's words became lost in the jumble of voices as we were bundled towards the house. Later, when I was finally left alone and had time to ponder the evening's events, I separated them from the cacophony. They sent a shiver down my spine.

'He says it's not your time.'

Chapter Four

I couldn't fail to notice that even the gardens were suffering from the detrimental effects of the war. The box hedges would have been scissor-cut to precision just a few years ago, but now, neglected, unkempt shoots were spurting out in all directions, and dandelions were thrusting up through the gravel pathways.

A stone in my shoe caused me to pause by the fountain. Though once it had shot plumes of water high into the air in a magnificent display, it now sat dormant, with only a murky pool in its wide basin. I steadied myself against its crumbling edge while I unbuttoned my shoe and shook loose the chipping.

I looked up at my home and felt, as always, a familiar tinge of sadness. Once it had been a perfect example of Palladian architecture, the main house being three storeys high, with two-storey additions stretching out on either side in perfect symmetry, all elegantly dressed in golden Bath stone. But now it stood uneven, oddly unbalanced, with no vestiges remaining of the destroyed east wing. The charred shell left from the inferno had been like a leper's appendage, blackened and dead, its windows empty sockets, its walls stripped of grandeur like flayed bone. I could still recall the acrid taint of smoke lingering in the air the morning after, as firemen continued to damp down persistent embers, their hoses running like veins across the lawn, drawing from the lake. My father and I had visited the bereft

Burrows family, to express our sympathies and gratitude, and on our return we had stopped to observe the firemen's efforts, soberly aware that within those blistered walls, amongst the rubble and detritus, were Jim Burrows' remains.

The ruins were soon demolished for no one wanted an enduring reminder of the tragedy, but the red bricks used to seal the gaping wound stood stark against the buttery stone of the remaining house, like a scar that fails to fade.

I slipped my shoe back on and continued to the house, wishing I had not allowed my mind to stray onto such unhappy recollections. I did not like to dwell on the night of the fire; doing so evoked upsetting memories and raised disturbing questions that I had spent the last ten years doing my best to ignore.

I entered by the door that led into the rear hallway and began stripping the gloves from my hands. I could hear muffled voices as I approached the drawing room and realised Mother must be entertaining. I had no wish to be embroiled in one of her tedious meetings, so I kept my head down and picked up my pace as I passed the open doorway, but all to no avail.

'Oh, there she is. Stella!'

I made no attempt to stifle my exasperated sigh. I spun on my heel and headed towards the door. I stopped in the opening.

A tall man in uniform stood with his back to me, his brown hair neatly clipped to his nape, while Mother stood facing me.

'Look who has come to see us!'

For a split foolish second, I felt a burst of unimagined joy: Gerald – it had all been a terrible mistake! A rapturous smile pulled my lips and my heart leapt, but as the officer turned to face me, the smile dissipated, and my effervescent joy stilled, as reality reasserted itself.

'Hector. How lovely to see you.'

My brother-in-law, Hector Brightwell, smiled broadly and manoeuvred himself from behind the sofa to greet me. He held the tops of my arms as he kissed my cheeks. 'Hello, Stella.'

'I was beginning to worry that you wouldn't be back in time to say hello,' Mother said.

'I'm sorry, I didn't realise you were expected.' My absurd disappointment began to fade.

'Oh, I called by on the off-chance. Work brought me this way and I thought I should pop in and see you all.'

Hector had by some good fortune – I suspect linked to his family's considerable fortune and influence – secured a safe *uniformed* position in Whitehall for the duration. I tried not to resent him for this, something I found especially difficult after Gerald was killed. I did not dislike him – he was intelligent and affable, though a little stiff at times – and I could not fault his devotion to my sister.

'Well, it's very nice to see you, Hector. How is Madeleine?'

My sister had telephoned a few weeks previously to give us the most welcome news: she was expecting a baby. It had been the first time since Gerald's death that I felt actual happiness. Madeleine was cautiously buoyant, tempering her excitement with the acknowledgement it was still early days, but ever the pragmatist, at three months along she knew she would soon be showing so felt we ought to know.

'She is well, thank you, very well.' Hector retook his seat whilst I settled myself down and Mother poured out some more tea. 'She may have told you, she's gone to stay with my mother at our country estate, Greyswick.'

'Oh yes, she mentioned that in her last letter. The Zeppelin attacks on London must be terrifying.'

'I know they can be a bit hit and miss, but quite frankly I would rather Madeleine wasn't anywhere near them, especially given the circumstances. And in all honesty, I'm unable to spend much time with her, what with things the way they are.'

'Of course. Well, I'm glad to know that she will be safe. It is all such a worry.' My mother paused. 'And she is *well*, Hector?'

'Quite, quite well,' he assured her with a gentle smile. 'She's doing wonderfully.'

He and my mother talked on, but for me Hector's presence had brought back memories that were bittersweet. The last time we had been at Haverton Hall together was the wedding. By some miracle Gerald and I had both managed to wangle leave, enabling us to attend together. In a way I wish it had been the last time I had seen him. Perhaps it would all be easier if I could remember him like that – handsome in his dress uniform, laughing, a glass of champagne in his hand, carefree in the sunshine. But we were to meet once more, in tragically different circumstances.

Hector's apologies as he rose to depart brought me back to the present.

'I'll have your driver bring the car round,' Mother said, tugging the thick bell-pull that hung by the fireplace. Hector crossed to her and bade her a fond farewell, but as he came towards me, running his cap through his fingers, he stopped.

'Would you walk me out, Stella?'

'Of course.' I set down my teacup, taken aback by the unexpected request.

We walked through the hallway together, Hector opening the large front door to allow me out onto the steps first. The sky had clouded over to an impenetrable white layer. Looking up,

I could see the gauzy glow of the sun trapped behind it. A stiff wind cut through my clothing, and I hoped he wasn't going to keep me outside for long.

'I didn't just happen by today. I very much wanted to speak to you,' he admitted.

'Oh?'

He pulled the peak of his cap down low over his brow. 'It'll take my driver a while – shall we walk?'

We crossed the gravel driveway and ambled over the lawn at the front. In the distance the lake stretched across the horizon, the wind rippling its surface. I noticed that Hector drew to a stop before we got too near, perhaps fearing its appeal might prove irresistible to me.

'I've actually come to ask you a favour.'

'A favour?' I failed to mask my surprise. He might be my brother-in-law, but Hector was almost a stranger to me. I was already stationed in France when he met Madeleine at a fund-raising event in town. He was someone I read about in letters – a one-dimensional creation, a list of descriptive words. I met him for the first time at the wedding, when, selfishly perhaps, I was more intent on spending precious time with Gerald than with my new brother-in-law and the pompous entourage he brought with him. Since my return I had only seen him a handful of times, all brief encounters, where pleasantries were exchanged but little familiarity gained. But now he had come for the sole purpose of exacting a favour from me.

'I was wondering whether you might consider visiting with Madeleine for a while – at Greyswick.'

It was hardly an onerous request. Nothing would give me greater pleasure than to visit my sister, and no doubt we would have come to the arrangement ourselves in a few weeks. I hadn't seen her now for a couple of months and I missed her company and support, but I was alerted by the undercurrent I detected in the question.

'Hector, of course I will. Is everything all right?'

His eyes pinched as he focused on the skyline. I realised I was holding my breath, waiting for him to break the silence.

'I'm worried about her.'

'Why?'

He seemed loath to answer. He pulled his cap from his head and raked his fingers through his neatly combed hair. I could tell he was biding his time, contemplating his response. I felt a spike of unease.

'She doesn't seem to be at all herself.' The words spilled from him. He stopped. I was impatient to hear more, my concern acute now; my fingers flexed as I resisted the urge to shake him. Sensing my rising agitation, he stumbled on. 'She's so quiet and withdrawn. Mother's constantly complaining about how jittery she seems, scared of her own reflection.' He let out a sharp breath. 'I think she's terrified something's going to happen – to the baby.'

I relaxed at once on hearing this, rather relieved. It was perfectly natural of course that Madeleine should be unsettled. She had always been the more sensitive of us two, the one more prone to worry, to fear the worst – ironic really, given the way things had turned out.

'Well, I'm sure that's to be expected. It's an anxious time for her – for any new mother – but I'm sure it'll all be fine.'

'Well, that's just it, it might not be.'

The reassuring smile I had mustered wilted under his grim countenance. 'Why shouldn't it be?'

33

'We've been here before, you see.' But it was clear to him that I didn't see at all. He sighed. 'Madeleine lost a baby, Stella.'

My stomach plummeted. 'When?'

'Just before you came back.'

We stood silent, the air heavy with the solemnity of this awful revelation. 'Why didn't she tell me?' I asked at last.

'You were – you were so unwell. It was early on . . . She didn't want to burden you – after all, nothing could be done.'

I brought my hand to my mouth. Dear, darling Madeleine! When I had arrived back, eviscerated by Gerald's loss, Madeleine had flown to my side like the golden angel she was – compassionate, non-judgemental. She became my rock, my constant, unflinching companion. She had stoically weathered my rages and vicious words, stroked my head as I broke down and sobbed, and read quietly beside my bed as I lay motionless with grief. At a time when I had little inclination to carry on, she never gave up on me; even as others began to lose their patience, she alone defended me. And yet through it all she must have been nursing a terrible anguish. She had prioritised my recovery over her own devastating loss.

'Oh, Hector, I'm so sorry.'

'These things happen.' He couldn't prevent the tell-tale break in his voice. He took a moment. 'It's just, now – she's not herself at all. I think she's terrified of it happening again. She dealt with it so bravely last time, but she was devastated, Stella, absolutely devastated. To be honest, I think looking after you is what got her through. It was a welcome distraction from her own pain.'

His words stung me. He flushed, realising how they could be misconstrued. To cover his embarrassment he fussed about, setting his cap straight on his head, before thrusting his hands into his trouser pockets and rocking on his heels, waiting for the clouded moment to pass.

'Madeleine never wanted to go to Greyswick.' He broke the silence, an apologetic glint in his dark eyes. 'I had to plead with her to go. Now she's there, I think she has little else to do but obsess on the worst. She keeps asking to come back to town, but I would never forgive myself if she got caught up in a raid. She's safe at Greyswick, but I think she would benefit enormously from some company.'

'She has your mother.' The words slipped out before I could stop them. Hector picked up on my sardonic tone and winced.

'As you are well aware, my mother is not the easiest woman to get on with.'

I had only met Lady Brightwell once, at the wedding, and once was quite enough. She was a dour, self-important woman who revelled in the glory of her husband's honorary knighthood. I could see that she would not make an empathetic companion.

'Look, I would just be ever so grateful if you could go and keep her company for a while, take her mind off things. What do you think?'

'Hector, nothing would give me greater pleasure than spending time with Madeleine, especially after what you've just told me.' His motorcar drew along the drive behind us.

'Please don't say anything about me asking you to go and stay. I don't think she'd appreciate my interference.'

'It'll be our secret. I'll telephone her this afternoon and chide her for not inviting me to visit. After all, I've never seen your country seat.'

He smiled. 'I think you'll like it, it's a wonderful spot.'

We reached the car. His driver leapt from the front and opened the rear door.

'Oh, one more thing – Mother is a stickler for protocol and she doesn't see why a little thing like a war should lead to a fall in standards, so she still runs the house as if nothing has changed. Like you, we've lost most of the servants. She has conceded to allowing a maid to serve at dinner, but she still insists on full evening dress and so on. If you were able to bring someone with you, to lighten the load of your visit a bit, that would be tremendous.'

I laughed. 'Well, I wouldn't want to be responsible for upsetting the smooth running of the household.'

He swept off his cap to kiss my cheek. 'Thank you, Stella. You will look after her for me, won't you?'

'After all she's done for me? It's the least I can do.'

I watched the car pull away, sensing this unexpected tête-à-tête had bridged a gap in our relationship and I was surprisingly touched that Hector had taken me into his confidence. Madeleine would not lose this baby, I was determined of that, and I would do everything in my power to help her through the pregnancy. I would be her rock, as she had been mine. The prospect of new life invigorated my soul and my heart lifted at the thought of seeing Madeleine again.

As I walked back towards the house I looked up to see Annie watching me from a first-floor window. For an uncomfortable moment I remained trapped in her steady gaze, until she slowly turned away, vanishing from view. My blossoming happiness was marred by a disconcerting thought. Try as I might, I could see no alternative.

There was only one expendable servant at Haverton Hall.

Annie Burrows would be coming with me.

Chapter Five

A few days later, I stood on the platform of a small country station, waiting with ill-masked impatience for Annie Burrows to emerge from the swirling steam with a porter and our luggage in tow.

As the train heaved away, a uniformed chauffeur appeared, and having ascertained my identity, he guided our caravan out to the cobbled front, where a gleaming Rolls Royce awaited us.

It was, the chauffeur informed us, but a short drive to Greyswick. The car purred down narrow country lanes, the high hedges banked with a thick lace ruff of cow parsley, until soon we reached the village of Wick – a sweet little place, boasting an assortment of stone cottages, bronzed with age and weighed down with thatched roofs. There was a blacksmith by the village pond, and beyond stood a square turreted church encircled by a low stone wall, a neat Queen Anne rectory beside it.

We soon glided from the village, the road plunging through a wood before breaking out into open farmland, the cultivated fields either side of us sprouting with green barley shoots, while a ridge of hills shouldered the horizon. Finally, two grey-brick lodges appeared set either side of a great archway, its wrought iron gates already opened for our arrival. A thrill of anticipation stirred in my belly as we skimmed up a long driveway lined with beech trees, last year's prickly cases still scattered about the bases of their slender trunks.

The parkland about us was pleasant enough, with a few clusters of ancient oaks and a magnificent cedar whose low-slung branches hovered just above the ground. Unlike our park, it was devoid of livestock, but then Brightwell had made his fortune from mining not farming. As the avenue of trees gave way to iron railings, I caught my first glimpse of a large grey edifice in the distance. Gradually its intriguing outline began to take shape until, at last, the driveway billowed out into a gravelled carriage sweep and Greyswick loomed above us.

My first impressions were not favourable. It had been set square on to the drive, designed to impress and perhaps even overawe those who approached, though it was blatantly apparent the house would have enjoyed a far better aspect had it been positioned more with aesthetics, rather than vanity, in mind.

The chauffeur opened my door and I shuffled out, taking a good look at the monstrosity before me. The house was an incoherent fusion of architectural styles. The gabling appeared faux-Jacobean, but the enclosed porch would have suited a Victorian church, while the mullioned windows, Gothic by design, clashed horribly with the ill-advised clock tower, which was itself reminiscent of a Venetian palazzo. The extensive roof line had been trimmed with an open balustrade, underneath which, I was rather startled to observe, leered a menagerie of gruesome gargoyles. The whole extraordinary effect was, I thought, appalling.

I had just concluded my rather devastating assessment when the front door was yanked open, and my name came squealing through the air. Madeleine charged down the steps in a most undignified manner and threw herself into my awaiting arms, knocking my hat quite askew.

We clung to each other, giggling like school girls. I relished being with my younger sister again – she was my superior in every way. Whereas I was argumentative, quick-tempered and cutting, she was charm and grace and kindness personified. She was also beautiful in that classic Grecian goddess way. Her golden tresses could be effortlessly curled and arranged, while my coarse brown muss had to be teased and heated and twisted to destruction – only to resemble an ill-formed bird's nest when done. And yet, despite her obvious advantages, I had never been jealous of her – I simply adored her. Undoubtedly, the fire had drawn us closer together. We came to depend on one another as never before, comforting each other as we mourned our sister. The tragedy made us appreciate from an early age that the sibling bond was a precious one, to be nurtured and cherished at every opportunity. We had never taken each other for granted from that moment on.

As I broke away, a cold vein of concern tempered my happiness. Studying her properly I was shocked to see the transformation in her. Always the personification of an English rose, the face before me now was deathly pale. Madeleine's skin was drawn tight over her high cheekbones; her eyes were sunken and shrouded with grey. She hardly resembled a young woman in the bloom of pregnancy, though the swelling about her girth reassured me all was still well.

'My dear,' I collected myself at last, 'you look so pale.'

A hint of colour crept across her hollowed cheeks. 'I have not been sleeping so well of late,' she admitted, 'but I am quite well.' She squeezed my hand. 'Oh, Stella, I am so glad you have come.' She made no attempt to hide the relief in her voice, but neither did she attempt to explain it. 'Now come in, you must be exhausted!'

Arm in arm we mounted the steps to the front door.

'I am so pleased to have you here,' she said again, drawing me still tighter to her side.

'I thought you might be finding life in the country strange after London.'

Her steps faltered. 'Yes . . . yes . . . it is a little strange here.'

We crossed an unlit vestibule, before passing through stately double doors into a grand hall. It was an impressive room, with dark wood panelling and a chequerboard floor of marble tiles, its ceiling intricately decorated with plaster mouldings. To my left and right broad archways supported by alabaster pillars acted as gateways to dark corridors beyond, while before me, spilling out across the floor, were the sweeping steps of a heavy oak staircase, its massive timbers carved with fruits and flowers. It wrapped itself around the back wall, gently ascending to the floor above, crossing below a magnificent stained-glass window that stretched upwards out of sight. This patchwork of glass was the only avenue for natural light to enter the hall, and the sun's penetrating rays cast a myriad of coloured shards upon the polished flight of stairs but failed to dispel the gloom that pooled at the edges of the room.

'Goodness,' I murmured, gazing about me.

Before Madeleine could comment we were startled by rustling from within the umbra. A woman materialised from the shadows, the full skirts of her stark black dress swishing as she drew near. I was struck by her unusual stature and sturdy build – and by the set of keys strung upon a gaoler's ring which hung from the belt about her thick waist.

Madeleine stepped closer to me.

'Mrs Henge.' There was an uncharacteristic tremor in her voice. 'This is my sister, Miss Marcham. Mrs Henge is the housekeeper here, Stella.'

'Welcome to Greyswick, Miss Marcham. I hope you will enjoy your stay.'

It was a low-pitched voice, staid and unobtrusive. Yet there was a perfunctory iciness to her demeanour that I found rather unnerving.

'Thank you, Mrs Henge. I'm sure I shall.'

'If there is anything you need, please do not hesitate to ask.' She marshalled her features into a contrived look of apology. 'We are, of course, short staffed, but I will endeavour to make sure that you have everything you need in as timely a fashion as possible.' There was something in her tone that conveyed the impression I was a personal inconvenience. I found myself prickling with indignation.

'I have brought my own maid with me, Mrs Henge. I trust, therefore, that my presence here will not prove too burdensome.'

She must have detected the underlying resentment in my clipped voice, for she responded with a subtle hike in one of her steely grey brows.

'Not at all, Miss Marcham.' Her eyes flickered over my shoulder and narrowed. 'Do I take it that this is your maid, miss?'

My heart sank with misgiving as I turned to follow her supercilious gaze. Annie Burrows stood silhouetted in the doorway behind us, staring at the imposing staircase rising majestically before her.

Chapter Six

'Maids don't usually enter by the front door, Annie,' I said, exasperated by her faux pas.

I was struck by how pale she looked, and hoped she wasn't ailing. She would become a burden if she fell ill, but I knew how easy it was to succumb to a chill in these cavernous houses. There was indeed a rather nippy draught blowing down the staircase. It had filtered through the fine weave of my blouse and my skin was bristling against it. For all its splendour, I suspected the intricate framework of the stained-glass window did little to keep invasive breezes at bay.

Stifling my irritation, I turned to the housekeeper. 'Please understand, Mrs Henge, Annie has never been away before. It seems she's rather overwhelmed.'

'Good staff these days are proving difficult to find, Miss Marcham,' Mrs Henge observed, before issuing Annie brusque instructions to go below stairs via the green baize door located in the far corner of the hall.

The maid dipped a curtsy. I saw her sneak a further glance at the staircase as she scuttled away.

'I'll make sure the girl settles in, miss – without delay,' the housekeeper assured me in a rather forbidding manner.

'Mrs Henge, might we have some tea brought to the drawing

room?' Madeleine asked, bringing a welcome conclusion to the awkward episode.

'Of course, Mrs Brightwell. I shall have Maisie bring it directly.' With a curt dip of her head, the housekeeper melded back into the shadows. We heard the baize door close behind her.

'Did you have to bring that girl here?'

Madeleine's quiet question took me by surprise.

'Annie is one of the few servants we have left,' I laughed. To my consternation, she looked away, biting her lip. 'There was no one else, Madeleine. God knows she would not be my first choice, but all the others have gone.'

She mustered a smile. 'No matter . . . it's just . . .' She shook her head, mocking her own foolishness. 'It really doesn't matter, I'm being silly. She's such a bit peculiar, that's all.'

'Your Mrs Henge seems like an old stalwart – I'm sure she'll brook no nonsense. You watch, she'll keep Annie in line.'

She forced a laugh. 'Mrs Henge has been with the family for so long she's practically part of the furniture.'

'I didn't even see her standing in the shadows there when we came in. She gave me quite a fright.'

'There are lots of shadows in Greyswick. Mrs Henge seems to occupy most of them.'

To my relief, she shrugged off her odd humour and returned to sorts, taking my hand to lead me under the left arch into the panelled corridor beyond. Doors were set opposite each other along its length, and at the end was a single sash window. There was something bleak and institutional about the design of the house and its failure to incorporate much natural light. I found the enclosed corridor dismal and claustrophobic, and I felt I was navigating the bowels of the building, not the communication passage to its principal rooms.

But it was the tasteless opulence of the salon Madeleine ushered me into that shocked me the most. My jaw gaped in horrified wonder at the gaudy wallpaper and the vast, over-stated swags of material draped around the French windows lining the outside wall. Gilt-legged sofas flanked the monstrous marble fireplace, while Chinoiserie cabinets stood like exotic guards either side of the doorway, with even more oriental pieces gamely distributed about the room. It was a far cry from the tired but gentle splendour that reigned at home. At least, I found myself ruefully appreciating, it was light.

'Goodness,' I muttered.

'Oh, I know, it's hideously crass, isn't it? It's all right, Lady Brightwell and Miss Scott are out visiting. We are free to say what we want.' Madeleine dropped down onto one of the uninviting sofas, indicating for me to join her. 'Hector's parents were rather nouveaux – the house was just another attempt to assert their acquired wealth and position.' She wrinkled her nose. 'Does that make me sound horribly stuck-up?'

'Not at all.' I stared up at the varnished oil painting that hung above the fireplace. 'Is this Sir Arthur Brightwell himself?' Hector's father had died in a motor accident just before the war, so I had never met him. I studied the portrait with open curiosity.

'It is indeed. It's the only one of him left on display – Lady Brightwell ordered all the others to be taken down when he died. She said she couldn't stand him staring down at her, watching her every move. Hector insisted this one remain. It is only fitting, after all.'

The image portrayed was that of a self-assured middle-aged man, dressed in a red hunting coat, buckskin breeches and gleaming riding boots, his knighthood medal proudly displayed on his chest. In his heavy features I could detect traces of Hector, but his eyes, in the portrait at least, lacked the warmth that was always evident in his son's. His fingers gripped the handle of a pickaxe, the scooped metal head resting on the ground by his feet along with a few lumps of gleaming coal, the black gold from which he had derived his fortune. I took another step forward and peered into the background. Brightwell stood on the crest of a hill, and in the valley below him I could see Greyswick, or that is, I could see part of it. In the detail, the house beyond the clock tower was overlaid by a crisscross of scaffolding, and an army of workers the size of tiny ants could be seen labouring around it. I expressed my surprise.

'Greyswick wasn't actually finished when the portrait was done,' Madeleine explained. 'Obviously the artist has taken some licence with the landscape, but I believe the representation of the house at that time to be accurate. It was his wedding present to Lady Brightwell, but it wasn't completed until a year or so after Hector was born. No expense spared, and little taste engaged. But don't you dare tell her I said that,' Madeleine concluded.

I laughed and settled myself down opposite her, just as she was responding to a gentle tap on the door. A young maid sporting a mischievous twinkle in her eye and bearing a laden tray slipped into the room.

'Thank you, Maisie, we'll take it here.'

The girl's inquisitive gaze stole my way several times as she set the tea things out upon an occasional table beside Madeleine.

She stood back as she finished and dropped a curtsy, before scooting from the room.

'How many servants do you have?' I asked.

'Not many. It's like at home, they've all left since the war. Hector has the butler in town with him, so there's just Cook, Maisie and Mrs Henge here now.' She handed me a cup of tea. 'There's Miss Scott as well, of course, but I can hardly call her a servant. Do you remember her? She came to the wedding. Lady Brightwell always refers to her as her "companion" now.'

I did remember Miss Scott, a neat, birdlike woman, fine featured and rather jittery. Hector had introduced her as his nanny, and his affection for the old woman had been clear to see, as had her adoration of him. She had not been a conspicuous guest at the modest gathering, Lady Brightwell had very much played the dominant role, but she had struck me as kind and tolerant, characteristics which I suspected were essential for anyone fashioned as Lady Brightwell's aide.

'So how are you finding it here? It must be so different from London.' I set my tea down on the hearth while I used the poker to stoke some life back into the dwindling fire. The sun that had lent a pleasant air to the day was receding as evening advanced, and a distinct chill bit into the room. Madeleine gazed off into the mid-distance, her brow creased. She rallied as I sat back in my seat.

'Oh, you know . . .' she said, but the insipid smile that flickered on her lips didn't last long. She sipped her tea, I suspected, to cover a sudden pallor of unhappiness. I felt a twinge of disquiet. 'I wish I were back in London. With Hector. Being here is so – it's just not as I imagined.'

'Oh, Madeleine. Well, I am here now, and I intend to stay

for as long as you will let me.' I was cheered to see her spirits restored by this promise. 'How have you been, anyway?'

'Well, the horrid morning sickness has passed,' she said, an attractive glow finally brightening her cheeks. 'I've been tired, but then I haven't been sleeping well, I suppose.' That nagging furrow reappeared between her brows, but she banished it with a shy smile. 'I think I felt it move, you know, the other day. It was a funny squiggly feeling. Mother said it was a good sign.'

'I should think it's a wonderful sign!'

'And how have you been, Stella?'

She didn't need to elaborate. We both knew she was prodding at the fresh scab on my tender wound, conscious that over-investigation would split the delicate surface and expose the vulnerable flesh beneath. I didn't want to disappoint her as she looked for signs of healing.

'Better. I cry a little less, I manage a little more.' There was a sober pause. 'I couldn't have done without you, Madeleine. I do hope you will let me return the favour now.'

Her eyes glistened. 'Oh, darling, I will take your help now. I am so glad you have come.'

Both of us laughed at our mawkish sentimentality. I poured some more tea and as we moved onto less emotive topics, our good humour was soon recovered.

I was very keen to see more of my surroundings, but Madeleine seemed strangely averse to leading me on an exploration of the property. After much wheedling and cajoling, however, she finally acquiesced and agreed to give me a complete tour of what she referred to as 'the dratted house'.

As we moved from one excessive room to the next, I realised that her earlier summation had been most apt. It was impossible to deny Greyswick's luxurious finish and yet it lacked a quality to its splendour found in more established houses like our own. The calculated effort put into its grandeur had reduced it to a caricature of the very thing it aspired to be. Many of the rooms now lay dormant, particularly those in the 'new wing' – a garishly gilded ballroom, the smoking room, the study – none of which had been utilised since Sir Arthur's death – and a lady's parlour, neglected by Lady Brightwell in favour of the morning room, which lay at the other end of the house.

Once our tour of the ground floor had been completed, Madeleine led me upstairs. The bedrooms occupied by Lady Brightwell and Miss Scott were located in the new wing, whilst our rooms were to be found in the original part of the house. The upper corridor was only half-panelled, with claret-flocked wallpaper stretching up to the stuccoed ceiling, while a blood-red runner was centred over the treacle-coloured floorboards. Once again, the only natural light came from the arched window in the end wall, and it failed to pierce the blighted dimness of the landing.

'Our rooms are here. I had Mrs Henge put you in the one next to mine,' Madeleine announced. 'I did so want you close by.'

I expressed my pleasure at the arrangement and Madeleine was about to open the bedroom door when I stopped her, my curiosity having been aroused by the straight flight of stairs beside the arched window. As I carried on towards them, I saw they connected to a short galleried landing above.

'What rooms are up there?' I asked, turning back to her.

Madeleine clutched the door handle.

'Just disused rooms,' she said at last. 'I have no need to go up there.' The words tripped over themselves in their haste to be out. She pushed open the door, entreating me to come. 'It's getting late, you should dress for dinner. The bell-pull is by the bed, you can ring for Annie. I hope you like the room – it has its own adjoining bathroom, you know. Do try to hurry, Stella – it's best not to be late down.'

I had to fish behind the swag of frilled curtain that hung from the canopy of my bed to find the bell cord. When Annie appeared a few minutes later I thought her rather subdued, but I dismissed her reserve as nerves.

She remained silent as she helped me into my black evening dress. I hung my locket from the hinge of the dressing table's triptych mirror for safe keeping while she fastened strings of pearls about my neck. I decided to make an effort and engage her in conversation. We were, after all, to be thrust into each other's company and I wanted the situation to be as tolerable as possible.

'Are you settling in all right?' I winced as she grazed my scalp with one of the pearl-headed pins she was using to dress my hair. She made no apology and I couldn't tell whether she was unaware of her carelessness or simply choosing ignore it. Her cool gaze met mine in the mirror as she finished and it crossed my mind that it might not have been carelessness at all. I pushed aside my misgivings and decided to give her the benefit of the doubt. She stepped back as I got to my feet. 'All of this must seem rather daunting,' I said.

'Everyone is being very kind to me, miss.'

'Good.' I began to squeeze my fingers into a tight-fitting evening glove, smoothing the satin up the length of my arm.

'Do lend a hand when you can. I don't want our visit to be a burden on anyone.'

'Yes, miss.'

'Is your room comfortable? I presume you're up in the attic? I hope it's not too ghastly up there.'

Annie hesitated for a minute, busying herself with hanging up my discarded day clothes for longer than I felt necessary.

'It's comfortable enough up there, miss.'

There was something in her tone that piqued my curiosity and I was about to question her further when there was a knock on the door. Madeleine stuck her head around its edge.

'Are you ready to face them?'

I laughed, pulling my glove up the final inch so that it lay just below the crook of my elbow. 'You make it sound like we're going up against a hostile crowd!'

'Yes, well . . . dinner here can sometimes feel like that – don't say I didn't warn you.'

I found her lack of humour to be rather disconcerting.

Chapter Seven

Lady Brightwell and her companion, Miss Scott, were awaiting us in the drawing room, both sipping sherry from cut crystal glasses, as they warmed themselves by the roaring fire.

'Visiting is so exhausting!'

I was unsure whether Lady Brightwell's exclamation as she rose to greet me was in reference to her busy day, a declaration of sympathy, or a complaint aimed at my very presence. I bent to kiss her creped cheek. She was small in stature, though she gained an extra inch or two from the artistic arrangement of her abundant grey hair, but what she lacked in height she more than made up for with her forceful persona. Large blue eyes ringed with gold inspected me thoroughly from under their broad arches as we exchanged the usual pleasantries, her thin lips barely breaking into a smile.

It was left to her companion, Miss Scott, to make me feel welcome.

'So nice to see you again, Miss Marcham!' She was a few years older than her employer, finer-boned and far sprightlier. Her eyes glowed with kindness from behind her round, wire-framed glasses as she warmly clasped my hand. I found I breathed a little easier in her company.

Mrs Henge's appearance cast a dark shadow into the room,

as she informed us that dinner was served. Lady Brightwell led us out into the draughty corridor to the dining room, leaning heavily on her silver-capped cane, a necessity since the stroke that had afflicted her twelve months previously.

Our steps echoed off the wooden floorboards as we took our places at the enormous rosewood table. I thought we looked rather absurd, the four of us clustered at the one end while its gleaming top stretched into the distance. Every cough, chink of cutlery and ting of wineglass seemed to reverberate off the barrel ceiling above us, which was itself an extraordinary sight – a dazzling collection of hand-painted panels, all executed in the Italianate style and excessively trimmed with gilt. The room was lit by four huge chandeliers boasting tier upon tier of crystal drops the size of my fist, their brilliance rendering the flickering flames of the candelabras before us obsolete. Yet none of this opulence served to make the room more comfortable, and though the fire was lit, it was not enough to take the edge off the cold that had my skin stippling in protest.

As Maisie placed soup bowls before us, Lady Brightwell launched into complaint after complaint about her day spent with friends, which had been soured by dull conversation, chipped china and over-cooked asparagus. I tried to offer sympathy where appropriate, but she would not permit any interruption, so in the end I kept quiet, relying on the contents of my wineglass to see me through the ordeal.

There was a brief respite as the table was cleared, with Lady Brightwell making a few curt enquiries into my parents' health and my own present occupation, the latter of which I deftly side-stepped. Unfortunately, the arrival of the main course brought to mind yet another unsatisfactory element of her day, and her disgruntled diatribe was reignited, quite spoiling my enjoyment of the sweet Dover sole and later the wonderful gateau the cook had prepared.

There were several times during this extraordinary mono-logue of misery that I attempted to catch Madeleine's eye, desperate to share with her the absurdity of it all, but she fixed her gaze firmly on the table. She appeared completely withdrawn as she played with the stem of her wineglass, from which she sipped sparingly.

It was whilst Lady Brightwell was midway through a com-prehensive character assassination of the 'dear friend' she had visited, that the heavy dining-room door suddenly slammed shut. The sound thundered through the air, surprising everyone. Madeleine jumped so violently she toppled her glass, spilling her wine over the table. She pushed her chair back, aghast, and I feared she was about to burst into tears.

'Oh Madeleine! How careless of you,' Lady Brightwell cried as I sprang to mop up the spillage with my napkin. Miss Scott got up to help me. She righted the glass and assured Madeleine no harm had resulted. I was shocked to see my sister visibly trembling as she stared at the closed door.

'There really has been no damage done,' I said, echoing Miss Scott's reassurance. I spotted one of the curtains lift and immediately deduced the cause of the door's sudden movement. 'It was probably just a through draught.' I excused myself from the table and pulled back the offending curtain, the rings raking sharply against the brass pole. 'Yes, look! The window has been left open – no wonder it was so cold in here.' The sash clattered against the frame as I pushed it down.

Madeleine remained pale and shaken. Rather foolishly we

leapt again as the door swung open, but it was only Maisie. Lady Brightwell was quick to reprimand her for not having closed the window. The young maid apologised as she gathered our dishes and meekly withdrew.

I breathed a sigh of relief when our little party retired to the drawing room. Madeleine joined Lady Brightwell on the sofa by the now sedate fire while Miss Scott and I took two chairs a short distance away. It was not long before Lady Brightwell succumbed to the somniferous effects of the flickering flames as they comfortingly crackled around the pine logs. Madeleine opened her book, but I noticed she spent more time staring into space than losing herself within its pages.

Miss Scott pulled out her knitting from the bamboo-handled bag resting alongside her seat. She smiled serenely at me as her dancing needles clicked a tattoo with practised dexterity.

'Do I see a matinee coat?' I asked.

Her face lit up and she held the skilled weave of wool up for my perusal. 'It is indeed.'

'What a charming pattern.' I glanced at Madeleine, now drowsily absorbed in the pages of her novel. 'It's an exciting prospect, isn't it? A new life coming into the world.'

The older woman looked wistful and sighed. 'The most wonderful thing.' The needles began to clack softly once again, but then came to a stop. She appeared to wrestle with some inner dilemma, but her mind was soon made up. 'Miss Marcham, may I say how sorry I was to hear about your fiancé? Such a terrible loss for you. I know I only met him briefly at the wedding, but he struck me as being a most lovely young man.'

Startled, I felt a lump block my throat. 'He was.'

'Had you known each other long?'

'We met as children,' I said, picturing the solemn little boy who had gifted me a jam jar of water boatmen one summer. 'We shared a godmother,' I explained. 'She would take us out on theatre trips and to tea at The Ritz.' I thought back to a Christmas party where a bout of tonsillitis prevented me from partaking in the festivities, and how an eleven-year-old Gerald had sat at my bedside, entertaining me with card games, insistent he would rather spend time with me than join in with the fun downstairs. In time, I came to learn such loyalty was as characteristic of the man as it had been of the boy. 'We lost touch, for a while – his family moved abroad – but our godmother brought us together again some years later. She always thought we were meant to be.'

'You certainly looked very happy together.'

I nodded to dispel unwelcome tears. 'Well, at least Hector is safe,' I said, keen to change the subject.

'Thank God, yes!' She regarded me intently as she rested her knitting on her lap. 'A most fortunate posting!' With the quick movements of a sparrow, she tilted her head towards her sleeping employer, before tilting it again to check Madeleine was not eavesdropping. She lowered her voice, drawing me into her confidence. 'I have to admit I did stress to Lady Brightwell that if she could bring any pressure to bear to find him something safe, then she should.' She released her knitting needles and laid her dry hand on mine. 'Oh, I know some people would say it was wrong to do so – to use one's connections in such a way. Lady Brightwell struggled with the idea for some time, but I told her firmly, she would never forgive herself if something happened and she had not done everything in her power to protect him.'

She appealed for my understanding, if not my sympathy

– perhaps even my approval. I itched to withdraw my hand – there was something sullying about this confession, and I wanted no part of it. After an awkward pause she leant back in her chair and resumed her knitting before continuing.

'Lady Brightwell saw sense in the end of course and was able to make some suitably discreet arrangements. I'm not even sure Hector is aware, but I for one sleep easier knowing he has been kept from that dreadful slaughter over there. Such a waste of young lives!' She remembered herself and quickly added: 'As you, more than anyone, must know.'

I looked across to the dancing flames. I was right – Hector's family had indeed intervened to keep him from harm's way. Gerald's family could perhaps have done something similar, but they had not. I took little comfort from the knowledge that Gerald would never have accepted anything but a frontline command. I wondered how Hector would react if he knew the truth.

Madeleine's head nodded tellingly. Closing her book, she covered a yawn.

'I'm so sorry,' she said, keeping her voice low so as not to disturb her mother-in-law. 'I am falling asleep! I think I'll retire.'

But as she rose, Lady Brightwell awoke with a start. She straightened in her chair.

'Where are you going?' she demanded, her voice thick with sleep.

'I'm sorry, Lady Brightwell, I'm very tired. I should quite like to go to bed.'

'We usually retire together. Oh well, I suppose in your condition you need your rest. Off you go then.' She waved dismissively, blue veins bulging down the back of her hand. Madeleine stopped as she reached my chair.

'Will you come up with me?' It struck me as more of a plea than a question, so whilst I did not feel particularly ready to turn in, I got to my feet and bade my companions goodnight.

Madeleine left the drawing-room door ajar, permitting a splinter of light to penetrate the dark corridor. She slipped her arm through mine, gripping onto me as we made our way towards the hall. I had expected the electric bulbs to be ablaze, but instead only a little moonlight alleviated the darkness. Madeleine informed me that Lady Brightwell insisted they exercise economy during these tumultuous war years. Whilst I applauded her patriotic sense of duty, I felt unnerved by the shifting shadows that cloaked the vast house.

We made our way upstairs, past the stained-glass window, the moon casting faint and fragmentary light upon the steps. As we reached the landing, I was surprised but relieved to find economy had been relaxed on the first floor – glowing wall lights lit the way to our bedroom doors.

'It's such a comfort, having you here in this house with me,' Madeleine said at last as we stopped beside her room.

'I can see what a trial these last few weeks must have been for you. I'm sure Lady Brightwell has her merits, but ease of company is surely not one of them.'

'One gets used to her.' She hesitated. 'The nights here are the hardest.'

'I can see that,' I said. 'At least during the day you can find reasons to avoid her company, but you'll always have to suffer her at dinner.'

By the funny look she gave me I realised we had been

speaking at cross-purposes – she had not been alluding to Lady Brightwell at all.

'I hope you manage to sleep well, Stella. Goodnight.'

Before I could respond, she closed the door against me. I was a little taken aback by her abrupt behaviour, but I dismissed it as acute tiredness and let myself into my room. I kicked off my shoes and padded to my dressing table to begin unwinding my hair.

It didn't take long to disrobe and pull on the nightdress that Annie had left neatly folded on the bed. I turned off the main light, leaving only the bedside lamp glowing from under its fringed shade. Weary now, I threw back the covers.

Lying on my sheet was a toy soldier.

It was surprisingly heavy given its diminutive size. Puzzled, I turned it over in my hand, studying its perfectly painted red tunic, white belt and black trousers, a red stripe down their sides. The facial features were worn but the detail of its domed bearskin was still discernible, perfect in miniature, while the rifle that rested proudly against its shoulder was slightly bent at the end. Its black boots were soldered onto a small square of lead, painted a vivid green.

My breath lodged in my throat as Gerald's face sprang into my mind's eye. I stood perfectly still, my skin prickling as a flare of hope quickened my pulse. Was this a message for me? A poignant sign from beyond the grave?

'Gerald?' I whispered.

The only response was silence. Unable to surrender the blissful fantasy, I turned around to peer into the inky corners of my room. There was nothing there. I was completely alone. Cold reality reasserted itself once again. The soldier was nothing more than a child's toy after all.

Mocking my own absurdity, I turned it over in my hand, noting as I did so the letters *L* and *B* crudely scratched into the base. I set it down on the bedside table, wondering how it could have found its way into my bed, but then I recalled Maisie's mischievous glint and I wondered whether she had left the soldier, as some sort of jest.

Still bristling with self-contempt, I decided to pay no further thought to the toy's puzzling presence. Instead, I settled myself amongst the damply cold sheets and turned off the light, gratefully succumbing to the gradual creep of slumber.

Chapter Eight

The sound of a match being struck woke me. A thin cord of light edged the curtains, hailing the arrival of a new day. I propped myself up to observe Annie, on her knees leaning into the grate, attempting to bellow the flames with her own gentle puffs. She settled back on her heels and watched the newspaper curl, char and crackle, before hungry flames began licking at the lumps of coal and kindling.

'Morning, Annie.' My voice was croaky. 'What time is it?'

'Seven o'clock, miss.'

'Draw me a bath, would you?'

Having a bathroom attached to my bedroom was a luxury I didn't have at home, and I intended to make the most of it. Sir Arthur had been insistent his guests should stay in comfort and his servants be better employed than in the transportation of water. Some saw such expenditure on indoor plumbing as extravagant but having spent years scurrying up and down freezing corridors to avail myself of the lavatory in the middle of the night or to take a bath on a bitter winter's morning, I thought it a most worthwhile investment.

Hearing the squeak of taps and gushing water, I pushed back the thick covers and swung my legs from the bed. I yawned and stretched with feline indulgence.

'All ready, miss. What clothing would you like me to set out?'

'Oh, my black dress . . .' I realised all the dresses I had brought were black. 'The one with the scooped collar,' I clarified. 'And the lavender cardigan too.'

When I emerged from the bathroom Annie was standing beside my bed, closely examining the toy soldier clasped in her hand.

'Annie?'

My sharp tone jolted her from her reverie. The figure flew into the air and landed with a soft thud on the carpet. Unabashed, she bent to retrieve it.

'I don't suppose you know how that came to be left in my bed, do you?'

She carefully set it down upon the table. 'No, miss.' There was something in her bland expression that led me to suspect she was being less than forthcoming.

'I don't appreciate being the butt of anyone's joke.'

Her eyes flickered up to meet mine. 'I'm sure you're not, miss.'

'Well, I'd appreciate it if you could have a quiet word with Maisie and make sure she understands that too.' I picked up my undergarments and began to dress, taking her assistance where required. 'Is Mrs Brightwell up?'

'I believe so, miss.'

I dismissed her, reminding her she was at Mrs Henge's disposal and so should strive to make herself useful. Once she had gone, I fastened my locket and went to turn off the bedside light. I don't know what compelled me to pick up the lead soldier, but I did, slipping it into my cardigan pocket before I left the room.

Receiving no reply when I tapped lightly on Madeleine's door, I surmised she must already be taking breakfast so I hurried to join her.

I descended into the gloom of the hall, quickly crossing the chilly cavern into the bleak corridor beyond, the echo of my footsteps softening as marble gave way to polished wood. I had only proceeded a short way when a rapid swishing of skirts revealed I was being pursued. My heart leapt into my mouth as Mrs Henge called my name.

'Goodness! Mrs Henge, you quite startled me!'

Her face remained impassive. 'Miss Marcham, I did not mean to alarm you.'

I laughed at my own skittishness, but she met my self-deprecatory humour with a flicker of disdain. I flushed.

'Was there something you wanted?'

'I merely wished to check that you had settled in and have everything you need.'

'I do indeed, thank you.'

She expressed her satisfaction with a slight nod. She folded her hands before her. 'If I may be so bold, Miss Marcham, may I say how pleased I am to have Mrs Brightwell with us. I very much hope she will, in time, come to see Greyswick as her home and feel some fondness for it.'

'You make it sound as if Mrs Brightwell doesn't like it here.'

'Sometimes, it seems, Mrs Brightwell is not – comfortable – here.'

I could see how Madeleine might struggle to feel 'comfortable' in the house her mother-in-law continued to reign over like a grand matriarch, but I found it interesting that Mrs Henge had also detected Madeleine's disquiet. For the first time, I had a proper opportunity to study Greyswick's housekeeper, now she was finally out in the open and no longer draped in shade. She was not as ancient as I had first perceived, though I suspected her late middle years were calling. The heavy set of her features, her Roman nose and broad chin suggested she had never enjoyed great beauty. Her hair was a uniform grey and her skin had long lost the suppleness of youth. It sagged now, weary lines fanning from her eyes, while deep channels carved down the sides of her mouth. The one extraordinary feature she did possess, however, were her eyes. They were the clearest grey I had ever seen, like thick sheets of pond ice, with only the merest hint of colour in their transparency. I wondered what treacherous depths they concealed.

'My sister tells me you have been with the family for a long time, Mrs Henge.'

Her lips quirked in a way that felt strangely measured, practised somehow. 'I have indeed, miss. I was with Sir Arthur from the time he was a young man just starting to make his way in the world. It has been an honour and a privilege to serve in such an esteemed family for all these years. I hope I may continue to serve long after the next generation arrives.'

'An old retainer is a highly valued asset.'

I thought of how I cherished dear Brown and Mrs Scrivens. I so often took their service for granted, and yet I knew they were completely irreplaceable, and much loved. Swelled with tenderness, I laid my hand on Mrs Henge's arm, but she flinched at the unanticipated touch, and I quickly withdrew it, somewhat embarrassed.

'They are very lucky to have you, Mrs Henge,' I said, hoping to mitigate for any discomfort I may have caused.

'Annie is being most helpful, miss.' I think both of us welcomed the change of subject. 'She's a queer sort, if you don't mind me saying, but she's a good worker, I'll give her that.'

'Well, it's a strange house to her, Mrs Henge, and she is not the most experienced of girls, but I'm sure she'll do her best.' I thought of Mrs Scrivens' concerns. 'She has a few foibles, but we all have our idiosyncrasies after all. Now, if you'll excuse me, I'm hoping to catch my sister at breakfast.'

'Mrs Brightwell is indeed still in the dining room, Miss Marcham. Lady Brightwell and Miss Scott have already left for the day.'

'What busy lives they lead,' I observed dryly.

It was impossible to read the housekeeper's leaden expression. She offered a courteous dip of her head and turned back to the hall. I remembered the toy soldier and was about to call after her but then decided not to. It was probably nothing more than a foolish prank by the housemaid, and I had no desire to get the girl into trouble. Perhaps I would have a quiet word with her myself, if Annie was disinclined to do so, or indeed if I found myself in receipt of another such bedtime gift. I pressed on to the dining room.

Madeleine shuffled round in her chair to beam at me as I entered.

'There you are at last! Did you sleep well? I slept wonderfully – I knew I would rest better with you here.'

She caught my hand as I leant down to kiss her and brought it to her lips. I was heartened to see her restored to her usual humour. She chattered merrily as I helped myself to bacon, eggs and kidney. Deciding to indulge, I slipped a muffin onto my plate.

Madeleine was very keen to visit the local town as there were a number of purchases she needed to make and required my advice. I was quite happy to fall in with whatever plans she had and we decided to take the omnibus, as Lady Brightwell had already commandeered the car.

I was full to bursting by the time I popped the last morsel of jam-slathered muffin into my mouth. Madeleine had been fidgeting to be gone for the last five minutes, and the moment my lips closed she pushed back her chair.

'Come along, Stella, we simply can't miss the 'bus.'

Still chewing, I got to my feet, and as I did so, I felt the weight of the toy soldier pull at my pocket.

'Oh! I almost forgot, I had the most peculiar bedfellow last night.'

Madeleine burst out laughing. 'I beg your pardon?'

Grinning, I ceremoniously stood the figure on the table. The smile froze on Madeleine's face as the spark faded from her eyes. The edges of her mouth relaxed until her lips were pressed into a thin line.

'Where did you find him?'

I fought a sense of foreboding as I offered my response. She nodded distractedly, before flinging her napkin onto him.

'I can't stand the things.' She turned on her heel, her movements taut as she strode for the door. 'Anyway, we'd best hurry. That omnibus won't wait for us.'

I made several attempts to broach the subject of the soldier throughout the course of the morning, but Madeleine was always quick to change the subject. Her demeanour remained cheery and light, but I couldn't help noticing a strain about her eyes and a tension to her smile, that hadn't been evident before the figure's appearance. I found the whole situation most curious.

It was late afternoon before we clambered down from

the 'bus and began the long walk up the drive to the house. Madeleine grew quieter as we approached the grey mansion.

Mrs Henge must have been watching for us – she hauled open the front door before we reached the top step. She stood in patient attendance as we unburdened ourselves of hats, coats and parcels.

'I am quite worn out from all that,' Madeleine confessed. Her subdued manner was reflected in her pale cheeks and dull eyes. 'I think I might take a lie down for a while. Will you come up with me?'

We used the last of our reserves to climb the vast staircase, too drained even for conversation. As we entered the corridor leading to our rooms our steps faltered to a standstill. Annie Burrows was crouched outside my bedroom door. There was a furtiveness about her which immediately aroused my suspicion. It appeared I was not alone: Madeleine tensed beside me.

Noticing our arrival, the young maid shot up. She dipped a brief curtsy, before scuttling past us, her right hand clenched by her side. We watched her disappear through the servants' door concealed in the panelling of the landing.

'I wish you hadn't brought that girl here. This house is unsettling enough without her gracing its corridors.' Madeleine shuddered and turned, her pace quickening as she continued to her room. I had to hurry to catch up.

As we reached her bedroom door, she swung round and gave me a fierce embrace that quite knocked the wind from me. 'Oh, ignore me! I'm sorry if I've been a little off. I'll feel much better after a nap.'

'It's been a tiring trip. Get some rest. I might even catch a wink or two myself,' I confessed. The prospect of sleep was quite alluring now that my bed was within easy reach, but I found myself hovering in her doorway. 'Madeleine, the toy soldier – I dismissed it as a prank by the housemaid. I failed to mention it to Mrs Henge when I had the opportunity – was I wrong to do so?'

'Telling Mrs Henge wouldn't have helped.'

'But . . .' I struggled to believe the housekeeper would tolerate such behaviour if she were made privy to it. 'I know it's a harmless jest, but it's not appropriate. Someone needs to say something to the girl. I take it Maisie has left them for you too?'

'It's not Maisie, Stella – Maisie's a good girl. Please, don't let's say any more about it, there's no need to trouble yourself.' She began inching the door to. 'We both need some rest. Come and get me when you're ready, we'll go down to dinner together when it's time.'

Try as I might, I could not understand Madeleine's reluctance to resolve the matter. It appeared there was an underlying nuance to the whole situation that I was missing completely.

I closed my bedroom door behind me. It was a relief to cast my shoes from my aching feet. I removed my dress, not wanting to crease it, and draped it over the bedroom chair. I held my breath as I yanked back the bedcovers, half-expecting to find another toy figure. I was relieved to see nothing but a crisp expanse of white sheet. I lay down, hoisting the covers over my shoulders, wondering whether I should set my alarm clock. I soon regretted not drawing my curtains against the bright sky, but I couldn't be bothered to heave myself out of bed now that I was settled. So I closed my eyes and ignoring the vibrant glow beyond my eyelids, I concentrated on slowing my breaths.

Just as my consciousness was ebbing, the image of Annie's

furled fist came back into view. It was then I realised what I had failed to see.

A slash of scarlet wrapped in the cream skin of her palm.

I awoke with a start, my hand flying to the side of my head, my hair roots tingling. I almost expected to knock someone's hand aside, so vivid was the impression of my hair being stroked – but my fingers merely dug into thick hanks. My heart raced as I scrambled upright. The room was unchanged: my dress still lay folded over the back of the chair and the curtains were still drawn from the window, though the sky outside was smothered with cloud now and the room felt heavy without the lift of yellow sunlight. Only the steady ticking of the clock on the mantelpiece and my own ragged breaths punctured the dense stillness. I pressed my palm to the side of my head, confused. The sensation of the gentle touch had seemed so real, yet I must have imagined it.

My breath caught. The door was wide open.

I scrabbled from the bed and stood shivering in my slip, staring at the opening. The door had been shut when I had taken my nap, I was sure of it. I snatched up my wrapper and pulled it on. Had someone been in while I slept?

My breath shuddered from me as I crossed the room, the carpet soft under my stockinged feet, until I stood on the threshold. My attention was immediately caught by creaking wood. I looked up the corridor. Annie Burrows was halfway up the staircase at the end.

'Annie! Where do you think you are going? Are you supposed to be up there?'

A jerk of her head revealed a fleeting look of irritation, before her expression quickly closed. She began to backtrack, the stair treads grumbling underfoot as she descended. She stood at the bottom as I bore down on her, her head hung low, but I noticed her eyes swivel up towards the landing above us.

'Were you just in my room?'

'I wasn't, miss.'

'Was anyone else?'

Her eyes skidded again towards the empty staircase before meeting mine. 'No, miss.'

Her curious behaviour aroused my suspicion, but I could see nothing amiss. The mahogany steps rose steeply, siding onto a wall lined with paintings, before opening out onto a short galleried landing, which hosted two doors set in the wall facing me, while the landing itself ended rather abruptly with a further half-glazed door. My damp palm cupped the newel post. I was surprised at how cold it felt. I mounted the first step, focused on the landing above. I had an irresistible urge to explore. I took another step, the wood creaking as it took my weight. An icy draught brushed my cheek sending a shiver down my spine. I took another step and then another until I reached the collection of small oil paintings that hung above me.

Most of them were whimsical rural scenes – sheep being driven down muddy country lanes; a milkmaid sitting with her ruddy cheek pressed to a cow's side, her fingers closed on its teats. But as I drifted on, I came upon a much larger painting in an exquisitely carved, gold leaf frame. I stopped. I was acutely aware of Annie's inquisitive gaze as I tilted my head back to appreciate the striking work of art. It was a portrait of an angelic young boy, his cheeks rosy, blond curls looping round his petite ears, his blue eyes soft and loving, his rosebud mouth prettily pursed. Dressed in a blue sailor suit, his right hand rested on a metal hoop, whilst the fingers of his left brushed the head of the King Charles spaniel that was looking up adoringly up its master with bulging brown eyes. There was something about the portrait that was both touching and totally entrancing.

'Stella!'

The urgency in Madeleine's voice sliced through the air, startling me from my strange captivation. She stood stock-still outside her bedroom door.

'Come down, Stella. There's nothing to see up there.'

I was unwilling to tear myself away from the portrait. 'Who is this painting of, Madeleine? Is it someone in the family?'

'Come down, Stella, will you?'

I felt a devil of resentment inside me as I began my descent.

'Is he one of the family?' I persisted.

Annie was standing meekly with her hands clasped before her, but her eyes strayed to Madeleine, as if she too were curious to hear the answer. Madeleine fidgeted, folding her arms across her body, hugging them to her.

'Yes,' she answered as I reached the last step. She visibly relaxed as my feet finally settled on the carpeted landing.

'Who is it? It's a charming portrait.'

'It's Lucien.'

'Lucien?'

'Hector's half-brother, Lucien Brightwell.'

'I didn't know Hector had a brother.'

'Half-brother,' she corrected me. She was clearly reticent about providing more information, but I pressed her for it. 'His mother was Sir Arthur's first wife, she died in childbirth. Lucien died of influenza just after Hector was born.'

I always remember my grandfather advising me to pay attention to the silences in a conversation, rather than the words. When I asked him why, he had removed his ever-present pipe and bestowed his wisdom upon me. The things that are most important are often left unsaid – they fill the pauses, he explained, the rest is often inconsequential. As I stood now observing my sister's uncomfortable silence, I knew there was a lot more to be gleaned – a story she did not want to share – and I couldn't help wondering what and why. I had never known her to exclude me from a secret, yet since my arrival at Greyswick I couldn't dispel the feeling that Madeleine was hiding many things from me, and I feared no good would come from it.

'Mrs Henge will be ringing the gong soon,' she said. 'We really ought to get on.'

'What rooms are up there, Madeleine?' She had been most determined to steer me away from what lay beyond the staircase and I wanted to understand her reason.

'Nothing of importance.'

'Just an entrance to the servants' quarters.' Annie's interjection startled us both. 'And, of course, the old school room – and nursery.' Her lowered lashes fluttered up as she spoke. 'Or so I believe, miss.'

Madeleine glared at her. 'That's right,' she said, her voice discordant, like an overstrung instrument. 'But I do not like them. I have chosen a room on this floor for a nursery. And that's that.'

'Well, that's your prerogative I would have thought,' I replied.

'Yes, yes, it is. Now really, we should get ready for dinner.

Lady Brightwell does hate to be kept waiting. I must ring for Maisie.'

And before I could say anything more, she disappeared into her room, closing the door firmly behind her, leaving me to examine the pregnant pauses left in her wake.

Chapter Nine

The next morning the heavens opened, and the winds whipped up a fury, dashing rain against the windows and rattling the sashes, as if furious to be denied entry. Madeleine and I settled ourselves in the library to write letters, as there was no chance of us escaping the confines of the house in the face of such onslaught.

Like the rest of Greyswick, the library was a room designed to impress. Its enormous windows were draped in excessive quantities of gaudy material, quite inappropriate given the nature of the room, and the bookcases which lined every square inch of wall had been specially commissioned, as had the large oak reading tables at which Madeleine and I now sat.

After finishing my first letter – one to Mother – I drifted around the room, my fingers running across the ornate bindings of books that ranged in subject from theological texts to fashionable scientific theories. Having drawn out a few to investigate further, however, I noticed that none of the pages had been slit: the books were unread. Like so much else in Greyswick, it appeared they were merely for show.

I was next attracted to a large glass case containing a display of stuffed birds, arranged against a backdrop of dried grasses, gorse and fern. I was not generally a great admirer of taxidermy, but the exhibit was striking, and demanded my scrutiny. A large coot took centre stage, overshadowing a white-throated dipper, whilst behind it, a small falcon had swooped down upon a chaffinch, whose beak was open in distress, its wings raised in fruitless defence. The magpie and mistle-thrush positioned on an angled branch at the back of the case showed no interest in the poor creature's predicament – instead their black eyes appeared focused on me. But it was the beautiful bird clinging to the furthest fork of the branch that evoked my sharp intake of breath.

A kingfisher gazed out through the glass side of the cabinet, his dagger-like bill elevated, his golden chest puffed with pride as he turned his stunning blue back on the display's other subjects. I pressed my fingertips to the glass.

'Halcyon days . . .' My brow creased as a bittersweet memory flooded my mind. I closed my eyes, fighting against the pain, to savour it.

It was the summer of 1913 and a letter had arrived from my godmother, asking whether I remembered Gerald Fitzwilliam at all. I did, of course, though I hadn't seen him for years. His family had moved to Australia not long after Lydia died, and though Aunt Irene referred to him in passing every now and then, he had rather slipped from my mind.

I still had his letter, though, the one he sent me just after Lydia's death. It was the sweetest thing. He wrote to say how sorry he was, and how he hoped I was bearing up, though he realised I must be hurting terribly. He had gone on to say how Lydia had been one of only two girls in his acquaintance whose company he had always enjoyed (in brackets he had assured me that I was the other one. He had made no mention of Madeleine).

It was such a rarity for me, as a child of ten, to receive a proper letter in the post. The only correspondence I tended to get came on my birthday and at Christmas, when aunts and uncles might send a brief note with a small cheque enclosed, in lieu of a more exciting present. That he had taken the time to do such a grown-up thing had made me feel very special indeed, and the simple kindness expressed in those few lines stayed with me for years.

Aunt Irene went on to inform me that the Fitzwilliam family had returned to England the previous autumn, and that Gerald was just finishing his first year at Cambridge. She intended to visit him that weekend and, recalling how famously we had got on as children, she asked whether I might like to accompany her on the trip – 'for old time's sake'. Having little else to occupy me, I happily agreed.

She called for me early that Saturday morning, and we had motored off to the Fens. I had never been to Cambridge before, and it was exciting to be somewhere so steeped in history, and see the students walking through the town's hallowed streets, striking in their black gowns.

We had arranged to meet Gerald at his college, and for some strange reason I felt a flutter of nerves as the car drew to a stop. He appeared as soon as the car door opened and before I was even out, he was being heartily embraced by our godmother. Any view of him was blocked by the huge flowered hat she had donned for the occasion. Finally, after much kissing and hugging, Aunt Irene released him and stepped away, enabling me to see my childhood friend for the first time in seven years.

It would perhaps be trite to say he had grown, but goodness – how he had grown! He was tall, broad-shouldered, and quite breathtakingly handsome. There was still evidence of the boy I had known, though: his thick hair the colour of rich brandy, those eyes that twinkled with mischief, and the lightning-flash grin.

He escorted us first on a tour of his college and later the town. He was attentive, intelligent, his manners were impeccable, his charm was undeniable, and his humour most refreshing.

It was a glorious summer's day, and Aunt Irene had packed a picnic for us to enjoy. Rescuing the large hamper from its strapping on the rear of the car, Gerald suggested he take us punting down the river, so that we could feast in a quiet spot on the meadow. The punt dipped and wobbled as Gerald helped Aunt Irene and myself in, and I was most relieved when I was at last safely planted on the bench seat and no longer in danger of toppling us all overboard.

It was idyllic, gliding up the wide river, shadows falling on our faces as we passed under the arches of historic stone bridges. Gerald proved a most able punter, manoeuvring us around other boats and easing us on our way.

When we reached the meadows, he found a spot on the bank suitable for us to disembark. He leapt off first to secure the punt with a rope, then handed Aunt Irene and me back up onto terra firma, before retrieving the picnic basket.

We found a lovely spot where willow trees wept into the river, their tendril branches tentatively dipping beneath the murky surface. The tartan rug billowed on the breeze as Gerald shook it out before laying it down amongst the buttercups, daisies and purple fritillaries.

Aunt Irene and I knelt in our light summer dresses and began to unpack, setting out the plates, wine glasses and cutlery before arranging a veritable feast of delights, all lovingly prepared by Aunt Irene's cook. There was jellied chicken, cold salmon, potted shrimp, boiled eggs, tiny tomatoes, pickles, bread, melting butter and wedges of hard cheese that were beginning to soften in the heat. Gerald threw himself down and pulled off his boater, a red line across his forehead where the rim had cut in. Laughing, he ruffled some life back into his flattened hair and proceeded to uncork the wine. Reminiscing about the past, and filling in the missing years, the three of us ate and drank and talked until we could manage no more.

Fully sated, Aunt Irene declared herself quite exhausted, and using Gerald's folded blazer as a cushion, she lay back on the blanket and closed her eyes. We smothered our laughter as she began to snore peacefully.

I decided to stretch my cramped legs, so I stood up, brushing the crumbs from my skirt.

'Shall we wander over to the river?' Gerald suggested, scrabbling to his feet.

'Yes, all right,' I smiled, a little giddy from the combination of heat and wine.

We ambled quite companionably through the long grass that was alive with the buzzing of bees and chirping of crickets, until the river flowed before us.

'It is so good to see you again, Stella,' Gerald said, glancing down at me. 'In a strange way, it seems like only yesterday.'

I smiled, plucking a stem of grass for want of something to do with my trembling hands. I knew exactly what he meant. In just a few hours, the years had fallen away, until only that easy familiarity we enjoyed as children remained. It set my heart beating a little faster.

'Did you see that?' he exclaimed. Seeing my puzzlement, he grabbed my hand and led me closer to the river edge. 'Look! There!'

I followed his finger just in time to see a bolt of blue shoot into the brown depths, only to appear again seconds later.

'A kingfisher!' I declared with delight. 'Why, I don't think I've ever seen one before!'

The plump bird rested on a low hanging branch, preening.

We sank down to a crouch to observe it. I was somewhat distracted by how natural it was, for my hand to be in his, and by how comfortable it felt to be beside him once again.

'It's reputed to be the first bird to have flown from Noah's Ark.' He kept his voice low, eager not to disturb the exquisite creature. 'Myth has it, it got its colouring that day, from the blue sky on its back, and the orange setting sun on its breast. Its Greek name is *halcyon*. They see it as a symbol of peace and prosperity . . . and love.' He looked at me and smiled.

'It's beautiful.'

We both gasped as in a flash of colour, the little bird was gone, darting off down the river. We rose from our haunches. Gerald's hand continued to clasp mine.

'I'm glad we saw it together,' he said.

'Oh, here you are. Fancy abandoning me in this heat!'

We swiftly dropped hands and turned to see Aunt Irene standing a little way behind us, cooling herself with a lace fan. 'Sadly, my dears, I think it is time to draw this blissful day to an end, if I am to get Stella back to her parents as promised. Do come and help me pack the picnic basket. I think there's a drop of wine left in one of the bottles – it would be such a shame to waste it.'

With faces flushed from more than just the heat of the day, Gerald and I led the way back to the picnic blanket. My heart felt heavy at the prospect of our imminent separation. Aunt Irene, in contrast, seemed more gay than ever, as she directed our clearing up, a sly smile creeping across her lips and her sharp eyes observing our every interaction.

It wasn't long before we were back at the car, with the basket stowed and us saying our farewells. Aunt Irene kissed her godson fondly and promised to visit again soon, before ducking into the back seat, leaving me on the pavement, waiting to say goodbye. I was rather thrilled when Gerald bent to kiss my cheek, catching my fingers in his hand as he did so.

'May I be terribly forward and ask whether I might write to you?' he said.

My heart seemed to explode as I tried to control the unlady-like grin that burst across my face.

'Oh! I would like that very much.'

His return smile was instant. He squeezed my fingers. 'Good. I think we have a lot of lost time to make up for.'

I felt six inches taller as I climbed into the back seat next to my godmother. We both turned to wave out of the rear window as the car pulled away and as Aunt Irene settled back for the journey home, she made no attempt to hide her approving smile, nor her brief nod of satisfaction, as her eyes twinkled with glee.

'Halcyon days indeed.' I withdrew my fingers from the glass, my heart aching. Halcyon days the like of which I would never enjoy again. My throat burnt with contained tears as I bit my lip and turned away from the kingfisher, silently cursing him for his betrayal.

I was shaking by the time I slid back into my chair, battling to control the unruly sway of my emotions. I snatched up my pen, determined to divert myself with industry, and quickly dashed off a greeting to a Sister I had worked with in France. I paused, my nib resting on the paper, as I remembered how kind she had been on that awful final day. My grip tightened on the pen. I was barely aware of the force I was exerting, when the fine tip broke under the pressure.

'Oh Stella! How careless of you!' Madeleine chided, having heard the snap of the metal, but her tone changed in an instant as she looked up to see my mounting distress. 'Stella? What is it?'

I shook my head, breathing deeply to suppress a deluge of tears. 'I'm sorry ... I'm being silly ... lost in unhelpful thoughts.'

'Oh Stella ...' Madeleine rested her hand on my arm.

I patted it reassuringly before clearing my throat. 'Well, that was rather silly of me. Where might I find a new nib?'

Clearly sensing my desire to move on, Madeleine got up in pursuit of a replacement. She rifled through a set of desk drawers, and the writing box on the window sill, but without reward.

'I do know that mother-in-law has spare nibs in her bureau in the morning room – shall I go and look for you?' she asked.

Keen to have a moment to myself, I assured her I was happy to go. She told me where they were to be found and with a concerned smile, sent me on my way. I closed the door behind me and paused while I afforded myself time to come to terms with the past. Only when my doldrums were banished, and I felt sufficiently restored, did I set off towards the morning room, ready to face the world once again.

I knocked lightly when I reached the door. On receiving no answer, I gingerly turned the brass handle. I was most relieved to find the room unoccupied.

I had seen it only once before, little more than a cursory glance on Madeleine's whistle-stop tour that first day. In stark contrast to the rest of Greyswick, it was a pretty room, painted a vibrant buttercup yellow, and was perfectly positioned to enjoy the sun which streamed in through the floor-to-ceiling windows now the storm had abated. Great cut-glass bowls of pot pourri embellished the other window sills, leaving the hint of a faded summer in the air. The armchairs cosily arranged around the fireplace were covered in chintz, and the shelf of the mantelpiece was draped in velvet as if from a bygone era, and it crossed my mind that the décor may have been unchanged since Lady Brightwell first took occupancy of the house.

I took a moment to examine the abundance of silver picture frames placed about the room. They contained sepia images of largely unfamiliar faces, though some bore sufficient resemblance to Lady Brightwell to suggest a familial connection. There were some pleasantly candid photographs of Hector and Madeleine, as well as the lady herself – there was even a rather charming one of Miss Scott – but I noted with some curiosity there were none of Sir Arthur. He didn't even figure in the ensemble shots taken at house parties and Christmases past. It smacked of a purposeful omission, as if a concerted attempt had been made to erase his presence, but before I could ponder further on this apparent slight, I found myself drawn to the commanding painting that hung above the mantelpiece.

It was a stunning portrait, skilfully done, and though the years may have aged her, it was instantly recognisable as a young Lady Brightwell.

She was standing in profile at a large fireplace, the fingertips of her right hand just visible as they rested on the broad marble mantel. There was a gilt-framed mirror hanging above it, and though the suggestion was a desire to see her reflection had brought her to that spot, her face was angled away from the glass – Lady Brightwell herself was looking directly at the artist. She was dressed in an exquisite red evening gown, the sharp lines of her shoulder blades just visible above the buttoned back that clung to her torso, pulling into a minuscule waist before rucking up in elaborate folds over a bustle and tumbling in waves to pool on the floor. Her chestnut brown hair, threaded with strands of gold, had been gathered up with diamond-headed pins until it overflowed, covering her neck with a cascade of curls. But it was the expression on the stunning young face that struck me the most.

This was no whimsical pose. There was no coquettish regard for the painter, as he painstakingly preserved her for posterity. The expression on her face was arrogantly self-assured. This was a young woman confident of her looks, from the fine line of her nose, to her arched brows and sculpted cheekbones, a young woman who knew her mouth was the perfect shape even if her lips were a little too thin. She was aware her beauty was arresting, and her eyes shone with an unveiled challenge to the artist, daring him to record her otherwise.

'She is a very beautiful woman, is she not, Miss Marcham?'

I whirled around at the intrusion. Miss Scott was standing at the open door. I hadn't heard her enter and fumbled my apologies. She smiled as she drew near.

'Please don't apologise. She is very distracting.'

'It's a wonderful portrait.'

'She was just eighteen when that was done. Oh! She made me do her hair four times before she was satisfied with it. She was quite determined to look perfect.' She drank in the picture, her face rapt, as if relishing it for the first time. 'And she did look perfect,' she finished, her voice soft.

'You've been with her for a very long time then, Miss Scott?'

'Since she was seventeen, and I was not much older myself. She was headstrong and determined even then, and a much-toasted debutante. I've witnessed rooms fall silent by the mere act of her walking into them.'

I looked again at the portrait and had no doubt that the companion's recollections were accurate.

'She is quite a forceful character,' I said without thinking. I saw a flicker of discomfort on the older woman's face.

'You mustn't judge her too harshly, Miss Marcham. What you see above you is a carefully choreographed image. What lies beneath the surface is often too profound to be caught in oils and brush strokes. The events of a lifetime have moulded her into the woman she is today.'

The admonishment was gentle but left me feeling gauche. The affection Miss Scott felt for her employer was clearly deep-seated and genuine, however difficult that might be for me to understand – and she clearly had the patience of a saint to suffer the woman's foibles.

We both turned when we heard a slight cough behind us. Mrs Henge stood framed by the doorway.

'Forgive me for interrupting. I just wanted to check this

morning's tea things had been cleared.' I was surprised to detect an uncharacteristically soft timbre to the housekeeper's voice as she addressed us, Miss Scott her primary focus. One glance revealed the china was still very much in evidence – abandoned on a squat table. Mrs Henge's lips pursed in displeasure and I pitied poor Maisie, who I suspected had overlooked the task amongst a multitude of other chores.

'Oh dear, it's a bit of a mess, isn't it?' Miss Scott declared without recrimination, as Mrs Henge advanced on the china. I explained then that I had come looking for a pen nib. 'Oh, you'll find one in the bureau, Lady Brightwell always keeps several spares, let me find one for you.'

'This is such a pretty room,' I declared, as she bustled over to the desk and pulled open an inner drawer. 'It has such a different feel to the rest of the house.'

'Well, it was the only room she was given free rein in . . . Ah!' She triumphantly brandished a new nib. 'Will this do?'

'Perfectly, thank you.'

Handing me the nib, she delved into a large bag resting in the corner and withdrew a ball of wool, which was clearly what had brought her to the morning room. I cast a final appreciative glance at the painting.

'Was it for a special occasion?'

Miss Scott smiled. 'Her eighteenth birthday – it was the last portrait done before her engagement.'

'And you came with her here to Greyswick on her marriage?' I asked.

'I did indeed, and I have been by her side ever since. Only once have I been away from her in all that time – and only then because there was no other way around it.' Her voice had grown wistful. From the corner of my eye I noticed Mrs Henge glance up, just before she lifted the laden tray.

Miss Scott and I fell in step to leave. Mrs Henge stood aside to let us pass.

'Well, I can see you have quite a bond,' I observed, slowing my pace to allow Miss Scott first access to the doorway.

'Oh yes,' the companion assured me, clutching her wool to her stomach as she left the room. 'I could never leave her.'

As I reached the doorway I glanced back to acknowledge the housekeeper. Mrs Henge made no attempt to return my smile, indeed she appeared distracted and unaware of my existence.

It was only much later that I succeeded in defining her expression. I realised the look she had borne was one strangely akin to pain.

Chapter Ten

Over the next few days my sister and I were constant companions. Madeleine grew increasingly at ease, and at times, as we walked arm in arm through the gardens observing the blossoming spring, she appeared completely carefree, her hand resting contentedly on her growing belly.

As a household we all began to muddle along quite nicely: I became inured to Lady Brightwell's grizzling; Miss Scott started another matinee coat; Mrs Henge continued to efficiently haunt the corridors; and Maisie lent a breath of fresh air to each day. I came to look forward to her impish smile and revised my earlier judgement of her, recognising her now to be a sweet, spirited girl.

The only fly in the ointment was the continuing odd behaviour of my own maid. For some unfathomable reason, Annie Burrows had become fascinated with the nursery staircase, indeed, it seemed to exert some irresistible draw upon her. On numerous occasions I found her loitering at its foot, peering at the landing above, and once I even caught her halfway up, whispering into thin air, evoking uncomfortable memories of her father on the night of the fire.

As a child, I had made the conscious decision never to share what I had witnessed with anyone – not even Madeleine. I had been terrified of inadvertently causing further pain and my suspicions were only supposition after all, suppositions which in time – with maturity and logic – I came to dismiss completely. The re-emergence of such recollections now was as unsettling as it was unwanted. I did my best not to dwell on them.

One afternoon Madeleine and I had happily ensconced ourselves in the orangery. The light outside was that heavy gold hue that often presages a storm. We were quite comfortable on our wicker chairs amongst the aspidistras, looking forward to the cloudburst that was sure to come, anticipating the satisfying thunder of rain on the glass panels above us.

We were both engaged in embroidery, though the pastime was Madeleine's forte not mine. I fumbled hopelessly with the needle and thread as I tried to create the image of a swan, but I failed to count the squares correctly and ended up having to unpick it all. I counted to ten under my breath in a bid to calm myself and rethreaded my needle.

'Bother!' Madeleine had been digging around in her embroidery case. 'I must have left that lovely skein of blue we bought in town the other day in my room. I want it for the sky.'

Seeing an opportunity to escape my torturous needlework, I set down my things and insisted on retrieving it for her. I waved away her protests and promised I would be back directly. Madeleine laughed at my enthusiasm for the errand before merrily stitching on, humming an Irish air as I made my getaway.

As I proceeded to her room I was struck by how different the house felt when the ominous weight of night was not upon it: the corridors innocuous, the shadows cast by daylight somehow shallower and less daunting. It was much pleasanter altogether, and I made the journey to her room far more valiantly than I would have done on my own at night.

She had assured me the thread was on top of her dresser, but when I arrived, there was no sign of it. I looked to see if she had left it elsewhere, and immediately saw the music box sitting on her tallboy. My fingers lingered over the black lacquered wood, beautifully inlaid with mother of pearl. I lifted the lid, and tinny strains of 'Für Elise' filled the room. There was a tiny metal pin that turned slowly round as the music played, but the dainty ballerina who had once spun so elegantly upon it now lay motionless against the plush lining of the box, the gauze of her pink tutu crumpled beneath her. I remembered the day Lydia's clumsy fingers had snapped the ballerina from her stand and how her tears of regret had failed to earn the forgiveness of her incensed elder sister. And I remembered too how on the day Lydia died, I had found Madeleine cradling the box, the broken ballerina in her hand. 'Why did I shout at her so, Stella?' she had sobbed. 'It's just a silly trinket. It didn't really matter! It didn't matter at all . . .'

I closed the lid of the box, and returned to the present, and that troublesome missing thread.

Thinking she may have slipped it into her bedside cabinet, I crossed the room and pulled open the drawer. There, tumbled together in a mêlée of limbs and rifles, were at least a dozen lead soldiers.

Coming so soon after my mournful memory, the discovery upset me more than I could say. Children's treasured possessions: things not be shared lightly. I curled my fingers around a rifleman. He was down on one knee, his rifle thrust before him, the bayonet sharp. I turned it over and smoothed my thumb across the scratched lines I knew I would find on the painted base – *LB*. My fingers flared open and he clattered down onto the bodies of his comrades. Why did Madeleine have a drawer full of soldiers next to her bed? Had she indeed found them, as I had found mine? Or had she gathered them for some purpose known only to herself?

As theories careered through my mind, I abandoned my search for the thread. I rested my forehead on the door as I pulled it shut. The cool wood against my warm skin was as comforting as a damp cloth to a fevered brow. I took a steadying breath.

I would have to discuss the soldiers with Madeleine, whether she wanted to or not. As I turned away from her door I caught sight of Lucien's portrait and for some reason I stopped. It drew me like a moth to a flame – I longed to study it one more time. My feet seemed to possess a life of their own as I took step after step until Lucien loomed above me. I drew close to the canvas. I could see the cracking in the oil paint on his rosy cheeks, the white fleck in his blue eyes, the curl of the spaniel's fur, the metallic sheen of the hoop and the silver buckle on the side of his shoe. My eyes searched every inch of the painting until I found what I was looking for, tucked into the bottom corner, almost concealed by the overlying shadow of paint: the army of lead soldiers.

I recoiled, bumping against the handrail. I couldn't explain my strange reaction to the sight of the toy figures. It was only natural that a little boy would want to be painted with his prized posessions, but what was Madeleine doing with them? Before I could begin to draw any conclusions, a girl's whisper stilled me. My head snapped towards the landing that stretched above me. I noticed the first door was ajar.

Gripping the banister, my gaze unwavering, I took a step up. The polished tread betrayed me with a creak but the whispers, little more than persistent breezes, continued. My chest grew tight as I mounted another step and then another, until at last I reached the landing. I stood before the first door and listened to the whispers, so soft I couldn't catch the words – but I knew the voice.

I pushed the door wide.

'What are you doing in here, Annie? Who are you talking to?'

'I . . . no one, miss.'

'I clearly heard you, Annie.'

'Just myself then, miss,' she replied, her expression shuttered.

Unable to contradict her, I turned my attention instead to my unfamiliar surroundings. I was in an eaves room of reasonable size, though it felt smaller due to the intruding angle of the ceiling, from which a single dormer window projected. Judging from its furnishings it had once been the school room – two hinged desks with attached plank seats stood side by side facing the teacher's table, the wall behind which was adorned with a large, coloured map of the world. Above the small fireplace hung a framed, embroidered sampler stitched with a religious quote from the parable of the talents – it induced the reader not to squander their God-given gifts.

I surveyed my surroundings avidly, as if I had stumbled upon a secret treasure trove. I disturbed a lamina of dust as I ran my fingers over the cloth-covered story books lined up on the shelf and I couldn't resist peeking beneath the desk lids, curious to discover any hidden artefacts.

'The school room . . .' I murmured to myself.

'The nursery is next door, miss,' Annie said, her tone beguiling. 'Would you like to see it?'

'Yes,' I murmured. 'Yes, I would.'

She led me back to the landing. I fancied she threw me a sly glance as she pushed open the second door and stepped aside. I detected a faint yet discernible odour, an unpleasant fusion of mothballs and damp, but it was otherwise a plain, inoffensive room, similar in size to the school room, with the same sloping roofs. Dust motes floated in the shaft of sunlight streaming through the dormer window, but the sun's rays brought no warmth. Pushed up against the wall behind the door was a full-sized metal bedstead, a green ribbed coverlet tucked in around the hump of a pillow and fastened tight under the mattress. At the foot of the bed the chimney breast jutted out into the room, with a simple fireplace as before, though above this one hung a faded sampler declaring 'We Are All God's Children'. On the opposite wall was a child's iron bedframe made up as the adult one, and next to that was an empty wooden cradle.

It may have been my imagination, but I couldn't help feeling an oppressive aura about the room that went beyond the fustiness of the air and the pervading chill that sent goose-pimples down my arms. It felt somehow inhospitable, and I understood now Madeleine's reluctance to use the room for her own baby. Indeed, I felt greatly relieved her child would be housed elsewhere.

The light streaming through the window vanished as scudding clouds covered the sun, casting a grey pallor over the room. There was a soft clatter. A small marble rolled across the floorboards towards us, skipping over the edges of each adjoining board. Its blue centre, the shape of a cat's eye, spun hypnotically within the green glass ball. I was transfixed by its progress until it finally came to a stop by the tip of Annie's shoe.

'I must have knocked it down,' she said. 'Have you seen enough, miss?'

I nodded and allowed her to usher me from the room. She pulled the door shut behind her. I hesitated at the top of the stairs. I was filled with an irrational yet overwhelming sense of fear.

'They're so terribly steep,' I muttered.

'It's a long way down, isn't it, miss?' Annie was so close behind me I could feel her breath on my cheek. Discomfort shunted me forward.

My fingers tightly gripped the cold curve of the banister. Steadily I made my way, the air growing warmer with each descending step. I experienced a peculiar sense of relief when I set both feet on the carpet at the bottom.

Later, when I had finally managed to dispense with my lingering unease, I thought back on the marble. Curiously, it had not appeared to be rolling away from Annie.

I could have sworn it was rolling straight for her.

Chapter Eleven

I made no mention to Madeleine of my exploration of the nursery floor, nor did I broach the accidental discovery of the toy soldiers in her drawer. This last bit of intelligence festered within me for the rest of the day and long into the evening. I found my nerves brittle, my manner off-hand, and my thoughts conflicted. By dinner time, a tight knot had developed in my stomach and I barely touched a thing. Instead, I snatched glances at Madeleine, wondering what secrets lay concealed behind her innocent expression.

I was relieved when she finally declared she was ready for bed. She looked to me, as ever, to escort her through the treacherous darkness to the safety of her room. She had of course noticed that I was not myself, but I allayed her concerns by attributing my low-spirits to a nagging headache.

I could not sleep. I was deeply troubled by the tangle of soldiers and what could be inferred from their mysterious presence in Madeleine's drawer. The peculiar atmosphere of the landing rooms also played on my mind, and though the house was at peace under the cover of night, I found myself straining to catch every whisper of draught, every tell-tale creak. Each time I closed my eyes I saw images of Annie Burrows and spinning marbles, Lydia and Lucien, Madeleine and her miniature lead army, all set against a terrifying backdrop of searing flames and choking smoke. Sleep was an impossibility. I longed with every particle of my being for Gerald's steadying presence.

I must have eventually succumbed to exhaustion for I woke in a befuddled daze, daylight straining at the curtains. The fire's gentle crackle revealed Annie had already been in, but I had clearly slept right through her visit, dead to the world. I turned over and groggily looked at my watch – I was thoroughly aghast to see that it had already turned eight.

Madeleine had warned me the evening before that I would be expected to join the house party for church. Lady Brightwell, it seemed, was as stringent as my parents in that regard: guests and servants alike were expected to attend the Sunday morning service. I was already running late as I reached for the bell-pull.

I found myself keeping a close eye on Annie as she laid out my clothes, tidied away my things and gathered items for the wash. I don't know whether she was aware of my constant surveillance, but sometimes I thought I saw her use the mirror to spy on me. We moved cautiously about the room, like two circling pugilists, each waiting for the other to make the first move.

I was last down, of course. Madeleine looked up in obvious relief as I began my descent to the hall, where Lady Brightwell and Miss Scott were already waiting, ready to depart, armed with umbrellas.

'You join us at last.' Lady Brightwell made no attempt to hide her disapproval at my tardy arrival. 'We had almost given up on you.'

'I'm so sorry. I didn't sleep well last night, the unfortunate consequence being I overslept this morning.' Annie appeared with my coat, hat and a furled umbrella.

'Was it the headache?' Madeleine enquired as I fumbled with my buttons. 'You poor thing.'

'Well, we must be off. I have never been late for a service in thirty years, I have no intention of starting now,' Lady Brightwell declared, leading us out to the car.

'She has never been late because the vicar has never dared start without her,' Madeleine muttered as we fell in behind.

As the Rolls rumbled over the cattle grid we passed Annie, running to catch the rest of the servants, who were taking a shortcut across the park to the village. I settled back in my seat and felt for my locket, hidden below my clothing. I fished it out, so it lay against the black weave of my coat.

Miss Scott leant forward. 'Your locket is very pretty, Miss Marcham, it has caught my eye now on several occasions.'

'Thank you.' I smiled. 'Gerald gave it to me.' The detail was instinctive, but my smile wavered as I delivered it.

'It must be very precious to you then.'

'Yes, yes, it is. Most precious.'

I touched the gold oval, relishing its solidity, as my memory took me back to a perfect late summer's day, August 1914. It had been a small gathering, just a few friends and neighbours, tables set out on the lawns. We women had declared there was to be no talk of war, but the subject proved irresistible to the men. They had huddled together, voices muted, their faces grave.

Gerald had broken off from them as the afternoon grew languid. I was sitting on a blanket, gossiping with Madeleine, when his shadow fell across my face.

'Walk with me?' He held out his hand in invitation.

I laughed as he hauled me to my feet. He drew my arm through his and we ambled towards the lake. My dress was white and light, floating about my ankles with every step. Gerald was dressed in cream trousers and a cream blazer trimmed with navy, his shirt collar open at the throat. It was, everyone had agreed, far too hot for neckties.

It was fresher by the lake, a slight breeze rippling the sparkling surface. Our steps sounded hollow as we walked the length of the wooden jetty. When we reached the end it felt as if we were standing in the middle of the lake itself – the shore, the others, far behind us. A moorhen glided out from the bank, periodically dipping his red beak into the water. I leant on Gerald, light-headed under the oppressive sun. My scalp itched with the heat, and I could feel a trickle of sweat running down my nape.

'I've signed up.'

I knew the announcement was coming, of course. They all were – the eager young men, keen for adventure. There had been a desperate rush, all fearful they might miss it – their one opportunity for a jolly good fight, a rather marvellous war. I didn't react. I just stared out over the lake. I didn't even have any words in my head – I had to *think* what to say. In the end, all I came up with was a paltry 'Oh'.

We stood in silence, watching the moorhen change direction.

'I wanted to speak to you, before I went.'

I hardly dared to breathe.

'Stella – I was wondering whether, when I get back, if – well – oh dash it! Marry me, Stella.' There was a desperate urgency to his final words. My heart exploded, my smile so instantly broad I thought it would tear my cheeks apart.

'Of course, I will!' It was a whisper, a laugh, a joyous exclamation and the radiance that broke out on his face mirrored my own.

'I'm sorry, I had intended to go down on one knee and everything!'

'You would have ruined your cream trousers!' I teased as he clutched my hands.

He adopted a look of mock seriousness. 'I do have something for you.' I couldn't stop smiling, my giggles rising like bubbles in a champagne glass. 'Close your eyes and hold out your hand.'

Biting my lip, I did as he ordered, proffering an open palm. I instantly realised that the velvet box placed on it was considerably larger than anticipated and my eyes flew open. My eyebrows twitched with confusion. Gerald watched me steadily as I lifted back the lid. Nestled against the satin lining was a beautifully scrolled gold locket. I felt the smile falter on my lips.

'I think a ring is more traditional in these circumstances,' I concluded lightly.

'Yes, yes, it is, but . . .'

He turned away from me, taking a couple of steps closer to the edge of the jetty. He thrust his hands deep into his pockets. I fought to subdue the ominous feeling that was threatening to dampen my happiness. When eventually he turned back to me the youthful joy had dissipated from his handsome features to be replaced by grave contemplation. The afternoon grew chilly.

'I'm going to war, Stella.'

'I know . . .' The weight of the announcement came to bear. I swallowed back a rising sense of panic. 'But it won't be for long. Everyone says it'll be over by Christmas.'

'Yes well, that's the thing about war. It has a way of being rather . . . unpredictable.'

'Well, it doesn't matter how long it lasts . . .' I took a tentative step towards him, the jewellery box in my hand. 'I will always love you, Gerald – you being away won't change that.'

'But it might change me.' He saw my look of shock and corrected himself quickly. 'Not my feelings for you, Stella, nothing will ever change the way I feel about you, but I don't know what's going to happen. I might be horribly injured, I might not even make it back at all—'

'Don't say that!'

He bridged the distance between us in one easy stride, gripping my arms to prevent me turning away.

'Darling Stella . . .' I refused to look at him. I couldn't understand why he was being so cruel, ruining this wonderful moment with talk of devastation and death. 'Stella.' I relented and sullenly met his gaze. 'I cannot tie you to me, not like this. Not knowing what I might be inflicting upon you at the end of this war. But there is nothing I want more in the world than to marry you, to have you as my wife and spend the rest of my days with you. I love you, Stella.'

I swallowed back the sob that threatened to undo me. I forced myself to be brave.

'So, what is this, then?' I asked, holding out the locket box.

He smiled, reassured by my attempted return to form. His finger tapped the end of my nose. 'You're being slightly petulant.' He lifted out the locket and stepped behind me, dangling it before my chest. His fingers rested against the back of my neck as he struggled with the clasp. 'This is a symbol of my intent, Stella Marcham.' I gasped as his lips pressed against the sensitive skin just below my hairline. Firm hands on my shoulders turned me round. He pulled me close until our bodies touched, his face just inches from mine. 'I intend to come back to you, I intend to marry you, I intend to spend the rest of my life with you.' He came even closer. 'I intend to make you a very happy woman.'

He kissed me then. I melted into his touch. My fingers threaded into the hair at the back of his head, drawing him ever closer to me. When we broke apart, I smiled with deliciously swollen lips.

'I like your intent,' I whispered. 'I accept your intent – and I'll match your intent, every step of the way.'

Chapter Twelve

The car pulled up before the church just as the troop of servants appeared from a pathway down the side of the graveyard. There were a few spots of rain in the wind as we got out, and I took the umbrella for good measure. The memory of Gerald's proposal had left me feeling melancholic and for once, I welcomed the opportunity for quiet reflection that the church service offered. Annie Burrows appeared last from the pathway, following a plump woman who was carefully tucking two posies of wild flowers into a bag looped over her forearm. Her eyes narrowed as she caught me watching her.

Following Lady Brightwell to the front door of the church was rather like following Moses across the Red Sea. The crowd of villagers who had congregated outside parted, their heads dipped deferentially as we passed through their midst. I think Madeleine found the whole experience rather embarrassing, shyly meeting people's eyes and murmuring 'Good morning' as she followed in her mother-in-law's wake.

Lady Brightwell, though, displayed little short of divine authority. She glided through the aisle and up the nave, Miss Scott darting forward to hold open the swing door of the Brightwell boxed pew, positioned at the front. Miss Scott herself only sat when she was quite satisfied she had met her employer's every need and comfort.

I followed Madeleine into the pew behind. I sighed as I sat down, tucking my umbrella into the corner out of the way. Madeleine unhooked the embroidered hassock and set it on the cold flags, dropping down to offer a prayer. I had no interest in engaging with the God who had abandoned me, so I remained in my seat, worshipping my memories of Gerald rather than a deity I could not see.

It was an unexceptional service. The vicar was ancient and stumbled over his words, his eyes straining to read the sermon, the glasses balanced on his stubby nose clearly unfit for purpose. The organist too was either decrepit or inept, labouring every note until even 'What A Friend We Have In Jesus' was reduced to a dirge. I leapt to my feet for the parting blessing, eager to escape.

Lady Brightwell stopped outside the porch to engage the vicar in a long discussion about the state of the hassocks. Miss Scott, clutching her handbag, leant in to me as the departing congregation shuffled around us.

'I miss the bells,' she said as Madeleine joined us. 'I was just saying, it's not the same without the bells, is it, my dear?'

Pealing church bells were a distant memory. Sundays had been silent for three long years, and would be, I feared, for longer yet. I left Madeleine to console her mother-in-law's companion and drifted away to scan the faded inscriptions on the headstones haphazardly placed about the graveyard.

I hadn't gone far when I noticed a soldier. He had his back to me, standing stiff and straight before a humble-looking grave, his head bowed. My heart ached; there was something very poignant about the simple sight – a fighting man grieving the lost. Sensing my presence, he began to look my way. I put my head down and walked on, shivering in the cool breeze that whipped up a clutch of dead leaves, buffeting them along the path before me.

A large chest tomb caught my eye and I wandered over to it. The flat tablet of stone that sealed the top rested on ornate pillars, one at each corner. An exquisitely carved stone angel, her head bowed in prayer, her wings closed behind her, knelt at one end, the folds of her robe pooling around her, her arms crossed over her chest. I stopped to read the inscription cut deep into the stone side, and learnt I was standing at the final resting place of none other than Sir Arthur Brightwell himself. The grass about the sarcophagus was unkempt, the edges of the stone lid were beginning to flake, and there was no indication that anyone had been near it for some time.

Moving on, I noticed a few feet away a more traditional headstone, its arced top ornately carved with cherubs and flowers. My pulse stuttered as I read the simple inscription:

IN LOVING MEMORY

LUCIEN ARTHUR BRIGHTWELL

AGED 5 YEARS AND 10 MONTHS

A wilting posy of simple wild flowers lay at the foot of the headstone. I crouched down to touch the faded offering. How curious the boy should be remembered and yet the father should not.

I became aware of someone hovering behind me, and I glanced over my shoulder to see the woman Annie had followed, waiting patiently for me to move on.

'Oh, I'm sorry,' I said, rising.

'Oh no, miss, that's quite all right. I'm just not used to seeing anyone else here, that's all.'

I noticed that she was clutching one of the bunches of flowers I had seen her with earlier, the top of the other just visible over the rim of her bag.

'You left the flowers?'

Her round cheeks diffused with pink. 'Oh, they're nothing much, miss, just a few pretty wild flowers I pick on the way here each week.'

'Oh no, I think they're lovely.' I stepped away from the grave. 'What a very sweet thing to do.'

She brushed off my praise, covering her embarrassment by busying herself replacing the old posy with the new. I looked away, affording her some privacy, as she quickly closed her eyes and silently muttered some brief words, before drawing her finger in the figure of a cross over her buxom breast. I smiled warmly as she stepped back.

'We shouldn't forget the dead, miss, especially when there's no one else who cares to remember them.'

'You're employed at Greyswick? I saw you arrive with the other servants. I'm Stella Marcham.'

'Of course you are, miss. Oh I've seen you but no, you won't have seen me. I'm Cook. I did have a name once, but Cook is all I'm known as these days.' She took the demotion from an individual to an unnamed servant with surprising good humour, as if she had always expected little from life and it hadn't disappointed her.

'Oh! Cook! Your apple sponge is divine.'

She chuckled modestly, but I could see she appreciated the compliment.

'You knew Lucien then?'

'Oh yes, miss – sweetest boy ever, well, next to Master Hector, of course. Years ago now, mind, I was a mere slip of a thing when the accident happened.'

'Accident?' The word felt clumsy on my tongue. 'I thought he died of influenza.'

'Well, he was recovering from the Russian 'flu, miss, to be sure, but it was the fall that killed him.'

'What fall?' Strands of unease were winding together to form a solid ball in the pit of my stomach. Why had Madeleine not been more explicit? She had made no mention of a fall, attributing the boy's death to illness alone. The sun disappeared behind bruised clouds. The air was getting damper and the atmosphere increasingly foreboding.

'He fell down the stairs, miss. They think he must have been faint from the 'flu and lost his balance at the top of the nursery staircase.'

I reeled in shock, reaching out to catch hold of the boy's headstone to steady myself. I recalled the fear I had experienced at the top of that very staircase and the threatening glint of the steps as they stretched perilously before me.

'Are you quite all right, miss? Do you need to sit down?'

'No, I'll be absolutely fine. The poor boy – I had no idea.'

'Oh, it was a terrible tragedy, miss, shocked us all to the core. His poor nanny was quite beside herself, she'd only left him for a minute.'

I thought of Madeleine's reluctance to stray beyond the nursery staircase, her insistence she would not be using the rooms for her own child and her apparent fear when I had mounted the steps myself. I began to understand her concerns.

Misfortune stalked the halls of Greyswick – it had stolen a child. It was little wonder Madeleine found herself so fearful, given her baby would soon be born within its walls. She was no doubt terrified of misfortune's greed, and the oil painting of Lucien Brightwell served as a daily reminder of the last time that hunger was sated. It was a dire warning of how vulnerable her fledgling happiness was. I was struck by a ghastly thought: could someone be using Lucien's lead soldiers to cruelly reinforce this insecurity?

'Are you sure you're all right, Miss Marcham?'

'I'm so sorry, Cook, I don't know what came over me. I was running late this morning, I didn't have time for breakfast.'

This information appeared to reassure her. She nodded wisely. 'That'll be it, we all need some sustenance after the night's fast. I'll make sure that girl of yours brings you a tray of something good and sweet as soon as you get back, miss. A little sugar and a nice cup of tea will soon perk you up.'

'That sounds wonderful, thank you.'

'Now, if you're quite sure you're well, I've got another posy to deliver before I can head back.'

'Oh please, don't let me detain you.'

She moved away, threading a clearly familiar path through the headstones until she reached one overshadowed by a holly tree. It was the same one I had seen the soldier at earlier, though he was now nowhere to be seen. I watched as she exchanged posies, the new for the old, then I hurried back towards the church door.

Lady Brightwell was already leading the return to the car, Miss Scott beside her, while Madeleine trailed behind. I dashed to join her.

'Oh, there you are—'

'Did you know? That Lucien had fallen to his death down those stairs?'

'Lucien? Oh, gracious, Stella, now? Really?'

'You did know then, that it wasn't the 'flu at all,' I persisted. With a huff she briskly carried on down the path, and I had to quick-step to catch up with her. She caught the dogged look on my face and frowned but knew it would be pointless to try and fob me off. She let out an exasperated sigh.

'He had been ill with the Russian influenza, the whole household got it,' she explained impatiently as we approached the gate. 'But it was the fall that killed him. His nanny wasn't watching him, and they think he must have left his bed to find her and just . . .' She lowered her voice, drawing me closer. 'That's why Miss Scott ended up looking after Hector. Lucien's nanny was immediately dismissed for neglect and Lady Brightwell wouldn't trust anyone else to care for him.'

She exclaimed as a spot of rain landed on her cheek. It was quickly followed by another, then more in rapid succession. Madeleine readied her umbrella. She paused when she saw I was failing to follow suit.

'Where's your umbrella? You haven't left it inside, have you?'

Cursing, I realised I had done just that. Promising to catch her up, I ran back through the rain. The studded oak door creaked as I rattled the latch and pushed it open. The church stood empty, and my footsteps echoed on the flagstones as I hastened up the nave to the boxed pew. My brolly was where I had left it, tucked into the corner. Tutting at my carelessness, I retrieved it and made my way out.

The last of the congregation had dispersed from the

churchyard. I stood in the porch, dismayed at the sheets of rain now falling, hoping that Lady Brightwell would be gracious enough to hold the car for me. I shook out my umbrella and was just in the process of putting it up when I spotted a solitary black-clad figure approaching the tomb of Sir Arthur Brightwell. There was something in their furtive movement that piqued my interest. I lowered the brolly and tucked myself against the inside edge of the porch, peering round the blackened stone through the gauze of rain.

The woman was holding aloft an umbrella to protect herself from the downpour. I did not need to see her face – the solid black clothing, the stature and broad shoulders gave Mrs Henge away immediately. She took a step closer to the sarcophagus, the rain streaming over the curve of her brolly. She stood for an age, staring at the damp-darkened stone. I found this quiet display of homage by a long-serving servant strangely touching and I was about to leave her to it when she tipped up her chin and brought it down abruptly. I gasped, recoiling into the protection of the porch, stunned with disbelief.

Even from this distance, the globule of spit flying from her mouth was shockingly clear to see.

Chapter Thirteen

Later that afternoon, Madeleine became extremely upset. We had all gathered in the drawing room after lunch. The rain persisted in its steady downpour, draining the day of light, forcing us to utilise the oil lamps to take the edge off the depressing weather-induced gloom. The fire spat and crackled as we engaged in our individual pursuits: I was reading, Miss Scott was clacking her restless needles, Lady Brightwell was snoozing, and Madeleine was finishing off her embroidery panel.

The clock had just struck two when Lady Brightwell roused herself.

'Madeleine, have you finished with my copy of *The Lady*?'

'Oh yes, of course.' Madeleine set down her embroidery. 'I'm so sorry, I meant to return it. It's in my room – let me fetch it for you now.'

She hurried out.

The wind picked up and changed direction. Rain struck the windows like handfuls of pebbles, distracting me from the pages of my book. I rather liked the comfort of being all tucked up by the fire when it was so horrid outside.

The door opened and Madeleine walked back into the room. She came to an abrupt standstill. I looked round and immediately saw she was as white as a sheet, tears layering her blue eyes, her mouth tight with self-control. She was clutching a picture frame.

'Madeleine – are you all right?'

Miss Scott and Lady Brightwell both looked up on hearing the concern in my voice.

'Look.' Emotion cracked the single word as in a flash she held up the large frame to face us. It was a photograph of Hector, a studio-taken head shot of him looking proudly at the camera, dashing in his officer's uniform. I had seen it before – it hung on the wall above the tallboy in her room. It was her favourite photograph.

The glass of the picture frame had been smashed, but it wasn't chaotically fractured as one might have expected. It appeared as though something had been drilled into the very centre of the pane. The cracking fanned out in concentric circles, like a perfectly formed spider's web, dissecting the handsome features of the sepia image below.

'Oh no!' Miss Scott cried out. 'You've broken it! What a terrible shame. It's such a nice frame and I adore that photo of Hector. Why, I have a smaller version of very same one by my bed.'

Madeleine was clearly struggling to maintain control. 'I didn't break it.' There was uncharacteristic venom in her denial that took me by surprise.

'Oh dear,' Miss Scott sympathised, seemingly oblivious to the simmering anger.

'Has one of the maids broken it while cleaning?' I suggested, setting down my book.

'How can they have?' Her head snapped towards me and I drew back, seeing the vehemence behind her tear-blurred eyes.

'It hangs on the wall above my tallboy, Stella! How could anyone knock it down from there?'

'One of the girls probably caught it with a feather duster,' Lady Brightwell interjected.

I saw the loaded look she exchanged with an uneasy Miss Scott; there was an undercurrent to it that I didn't understand – all I could see was Madeleine's profound distress. It was of course upsetting that the picture had been broken, but it was easily rectified. I couldn't understand why she was so angry, when by nature she was such a placid, forgiving soul.

She took a step further into the room, thrusting the frame at her mother-in-law, her hands shaking. 'Look at that damage! Even if it had been knocked from the wall, it would have just shattered, the way glass does. This isn't a simple fracture – look at it! This glass has been deliberately broken.'

Lady Brightwell huffed and refused to engage. Once again it was left to Miss Scott to placate her.

'Oh, my dear, I'm sure it was a simple accident. To say it was deliberate . . . why, that is quite an accusation to make. Why would anyone do something to upset you?'

'Someone has deliberately been trying to upset me since the day I arrived.'

It was most unfortunate that Maisie chose this inopportune moment to enter with a fresh tray of tea things. The poor girl detected the hostile atmosphere as soon as she pushed the door open with her hip. She stood, wide-eyed, holding the tray before her like a sacrificial offering.

'Mrs Henge said you'd probably be wanting a fresh pot of tea by now,' she stuttered, darting glances between us all and finding sparse welcome in our grim expressions.

'Indeed. Your appearance is most fortuitous, Maisie, as our last remaining housemaid.' Lady Brightwell's beady eyes glinted dangerously in Madeleine's direction. 'Set the tray here, girl.'

Maisie hurried forward, the china chinking a mismatched tune. She did as she was bid and began to unload the tray, exchanging the cold pot and empty milk jug. She stood once the task was done, looking apprehensive.

'Now, Maisie, do tell me . . .' Lady Brightwell's long fingers folded around the arm of her chair, the stones of her rings dwarfing her age-withered hands. Her gaze flickered over Madeleine, her eyes narrowing, like a cat preparing to toy with a mouse. 'Have you been in Mrs Brightwell's room today?'

The question hung in the air. Maisie looked confused, then wary, suspecting a trap.

'Yes, my lady. I went in to light the fire first thing and help her dress. I haven't been in since, though.'

'Are you sure? If you are honest no one will be cross with you.'

'I am being honest,' the young maid said, indignant at the suggestion she might be otherwise. 'I was only in Mrs Brightwell's room this morning and once she was dressed I left. I haven't been back since.'

'It's not Maisie.' Madeleine's statement was barely audible. 'We both know it's not Maisie,' she said again, bolder this time.

Lady Brightwell paid her no heed; her fingers flexed, like a cat extending its claws. 'To the best of your knowledge, has anyone else been in Mrs Brightwell's room today, Maisie?'

The girl smirked. 'Well, forgive me, my lady, but it's not like Cook leaves the kitchen and there's only me and Mrs Henge that see to the house these days,' she looked at me, 'save for your girl

Annie, miss, who's been helping out. But I don't believe she's been up to Mrs Brightwell's room today either – she's had no cause to.' I felt a stir of unease at the mention of Annie's name. 'Perhaps Mrs Henge had reason to go in.'

'I see.' Lady Brightwell devoured the girl's answer, smacking her lips with satisfaction. 'So, neither you nor Annie have been up to Mrs Brightwell's room?'

Madeleine hugged the broken frame to her chest. She looked utterly miserable. 'Please stop . . .' she murmured, but Lady Brightwell carried on regardless.

'You know, Maisie, honesty is always rewarded. If an accident has occurred with one of Mrs Brightwell's possessions – perpetrated by you or another – as long as a confession is made, there would be no punishment.'

'There's been no accident, my lady.' Maisie looked thoroughly confused now. 'I'm very sorry, my lady, but really I don't know what you're talking about, begging your pardon.'

'Thank you, Maisie. You may go.' The bemused girl bobbed a curtsy and began to withdraw. 'But Maisie, you did say Mrs Henge might have had reason to enter Mrs Brightwell's room?' Lady Brightwell called out.

At this, Madeleine's head shot up. 'Oh no please! There's no need—'

'Do you know where Mrs Henge is, Maisie?'

'Well, yes, my lady, Mrs Henge was just in the hall a few minutes ago. I saw her when I was on my way here.'

'Please send her in.' Lady Brightwell sat back in her chair.

'Oh, please don't ask Mrs Henge, there really is no need, I'm sure she wouldn't have had anything to do with it . . .' Madeleine begged, like a condemned prisoner pleading for mercy.

My stomach churned. I decided to stop this ridiculous charade that seemed to me little more than a cruel exercise in humiliation, but as I tried to object Lady Brightwell held up her hand.

'Madeleine has once again made some very serious accusations and they must be investigated.'

The door opened and Mrs Henge, a new player in the drama, walked in to take her place centre stage, expressionless, self-contained and confident.

'You called for me, my lady?'

'Mrs Henge, Mrs Brightwell has just gone to her room and found the glass in the framed photograph of her husband quite smashed. She believes it to be the result of intentional vandalism.'

'I'm sorry to hear that, Lady Brightwell, but I assure you, the picture could not have been broken by anyone today. No one has been in the room, save Maisie when she was called to attend Mrs Brightwell this morning.' The housekeeper now turned to face my sister. 'I'm sorry, Mrs Brightwell, you must be mistaken.' Madeleine flinched as if she had been struck. Even though I longed to go to my sister's aid, I remained seated, transfixed by the extraordinary scene playing before me. Mrs Henge held out her hand. 'If you would care to give me the frame, ma'am, I will ensure that it is mended or replaced, whichever you prefer.'

'No.' Madeleine clutched the precious photograph closer to her chest. I was horrified to see a single tear trickle over her pale cheek. 'No. I will see to it, thank you.'

Mrs Henge raised her eyebrows before turning back to her employer. 'Is there anything else, my lady?'

'No, Mrs Henge. I think the matter has been satisfactorily concluded. You may go.'

Lady Brightwell let the ominous silence breathe through the room after the door closed on the housekeeper. She tapped impatiently on the arm of her chair.

'You really must accept, Madeleine, that there is no one in this house conspiring against you. Such unpleasant fancies are unhealthy figments of your imagination.'

Madeleine raised her head, her mouth trembling, fresh tears marring her cheeks. She tilted up her chin in defiance. 'Well, all I know is I certainly didn't break it, which begs the question – who did?'

And before anyone could answer, she fled the room.

Chapter Fourteen

I was already on my feet and halfway across the room as the door slammed behind her.

'Please sit down for a moment, Miss Marcham,' Lady Brightwell said.

'I will not sit down. I am going after my sister.'

'Sit down, would you?' she repeated wearily. 'Going after Madeleine will not achieve anything.'

'She's upset!'

'And your sympathy won't change that.'

'Why did you do that? That was a horrid thing to do.' `

'I really do wish you would sit down, Miss Marcham. This seems to me the perfect opportunity for us to speak.' She refused to be infected by my temper, but her equanimity was no cure for my anger.

'It was despicable of you to humiliate Madeleine like that.'

Her patience snapped. 'Miss Marcham, I assure you that was absolutely necessary. God knows we have tried every other tactic with your sister over the past few weeks. We have exhausted all niceties and attempts at rationale – it seems ridicule is the only method we have left to rebut her absurd claims.'

Her words set off an alarm bell in my mind. A persistent inner voice suggested that I should listen to what she had to say. This arousal of my curiosity began to undermine my defiance.

'Please, Miss Marcham.' Miss Scott now lent her kindly voice to the appeal. 'Won't you sit with us? We have been looking for an opportunity to speak to you.'

She removed her spectacles. It was strange to see her without them. The glasses were so old-fashioned they aged her, blunted her somehow, but without them, I could better see the beautifully preserved planes of her face, the high cheekbones and dainty nose. I found myself weakening under her gentle persuasion.

'Why do you want to speak to me?'

'For goodness' sake, girl, I cannot conduct this conversation with you towering over me.' Lady Brightwell's jewelled hand smacked the arm of the sofa. 'Sit!' she commanded, gesturing to the empty seat opposite. With an exasperated sigh I finally relented.

'Tell me, Miss Marcham, how have you found your sister since your arrival?'

The formality of her address seemed officious, intimidating even, and I began to suspect I had been unwittingly lured into the witness box.

'I find her very well.'

'Really, Miss Marcham?' The questioning note in Lady Brightwell's voice conveyed her incredulity. A log slipped in the fire, spitting out a cascade of sparks. One landed on the very edge of the grate and I quickly suppressed it under the toe of my shoe, grateful for its fleeting distraction – an opportunity to formulate my thoughts.

'She is . . . she is perhaps not quite herself . . . a little anxious, I would say.' My cheeks flushed under Lady Brightwell's perceptive scrutiny. I felt like Judas on the brink of a betrayal I would come to regret.

'Anxious,' Lady Brightwell echoed. 'Yes. May I be completely frank with you, Miss Marcham? I have myself become very concerned about Madeleine. I am sorry you had to witness that drama, but it is only the latest in what has been a rather long and increasingly tiresome series of events. You see, the picture, it is not the first *incident* since Madeleine's arrival.' She paused, and my apprehension increased. 'She has made several accusations against the household staff. She has become increasingly . . .' She looked to Miss Scott for inspiration.

'Belligerent,' the companion concluded. 'She is convinced someone is acting maliciously against her – which simply isn't true, I assure you.'

'Madeleine has been to stay with us before and we've never had an issue. Until now.'

'Lady Brightwell, forgive me if you find me blunt, but I hardly think humiliation will help the situation. If anything, you have only succeeded in making her feel more isolated and self-conscious, when by rights she should be the mistress of this house.'

'You are blunt.' Spots of colour appeared high on her cheeks. To my surprise, she sighed heavily. 'Perhaps you are right. Perhaps I was wrong to do that. But you must understand, Miss Marcham, it has become extremely difficult to maintain the equilibrium of this house with your sister making unpleasant accusations.'

We sat silently as the rain splattered against the windows, the wind building again outside. Lady Brightwell seemed lost in troubled thoughts.

'I do empathise with Madeleine.' She surrendered the words with some reluctance. 'I appreciate she is going through an extremely testing time, and I have no doubt she would rather be with my son in London, but unfortunately, needs must.'

Miss Scott smiled gently. 'We do so want her to be happy here, my dear. As you rightly suggest, Greyswick is her home too.'

'She can be mistress of this house, Miss Marcham,' Lady Brightwell adopted a more strident tone now, 'but it is no small undertaking, and forgive me for saying this, but she has not yet proven herself up to the task.'

'Perhaps she hasn't had the opportunity,' I pointed out.

'Perhaps now isn't the right time,' Miss Scott sweetly countered. 'She has so many changes to contend with at the moment, it must be so daunting for her.'

Lady Brightwell nodded sagely. 'Indeed. I believe all of this trouble with Madeleine stems from her being in her *delicate* state. I appreciate she has a great many anxieties – a baby on the way, Hector in London, fears over the safe-keeping of them both . . .' We locked eyes as I realised Hector had confided in her about Madeleine's miscarriage. 'We are living in very difficult times, Miss Marcham – daily life is challenging for us all, but we must rise to that challenge and meet it head on. We must all be strong – I'm sure you can appreciate that. Madeleine must learn to be robust.' The last word escaped her like air hissing from a punctured tyre.

'I do appreciate what she's going through,' she continued, her demeanour softening as she leant towards me, her sagging features golden in the firelight. 'I will confide in you now, Miss Marcham, I know exactly what it is to be unsettled – distressed even – by the gravity of pregnancy, by the prospect of birth. I myself did not take to motherhood – it is not all joy, having a baby. One surrenders a part of oneself and some cope with that better than others, I suppose.'

She paused again, and Miss Scott's hand strayed across to lightly brush her forearm, willing her the courage to continue. Lady Brightwell, warmed by the comforting gesture, cleared her throat.

'In my own case, illness initiated labour, a . . . very traumatic labour. It was touch and go whether I would survive, whether even the child would survive. Of course, I did and, thanks be to God, so did he. But that whole experience took a profound toll on me. I was not myself for some time after. I'm ashamed to say that I succumbed to a form of hysteria.'

She was clearly embarrassed to recount these details, humiliated by her perceived weakness, but she took a deep breath, and the vulnerability I had fleetingly witnessed vanished. Her voice was forceful once again.

'I was a young woman, in a strange house, with a new baby and a stepchild who resented me. My husband was away much of the time and I felt completely alone. Even dear Miss Scott was not with me.'

'Oh, my lady . . .' Miss Scott began, but Lady Brightwell silenced her with a wave of her hand.

'They were your parents, Scottie, you had to go,' she said, before addressing me once again. 'What I am trying to say, Miss Marcham, is that I am not, as I think you are inclined to believe, totally oblivious to Madeleine's vulnerabilities at this time. I sympathise, I truly do, but I implore you to bring her to her senses and prevent her from leaping to ridiculous conclusions every time something untoward happens. Can you do that for me, Miss Marcham?'

I smoothed my skirts over the curve of my knee. 'I came here, Lady Brightwell, to lend comfort and support to my sister in any way I can, and that is what I intend to do.' I eyed her sharply. 'Are you completely sure there's nothing in what Madeleine says? That someone isn't—'

'I assure you, Miss Marcham, there is not.'

'Then obviously I will do my best to allay any fears she has in that area.' A lingering uncertainty niggled at me. 'You are quite sure the younger staff—'

'Miss Marcham, if you are in some way looking to point the finger of blame at Maisie, you are quite wrong to do so. Maisie's mother worked in this house, and now her daughter proudly follows suit. She may be high-spirited, but I am confident she would never do anything to jeopardise her position.'

'I think I would like to go to my sister now.'

As I reached the door it occurred to me I did not know the full nature of Madeleine's accusations.

'May I ask what sort of things Madeleine has complained of?'

'Oh,' Lady Brightwell harrumphed. 'All sorts: odd noises, people sneaking into her room, things left on her bed . . .'

A trickle of ice ran down my spine. 'What type of things?'

'Ummm?' I could see she was only half-listening now. Our discourse had ended, and her interest was waning.

'Lady Brightwell . . .' I pressed. 'What type of things?'

She let out a sharp bark of laughter. 'Toy soldiers, would you believe? Really! The notion of it. Quite, quite absurd!'

Chapter Fifteen

Madeleine failed to respond to my knock, but I let myself in anyway. Hector's portrait lay face up on the bed, while she stood at the window, her back to me, her arms wrapped across her front. She didn't turn around when I softly called her name, but a hand strayed to wipe her cheeks.

'Did you have a nice chat?'

'We need to talk, Madeleine.'

'I don't want to talk. There's no point. Whatever they've told you, must be the truth.'

'Madeleine—'

'Stella, *please*!' At last she faced me, and she was unable to hide her distress any longer. Her eyes were red and swollen, her nose inflamed, her mouth blown with misery. A breath shuddered from her and she threw her head back, as if hoping gravity might stop the pooling tears from falling. 'Please, let's not talk about it.'

'Tell me about the toy soldiers.'

She groaned and swung back to the window. 'I don't want to. I don't want to talk about any of it.'

'Madeleine, did you put the toy soldier in my bed?'

'No! Of course not, whatever would make you think that?'

Having gained her attention, I walked around the bed and pulled open the bedside drawer. I didn't need to say anything.

'I didn't put it in your bed. I know what you're thinking, but I didn't.'

'Where did these come from?'

'They have all been left for me. In this room.'

'By *whom*, Madeleine?'

She made no attempt to answer but adopted a guarded expression as she turned back to the window. I joined her there, determined not to be ignored, determined to have her confide in me.

'You think someone in the house is doing this to you on purpose.' A solitary tear tumbled over the scalded rim of her eye and trickled slowly down her cheek. 'You think there's someone invoking Lucien's death to make you afraid, afraid for your baby.' She bit her lip and swallowed hard. My own heart ached at her display of dignified misery. 'Madeleine, Hector told me about last time.'

Her face crumpled. I rested my arm about her shoulders and drew her against me. Gradually her stiff body eased into my embrace, her resistance weakening as she unfolded her arms to cling to me. I kissed her head and offered words of solace as her body heaved, until at last she regained her self-control and pulled away from me, drying her cheeks with her hands.

'I am right, aren't I?' I said at last. 'You suspect someone's trying to hurt you – make you feel vulnerable?'

'That's what I thought . . . at first.' She slumped on the end of her bed, her fingertips subconsciously catching the picture frame.

'What do you mean "at first"?' I asked as I dropped down beside her.

In a faltering voice, she explained how she had discovered a toy soldier tucked within her bed on the second night of her stay. She dismissed it without much thought, but the night after, another one appeared – again she ignored it as nothing more than a foolish prank. But by the time the fifth one appeared she'd had enough, and the toys' association with Lucien – knowing of his mother's tragic death and his own fateful fall – troubled her, and suddenly the ill-conceived joke wasn't so funny any more.

She took the liberty of having a quiet word with Maisie, the obvious culprit, but when the girl vehemently denied any wrong-doing, she mentioned it to Mrs Henge, who in turn brought the matter to Lady Brightwell's attention. The servants had been summoned and questioned and all had denied any involvement. Madeleine was left embarrassed, but worse, she was aware of her mother-in-law's scepticism. She resolved to say nothing more, but as the toy soldiers continued to appear, she began to suspect a sinister intent.

'And then other things started happening,' she said quietly.

'What other things?'

Restless, she pushed herself from the bed. 'Someone had been in my room.'

'Madeleine, you live in a house with servants and family – no doubt many of them have reason to be in your room,' I pointed out, subduing a flicker of disquiet as I recalled my open door, and the sensation of fingers in my hair.

She whirled round. 'While I'm asleep? And I don't mean sneaking in to light the fire in the morning.' She began to prowl about the room, her agitation mounting. 'Again, everyone denied all knowledge. I took to locking my door, but it would be open come morning – the key still in the hole. I even took to rolling back the carpet, so if someone unlocked the door from the other side, I would hear my key dropping onto the floorboards. It never did.' She hurried back to the bed, sinking down beside me, her body urgently angled into mine. 'Stella, no one on the landing would have been able to unlock the door without dislodging my key first.'

'Madeleine, what are you trying to say?'

'Things happen in this house that defy explanation . . .' Her voice fell to a whisper, as her eyes slid surreptitiously about her, distrusting the very walls that enclosed us. 'I am afraid . . . I am afraid of this house.'

'Oh, Madeleine . . .' I took her hands and squeezed them, thinking how young and vulnerable she looked, having delivered her terrible admission. 'It's just a house – just bricks and mortar. You risk exaggerating these things – twisting them into something they're not. I suspect the toy soldiers were a nonsensical prank gone wrong. I've seen the glint in Maisie's eye, she's a mischievous one – not malicious, I don't think, but immature and perhaps thoughtless. Of course she's going to deny any wrong-doing, she doesn't want to get into trouble. As for the door, I'm sure there's a sensible explanation – a loose-fitting lock, perhaps . . .'

She withdrew her hands from mine. 'No, you are wrong, Stella. I have spent all my time here thinking these things through as logically as I can . . .'

'You are too close to them, too emotionally involved, you cannot see the wood for the trees . . .'

'No, Stella, there is something not right about Greyswick. Even you have sensed it, I know you have. Why else do you find yourself so drawn to the nursery staircase and those rooms I have tried so hard to keep you from?'

I had no answer for her, just a rising sense of unease. Memories of Annie Burrows whispering in the nursery forced their way to the fore, but I pushed them back, not wanting to dwell on her strange behaviour, so disturbingly reminiscent of her father. I did not want to dwell on any of it. I had exiled my recollections to the shadowy corners of my mind years ago and I would not cast any light onto those thoughts and suppositions now. I was afraid of what I would find there; something, I suspected, far more disconcerting than cobwebs and dust.

Madeleine got up and returned to the window, bracing herself against the frame. She had spent weeks stockpiling her precious secrets – now she was contemplating sharing her cache with me – if I deserved it, if I could be trusted. She decided to take the risk.

'I hear crying, Stella.'

She was an empty shell when she turned to gauge my reaction, as if someone had scooped out her tender heart and sweet filling, leaving just her exterior, rendered unnaturally hard without her innate gentleness to soften its edges. Alarmed, I asked her what she meant.

'I hear crying at night. It's a heartbreaking sound . . . it drills into my head and I can't shake it loose.'

'What?'

'I don't know what he wants with me.'

'Who, Madeleine?'

'No one else hears him, Stella . . . only me . . . and only now.' She cupped her belly.

'Madeleine, what are you talking about?'

'I'm too frightened to go to him. I'm too frightened of what I'll find if I open that door. Do you see now, Stella, do you understand why I cannot rest in this house?'

Tears glazed the blue irises dancing across my face in search of understanding, as she fought to subdue the emotion swamping her without warning, tearing at her throat, trembling through her limbs. I was appalled by the transformation.

'Dear God! Who, Madeleine? Who do you think you hear?'

In those taut seconds I awaited her answer, my very surroundings seemed to contract, as if the room itself was holding its breath, waiting for her revelation.

'Lucien Brightwell, of course.'

Silence stretched between us. A word unspoken filled the void, one I could not ignore.

'Madeleine, are you trying to say you think this house is *haunted*?' She nodded her head: short, sharp tremors of movement. 'Is that what you've told the others?'

'No, how could I?' She sniffed and wiped again at her cheeks. 'What would they think if I said that? They already think I'm mad – perhaps I am.'

'There are no such things as ghosts, Madeleine . . .' But even as the words left me, my conscience called. Jim Burrows' face backlit by flames flashed before me. I tried to banish the image, but in the deepest recesses of my mind, a slumbering monster stirred. 'Whatever you've experienced, I'm sure there is a perfectly reasonable explanation.'

'I thought so, too, at first. But not any more. I've exhausted all the "perfectly reasonable" explanations. Either this house is haunted, or I am losing my mind. It's not much of a choice, is it?' She collapsed into a chair by the dead fire, the bed of ashes lending a sooty tang to the air.

I was struggling to grasp it all. 'What makes you think it's Lucien Brightwell?'

'It's a child I hear, Stella. Only Hector's family have lived in this house and Lucien is the only child to have died in it.'

'Perhaps there is a living child here – someone the servants are concealing, and it's them you hear?'

'Don't you think I've thought of that?' Her head snapped towards me, anger and disappointment conflicting in her stormy eyes. 'There is no child at Greyswick, Stella, I assure you of that. No *living* child.' She looked back into the ashes, her zest extinguished. 'You don't believe me.'

'I just don't understand why no one else has experienced anything.'

'Maybe they have, but they're like you – in denial.'

Her words cut me, their inferred lack of support wounding me deeply, yet as I continued to try my best to reason with her, to reassure her of the absurdity of her conclusions, it was my own duplicity that troubled me the most.

Neither of us could face dinner, so as dusk stole the light from the room we had Maisie bring up a tray, sending our apologies to Lady Brightwell. We talked more on the subject, but it was futile: we were both entrenched in our positions, with neither of us willing to give ground. In the end we lapsed into stalemate and engaged ourselves with other distractions until it was time to retire. I kissed Madeleine's cheek as I left and begged her to get some rest.

'Sleep is so elusive here,' she murmured, as she slowly closed the door.

I chose not to have Annie help me. I undressed myself and climbed into bed, but when I extinguished the light, it was impossible not to imagine what lurked in the shadows, and for the first time I found the darkness threatening, as if our conversation had given the night carte blanche to create whatever terrors it wished.

The stubborn memories that troubled me did not help my state of mind, as I dwelt on dead men and dead children, until at last I threw myself onto my side and hiked my blankets over my head, determined to sleep.

I am looking for Gerald. He is not dead, he is merely lost – I must find him. I am running through a tent – it stretches for miles, I cannot see its end. The canvas snaps and cracks as the wind billows it in and sucks it out with every howling gust. The duckboards beneath my feet are slick with blood, and it is all I can do to stop from skidding through the coagulated pools. There are so many beds – I must find him. Gerald! I want to scream his name, but it lodges in my throat. I hear him crying. He is sobbing for me. I am coming! Please do not cry, my love! I am coming!

My eyes flew open. I peered into the darkness as my consciousness drunkenly staggered into the present, my breaths cutting my lungs with short, sharp thrusts. I propped myself up on my elbows, the bedcovers slipping from me, as I struggled to anchor myself in place and time. Gradually, I began to recognise familiar articles in my room and their tangibility reassured me. With a sigh I collapsed back upon my pillow, reality reasserted, my hopes of Gerald sinking like lead to the pit of my stomach.

I rolled onto my side and shuffled to get comfortable, willing myself back to sleep, desperate to shun the images of my nightmare. My muscles began to relax as my body moulded into the mattress.

Then I heard it.

I sat up, staring into the darkness. Had I been mistaken? I focused again, trying to bore beneath the still surface of the silence to discover the faint sounds trapped beneath. My breathing was too noisy, so I seized my lungs. I squeezed my eyes shut – there could be no distractions. I had to concentrate, I had to be sure. I waited, all my senses redundant bar one.

I gasped, my eyes wide.

I was not mistaken.

It was there – faint, but distinct.

I heard it. Just as she said.

A child.

Crying.

Chapter Sixteen

I lay rigid in my bed, barely able to even breathe, captivated by the sobs that softly filtered into my room – though I lacked the courage to contemplate from where. Every sinew of my body was taut, ready for flight, prepared for self-preservation. My heart pounded so loudly against my chest I could almost pick up its vibrations through the still air.

I longed to pull the covers over my head and hunker down into my mattress, to cower from the ghastly unknown, but somewhere amongst the fear-induced fuddle of my brain was a petulant voice demanding I get up. It played its trump card: I owed Madeleine.

There had to be a rational explanation, I told myself firmly as I pushed back the covers. I sat, shivering in the darkness, waiting for the plaintive sound to pierce the air. When it finally came I almost persuaded myself it was nothing more than the wind sighing through a loose sash. But then it came again, and I knew it was not.

My legs were quivering as I got up, my joints liquid now rather than cartilage, muscle and bone. I groped towards the door, drawn to the sliver of light running along its bottom, a beacon in the darkness. It was the final barrier to whatever awaited me beyond my room. I had long since turned my back on God, but now in my hour of need, familiar sacred words found their way to my lips, as I turned the handle and inched the door ajar.

The warm light from the wall sconces spilt comfortingly into my room. I edged myself against the door jamb, the artery in my neck pulsing. The crying was clearer now. This was no breeze through an ill-fitting window. It was unmistakable, and the sheer visceral quality of it took my breath away. I was startled by the click of Madeleine's door lock. A moment later, her pale face appeared.

'You hear it?' she whispered. I couldn't speak. I simply nodded. She leant against the door frame. 'Thank God.' She observed my terror with pity. 'It comes from the nursery.' Experience had made her stoical.

I nodded again. I had not attempted to look up the corridor. A basic instinct had advised me against it, but I knew I must. The wall lights stopped just short of the nursery staircase, their soothing golden glow failing to reach its treads. Instead the dark mahogany steps wallowed in a milky pool of moonlight cast through the window at the end.

The staircase called to me like a siren, drawing me in, exerting an irresistible pull. I stepped out onto the landing.

Another plaintive sob split the silence. I fought the desire to flee; instead, I thought of Madeleine, and the unwavering loyalty she had shown me when Gerald died – she had defended me when I was incapable of protecting myself. The roles were reversed now – she needed my protection, my courage, and she would have it.

'I'm going up.'

'Oh, Stella, no . . .' An internal struggle raged behind her look of horror. Conquering her fears, she slid from her doorway to join me. She looked ridiculously spectral herself, in her high-necked white nightgown that skimmed the floor. But then, I realised, so did I: ghosts in the night.

'I am going,' I reiterated, hoping if I said it enough times, I might eventually leave the protection of my doorway. Sure enough, my feet shuffled forwards.

Madeleine's fingers caught at the floating fabric of my nightdress in a half-hearted attempt to stop me, but I easily pulled free from her fragile grip. Every ounce of common sense I possessed was screaming at me to turn and run as I made my wary advance.

Breathing hard, I grabbed the banister and mounted the first step. The polished wood was cold and unwelcoming beneath my bare feet. Moving upwards took concentrated effort, like wading through water. Somehow, I managed another step, and then another, each creaking in protest as they took my weight, vexed by my presence. I came abreast of Lucien's portrait, wreathed in shadows. The whites of his eyes glinted through the darkness.

I was petrified as I took the final step onto the gloomy landing, the doors closed against me. There were audible gasps and splutters in the sobbing now, and it was utterly inconceivable to me that I might not find a living soul within the nursery, so vivid – so vulnerable – were the sounds emanating from that room. The air was stagnant and achingly cold. I stared at the door, daunted by the prospect of my next move. Another sob seeped out, ebbing and flowing. I had never heard such a wretched sound.

Something at the servants' entrance played in my peripheral vision; a jagged breath snagged in my throat. The violence of my quivering limbs paralysed me, but though my neck was rigid, I forced myself to look. Behind the obscured glass, a blurred face appeared in a golden orb. The door handle dipped down.

Annie Burrows emerged from the pitch of the servants' corridor dressed only in her cotton nightgown, holding aloft a candle in a brass holder.

'Annie!' My shoulders sagged with relief. 'Did you hear anything?'

'Crying.'

But now only silence filled the frigid air.

We waited, time dragging, while the icy boards bit hungrily into the naked soles of our feet. The flickering light cast by Annie's candle played upon her cheek, illuminating a strange intensity in her expression. My heart kicked stronger against my ribs. Her company provided paltry comfort.

Just as I decided to call a halt to this unsettling vigil, it came again: a faint sob, the death throes of hysteria. I knew what needed to be done, but I cowered from the task. Without consultation, and showing none of my fear, Annie stepped forward and turned the handle. The nursery door swung wide.

The room was empty. A shaft of moonlight was the only intruder, beaming in through the mullioned window, to highlight the furnishings. Collecting what fragments of courage I had left, I stepped onto the threshold. An arctic breeze leaked from the room, swirling around my bare ankles, sending shivers up my legs.

'There's no one here,' I murmured, mystified. The maid said nothing. Her candle flame guttered. 'How can that be?'

I backed away, confused and perturbed. Annie drew the door to behind her. I heard my name drift up the staircase, and gathering myself, I hurried to the top step, resting my hand on the banister. Madeleine had bravely progressed as far as the newel post below. She was looking up at me, a diaphanous sprite in the silver moonlight.

'What's happening?'

'It's empty. The nursery – there's no one there,' I whispered back.

At precisely that moment I felt an inexplicable shifting of pressure in the atmosphere. Annie cried, 'Don't!' and the next thing I knew I was plunging forwards. Madeleine screeched my name. My fingers anchored me to the banister and I crashed into the railing.

'Stella, my God! Are you all right?'

I was stunned and winded, but thankfully still in one piece. Annie's face loomed at the top of the staircase.

'Why did you say that?' I gasped. 'Why did you say "don't"?'

But I didn't need her to answer – I already knew.

Annie Burrows had not been speaking to me.

Chapter Seventeen

'Who were you talking to?' I demanded, terrified of her answer.

'Stella, do come off the stairs before you fall again,' Madeleine pleaded.

'I didn't fall.'

The maid shifted uneasily.

I gripped the handrail for dear life, my feet firmly planted. I was about to press the girl again when I was distracted by the servants' door opening. My heart sank as Mrs Henge emerged onto the landing dressed in a plaid dressing gown, its rope cord tightly knotted at her waist. Her grey hair hung in a thick plait over her breast, jarringly feminine and at odds with the masculine cut of her general appearance. She flicked a switch by the door and I flinched as bright light flooded the landing.

'Annie Burrows, what on earth are you doing out here?' she demanded. A grey eyebrow pitched upwards as she caught sight of me, hovering on the staircase. Her face fell into its usual impassive mask. 'I didn't see you there, Miss Marcham. I thought I heard a cry.'

'Crying,' I corrected her.

'No, miss, a single cry – a shout, if you will.'

My chest grew tight. 'My sister, she thought I was falling: she called out my name.'

'I see.' Her curious gaze fluttered over all of us. 'You are quite well, miss?'

I nodded.

'Very well.' It was impossible to know what she was thinking. She asked no questions, accepting without comment the eccentricity of us clustering in the dark on a disused landing. She turned to go.

'Mrs Henge!' Her name leapt out before I could stop it. I cursed my stupidity, but the damage had already been done: her focus was upon me. 'You didn't hear anything else? Just that single shout – you are quite sure you heard no actual crying?'

'No, miss, I did not.' With a curt nod of her head, she was gone. Annie tried to slip away after her, but I had no intention of letting her escape that easily. I sprang up to the landing and caught her arm.

'I haven't finished with you yet.'

'I can't help you, miss.'

'Who were you talking to?'

'No one, miss.'

My face was just inches from hers. 'I felt them, Annie.'

She struggled against my grasp, but I merely tightened the cuff of my fingers. 'Whose hands pushed me down those stairs?' She shook her head violently. I increased the pinch of my grip. 'Who was it?'

With a small cry, she yanked her arm free and stumbled back, rubbing at the tender flesh, her bottom lip jutting out, stubborn and resentful. 'I don't know what you're talking about.'

'I think you do.' And the hibernating creature that had lain dormant in the darkest corner of my mind finally roused. Its vague pulse strengthened. It stirred. It was waking now, and nothing could stop it. 'What is it about you and your father, Annie Burrows?'

'Stella! What are you still doing up there? Won't you come down now? Please.'

Gifted the distraction of Madeleine's appeal, Annie made a dash for the servants' door, but I recovered in time to slam my palm upon its glass panel.

'I know what I felt, Annie.' My eyes searched her face. 'Help me, please.' My whispered plea split precariously, as the terror of the evening's events finally struck home.

'Like I said, miss, I don't know what you're talking about,' she hissed as she yanked back the door, dislodging me. Before I could stop her, she was gone, the blurred glow of her candle flame retreating into nothingness.

I sank my face into my hands. Had I imagined it? Had I imagined all of it? Had the sobbing soldiers of my nightmare invaded reality?

I might have been able to convince myself of just that – had it not been for the two small palm prints still burning on the base of my back.

I was shaking uncontrollably by the time my feet sank into the landing carpet. Madeleine took my hand.

'My God, you're freezing. Come, let's get you wrapped up.'

She put her arm around my shoulders and led me to my room, banishing the fearful dark with a flick of the light switch. She left my side while she retrieved my wrapper and I picked up my cigarettes from the mantel, slipping one between my lips. I tried to strike a match, but my trembling hands made it impossible.

'Here, let me.' Madeleine set my wrapper down on the back of the chair and gently took the matchbox. The match took with the first strike, a phosphorous taint filling the air as the flame burst forth. She cupped it with her hand and guided it to the end of my cigarette. I drew in, relishing the soothing sensation of the smoke pooling into my lungs. The cigarette dangled from my lip as Madeleine slipped the wrapper over my arms and belted it around my waist as if I were a child, incapable. I collapsed into an armchair. She took the one opposite, perching on its edge, her hands clasped together as if in prayer.

'Stella, are you all right?'

I nodded, drawing greedily on the cigarette, holding onto its vapours for as long as I could, only releasing them when I spoke. 'It was completely empty, Madeleine, the nursery. There was nothing there.'

'But you heard it, you heard the crying?'

I nodded again. I decided not to mention my disconcerting suspicion that Annie and I had not been alone on the landing.

'Is it wrong of me to feel so happy?' Her flat voice contradicted her words. 'I am so relieved that it's not just me. After so many weeks of being met with ridicule . . .' Her fingers twisted in her lap. 'I'm just so relieved.' I detected the smallest of lifts in her tone; I tried to summon a smile but couldn't. While my trembling was finally beginning to subside, the furore in my mind was mounting – and still the icy imprints burnt my skin.

'I am just very sorry Mrs Henge had to discover us,' Madeleine continued. 'She will no doubt mention it to Lady Brightwell. But we know what we heard, don't we, Stella?'

I ground my cigarette stub into the stone of the fireplace and tapped another from the box. I managed the match myself this time, its rasp renting the silence that had descended between us.

'Who do you think it is?' Madeleine whispered at last, drawing closer. 'Do you really think Lucien Brightwell could be haunting this house?'

I pulled on the cigarette, staring sightlessly into the dark grate, the skin on my lower back tingling with recall: short fingers, squat palms – a child's hands.

'It's possible.'

Madeleine sat back in her chair. I realised for the first time that she was still dressed only in her nightgown and must surely be feeling the cold. Guilty she had once again cared for my needs whilst neglecting her own, I got up and retrieved a cardigan from my chest of drawers. Wordlessly I handed it to her, leaning against the fireplace, smoking, as she stood and added the extra layer. The bruised sacks beneath her eyes contrasted sharply with her chalky complexion. She looked exhausted. I finished my cigarette and stubbed it out.

'You should get some rest, Madeleine. There's nothing more either of us can do tonight.'

She agreed, but made no attempt to leave, still preoccupied with the night's events. 'I almost can't believe it's true – that this house is haunted.' The flimsiness of her self-esteem caused my heart to ache. What hell she must have been through, being made to question her own sanity? Of course, I knew something of that, but grief was generally accepted – believing in ghosts was not. 'And Annie heard it too, did she? Then we can't all be wrong, can we, Stella? They must believe us now.'

Annie Burrows. A finger of ice played over each bump of my vertebrae. She had heard the crying all right, but what had she seen? It had not been just the two of us inhabiting the darkness. The nursery had been empty, as far as I could see, but I now suspected Annie's perceptions went further than mine.

It had been there all along – my childish deductions were seeming less fantastic with each passing second. I was increasingly convinced Annie had drawn aside the porous veil that separates this world from the next, just as I once believed her father had on the night of the fire, enabling him to rescue Lydia. She had seen something on that landing – as absurd as that might seem to my rational self.

I escorted Madeleine back to her room, neither of us daring to look at the nursery staircase, no longer innocuous in the opalescent moonlight.

Madeleine hesitated on the threshold of her room. 'If it is Lucien, Stella, what do you think he wants?'

I thought of the force that sent me stumbling down the stairs.

'I don't know,' I answered at last, 'but I think we need to find out.'

And I knew precisely where to start.

Chapter Eighteen

I spent what was left of the night smoking cigarettes, until the room stank and so did I. It did nothing for my nerves at all.

I found myself unable to dispel the images gathered from the night of the fire. They crept into my mind's eye unbidden and once there, I could not escape them: flames licking at the walls, panes exploding from windows, the cascading fragments twinkling against the night sky. I remembered the servants and labourers forming a bucket chain until the fire brigade arrived – but their efforts were futile, like fighting a wildfire with teardrops.

And I remembered Madeleine and me, searing heat snatching the oxygen from our lungs, tears streaming down our soot-smudged faces, unable to answer our parents' desperate pleas as to where Lydia was. We simply didn't know. To her eternal regret, Nanny had acquiesced to our demands for a round of hide and seek before bed – and Lydia was a master of the game. She was cunning when it came to concealing herself, and far too stubborn to be tricked out of hiding by calls that the game was over, that tea was ready . . . that the house was on fire. And yet Jim Burrows, a groom who had never set foot in Haverton Hall, would discover her in an upstairs cupboard within minutes of entering the deadly furnace.

I was still awake when Annie crept into my room at the

start of the new day. Wrapped in my eiderdown I was tucked into a chair, sitting in wait, camouflaged by the early morning gloom. Unaware of my presence, she began seeing to the fire. The paper crackled as the flames took hold. I waited for the golden glow to illuminate her face before I spoke.

'Who were you talking to last night, Annie?'

Startled, she cried out, her hand flying to her chest – extraordinary considering her calm demeanour in the night. On that freezing landing in the dark she had failed to show fear or even any natural trepidation. I added all this to the evidence filed against her. The eiderdown rustled as I pitched forward.

'You need to tell me the truth.'

She fussed about the grate, tidying up after herself, sullen and silent.

'I remember the first time I ever saw you,' I said, nestling back in my chair. 'It was just after the fire. We came to pay our respects, my father and I, we came to your cottage – do you remember any of this?' My mind strayed back to that leaden July day – my father ducking under the lintel of their front door, leading me into a small parlour crammed with stunned mourners. Someone had ushered us through to the kitchen, where Jim Burrows' widow stood with her back to us, leaning against the wooden drainer, her sinewy arms tanned the colour of ripe hazelnuts. My father had clasped her hand and spoken kindly to her in muted tones, as tears fell down her cheeks with silent dignity.

There had been a bustle of movement, and Annie, then only five or six – about the same age as Lydia – had weaved her way through the forest of legs to confront our mourning. She had stood boldly before us all, her grubby hands on her hips, wearing a grass-stained pinafore, her ginger curls an unruly mass.

'You kept insisting your father was sitting in the kitchen,' I murmured, lost in the past, immersed in my recollection of how we had all dutifully shifted our gaze to the poignant empty rocker and how she had stamped her feet in frustration as she regarded our stricken faces, and crumpled into hysteria when her cajoling of the empty seat failed to elicit a response.

'I was just a child, miss, a grieving child, prone to say anything.'

'Oh, I think there's more to it than that, Annie.' There were hard chips of flint in my rough voice. I was exhausted – my head throbbed, my lungs were tight, and my mouth was tacky and tasted revolting. I was in no humour to dance around the mysterious maid. 'You see, I saw your father the night of the fire, just before he ran into the house. No one could ever understand how he found Lydia so quickly – but I know how he did it.' She disclosed a flicker of interest at last. I took a deep breath to steady my racing pulse. 'I think he had help.'

She got up, brushing herself down with precise strokes, buying time while she collected her thoughts and assembled her defence. When she deigned to give me a response, she was cool and collected.

'I dare say there were a lot of folks shouting out bits of information that night, miss. He must have picked up on something and acted on it. He just got lucky.'

'That night was chaos.' My words were forced through gritted teeth. 'No, your father had much clearer direction than a few jumbled comments and a little luck. I heard him, Annie.

He was speaking to someone over his shoulder, someone behind him . . . but there was no one there, at least, no one I could see.' She licked her lips, betraying her nerves. I steeled myself to conceal my own. '"You'll have to take me to her,"' that's what he said. Someone . . . some*thing* . . . guided him to Lydia, and that's how he found her.'

It might have been my imagination, or possibly a trick of the light, but I swear the blood drained from her cheeks. She quickly recovered.

'As I say, miss, I'm in no position to comment. I was just a child when it happened.'

I refused to tolerate her chicanery. Fuelled by frustration I left my chair, the eiderdown slipping from my shoulders to pile on the floor along with my shucked-off my patience. 'For God's sake, we both know there was something else on that landing last night. I *felt* it, Annie – its hands on my back. I know you saw it – you tried to stop it.'

'Forgive me, miss, if you've mistaken my words in any way.' Her icy tone was bordering on insolence. 'I called out, because it looked like you were too far over the edge, and I feared you were about to lose your balance and fall.'

'I was not too close to the edge and I did not fall. I was *pushed*, pushed by whatever was on that landing with us, Annie, whatever it was that we heard crying. You're not going to deny you heard the crying now, surely?'

Our eyes locked. Defiant, her mouth remained shut, her secrets sealed within her. I was determined to prise them out, but before I could begin a fresh campaign Madeleine, to my great irritation, burst unannounced into my room. She looked remarkably refreshed considering last night's events had robbed me of rest. She brightened even further when she saw I was not alone.

'Are you discussing last night?' Her eagerness was childlike and irrepressible, her wariness of Annie shamelessly forgotten as she turned to quiz her. 'You heard it too, Annie, the crying?'

'I was woken by something, ma'am.'

'But it was crying? A young boy crying?' Madeleine persisted.

Annie considered her response, framing it with a carefully crafted flicker of uncertainty. 'I suppose it could have sounded like that, ma'am.'

'But you did hear something?' Madeleine faltered.

'Well, something disturbed me, ma'am, I'm not sure what . . . it's all a bit strange, to be honest.'

I could bear it no more. 'Oh, stop it Annie! Stop with the lies!'

She flinched. Madeleine appeared stunned by the ferocity of my outburst, but I didn't care. I was tired and moody and on edge and I was sick of doubts and questions.

'Why can't you just be honest, for once?' I snapped. 'You were woken by the crying and you damn well saw something on that landing.'

'I didn't.'

'Yes, you did! Just tell us, now, exactly what you saw.'

'I didn't see anything, miss. I don't know what you're talking about.' She blanched, tears welling. 'I don't know why you're saying these things to me.'

Her contrived emotion failed to dampen my resolve. 'Why are you trying to hide the truth from me, Annie? I know! I know about your father . . .'

'Please stop talking about my father.' The words escaped her as a broken whisper. 'My father is dead, miss. I beg you, let him rest in peace, he's done you no harm.' Salty rivulets spilt down her cheeks to drip from her jaw. She turned to Madeleine. 'Please, ma'am, might I be excused? I'm not feeling very well.'

Before Madeleine could answer, I informed her she was not excused, not until she'd told the truth.

'I am telling you the truth! The only truth I can tell,' she cried, before appealing to my sister's softer nature once again.

Madeleine, clearly discomfited, gave her leave to go, instructing her to send Maisie to attend me in her place. Sobbing, Annie darted through the door. Madeleine stopped me as I went to follow her.

'For God's sake, Stella, what's got into you?'

I offered her no answer, I merely carried on my pursuit, catching up with Annie on the landing.

'Please, miss, let me alone.'

'Not until you've told me what I want to know.' I grabbed her wrist. 'I need you to help me, Annie.'

She lunged towards me. 'I *have* helped you.' The heat of her resentment scorched me. 'I helped that day at the lake when I could have left you to drown. I can do no more.' Belligerent now, she wrenched herself free. 'I *will* do no more,' she said and without waiting for my response, she turned tail and ran, disappearing through the servants' door concealed in the panelling.

Her evocation of the incident at the lake left me as dazed as a boxer caught by an unexpected hook. I recalled her words that day – 'He says it's not your time.' Last night, I had dared to contemplate that strange message anew.

If I had hoped to elicit a confession from Annie I had failed completely. All I had done was force her further into that impenetrable shell of hers, a shell I now suspected to be constructed of lies and deceit. But in my heart, I knew I was right about her, and that conviction gave sustenance to the hope I had been nurturing all night: if Annie Burrows could see Lucien, then what other spirits might she be able to see? Perhaps it was unwise to encourage such thoughts, but had she not just thrown fuel on that fire herself? The hope of somehow communicating with Gerald once again gave me the courage and determination to pursue the truth.

'What on earth was that all about?' Madeleine asked, as I slunk back into my room. Thankfully Maisie interrupted us before I could answer, bobbing a curtsy as she came in, no doubt alert to the unfolding drama. I placated Madeleine with a promise to explain when we were alone.

My thoughts were chaotic as Maisie helped me dress, and I was grateful she was so adept at her task for I was too discombobulated to be of much help. I sat at the dressing table as she did my hair. She met my eyes in the mirror a number of times, smiling shyly, as she applied the silver-backed brush. I began to relax under her careful ministrations, and I forced away the uncomfortable questions circling my brain. I tried to distract myself by engaging in conversation – at least Maisie's answers would be reassuringly substantial.

'I understand your mother worked here once upon a time, Maisie?'

'Yes, miss. She was taken on when she was just a girl, when Sir Arthur first moved here. She left when she married my dad – they farm up the road now.'

'Was she a maid? Like you?'

'That's right, miss – I'm following in her footsteps.' She giggled. There was something utterly naive and charming about her. Her irrepressible ebullience evoked the first genuine smile I had managed all morning. 'When I was little,' she continued, deftly combing through a section of my hair, 'my mum would tell me all about the glamorous parties here – the wonderful food and beautiful ladies in their gorgeous gowns – and it sounded like a fairy tale palace. All I wanted was to be a part of it – even if it was a part where I was scurrying about with a tray in my hand.' She wound the section of hair and reached forward for a pin to secure it in place. 'My mum used to say to me' – she mimicked what I took to be her mother's voice with the relish of a music hall actress – '"You get yourself a job at Greyswick, my girl, and you'll be set up for life – just don't catch Mrs Henge's eye and avoid Sir Arthur's wandering hands."' She giggled at her own impression and then stopped abruptly, her cheeks flushing scarlet as her eyes widened in horror at her faux pas. 'Oh Lord, miss, I'm so sorry! I meant no harm, it's just I forget myself – my mum always warned me my big mouth would get me into trouble.'

I laughed and waved away her apology. 'Never fear, Maisie, my lips are sealed.'

She stepped back once she had finished, her embarrassment forgotten, her hands clasped behind her back.

'Thank you, Maisie. I think that will be all.'

'Breakfast is all laid out in the dining room as usual, miss,' she informed me as she dropped a quick curtsy and beat her retreat. I was somewhat stunned to realise it was not yet nine.

I faltered as I entered the dining room. I had expected to see Madeleine waiting patiently for me at the table, but I had not anticipated seeing Lady Brightwell or Miss Scott, as it was their habit to take breakfast early. Madeleine's stiff posture as she sat eating her kippers and toast betrayed her discomfort, and I received cool glances from both older ladies as I quietly closed the door and issued my greetings.

I began to explore the breakfast offerings, trying my best not to disturb the taut silence with the clanging of salver lids. I took some kedgeree and set my plate down opposite Madeleine, turning back to help myself to the tea urn.

'I was just saying to Madeleine, Miss Marcham, that you two girls must be exhausted this morning.' Lady Brightwell's words were clipped and dipped in acid. 'Mrs Henge tells me you were engaged in some midnight wanderings. Do tell me, what on earth were you doing up on the nursery landing at that time of night?'

I pushed back the lever on the urn. There was no benefit to be gained from sharing the night's events with an audience who were bound to be unequivocally hostile. I needed time to formulate my own conflicted thoughts and tackle the problem of Annie Burrows.

'I thought I heard something,' I said, taking my seat.

'And what was that?'

Madeleine shot me a pointed look across the table.

'Nothing in the end,' I responded as nonchalantly as I could.

'No, that's not true.' Madeleine's cutlery clattered against the edge of her plate. I tried to kick her under the table, but my foot wouldn't reach. 'We did hear something, all of us did.'

'Madeleine.' I hoped she would heed the warning note in my voice. Instinct told me we should keep our own counsel. Madeleine's instinct was clamouring for exoneration.

'We all heard crying. Myself, Stella, even Stella's maid Annie heard it.'

'Crying?' The word dropped like lead from Lady Brightwell's lips. Miss Scott's teacup clinked into its saucer.

'Yes. You see, it isn't just me after all. I've been saying for weeks that I've heard something and none of you believed me, but now Stella has heard it too – so you see, it can't just be me. There is something, some*one* crying in this house.' Colour blistered her cheeks. 'Tell them, Stella.'

'Well, Miss Marcham?' Lady Brightwell's question spliced the air like a razor-sharp blade.

Madeleine read my hesitation. 'Stella,' she begged.

I cursed my soft-heartedness. Despite my misgivings, I could not do it – I could not turn my back on her.

'Madeleine's right. It was the sound of a child crying that woke me.'

The brittle silence that met my declaration was shattered by the dramatic sigh of exasperation that escaped Lady Brightwell and a muttered 'Oh dear' from Miss Scott. Madeleine looked from her mother-in-law to the companion, her distress mounting as she realised the revelation had not been well received. It was as I feared: Lady Brightwell now thought us both deranged.

'For goodness' sake!' she declared, shoving her plate away in disgust. Miss Scott unhooked her spectacles. With a dour expression she proceeded to clean the lenses on a handkerchief pulled from her cardigan sleeve, shaking her head in disappointment as she did so.

'Miss Marcham!' Lady Brightwell summoned my attention by banging both hands on the table. 'Are you to tell me you are now condoning this nonsense?'

'I can only tell you what I heard, Lady Brightwell, and I heard, quite distinctly, a child crying.'

'Encouraged, no doubt, by your sister.'

'I know what I heard.'

'Then you are wrong, Miss Marcham. Do you not think if there were truly a child crying in this house then someone other than Madeleine would have heard it by now?'

'They have,' Madeleine said, emboldened by my support. 'Stella's maid Annie heard it too.'

'Be quiet, child!' Lady Brightwell's withering look caused Madeleine to shrivel in her seat. 'I am talking to your sister. Your sister, who – I had hoped – might possess a modicum more common sense than you yourself do. Clearly I was wrong.'

'I am sorry, Lady Brightwell, but I know what I heard. It was very distinct. Indeed, I find it astounding that you have never heard it yourself.'

'Miss Marcham, I have lived in this house since I was little more than a girl. We never had any of this nonsense until your sister came to stay this last time. I find it unbelievable for that very reason. And I'm sorry to say, I do not find you a reliable corroborating witness.'

'There is my maid, Annie.' It had not been my intention to offer the girl up, but my back was to the wall. I dearly hoped she would not be called upon to give testimony; I was under no illusion she would support me.

'A servant girl? You expect me to believe the nonsense of a maid?'

'I know what I heard, what we all heard,' I said.

'And do tell me, Miss Marcham, did you find a culprit, when you were prowling around in pursuit of this mysterious crying?'

'No. No I didn't . . . which in itself is telling, surely? I think it warrants investigation.'

'"Warrants investigation"?' she mocked. 'The only thing that warrants investigation, Miss Marcham, is your state of mind.'

I looked her squarely in the eye. 'We can't all be wrong, Lady Brightwell.'

'I would beg to differ.' She rose imperiously from the table. 'I will have no more said on this matter, but know this, Miss Marcham, if you persist, I may have to reconsider your ongoing stay at Greyswick. Madeleine needs a calm and stable influence about her at this delicate time. I suggest you reflect very carefully on whether you can offer her that, given your own circumstances.' She eyed my black attire and began to move away from the table. Relenting slightly, she hovered by me, her tone softening. 'I say this as a mother, Miss Marcham. I only want what is best, for everyone.'

She left the room with Miss Scott, her ever-present shadow. I sighed with frustration as the door clicked behind them, tossing my napkin upon my untouched breakfast.

'Madeleine, why did you have to say anything?'

'It would all have come out anyway.'

It was a valid argument. Clearly Mrs Henge had wasted no time in recounting our midnight escapade to her employer.

'Well, it didn't go very well, did it?' I pushed back my chair. 'From now on, let's keep our cards closer to our chests, shall we? Unless you want the old battleax to send me home with a flea in my ear.'

'Oh no, Stella . . .' Madeleine reached for my hand. 'You can't leave me, not now. I won't let her send you away, whatever happens.'

'You may have no choice in the matter,' I observed as I got to my feet, any appetite I might have entertained completely gone.

Chapter Nineteen

Madeleine required little encouragement to join me for a walk in the gardens. I think we had both had enough of Greyswick's claustrophobic atmosphere. Fresh air was what we needed.

A warm breeze greeted us as we escaped. We crossed the lichen-covered flags of the terrace and descended its shallow steps, crunching along the gravel pathways that segmented the parterre.

We walked without direction, the garden stretching endlessly before us. To the far left was a rhododendron-dotted arboretum – the gateway to the copse-covered hillside beyond – while to the far right was the brick wall of the kitchen garden. Madeleine and I pressed on until the gravel gave way to soft sinking lawn, the grass overly long and in need of mowing. Leading away from the lawns was an avenue of cherry trees, and we turned towards it. The wind soughed through the blossom-laden branches, and the multitude of pink bouquets shivered with delight.

'Something will have to be done, Stella,' Madeleine said at last. 'I cannot stay in that house with things the way they are. Something will have to be done.'

I noticed how the buttons of her coat were straining at her increased waist. I folded my arms, hunching my shoulders against the brazen breeze. My heart ached for Gerald. He would have given me steady, sensible counsel and defended me to his very last breath.

The cherry branches heaved and sighed. A flurry of petals danced on the wind until, tiring of them, it subsided, leaving them to drift to the ground. One landed on Madeleine's shoulder and I lightly brushed it off.

'I don't know what we can do.'

'What about Annie, Stella? What did you mean when you said she saw something?'

I broke away from her, wandering over to lay my palm on the rough bark of a silver-hued trunk.

'Stella?'

I thought of home. We had some cherry trees at the edge of the gardens, a small cluster. When we were small – before the fire – we three girls would collect the best of the fallen blossom, giggling as we filled the scoop of Lydia's pinafore to the top. Madeleine and I would take turns playing bridesmaid and bride, while Lydia – far too young for such parts – would walk before us as our flower girl, scattering our path with handfuls of petals. Madeleine had chosen not to have a flower girl for her wedding. Lydia had been irreplaceable in the role.

'Stella?'

I rested my back against the tree. 'I think Annie Burrows . . .' I stopped. 'This is madness . . .' I whispered the conclusion more to myself than to Madeleine, but it induced her to draw near and after years of silence, I finally shared with her what I had witnessed the night Haverton went up in flames.

'Stella, what are you trying to say?'

A laugh barked out of me, coarse and abrupt. 'I think I'm trying to say that Jim Burrows had help from a dead person that night, and I think Annie . . . I think Annie possesses her father's gift.' I confronted my sister's amazement. 'I think Annie

Burrows can see the dead – and I'm pretty sure she saw Lucien Brightwell on the landing last night.'

'What on earth makes you say that?'

I hesitated. I needed to be careful how much I told her. I had no desire to make her more jittery than she already was, but she deserved to know, at least in part, what had happened.

'Madeleine, I felt a child's hands upon me last night – I presume Lucien's hands. Just as he touched me, Annie cried out to stop him. Don't you see? How could she have known – unless she saw him?'

'Stella – do you think it's *possible*?'

'Oh, Madeleine! I drew my conclusions about Jim Burrows when I was an imaginative ten-year-old girl. I rejected them as foolish nonsense years ago – there are no such things as ghosts, how can there be? And people communicating with them? I've always thought it ridiculous – like dear Aunt Maud going to seances trying to contact Cousin Charlie. I always questioned the point of it all – Charlie was dead, just like Gerald. Dead and gone with so many others. But . . . *what if* . . .' I trailed off, not yet brave enough to confess my fledgling hopes, not even to Madeleine. I needed to keep them to myself a little longer. I couldn't let them distract me from the more pressing matter in hand. 'Last night has made me question everything. It's unearthed memories I had happily buried and forgotten. But the more I think about it all, the more it seems to be the only explanation – however absurd. Illogical, unbelievable, unlikely – but perhaps true.'

'And you were trying to make Annie confess this morning?'

'I wanted her to be honest with me. All those strange things people say about her at home, her quirks of behaviour, they all make sense—'

'If she sees ghosts,' Madeleine finished softly. 'I've never believed in them before, but now, after being in this house, with all that's happened – I can't find another explanation either.'

Looking up through the candyfloss canopy above me, I could just make out glimpses of pale cloud scudding across the washed-out sky. I sighed and shoved my hands deep into the pockets of my coat.

'Well, one thing's for sure, we won't find any answers out here.'

I pushed myself upright and re-joined the path. Madeleine slipped her arm through mine, tucking into my side as we retraced our steps, and soon the grey façade of the house glowered down upon us once again. Glancing up, I noticed how the gargoyles with their rain-streaked jaws appeared to be salivating over our return. The thought repulsed me.

As we reached the parterre, I spotted a khaki-clad figure loitering by the arched gateway of the kitchen garden. Though he was some distance away, I was certain it was the same soldier I had seen at the graveyard, and I wondered what business he could have here. Curious, I watched him as Madeleine and I began to mount the steps to the terrace.

Annie Burrows appeared through the garden gate. She started so violently at the soldier's unexpected presence that the contents of her laden trug tumbled to the ground. She dropped to a crouch to gather up the spilt vegetables. He stood over her – rather unchivalrously failing to help.

'Stella, what are you gawping at?' Madeleine was holding open the glazed door of the orangery, waiting for me. I was so distracted I hadn't even noticed her slip free of my arm.

'Oh sorry, I saw Annie by the kitchen garden . . .' But realising it was of no great interest I didn't bother to carry on, instead I offered an apologetic smile and hurried to join her.

We were just in the process of removing our coats when Maisie appeared, bearing a flush of excitement. 'Oh! Mrs Brightwell, I've been looking for you everywhere. If you please, ma'am, Mr Brightwell is on the telephone.'

At the mention of Hector's name, Madeleine's face lit up. With a joyous exclamation, she dashed after the maid to take the call in the study. I made my way from the orangery back through to the hall, doing my best to subdue the parasitic envy that writhed in my chest, aware I might never again experience the excitement of a lover's call. It did me no good to dwell on such things.

I decided I would await Madeleine in my bedroom. I slowly ascended the staircase, my shoes scuffing the wooden treads, my head hanging low, as I did my best to shake off my indulgent self-pity.

I did not see Mrs Henge waiting on the landing step. I gasped when I looked up and found her towering above me.

'Goodness, Mrs Henge! You gave me quite a fright.'

'Miss Marcham.' She was as stiff as ever, her expression blank, her clothing pressed to precision. The toes of her boots, poking out beneath her old-fashioned skirts, shone like polished coal. 'Lady Brightwell was most upset to hear about last night's events.'

'Then maybe you shouldn't have told her.'

'She is my employer. It is my duty to keep her informed.' She took a step down, deliberately crowding me. 'It is very strange how no one else in the house hears anything.'

I was forced to tip my head back to look at her, otherwise I

157

would have been staring at her midriff and the gaoler's ring of keys hanging from her brown leather belt. This overt attempt to intimidate irked me immensely.

'I find it extraordinary that no one else does. It was clear as day to me.'

She took another step down, forcing me to shuffle backwards to avoid brushing against her. My heels hung precariously over the edge of the step.

'All this talk, it's so distressing for Lady Brightwell. I think it's a shame, if you don't mind me saying.'

She leant towards me and I instinctively tilted back. I gasped as I felt my heels pivot downwards and my weight shift. Just as I grabbed the banister to steady myself, Madeleine called my name from somewhere below. I swear the corner of the housekeeper's mouth twitched as she retreated up a step.

'Stella, where are you?' Madeleine came racing into the hall. 'Oh, there you are!' She ran to the bottom step. 'Oh, Stella, the most wonderful news. Everything will be all right now.'

She clamped up as she spotted the housekeeper hovering over me like a vulture. Mrs Henge bowed her grey head, but I detected mockery in the gesture. Her black skirts swished as she swivelled on the stairs and made her ascent, before sweeping along the landing.

Madeleine watched her go, following her departure by climbing the steps between us. When she was completely satisfied we were alone, she snatched up my hand in excitement. 'Oh, Stella! At last, we can make everything right.'

'How?' I asked, still shaken by my encounter.

'Hector,' Madeleine beamed. 'Hector is coming home.'

Chapter Twenty

The prospect of Hector's imminent arrival brought untold comfort to Madeleine and she counted down the hours until he was expected the following morning. She was convinced he would take our side – I didn't share her confidence, though I kept that to myself. She kissed me on the cheek when she bade me goodnight and pulled me into a hug.

'All will be well once Hector is here. You must believe that, Stella dear.'

I was not surprised that it was Maisie, not Annie, who came to assist me at bedtime. Annie was apparently 'unwell', but I saw through her feeble excuse. I did not press the point. She was trapped in this house and shackled to me – try as she might, she would not be able to avoid my company for long.

As I extinguished my bedside light, I felt a twinge of fear at the all-encompassing darkness. I tried to settle, but my ears tuned in to the groans and sighs of the house as it eased itself down for the night. Cooling wood contracted with the catch of clicking joints; water coursed through pipes beneath my floorboards like blood through veins, and all the while the resonant *tick, tick, tick* of my mantel clock beat its steady pulse. I did not feel any peace descend. Instead the house itself seemed taut with anticipation, a giant sleeping with one eye open, ever watchful, waiting. Like me.

But though I listened intently for it, I did not detect any unnatural murmur, and in the end only sleep possessed me.

The next morning there was a buzz of excitement in the air. Madeleine was last down to breakfast, looking refreshed and lovely, wearing a particularly becoming dress in a shade of pale blue that accentuated the colour of her eyes and set off her blonde hair exquisitely.

She was a bundle of nerves – more like a giddy girl anticipating a rendezvous with her sweetheart than a married woman awaiting the return of her husband. Lady Brightwell soon got exasperated with her spaniel-like ebullience, and she and Miss Scott retreated to the morning room to await Hector's arrival. Madeleine spent her time flitting between me in the drawing room, and the redundant smoking room, which she insisted afforded the best view of the drive.

In the end, fearing she would wear herself out dashing between the two, I decided to remove myself from the equation. I declared I was going to rest in my room and left her to continue her vigil in peace.

I passed the next hour flicking through magazines, but soon tired of their frivolity and tapped out a cigarette instead. Perching on my window sill, I cracked open the sash, and sat smoking. At last in the distance, I caught a flash of sunlight glinting off the bonnet of an approaching vehicle.

Madeleine ran outside before Hector's car had even reached the carriage sweep. Gravel crunched beneath its wheels as it finally came to a stop before the porch. From my window above I watched a subaltern leap from the driver's seat to open the rear door. Hector emerged just as a ray of sunlight burst through the banking clouds, looking quite dashing in his uniform. He whipped off his peaked hat as Madeleine ran into his embrace, nuzzling her face into the cleft between his jawbone and shoulder. I looked away. I used to do the same to Gerald and could still recall the tang of his aftershave and the sweet notes of pipe tobacco that clung to his skin.

As I got up to get an ashtray, something unexpected happened. The far rear door of the car was thrown open, and much to my surprise, another passenger clambered out. The young man in question stood gazing up at the front of the house as he put on his trilby. Madeleine's surprise was also evident. I turned back to the window, watching intently now, as Hector gestured to him. The unanticipated arrival made his way around the back of the car. He swept off his hat as he approached Madeleine and held out his hand, his face serious despite his tempering smile. The three of them began to make their way indoors. I turned away, troubled by an inexplicable sense of foreboding.

I had intended to afford Madeleine and Hector some privacy to reacquaint themselves, but my inquisitiveness flared. I extinguished my cigarette en route to the door.

They had congregated in the hall. Maisie stood in attendance, relieving the men of their coats and hats as Madeleine chatted with forced gaiety. My steps slowed as I reached the turn in the stairs, and Hector glanced up. Conflicting emotions flickered across his face before he called out his greeting.

He came forward and delivered a perfunctory kiss to my cheek as I stepped from the last tread onto the tiled floor. My eyes slid over his shoulder to the new arrival, who appeared to be watching me with piqued interest.

'Oh, Mr Sheers, this is my sister, Stella Marcham.' Madeleine replaced Hector by my side. 'She is staying with us.'

'How do you do.'

Holding out his hand, he took a step towards me, a rigid, unnatural step that immediately drew my attention. It was not difficult to deduce its cause. A man his age would only be home for one reason – he had paid his dues. Though I meant no offence, he clearly resented my unguarded reaction and by the time I took his hand his features had hardened, any initial warmth lost.

'Tristan Sheers.'

His voice was low and clipped. He released my hand as soon as he had delivered one decisive shake. It appeared he had made his evaluation and I had been found wanting.

'Tristan is an old friend of mine. I thought it would be nice if he came to stay for the weekend,' Hector explained.

'Oh, you are most welcome, Mr Sheers,' Madeleine cried with brittle enthusiasm. 'The more the merrier! Well, shall we go through to the drawing room? I know your mother and Miss Scott are eager to see you, darling.'

Hector and Madeleine led the way. I walked beside Mr Sheers, who was surveying the house with great interest.

'So how do you two know each other?' I asked.

'School.'

'The army.'

The men's voices collided. I saw my own surprise and confusion mirrored in Madeleine's startled expression. Hector and Sheers fleetingly exchanged a complicit look, before Hector cleared his throat and answered for them both.

'That is, we were at school together, but then became reacquainted through the army.'

'Quite so,' Sheers mumbled.

There was something about this explanation that seemed unsatisfactory – contrived, even – and it did nothing to alleviate my foreboding, but I knew better than to pursue it, and so remained silent as we entered the drawing room.

There was a warm and enthusiastic welcome for the returning son from both ladies. Lady Brightwell, however, made no attempt to conceal her disapproval at the imposition of an unexpected guest. Indeed, she adopted such a sour expression and responded to Mr Sheers' polite enquiries so curtly I felt almost sorry for the man. But it soon became clear from the way he and Hector interacted that they were not at all well acquainted, despite their statements to the contrary, which only further added to the mystery of who he was and why he was here at all.

The conversation dwindled once we had taken tea. Hector stood up and suggested Mr Sheers might like to see the house, but when Madeleine automatically rose to join them, he flushed and told her there was no need for her to trouble herself. Emitting a mew of disappointment, Madeleine sank back into her chair and, visibly disheartened, watched as the two men withdrew.

'Did you know about this?' Lady Brightwell demanded as soon as the door had closed behind them.

'No, Hector hadn't warned me at all.'

'Have any of you heard him mention Mr Sheers before?' I was not the least surprised when all three indicated they had not.

'Well, it's most unlike Hector,' Miss Scott said. 'Mr Sheers seems like a perfectly nice man, but I don't see why he should need to come and stay here.'

'Perhaps it's something to do with his . . .' Madeleine motioned to her leg as she trailed off.

'Clearly the young man has made a great sacrifice for his country,' Lady Brightwell bit out, 'but I don't see why a rare weekend with my son should be spoilt by the imposition of a stranger.'

'But Hector's so kind,' Madeleine countered, 'maybe Mr Sheers has been having a hard time of it, and Hector thought a weekend in the country would be a pleasant distraction for him.'

'You are right, my dear.' Miss Scott set down her tea. 'Hector does have a tendency to a soft heart and if he saw an old school friend and fellow soldier in need . . .' She shrugged lightly. 'If he is a friend of Hector's, we should all make him feel welcome.'

'*If* he is a friend of Hector's,' I echoed, though only Madeleine seemed to catch my inference.

She picked me up on the comment later, as the two of us made our way upstairs.

'It just struck me as odd they didn't agree where they knew each other from,' I said.

'But Hector explained that.'

'If they knew each other at school, then why did Mr Sheers not offer that as his answer? It seemed strange.'

'I think you are becoming overly suspicious, Stella.'

She may have persuaded me on the matter had we not reached our rooms in time to spot Hector and the mysterious Mr Sheers in hushed conversation on the nursery landing. I felt a surge of vindication as Madeleine squeezed my arm.

We slipped into my room without drawing their attention. Something was afoot.

We idled away an hour or so, before wandering downstairs, Madeleine growing increasingly maudlin at being deprived of her husband's company. The two men had ensconced themselves in the library, and it was all I could do to prevent her loitering outside the door.

'What could they be doing in there all afternoon? I do wish Hector would spend some time with me. He'll be gone before I know it, and we'll have hardly spoken!'

I encouraged her to sit with me in the orangery for a while, but she couldn't settle and instead kept peering down the corridor to see if there was any sign of them. When at last the library door did open it was Mrs Henge who emerged – looking both smug and triumphant.

By the time she reached us she had reinstated her reserved demeanour, her hands forming their usual neat knot.

'Can I get you anything, Mrs Brightwell?'

'Oh, yes, please,' Madeleine stuttered, a nervous hand scooping some errant strands of hair behind her ear. 'Would you have Maisie bring some tea?'

The housekeeper nodded. The echo of her heels ricocheted down the corridor as she disappeared into the gloom. Her steps were just fading when the library door jerked open again, but this time it was Hector and Mr Sheers who appeared.

'Oh! At last,' Madeleine cried.

'I'm so sorry, darling, Tristan and I had much to discuss.'

'Stella and I were just about to take tea. Won't you join us?'

'Well, I . . .' Hector looked to his guest for guidance. Mr

Sheers' agreed tea would be a most welcome distraction, though a distraction from what, he didn't say.

We settled somewhat stiffly in the orangery. Madeleine dispatched a flustered Maisie back to the kitchen for extra crockery and refreshments. Hector took the wicker sofa with Madeleine, while Mr Sheers lowered himself into an armchair, his prosthetic stretched before him. I had no choice but to take the neighbouring seat.

'Did you enjoy your tour of the house, Mr Sheers?' Madeleine asked as she handed him his cup and saucer. 'If the weather's clement tomorrow, perhaps you and Hector might do a spot of shooting? There are some fine woodlands here and lots of pigeons!'

'I'm afraid I'm rather done with shooting,' Mr Sheers answered, dropping a lump of sugar into his tea. 'It holds no attraction for me any more.'

Madeleine turned bright pink and fumbled over her reply, gratefully returning her attentions to the tea tray.

'Where did you serve, Mr Sheers?' My question was a tad snippy in its delivery, but I had resented his response – it had been unnecessary and designed to provoke embarrassment.

'Belgium and France.' He pivoted in his chair to face me. 'I understand you served yourself, Miss Marcham.'

'Yes, I did.'

'You must have experienced some very difficult things.' His voice was quiet, kind almost, but deceptively so – or perhaps that was my paranoia. I was rankled by the fact he and Hector had clearly been discussing me behind my back.

'I'm sure we all experienced some very difficult things,' I retorted, my gaze sliding to his leg, though I rather hated myself for it. The corner of his mouth tweaked, and he toasted me with his teacup as if to say, 'Touché,' but in the next moment, an intense sadness deadened his expression.

'We have all suffered.' The words were so quietly delivered it was obvious they were meant only for me. Our eyes snagged and, just for a second, we recognised a shared loss, an empathetic grief that the other two would never be able to comprehend. He cleared his throat, his voice louder now. 'We often fail to appreciate the profound effect tragic events can have upon us, upon the very workings of our minds.'

This robustly delivered statement hailed a sea change. Hector stiffened, a look of distinct discomfort frozen on his face. He swigged some tea in a manner that suggested he would have preferred something stronger – a brew more likely to give him a bit of Dutch courage.

'Quite. You've looked into it a bit, haven't you, Sheers? The subconscious, wasn't it?'

I had the strange impression I was watching a rehearsed conversation being delivered by inexperienced actors, not yet fully au fait with their lines.

'The subconscious is a very powerful entity, often working beyond our control – and beyond our awareness,' Sheers replied.

Madeleine looked confused, but my inner warning bells were sounding. I decided to gamely play along.

'How fascinating, Mr Sheers. Have you been studying this field long?'

'Since I came back,' he said, which I took as half an answer – he had not yet divulged when he had returned from the war.

'Do you specialise in any particular aspect?'

'The astounding power of creation that the subconscious

appears to possess, often in response to our deep-seated thoughts and emotions. It is capable of great feats of fabrication which are so compelling that the conscious mind can be thoroughly convinced by them – in effect, the subconscious has the ability to completely hoodwink its conscious self. I find that fascinating.'

I sipped at my tea to conceal a surge of anger. Madeleine's brow furrowed. She clearly detected the acrimonious chill that had descended like an impenetrable sea fog, but she couldn't decipher the undercurrent that went with it.

'Did I miss something?' she asked at last, issuing a light laugh.

'I don't think Hector and Mr Sheers are old school friends at all, my dear,' I said, setting down my cup and saucer. 'I think Mr Sheers is here for another purpose altogether.'

She still didn't understand. Hector covered her hand with his own.

'I hate to say it, but Stella is right. I apologise that we have been somewhat duplicitous, but we felt – given the circumstances – it was necessary.'

'I don't understand.' There was uncertainty in Madeleine's voice as her eyes darted over the three of us.

'Miss Scott telephoned me the other day.' Hector spoke gently, as if to a small child. 'She was most concerned about you.'

'Why?' Madeleine asked in a tiny voice, her fingers plucking at her skirts.

'Oh, for goodness' sake, Madeleine!' I exclaimed, snapped patience projecting me to my feet. 'Can't you read between the lines? Mr Sheers is here to offer his expert advice because we have been causing trouble.' I spun round on our guest. 'Isn't that right, Mr Sheers?'

'What do you mean, Stella?' Madeleine asked.

How I wanted to shake some sense into her, shake her until the scales fell from her eyes! The very man she had trusted to help us had betrayed us after all.

'Mr Sheers has been brought here to confirm there are, in fact, no ghostly goings-on in this house – merely the imaginings of our weak and febrile female minds.'

Perhaps I was being overly defensive but being demeaned by two – male – sceptics, echoed horribly of the high-handed belittling I had been subjected to by Dr Mayhew and his Harley Street cronies. My vicious tongue with the powerful sting in its tail was the only weapon I had to defend myself, and I used it now to lash out at my brother-in-law.

'That is the long and short of it, isn't it, Hector?' I demanded. 'We're just two more hysterical women, prone to fancy and incapable of rational thought. I tell you, it's a damn good thing we are not trusted with the vote – God only knows what we would do with it.'

Chapter Twenty-One

'Oh Stella!' Madeleine uttered, aghast, but Hector glowered at me with such contempt that I knew I had hit the proverbial nail on the head.

'Do sit down, Stella,' he muttered.

'I'm right, though, aren't I? You're not old chums at all, are you? In fact, I'd bet my last shilling you barely know the man.'

I found Mr Sheers' continued scrutiny rather unsettling, and in the end I did flump down on my chair, but only to make it harder for him to study me like a prize exhibit.

'Very well, I'll come clean. I have indeed only recently made Tristan's acquaintance. He chanced to overhear a conversation I was conducting with a friend at my club and introduced himself as a result.' Hector reached into his inside jacket pocket and withdrew a silver cigarette case. Flicking it open, he shuffled forward in his seat to offer one to Sheers, but the man shook his head. Hector placed a cigarette between his lips and snapped the case shut, tucking it back inside his jacket. I swallowed hard. I was itching for one. He stood up, pausing to light it. 'The conversation he'd overheard was a discussion of the telephone call I had just received from Miss Scott. It turns out Mr Sheers here is somewhat of an expert in the supposed supernatural—'

This praise was clearly overstated, for Mr Sheers began to qualify the comment. Reining Hector in, he denied he was an 'expert'. Rather he professed an interest in people's desire to assume 'otherworldly' interference in events that could be easily explained by the application of a little common sense and a modicum of science.

'I'm no expert,' he reiterated, 'merely a hobbyist.'

Hector batted away his modesty. 'Yes, yes, but the fact is you've managed to debunk quite a bit of this nonsense.'

'I have managed to expose a few mediums as frauds, and there have been one or two "hauntings" I've been invited to investigate, which I've proven false.'

'But you don't do this in any professional capacity?' I asked. 'You're not affiliated with – oh what's it called? That society that looks into this sort of thing . . .'

'No,' he said quickly. 'I'm not connected in any way to the Society of Psychical Research. As I say, Miss Marcham, I am little more than a hobbyist in this matter, but I have been fortunate enough to conduct my own amateur investigations and exposés, on behalf of friends and acquaintances, mainly.'

'For money?' My question was tart and the query dirty. Hector inhaled sharply, and Madeleine looked appalled, but Mr Sheers merely allowed a slow smile to play at the corners of his mouth.

'Sadly not, Miss Marcham. I say again, it is just my curious hobby.'

'And yet you are confident enough of your abilities to interject into a stranger's conversation?'

'I might remind you, Stella, that Mr Sheers is here at my invitation. He has competently persuaded me in his "abilities", as you put it. He has a keen rational mind and has already cast light on what's been happening here.'

I was intrigued now and encouraged Hector to continue. He drew heavily on his cigarette, tapping the ash onto the flagged floor.

'We have spent the day examining the house for any anomalies in its construction that might explain some of the elements that have been troubling Madeleine, and, I understand, more recently yourself. We have also spoken to Miss Scott and Mrs Henge to ascertain what's been going on.'

'Don't you think you should have spent some time questioning the people who have actually experienced these things, rather than those who haven't?' I asked.

Hector snorted at this. 'I assure you, rational minds are the ones I want to hear from.'

But he had barely finished his sentence before Mr Sheers added, 'I haven't finished my investigation yet, Miss Marcham. I would indeed welcome the opportunity of speaking at some point to both you and Mrs Brightwell.'

'I don't think that's really necessary,' Hector complained, straightening up.

'I think it's only fair,' Sheers responded. 'To make sure everything has been done properly.'

Hector grumbled over the prospect, but I wondered whether Mr Sheers was cynically offering Madeleine and me enough rope to hang ourselves.

'Then I think you should speak to everyone in the house, surely,' I suggested. 'My maid, Annie, heard the crying as well, you know.'

Sheers agreed – he would indeed like to speak to everyone. This proposed expansion of his investigation, however, did not sit well with Hector, but noticing Madeleine's subdued demeanour, he rid himself of his cigarette and sat down beside her. He took her hand as he explained he wanted her to feel happy and safe. She bravely summoned a smile for him, but I could see she was split between her own state of mind and wanting to appease her husband – it was my belief she shouldn't have to compromise. I was relieved when, in the end, he relented and agreed to Sheers' plan.

The day's light had begun to ebb from the room. When the clock chimed the hour, Madeleine expressed her surprise over how the afternoon had slipped away and suggested we should all repair to our rooms to dress for dinner.

We resorted to stilted conversation about the weather as we made our way, the four of us traipsing down the darkening corridor towards the hall. I wondered if Mr Sheers detected any danger in the pervading shadows that seeped from the walls and spilt across the floor, but he showed no outward sign of unease. My own pulse quickened as another night loomed before me.

As we reached the hall the green baize door opened, and Mrs Henge appeared. She turned on the electric lights, and the hall and corridors blazed brightly for the first time since my arrival. It appeared while Hector graced us with his presence, economy was to be relaxed. Greyswick's creeping shadows were to be banished, for a few days at least.

The truth about Mr Sheers had spread by the time we gathered in the drawing room. Lady Brightwell, elaborately dressed in black silk and taffeta, and clacking with jet beads, immediately drew him into a loud conversation designed to be heard by us all, as she called upon him to concur with her own belief that ghosts were mere figments of hysterical imaginations.

She made no bones about looking at Madeleine as she stated this, provoking such a flush to my poor sister's cheeks that she clashed with the pink sateen of her evening dress.

'Do tell me, though, Mr Sheers,' Miss Scott asked, her own colour heightened from the rather rapid effects of her sherry, 'do you secretly hope to see a ghost one day?'

'Don't be ridiculous, Scottie!' Lady Brightwell scoffed. 'You can't see something that doesn't exist. There are no such things as ghosts. It's all a lot of tosh and nonsense – is it not, Mr Sheers?'

I didn't expect much from his reply – he had been brought in to disprove our theory, not lend credence to it, after all. I was paying scarce attention, therefore, when he surprised Lady Brightwell by asking whether she believed in God.

Flabbergasted at the impudence of his question, she spluttered over her sherry and replied in no uncertain terms that she most certainly did – indeed she hoped we all did, for the sake of our mortal souls. I stifled a snort at this, though the others fell over themselves to concur. Mr Sheers, I noticed, failed to commit himself. Instead, he waited for the bluster to abate before proceeding with his enquiry.

'Yet, you have never seen God, nor – I speculate now – any direct evidence of His existence?'

One could have heard a pin drop. Lady Brightwell's expression was thunderous. Her eyes narrowed as her mouth drew into a tight knot of displeasure.

'I *know* God exists, Mr Sheers, and like every good Christian, I will not challenge Him to present Himself – though I hope when my time comes I will have the good fortune of having my faith confirmed.'

'And perhaps I shall have to wait until death to know once and for all whether ghosts exist – or whether indeed they are simply attempts to rationalise things we cannot understand or explain,' he concluded with the hint of a smile.

Lady Brightwell promptly declared the subject closed. To everyone's relief the conversation was diverted to far more mundane matters, until we were called in for dinner.

When the gentlemen joined us in the drawing room after their cigars and brandy, Madeleine asked whether we might have the gramophone on. To my surprise, Lady Brightwell, mellowed by her son's company, agreed. Madeleine directed me to select a record, before coyly teasing Hector into dancing with her. Miss Scott clapped her hands in encouragement.

Lifted by the sudden gaiety, I made my way to the gramophone cabinet tucked away in the corner. I leafed through the records stacked inside and selected a popular waltz. Music filled the room and Madeleine and Miss Scott laughed with delight, as Hector, putting up a mock protest, allowed himself to be led into a clear space before the windows.

'I regret to say, I'm going to be very unchivalrous and not ask you to dance, Miss Marcham.'

I had been so entranced by the performers that I had quite failed to notice Mr Sheers' loping advance. I was startled to find him standing beside me.

'I would have turned you down even if you had,' I informed him. 'I don't dance.'

Not any more, at least. I hadn't danced since Madeleine's wedding – with Gerald. I felt a lump forming in my throat as I pictured myself laughing in his arms as he steered me around the newly weds in the ballroom at home, whispering in my ear that we would be next.

'*Promise me,*' I had whispered back.

'*On my life.*'

I blinked rapidly and turned back to the gramophone, where the record was coming to an end. Madeleine called for me to put on another – 'something jolly'. I forced a bright smile and busied myself putting the record away, before placing a new one upon the turntable, ignoring Madeleine's impatient pleas for me to hurry. The bouncy tune was greeted with much mirth, as Hector found himself pressed into a music hall number.

'I don't dance either.' Sheers tapped at his left leg. 'I'm not as light on my feet as I used to be.' He allowed himself a rueful smile, but I saw the sadness behind it. I didn't know why he had come to pester me, when he could have very easily remained seated by the fire. I certainly didn't need him to keep me company, but perhaps he felt it was his duty to do so, as I was a spare young woman, and he a spare young man.

'Do feel free to go and sit down, Mr Sheers. Knowing my sister, I'll be attending this contraption all night. She loves to dance.'

He chose not to take my hint and gave no indication that he had any desire to move away. He kept his attention on the performing pair, a faraway look on his face. Madeleine let out a peal of laughter.

'Have you started to draw your conclusions then, Mr Sheers?' I asked for want of something to say. He looked at me in surprise, as if he had forgotten the reason he was here. I offered him a tight smile. 'Are you going to tell my sister and me that it's all in our heads, as Lady Brightwell so fervently believes?'

176

'I am starting to collect my evidence, yes,' his tone was dry, officious even, 'but as you say, it wouldn't be right for me to draw conclusions without interviewing everyone involved.'

'But you already seem to know where you're going to end up.'

He smiled at my persistence. 'Let's just say I think the reasons for these things occurring are a lot closer to home than perhaps you appreciate, Miss Marcham.'

'And you'll be giving my brother-in-law the benefit of your advice, no doubt?'

'That is why I'm here, after all.' His answer was soft and low, and almost lost in the hubbub of music and laughter that had brought some life back to the room, a glimpse of its glory days.

'You don't entertain the possibility of any of it, do you?'

'I must confess you surprise me, Miss Marcham.'

'What do you mean?'

'I understand from Hector that you were with the VAD. A base hospital in France, wasn't it? I would have thought that, like me, you had seen enough death over there to know the truth.'

My heart hammered against my chest. 'What truth?'

He came closer, uncomfortably close, in fact. He was determined to ensure I not only heard the answer but felt its heavy burden also.

'That after that last breath leaves the body there is nothing. Nothing remains. Nothing escapes to a better world. Nothing lingers. There is just death, and all that is left is an empty carcass, a hunk of meat fit only for a hole in the ground. That's the truth of it, Miss Marcham – the unromantic truth. To believe anything else is delusional.' He averted his gaze to the merry couple colliding comically with furniture at the far end of the room. 'To believe anything else,' he concluded, 'would be madness.'

And with that, he returned to enjoy the warmth of the fire and the conviviality of the evening, the joint comforts of which failed to reach the lonely corner I found myself left within.

Chapter Twenty-Two

Though the night passed uneventfully, just as one could have predicted, I did not sleep well. I finally awoke feeling heavy, my limbs like lead weights crudely attached to my body.

I tugged the cord for Annie and she appeared a few minutes later, tight-lipped and cautious. As she began to lay out my clothes for the day, I told her in an off-hand fashion that Mr Sheers intended to interview her. Though she made no comment, I noticed her hands faltered in their task, becoming momentarily inactive, until she restarted their motion with concentrated calm.

'They are convinced we are making it all up, Annie: Mr Brightwell and Mr Sheers. Their sole purpose is to convince us that these events are little more than figments of our imagination.' Still she said nothing. 'Imagine that – men telling us we are mad, once again.' I tilted my head as I screwed the back onto my pearl drop earring. 'Will you be brave enough to tell them the truth, I wonder?'

She made no attempt to answer.

Madeleine was alone in the dining room when I went in for breakfast. The overcast aspect of the day insinuated itself into the room; beyond the window panes the air shimmered with rain. She came straight to me, her mien as glum as the weather outside.

'I tried to talk to Hector again last night, but Stella, he'll have none of it. He is certain we are making the whole thing up. He says Mr Sheers is convinced our subconscious thoughts are overpowering our rational ones, or some such mumbo-jumbo as that – that it's all in our minds!' She rested against the sideboard, her arms folded across her chest, as I helped myself to what remained in the silver salvers. 'Except we know it isn't, don't we? He wants to talk to you today, you know, Mr Sheers. You will tell him everything, won't you, Stella? You will be frank with him? You won't allow him to sway you or embarrass you into thinking he's right?'

'I don't think it will make any difference, whatever we say,' I told her as I settled myself down to eat. 'Mr Sheers has no intention of entertaining any extraordinary conclusions. He simply does not believe in ghosts.' Even now the word felt strange on my tongue and faintly ridiculous. 'I doubt anything will make him change his mind.'

'Then what was the point of him coming?'

I looked at her in surprise. 'To confirm Hector's opinion: that it's merely a lot of nonsense conjured up by two unstable girls.'

'No, no. He promised me he would listen to what I had to say. He promised to take me seriously.'

'He's indulged you by bringing in a second opinion.'

She gnawed at her fingernails, staring into the haze beyond the windows. 'What are we going to do, Stella?' I could hear the fear edging her words. 'If they don't believe us, and we have to stay in this house as it is . . .' She glanced back at me, before worrying her nail again.

'If they don't believe us, we will have to try and sort it all out for ourselves, won't we? Just as we would have done if they had never come.'

'Everyone is against us, Stella. Everyone in this house.'

'We still have each other.'

She smiled at my reassurance, a thin watery smile, but it wasn't long before she was tearing at the innocent nail again, staring blindly through the window into the uninviting day.

To make up for having ignored her for much of the previous day, Hector surprised Madeleine with tickets for the matinee performance at the local theatre, leaving me at a bit of a loose end. So, once the rain had abated, I decided to take a solitary walk in the grounds, eager to stretch my legs and blow away the cobwebs.

I had just returned and was casting off my coat into Maisie's waiting hands, when Mr Sheers loped into the hall and asked whether I might spare him a few minutes. My stomach clenched with nerves, but I did my best to conceal them as I agreed to his request. He led me down the corridor into the new wing, throwing open the door of the study, entreating me to make myself comfortable.

I took a moment to look about me as I approached the walnut desk that dominated the room. I was, to be quite honest, surprised he had set up camp in Sir Arthur's hallowed quarters. Even Hector had not chosen to utilise the study since his father's death, so strong was the patriarch's pervading presence, and indeed, there was something stifling about the room that put me ill at ease. Everything was too large, too overpowering, for the space attempting to contain it – the vast desk, the enormous globe on its polished brass stand, the gaudy gilt mirror and the stags' heads mounted on plaques. Everything struck me as being too conspicuous and ostentatious. It was hardly surprising that

Hector chose not to work in here – he would for ever be a little boy labouring in his father's shadow.

Mr Sheers, however, didn't seem the least bit uncomfortable with his surroundings, though he made no attempt to settle behind the desk. Instead, he gestured me to the two facing chairs arranged before it. As I sat in one, he took the other, removing a notebook from the desktop. His pen hovered over the blank page.

He asked me to start by revealing all the strange events that had occurred since my arrival, encouraging me to include any peculiar feelings, odd sensations, queer smells, indeed anything that might seem different from the norm.

'Is there any point to all of this, Mr Sheers? You as good as told me last night what you intend to deduce from this whole affair – my evidence is irrelevant. Your mind is set; your conclusion is already drawn. Nothing I say will change your opinion.'

He set the pen down. 'I'm sorry, Miss Marcham. I should apologise for being rather heavy-handed last night.'

'I'm not asking you to apologise, Mr Sheers, but you are clearly a man of conviction. This' – I waved my hand between us – 'therefore strikes me as a fruitless exercise.'

'I would argue that it's not fruitless, not at all. I'm still keen to know what you've experienced, and I want to understand *why*.'

'As long as the "why" fits in with your own theories,' I pointed out.

He smiled. 'Perhaps you will convince me otherwise.' He shrugged and begged me to indulge his curiosity. 'Let's see what conclusions we can draw together at the end.'

I sighed and huffed, before folding my hands in my lap. Then in a fluid fashion, bereft of emotion, I gave as thorough an account as I could. He interrupted intermittently, seeking clarification on certain points, and throughout his pen scratched across the surface of the paper with surprising neatness considering the speed at which it moved. I hesitated over my first reference to Annie, and he looked up, detecting my reticence immediately. My mind fogged over how much to say, how much to reveal, and I cursed myself for not having prepared more. So far, I had kept it simple: no assumptions, no deductions, just straight facts, stripped of theories. But now I had evoked Annie Burrows, and I didn't know what to say.

'Is there something more you want to tell me?' His voice was suddenly so gentle, I fancied he was going to take my hand and peer into my eyes, hoping for a glimpse of my secrets. I interlaced my fingers as I tried to think. He shuffled forward on his chair. 'Is it about Annie? I've spoken to her already.'

I demanded to know what she had told him, but he proved evasive. He was like a cunning detective, keeping witnesses apart, denying them the opportunity to collaborate on their stories. If only he knew that Annie Burrows had no intention of cooperating with me at all.

'I have nothing more to tell you,' I said at last.

A carafe of water and a cluster of glasses stood upon a silver tray in the middle of the desk, and I asked whether he might pour me one. He handed me the tumbler without comment. I drank deeply, nursing it in my lap once I had done.

'So, Mr Sheers? I have told you all I know. What do you conclude?'

He studied the notes in his book. 'It's all very interesting.'

'But you don't believe a word of it.'

There was a weighty pause. 'I believe *you* believe it.'

'Mr Sheers, I have spoken plainly to you, I would very much appreciate it if you could do me the same courtesy.'

My display of unfettered irritation clearly took him aback. The veneer of practised charm slid away, revealing something much more thoughtful and honest. He placed his notebook flat on his knee and leant forward, his dark gaze focused on me with unnerving intensity.

For a horrible moment I was transported back to those frightful Harley Street appointments arranged by Dr Mayhew. He had suggested to my parents I might benefit from the involvement of 'Head Doctors', as he so charmingly referred to them. I had resented the way they tried to claw into my private thoughts, my private grief, relishing any details I inadvertently let slip.

The resurgent memory unsettled me, but if Mr Sheers noticed my fleeting discomposure, he made no show of it. He settled himself back in his chair, his bearing detached and professional now.

'The incidents in this house began with your sister. Now, I understand that she has stayed here previously without any misgivings or unexplained occurrences, and yet since coming to stay this time that has clearly changed. We must therefore ask ourselves what else has changed in that time, and there is one obvious, happy alteration.'

He paused, like a school teacher waiting for his favourite pupil to provide the correct answer.

'She's expecting,' I said, unable to meet his eye.

'Quite. It is a well-noted fact that changes in female hormonal conditions or' – he took a moment to decide how best to proceed, before delicately picking his way through the minefield before him – 'or other . . . *emotional* conditions,' he said at last, 'can precipitate experiences that some would be keen to define as paranormal.'

I laughed in spite of myself. I bit my lips to stop lest he should think I was hysterical. I shook my head in disbelief, and yet at the same time, I wondered why I was so shocked. Was this not what I had expected all along?

'*Emotional conditions?*' I mocked. 'Hector has kept you well informed, then?'

'You are no longer serving in France,' he said, 'and you are decked in mourning. I would have made a calculated guess, even if Hector hadn't forewarned me.'

I sipped at the dregs of my water – my throat was dry, and I didn't want him to misinterpret any catch that might occur while I was speaking.

'I see very well what you are saying, Mr Sheers,' I said at last. 'My sister is pregnant and therefore clearly cannot be deemed rational, and I am beside myself with grief and so have no doubt lost my senses also. Hysterical females, such as ourselves, do not make convincing witnesses.'

'Please, Miss Marcham, bear with me. Don't you think it's strange this is all happening now? Is it really so astounding that your sister, your pregnant sister, should be struck to the core by the tragic tale of a little boy falling to his death? That a woman who is about to become a mother herself suddenly hears him crying, and yet finds herself powerless to comfort him? Surely that predicament is every mother's worst nightmare?'

'I have heard it too,' I pointed out, meeting his eye now.

'Yes, you imagine you have – the idea planted by your sister and left to develop in your own subconscious, to be fed by your grief-stricken state.'

I rose from my chair, determined to listen no more. I placed the glass firmly down on the desk as Sheers got to his feet.

'You are wrong, Mr Sheers. You yourself admit you are no expert and I can assure you your deductions in this matter are incorrect. I am sick and tired of men telling me I am unstable,' I announced, a revealing crack in my voice. 'Am I grieving? Yes, I am grieving. I have lost my fiancé. I held his dying body in my arms, unable to do anything to save him.' He attempted to interject, but feeling my composure slipping with frightening rapidity, I held up my hand to stop him. 'No – I tell you now, Mr Sheers, that does not render me mad. It does not. It merely makes me heartbroken. But I assure you, one can be heart-broken and remain fully in control of one's faculties. Perhaps in time you will come to see that.'

And with tears blinding me, I fled the room.

The unexpected knock on my bedroom door came just before dinner. I had still not recovered from my interview with Mr Sheers, and was feeling sullen and subdued. Thus distracted, I failed to respond to it immediately, but when it sounded a second time I came to my senses. Hector, dressed in his evening suit, stood in the doorway.

'Might I have a quick word, Stella?'

I would have loved for nothing more than to send him away, but I knew I couldn't. He closed the door behind him. He made no attempt to advance into the room, and remained where he was, tugging uncomfortably at the cuffs of his shirt.

'How are you?' he said at last.

'Actually, I have a thumping headache.' Since this afternoon, tension had built in my temples and now throbbed there as a constant reminder of the unpleasantness of the day.

'I'm sorry to hear that.'

He might have been content to stand to attention, but I was not. I drifted over to the chairs by the grate and sank into one. After a moment's hesitation, he took the one opposite, though he only perched, as if prepared for flight.

'I do appreciate you coming to spend some time with Madeleine.'

'It's been lovely to see her.'

'But I think perhaps it's time for you to go.'

The clock on the mantel chimed the hour, the shrill strikes thrusting knives into my aching head.

'Please understand, Stella, I have nothing against you, but the doctors have made it very clear that if we are to avoid what happened last time' – he looked beseechingly at me – 'what Madeleine needs right now is peace and quiet. She needs to be calm, Stella, and from what I can tell she is anything but. I had hoped your company would help but' – his hands flew up in exasperation – 'I have to say I'm very disappointed to hear that instead of settling everything down you've rather inflamed the situation with more of this nonsense.'

'Nonsense?'

'Yes, Stella, nonsense. If you're trying to be supportive let me tell you now – you're doing more harm than good.' Agitated, he sprang from the chair and strode to the window, raking his fingers through his hair. 'Look, I realise how hard these last months have been for you. I can't imagine what you've been through, losing Gerald the way you did. Losing anyone in this war is hard enough, but what happened to you . . .' He hesitated. 'I thought perhaps you were feeling better and spending time with Madeleine might be good for both of you, but clearly I was wrong. I'm sorry, Stella, but I have to think about what's best for my wife, what's best for our baby – and right now, being with you doesn't seem to be doing her any good at all.'

I was too upset to respond. The ticking clock spanned the silence while I composed myself.

'You're wrong, Hector. We're not making it up, it's not in our imaginations – there is something happening in this house.' I swivelled round in my chair to face him. 'Take her away with you, Hector, please! Take her back to London, she'd be safer there than here. I beg you, don't leave her here.'

A muttered expletive stopped me in my tracks. He was puce, his anger sparking. 'I'm sorry, Stella! This is the very reason I want you gone from here.'

'Hector—'

'I'm *sorry*, Stella. I very much hope there will be a happier time in the future, when we can all be together again, but that time is not now.' He strode past me, stopping as he reached the door. He gripped the handle, casting back over his shoulder. 'There's a train first thing tomorrow, I'd like you on it.' And with a final, fleeting apology, he opened the door and was gone.

Chapter Twenty-Three

It took me some time to recover. Though not wholly unexpected, I was still left dazed and somewhat dumbfounded by his decree. The dull call of the dinner gong galvanised me into action. The evening would progress, and I would have to be part of it – it was the done thing, after all. Pulling on my gloves I left my room and as I did so I had the misfortune of colliding with Mr Sheers.

'Was it your idea,' I demanded, 'to have me removed from Greyswick?'

'Miss Marcham, please. Given your sister's delicate state, I just felt it was best—'

'To get rid of me.' I was angry and resentful, and it was easier to lash out at this man, a stranger, than to cause trouble with my brother-in-law who, come what may, I was rather stuck with. 'Well, thank you very much for that. You have no idea the damage you have done. She will be here alone now, alone with no one to protect her.'

'Miss Marcham, she has her mother-in-law, she has Miss Scott, servants – she is hardly alone.'

I had no patience for his ignorance. 'You have no idea what you're dealing with.'

'I think I do, Miss Marcham.' He manner was grave and resolute. 'And I think you will soon find the situation greatly improved.'

'Once I've gone,' I carped. We reached the top of the stair-case. His features clouded with weariness, though I wasn't sure whether it was from my attack or the prospect of the physical feat now facing him. It was sobering seeing him grip the broad banister and lean heavily into it, pivoting his left leg, wincing as he took weight on it, moving his right leg down in a curious hop that he was at pains to minimise. Putting aside our differences, I offered him my arm, but he just glared at me.

'Thank you, I can manage.'

Cut by his curt dismissal, I stepped out past him without further ado and hurried down the stairs, leaving him to labour at his descent alone.

I heard my name as I reached the drawing room corridor and Madeleine came rushing to greet me. She threw her arms around me, holding me close, as if I were a lifebuoy in a surging sea, her only hope of survival. As I gently disentangled myself from her suffocating grasp, I could see that the rims of her eyes were raw, and her face puffy. Hector had told her everything, she informed me, her voice catching with emotion.

'We had a most awful row about it,' she confessed. 'I begged him to let you stay, Stella, but he won't hear of it. What am I going to do? Here without you? I can't bear the thought of it!'

Feeling empty and helpless I drew her back into my embrace, pressing my lips to her hair, as the shoulder of my gown grew damp with her tears. Aware Mr Sheers would soon be upon us, I pulled her towards an alcove and wiped her cheeks dry, smooth-ing her face with my palms, instructing her to calm herself.

'It is not too late, Stella,' she insisted, her mouth set with grim determination. 'I will not let them send you away. I will make them believe us.'

'Oh Madeleine, I will have to go,' I whispered. 'But you must come to Haverton, as soon as you are able, and stay for as long as you can.'

We pulled apart as Mr Sheers limped into the corridor. He slowed when he saw us, huddled in the corner. With a flicker of acknowledgement, he proceeded to the drawing-room door. I heard him sigh as he pushed it open.

Madeleine regarded him with contempt, her eyes glittering. 'All is not yet lost, Stella.'

Feeling an awful foreboding I caught hold of her arm. 'Promise me you won't do anything rash.'

She failed to respond. I followed her into the lion's den, braced for tumult.

'Darling! Come and join us,' Hector called out as we entered.

The jovial atmosphere died the moment Madeleine and I drew near. Our arrival was like a damp towel thrown over leaping flames – you could almost hear the hiss of the extinguished conviviality that had warmed the air.

I couldn't help but notice the satisfied look that darted between Lady Brightwell and Miss Scott, as they sat cosily by the fire, glasses of sherry in hand. I had no doubt the news of my imminent departure had been warmly welcomed by them both – one less troublesome girl to deal with.

Only Mr Sheers, who pushed himself up from his chair as we came in, bore the sobriety of the situation. Perhaps his conscience had been tweaked and he was beginning to rethink his part in the whole unsavoury affair. I no longer cared. I was being made to leave, and I was – as was true with so many things – powerless to do anything about it. I took a chair removed from the group and was heartened when Madeleine chose to eschew the vacant seat next to Hector to keep me company instead. The slight did not go unnoticed.

Hector poured us both sherry from the decanter on the sideboard. He remained tight-lipped as he handed us our glasses. He tried to catch Madeleine's eye, but she studiously avoided it, barely murmuring her thanks. A crease appeared between his brows, but he said nothing, and returned to his seat by the fire, engaging his mother in conversation about the woeful lack of gardeners.

It struck me how contrived it all was. Everyone in the room knew I would be leaving on the morning train, and yet no one would even reference the fact. It was a great open secret – a gaping wound that was destined to remain undressed. We would all simply turn away from its unpleasant gore and carry on as if nothing was wrong. The despicable politeness of it all made me feel quite sick.

Left to stew in my own thoughts, I began to resent Annie Burrows' part in it all, more and more. I wondered what she had told Mr Sheers. I had tried to discuss the interview with her when she came to dress me, but she had kept her answers vague, deflecting my enquiries with such skill she soon wore me down. I had no doubt she would have led him a merry dance, too, deftly side-stepping his questions, giving nothing away. She would have to go. I couldn't help but hold her at least partly accountable for the situation I now found myself in. If she had been more reliable, more forthright – dammit all, more honest! – then she could have added her voice to Madeleine's and my own. She had not.

I was so lost in my thoughts that I did not notice the rise in Madeleine's colour, or the manic glint in her eye. Perhaps if I had not been so self-absorbed I could have acted before it was too late. But I remained unaware of them until Madeleine cut across the room's banal conversation.

'Are we really going to act as if nothing has happened?' Her shrill voice was as demanding of attention as breaking glass. 'Stella is being made to leave – is no one going to mention her imminent departure?' Hector found himself pinned by her disdain. 'You make such a big show of saying this is my house, my home, and yet I have no say in it. I do not wish my sister to leave, and yet you take it upon yourself to banish her in disgrace.'

This uncharacteristic display of defiance was breathtaking. But though I was awed by the bravery summoned for the confrontation, I desperately wished she hadn't embarked on a battle there was no hope of winning.

'Madeleine—'

'No, Stella, I will not sit here and be reasonable. I tried that, and it got me nowhere. I am no suffragette but it appears if I want my voice to be heard in this house, I must take a more militant stance.'

'For God's sake, Madeleine,' Hector said, 'we've discussed all this—'

'Have we, Hector? Have we discussed it? A discussion requires more than one person's participation. It requires an exchange of opinions and a willingness to shed preconceptions, especially if the evidence is sufficiently compelling. There has been no discussion here. Stella and I have attempted to present our evidence, but the opinion of the jury was so predetermined against us we never had a chance.'

'You are absolutely right, my dear,' Lady Brightwell chirped up. 'As extraordinary as it may be to you, I have no intention of lending any credence to the ludicrous claim this house is haunted.'

'Mother, please . . .'

'Well, I'm sorry, Hector, but it's absurd. The person who has made a compelling case, to my mind at least, is Mr Sheers. This nonsense is little more than the . . .' she paused. 'What was it again, Mr Sheers?'

'The influence of suggestion and the power of the subconscious.'

He offered the summation with an air of reluctance. I wondered whether he was now beginning to regret nosing into a conversation that had been none of his business, interfering in something that went far deeper than a superficial fancy for the afterlife.

I had expected Madeleine to wilt under Lady Brightwell's condemnation, just as she had withered on so many previous occasions, but it seemed I had underestimated my sister. She had moulded herself into a thing of steel, inflexible and strong.

'I know what I heard, Mr Sheers, and it was not some creation of my imagination. And unless someone in this house is lying, things have happened which cannot be neatly explained away by your theory.'

Sheers made no attempt to correct her, he just carried on staring into the flames. It was Hector who tried to silence Madeleine, but she would have none of it.

'Hector, I've been telling you for weeks that I've heard crying coming from the nursery. And now, I have corroborating witnesses—'

'Darling, please.' He covered the distance to Madeleine's

chair in a few strides, dropping into a crouch to take her hands. 'This has all been explained to you. Stella loves you very much. She wants to believe you, so much so, her own mind creates the suggestions you have planted there . . .'

I objected to him telling me my own mind. 'You're wrong, Hector. I'm not so much of a fool as you take me for and I'm not so easily encouraged as you think. I didn't want to believe Madeleine – I didn't believe her, not initially. It was only after I had heard the crying myself that I realised she had been telling the truth all along. I too am utterly convinced a spirit lingers in this house.'

From the fireplace, Lady Brightwell released a derisive cackle.

'Stop it! Stop it now!' Madeleine jerked out of her seat, sending Hector sprawling. My sister, my sweet little sister with her swelled stomach, looked like Boudicca ready for battle. 'We are not mad. We know what we heard and what's more, we know *who* we heard.'

I cringed. My fists clenched, trying to hold onto the secret I feared Madeleine was about to let fly. I had been impressed by her determined courage to speak out, but now I was apprehensive. I felt like an army protected by a loose cannon – grateful for its presence but fearful of where the next round would land.

'Oh wonderful!' Lady Brightwell crowed, clapping her hands in glee. 'You intend to unmask the ghost.' I winced at her acerbity, willing Madeleine to keep calm, to retain our secret until we could nurture it for better use than this fraught defence. 'So? Who is it? Who dares to upset the tranquillity of my home?'

Time itself seemed to stop in breathless anticipation of the answer. It was not too late to avert the impending disaster. Madeleine delayed her response for so long that for a blissful moment I thought she had seen reason and drawn back from the edge of the precipice. But I was wrong. Her delicate pink lips curled as her narrow chin jutted up. She would not be cowed, there was no going back now. Her voice rang through the electrified air.

'Lucien Brightwell.'

And at precisely that moment, the lights went out.

Chapter Twenty-Four

Thanks to the fire, we were not plunged into total darkness. Miss Scott let out a cry of fright, and I heard Madeleine gasp, but Hector was quick to reassure us all it was little more than a blown fuse. Lady Brightwell remained phlegmatic. Sitting beside the fire as she was I couldn't help but picture her as a devil backlit by Hades.

Hector retrieved the matches from the mantel and fumbled his way around the room lighting the oil lamps. Before long, the golden cast of the fire had been supplemented by further puddles of light. He was just replacing the last glass bowl when the door opened, and Mrs Henge loomed from the pitch, her face illuminated in a most ghastly fashion by the flickering flame she carried before her.

'I brought some candles, Mr Brightwell, I thought you might need them.'

'Thank you, Mrs Henge. It's probably a fuse. I'll have to go down to the cellar to change it.'

'I believe there is a box of spare wires by the electric board, sir.'

'Very good, would you set these candles about the room? I'll go and sort this out.'

'Let me come with you,' Sheers offered, pushing himself up.

I recalled his torturous journey down the stairs and imagined the narrow damp steps that would lead into the bowels of the house. I got to my feet.

'Don't trouble yourself, Mr Sheers, I'll go.' Hector displayed a distinct lack of enthusiasm at the prospect of my company. 'You'll need someone to hold the candle, and no offence intended, Mr Sheers, but we don't want you coming a cropper on the cellar stairs.'

I realised too late how belittling my flippancy was. I had stolen his pride with my crass words. I may not have liked him, I may have resented his opinions, but I had injured him in a way so callous it was unforgivable.

Only Mr Sheers and myself, however, appeared aware of my misdemeanour. He made no comment but punished me by holding my appalled gaze until I squirmed, my jaw gaping as words of apology screamed in my skull but failed to reach my lips. Mortification robbed me of my voice.

'Well, hurry if you're coming, Stella,' Hector said offering me a candle, impatient to get on. Mr Sheers lowered himself back into his chair.

The black beyond the drawing room was indecipherable. Not a glimmer other than our wan flames pierced the umbra until we reached the hall, where beams of moonlight strained to reach the bottom of the staircase. I bumped into the oak table and cursed at the burst of pain in my hip. Hector touched my arm and I assured him I was quite well, but he cupped my elbow all the same and guided me to the green baize door. Our candles twitched and dipped, brushed by chilly draughts.

'Careful of the steps.'

He led the way down the flight of stone steps immediately beyond the servants' entrance. At the bottom I could discern the beginnings of a passageway, but it vanished into the darkness before it had barely begun. There was a doorway to our right through which I could see the twin glow of two candles, set upon a large table. They lit three faces: Cook, Maisie and Annie, all clustered round, each taken aback by our arrival. Annie's attention settled upon me, her expression enigmatic in the candlelight. The flames spluttered, and she looked away.

'Do you need any help, Master Hector?' Cook called out.

'No, no thank you, Cook.' A golden streak danced across Hector's features. 'It'll just be the fuse. I'll head down now and sort it out. We'll have you bathed in light in no time.'

The cellar door was tucked beneath the slope of the stairs. Hector lowered his burning wick to the handle and turned the key jutting from the lock.

'Are you sure you want to come down?' he asked me.

'You won't see a thing otherwise.'

The door groaned as it opened. Stubby stone steps fell away into the abyss and I felt a tremor of trepidation. Hector went first, his candle largely futile. Quelling my nerves, I followed him down.

The steps were narrow and steep. I took them one at a time, like a cautious child. The air was glacial and when I put my hand to the wall to steady myself, the stone beneath my palm was cold and clammy, as if the very foundations of the house were feverishly perspiring. The relief at finally reaching the rough stone floor at the bottom was overwhelming. Even with our candles, we could barely make out our surroundings. I sensed rather than saw the low brick-arched ceiling, the uneven gritty floor and the stone shelves set into the walls.

Hector's confidence ebbed under the oppressive darkness.

He mumbled that the electric board was at the far end of the cellar, an undiscernible distance before us – it could as well have been five paces as fifty. He began to shunt forward, his feet shuffling like a blind man's, his black evening suit blending into the enveloping murk. My heart hammered as I stumbled to keep up with him. A harsh vinegary smell hung in the chilly air and I could faintly hear a rhythmic dripping, like a water clock keeping time.

'There must be a blown bottle of wine down here somewhere,' Hector muttered.

Our progress was painful – stunted footsteps pressing into air that grew colder and colder until goose-pimples peaked down my arms and across my shoulders. I clenched my teeth to prevent them from chattering.

'Ah, I think . . . I think it's here.' There was palpable relief in Hector's voice as he held his candle aloft, its flickering glow just catching the edge of the electric board with its intricate array of wires. 'Yes, here we are . . .' Setting his candlestick down on the shelf below it, he peered up, trying to make sense of the twisted threads.

'Do be careful.'

'It's quite all right, I just need to switch this fellow out . . .'

His candle guttered and died.

'Dammit.'

The gloom drew ever nearer, only kept at bay now by my own spluttering flame.

There was an almighty clunk as the cellar door slammed shut. Hector cried out and I leapt from my skin like a Jack-in-the-box. My candle flame twitched and vanished. We were engulfed by darkness.

'Dear God, I can't see a thing!' Hector exclaimed.

My heart was pounding, but I cautioned myself to keep calm. I stretched out my fingers to interpret my surroundings. I felt a rough wooden crate, with smooth glass jars inside. I nursed a naive hope of discovering a matchbox, but there could have been a hundred matchboxes within my reach – finding one in this underground cavern without a glint of light was a task akin to finding the Holy Grail, and somewhat less likely.

'We must have light . . .' I tried to stave the panic from my voice. 'I'll go back upstairs and find some matches.'

'I'll fumble around down here and see if I can find some.'

I turned around. The awful blindness had stripped me of all efficiency and every facet of capability. I shuffled forwards, my arms outstretched, slicing through space before me. I caught something and sent it smashing to the floor. My shoes slid into a sticky substance and given the sweet burst of scent I deduced it to be a jar of jam. Cook would not be pleased.

'Are you all right?' Hector's voice drifted my way.

'I think I'm nearly there . . .' My fingertips inched across coarse stone, tracing the outline of a step. 'Yes! Yes, I've reached the stairs, Hector.'

It was then I heard the noise – the sound of metal on stone. There was a rhythmic quality to it, paced and regular, like something rolling. I heard it twang as it skipped over the rough floor.

'What the devil . . .' Hector started, but then cried out in alarm. I called his name, but he didn't answer. There was a crash and clattering. I called his name again, panic rising as I stumbled back through the darkness, fear tearing at my chest as I begged him to answer me.

The room exploded into light. I shielded my eyes from the startling brightness, wincing, blinded again – this time by the multitude of spots dancing in my pupils. The single bulb suspended from the ceiling swayed on its short cord.

My breathing steadied as I became accustomed to the light. Hector stood before me, rigid, his face pallid. Concerned, I called his name, but it died on my lips. Lying on the ground before him was a metal hoop, a child's toy, the same child's toy I now knew I had heard rolling down the length of the cellar before it clattered to the ground at his feet. My stomach lurched. I had seen that hoop before.

'Were you at the steps the whole time, Stella?' Hector croaked. I nodded. 'And there is no one else in here with us?'

At this he visibly rallied and whirled around to peer down the stretch of cellar behind him. There was no one there. We were alone.

'It cannot be . . .'

'Hector, what is it?'

'I felt something. I felt something, here, in the darkness.'

I could barely whisper my question as to what.

His timorous features mirrored my own.

'A child, Stella – I felt a child.'

Chapter Twenty-Five

He insisted we carried out a proper search of the cellar before we retreated, but we found nothing untoward, no traces of the little figure that had brushed past my brother-in-law in the dark. I knew we would not.

Hector hastened up to the realm of the living, his shoes scuffing against the stone steps, stumbling in his haste to be gone from this place. The kitchen was a flurry of activity as we dashed past it – dinner running late, delayed by the outage.

We didn't speak at all during our return journey. My heart was racing faster than my charging thoughts and Hector was too shaken by the whole mysterious encounter to trust himself. He paused as we reached the drawing-room door.

'What was that, Stella? What just happened down there?'

'I think . . . I think Lucien was in the cellar.' I gripped his arm. 'Will you believe us now, Hector?' He didn't answer me. I withdrew my hand, his jacket sleeve crumpled from the pressure of my touch.

The others greeted us like heroes, crowing their delight and relief at the return of power, but when we drew closer they were alarmed by Hector's diminished appearance, his deathly grey pallor and hollowed eyes. He gripped the back of a chair to conceal the trembling in his hands.

'Dear God, Hector!' cried Lady Brightwell. 'What on earth is wrong?'

Sheers didn't wait for the answer but loped to the sideboard and upended the whisky decanter. He handed the tumbler to Hector, who threw back the generous measure in one gulp.

'Something happened in the cellar,' Hector stuttered. He faltered over his account, his eager tongue tripping him up, shreds of rationale holding him back, but then relenting. I stood beside him, staring at the carpet. I had expected to feel something – vindication, triumph – but I felt strangely empty and even more afraid.

Lady Brightwell was the first to break the awed silence.

'No, no, Hector. I will put my money on it being one of those wretched gypsy children. They are camped again on the common – Colonel Griffyths is quite up in arms about it. There have been thefts across the district, and now it seems they have had the audacity to break into our cellar! I shall have the constable called immediately.'

'It was no gypsy child, Mother. We searched the cellar, there was no one there but ourselves, and no way in or out but the door – and that door had slammed shut before the hoop moved, before I sensed the child.'

Lady Brightwell continued to bluster, but when it became apparent that her son was not for being swayed, she fell silent. Miss Scott also looked perturbed, her ever-present knitting piled on her lap, her industry stilled by Hector's revelations. Madeleine drew him to sit down and he slumped rather pathetically into an armchair.

'Might I ask what the cellar is used for, generally?'

Mr Sheers' question startled us all from our individual thoughts. For a moment, no one answered, then a low voice drifted from the edge of the room. We had all forgotten Mrs Henge, tucked away behind the door.

'It's used mainly for storage, sir,' she said, coming forward.

Mr Sheers nodded thoughtfully. 'Do tell me, was anything else disturbed in any way while you were down there?'

Hector frowned. 'Disturbed? Well, Stella knocked something down when she was trying to make her way back to the stairs. What was it?'

'A jar of jam. I accidentally knocked down a jar of jam. It smashed on the floor. I couldn't see in the dark.'

'So, it's perfectly feasible you may have knocked the hoop your-self, Hector, without realising it? Knocked it loose, set it rolling? I presume it's been stored down there for some time, Mrs Henge?'

'Oh yes, sir.' She clasped her hands before her black skirts. 'A lot of Master Lucien's things were stored away in the cellar after his death. Out of sight,' she said quietly, 'for everyone's sake.'

'And the electricity board is at the far end of the cellar, a less utilised area, I should imagine?'

'Indeed, sir. Cook tends to use the front of the cellar for food and the like.'

Hector tidied up his pose. 'I know what you're getting at, Sheers, but look here, even if I did somehow knock that hoop – which is possible, I accept – how do you explain the boy?'

The edge of Sheers' mouth tweaked upwards. 'It's definitely a boy now, is it?'

Hector looked flummoxed. 'What do you mean?'

'When you related your experience initially, you said you felt "a child". Now that child has become a boy.'

Hector swatted away the comment. 'Boy, child, what does it matter? I'm telling you I distinctly felt someone there.'

'Felt?' Sheers pressed. 'You touched them? You touched something solid? Flesh and bone?'

'No, no, I didn't touch anything—'

'Then how did you feel a child there?'

'I didn't feel as you feel with your hand, I *felt him* – you know – sensed, I could sense something there.'

'But you didn't feel it, you didn't actually physically touch or tangibly experience it in any way?'

'Dammit I . . .' Hector sprang to his feet, his hands clenched in frustration at his sides. 'There was something there.'

'You imagined something there,' Sheers corrected him. He eased himself down onto the arm of his chair. 'I don't think there was anything down in the cellar with you, Hector,' he said gently, 'other than your own imagination.'

Hector glared, angry at the insinuation. 'Now, listen here, Sheers, I was there—'

Sheers held up his hand to staunch the flow of rebuttal and asked Hector to humour him. Lady Brightwell interceded on his behalf and implored her son to listen to what their guest had to say. It was apparent from the anxious set of her features she was desperate for Mr Sheers to provide a sensible explanation for the unsettling incident. She was not to be disappointed.

'Immediately prior to the blackout, you were in the midst of an emotionally charged debate with your wife about – well, we were all witness to it, you don't need me to expound further,' Sheers said. 'In absolute darkness, we lose one of our treasured senses: sight. It is instinctive to feel vulnerable – the rest of our senses heighten to compensate. So, in the cellar just now you were on high alert – and all the time, the acrimonious discussion is ringing in your ears and playing on your mind. The depth of your affection for Mrs Brightwell is clear to all; you don't want to do anything to upset her, you wish for nothing more than to support and protect her.'

Hector looked abashed, and Madeleine flushed prettily. I clenched my hands in my lap.

'It is perfectly possible you knocked the hoop – innocently stored out of the way – without even realising it. We all know the hoop features prominently in the only portrait of Lucien Brightwell hanging in this house. You are on edge; your mind is full of a small boy your wife fervently believes has returned from the dead, and then suddenly in the dark there is – what? A cold draught escaping through an ill-fitting brick? Well, there are hundreds of reasons why you might get a draught in a cellar – the point is this: in this heightened, preoccupied state, your subconscious interprets something which is completely innocent as something connected to the undercurrent of thoughts troubling you. It is offering you an escape route from the unpleasant argument with your wife. It is offering you a way to support her, as you so desperately wish to do. It is, in short, conjuring, for your benefit, the impression of a spectral being.'

His deduction was met with stunned silence.

'Bravo, Mr Sheers!' It was Lady Brightwell who spoke up, clapping her hands in delight, relief freshening her face. 'You have explained it all beautifully!'

'Well, now hang on a minute . . .' Hector cautioned. 'How do you explain the lights going out in the first place? Madeleine says the boy's name and we're plunged into darkness! I didn't touch the damn board and they all come on again!'

'On my tour yesterday you told me your father had the electrics run through the house when it was first built – when was that? Thirty years ago? Is it so difficult to believe there may simply be a temperamental fault with the wiring somewhere? There is such a thing as coincidence. I suspect your wife has invoked Lucien Brightwell's name on several occasions with no adverse effect whatsoever.' He paused, then smiled and held his hands aloft. 'There, I said "Lucien Brightwell" myself and I haven't been struck down yet.'

Further discussion on the matter was interrupted by a tentative knock on the door. Maisie dipped into the room to announce that, with apologies for the delay, dinner was now ready to be served.

'Dear God,' Hector sighed, rubbing at his forehead. 'How are we supposed to eat after this?'

'I could ask Cook to hold it a while longer if you wish, sir?' Mrs Henge offered. I marvelled at her unnatural ability to be present without anyone realising.

'No, no, Mrs Henge. We must eat,' Hector said. 'We should go in.'

The dining room was only lit by two silver candelabras set upon the table, but Hector put on the electric chandeliers the moment we walked in. I think everyone had had enough of meek illumination – we were all too aware of the peculiarity of shadows.

Once we had settled, and Maisie had skirted about delivering bowls of consommé, the conversation returned to the events in the cellar. Hector remained indignant at the suggestion that it was all in his mind, though in some ways it was a more attractive option than the alternative. Madeleine and I continued to express our scepticism over Mr Sheers' neat explanation, whilst Lady Brightwell became its most vociferous advocate. Miss Scott remained glum as she paddled her spoon around her bowl.

'I'm sure I shall not sleep a wink tonight,' she complained during a lull.

None of us, save for the indomitable Lady Brightwell, had much appetite, and no one complained when Madeleine asked for the soup bowls, largely untouched, to be removed. I was surprised to see Annie appear to serve the main course. Since our arrival, she had assisted in the kitchen, but left Maisie to wait at table. Her gaze skittered over us as she proffered a vast dish of boeuf bourguignon, her disquiet patently evident, though I was unable to determine whether it hailed from the responsibility of attending us, or news of the evening's developments.

'I want to buy into your theory, Sheers,' Hector said. 'But dash it all, it was so real. The most important thing to me is Madeleine's happiness – I want her to be able to stay here without any concerns or reservations. I don't think that's too much to ask.'

'And what I say isn't enough to convince you?'

'I'm sorry, Mr Sheers,' Madeleine addressed him across the table. 'It's not that I refuse to be proven wrong, but I need to be more thoroughly convinced.'

'To put it frankly, Mr Sheers,' I interjected, 'neither my sister nor myself think we are in any way deluded, and whilst I appreciate what you are saying, none of this has happened to you.'

'Very well, I have a proposal,' he said at last. 'I personally don't think there is anything supernatural occurring within this house, but if you are so convinced there is, I can suggest a possible solution.'

'Which is?' Hector asked.

We all focused on Mr Sheers, waiting on tenterhooks.

'It is my suggestion you arrange for the house to be cleansed,' he announced. 'In other words, an exorcism.'

Chapter Twenty-Six

There was a tremendous clatter from the sideboard behind me. Annie hastily retrieved the vegetable dish that had slipped from her grasp and began scooping up the carrots spilt by her carelessness.

'An exorcism?' Hector said. 'Do you honestly think that would work?'

Mr Sheers shrugged. His flippancy rendered me uneasy.

'If I am unable to assure you otherwise, then I think you should take a more aggressive stance. It strikes me this is a God-fearing house – ask the house of God to banish the demon.'

Madeleine watched in hopeful anticipation as Hector weighed up the proposal.

'It couldn't hurt to try,' he concluded at last, taking a gulp of wine.

'I will not have our vicar dragged into this, Hector. The humiliation is too much to bear,' Lady Brightwell protested. She bristled as Annie offered her the vegetable dish. 'Neither will I eat dropped carrots,' she informed the young maid with a withering look. 'You should know better than that, girl.'

Murmuring an apology, Annie withdrew to the edge of the room, but I was acutely aware of the tension emanating from her – what was its root cause, I wondered. Fear? Dread? Desperation?

'No, Mother, I think it's worth a try. I'll drive to Turley in the morning, see if the vicar there might be able to help, if it's gossip you're worried about.'

'I'm worried about us becoming the laughing stock of the entire area,' Hector's mother retorted. 'Mr Sheers has provided what seems to me a perfectly rational explanation – why you can't accept it I simply don't know. This evocation of Lucien is as ridiculous as it is distasteful.'

'Well, my mind is made up,' Hector asserted. 'I'm going to Turley tomorrow. Whatever it costs, whatever I have to promise the vicar there, I'll do it, to put an end to this once and for all – to put all our minds at rest,' he concluded, as he laid his hand over Madeleine's.

I think everyone was rather relieved when the evening eventually limped to a close, with Hector and Madeleine being the first to declare themselves 'done-in'. Their decision to retire served as a catalyst, with Lady Brightwell, Miss Scott and Mr Sheers all rising to follow suit. Miss Scott invited me to join their bed-ward bound caravan, but I declined. I had much to ponder, and the prospect of quiet reflection by the low fire induced me to remain where I was.

Lady Brightwell and Miss Scott duly exited. Mr Sheers returned his glass to the sideboard, and quietly wished me a goodnight before hitching his way to the door.

'It's a trick, isn't it?' I called out, stopping him in his tracks. 'You suggesting to Hector that he has the place exorcised? You don't believe for a moment there are any ghosts here, so why believe a vicar muttering some biblical phrases could restore the status quo?'

His intelligent eyes narrowed. He made no attempt to

contradict me, but the corner of his mouth quivered, and it was then I understood. I swivelled in my chair to better face him, angry yet strangely impressed at his deviousness.

'You think it is all in our minds' – I picked my way carefully as the concept began to unfurl – 'so us all being good Christian creatures, if we see a man of God bless this house and banish whatever malevolent spirit lingers, you think we'll believe it's all over and our collected subconscious will be hoodwinked into behaving.'

He didn't concede his ruse had been rumbled, nor did he apologise for the deception. Indeed, he said nothing, just studied me further for a moment, before once again wishing me goodnight. He had almost slipped through the door when I called out one last time.

'You should know, Mr Sheers, that I lost my faith in France.'

He stood still, his shoulders heaving with a resigned sigh. He offered me a parting reply as he closed the door behind him.

'So did I, Miss Marcham. So did I.'

Chapter Twenty-Seven

Annie came to attend on me the next morning just as the clock struck seven. She was pale and drawn, and I suspected she too had passed a sleepless night. She proved to be sullen and clumsy in her distraction, dropping a bottle of scent, misbuttoning my dress. I noticed her hand shook as she reached for the brush on my dressing table.

'Your mind is elsewhere this morning,' I said as I dismissed her.

She held my gaze for a beat more than was comfortable, and I fancied I could detect a hesitancy about her, as if she had something to say and was struggling to find the courage, but in the end she just dropped her chin and stared at the floor.

'I'm sorry, miss.'

She slipped away from the room, leaving a residual aura of anxiety, and I couldn't help feeling her apology was more loaded than I had power to understand. I recalled her growing disquiet in the dining room as the exorcism was discussed, and I wondered what she might know that I could not possibly begin to fathom, with my orthodox understanding of the world. I felt the first stirrings of misgiving. What did any of us really know about exorcisms? Would it just be a bit of harmless fun, as I suspected Mr Sheers believed – an innocent exercise to relieve our anxious minds? Or were there dire consequences of such ignorant interference that we couldn't possibly begin to imagine?

I was not alarmist by nature, but by the time I entered the dining room for breakfast, my concern had become so grave I resolved to speak to Hector. I was too late. Madeleine – glowing, relaxed and happily anticipating resolution – told me Hector had already left for Turley. The relief of finally having her husband's support was evident in every aspect of her being – the looseness of her limbs, the light in her face, the tinkling levity in her voice; overnight, she had been unburdened. But this buoyancy, this irrepressible optimism, weighed heavily on me, as I recalled Annie's pale face and shaking hands.

'Am I allowed to stay now?' I asked.

'Yes, my dear, Hector has agreed you can stay. We'll see this through, and you will remain at Greyswick.'

I summoned a weak smile and looked away.

Hector reappeared just as we had settled down to elevenses. Madeleine had extended an invitation to Mr Sheers to join us in the orangery. I was wary of him now, seeing him as a wolf in sheep's clothing. He was taking advantage of the others, abusing their faith to achieve his own ends, and it seemed rather underhand to me.

Hector's energetic arrival diluted any awkwardness, as he imparted the news we had all been waiting for. Laughing, he held up his hand to staunch Madeleine's excited questions and settled down on a cushioned wicker seat before regaling us with his morning's adventures.

The vicar had, it turned out, been very reluctant to become embroiled in our situation, but a little financial encouragement had persuaded him, just this once, to intervene on our behalf. He was to attend the house this afternoon, while Lady Brightwell was engaged at one of her War Committee meetings.

'Best get on with it, I say,' Hector concluded helping himself to a petit four.

'And are we sure this is the right thing to do?' I piped up. 'These things . . . they can go wrong, can't they? Can't they make the spirits angry?'

It came as no surprise that my cautious arguments were lost in the bullish conversation that followed.

Lady Brightwell and Miss Scott disappeared down the drive in the Rolls just before two o'clock, and not fifteen minutes later, Maisie admitted Reverend Dugdale to the drawing room.

He was, I estimated, in his late fifties. Not particularly statuesque, he had a weather-worn complexion and the beginnings of a paunch that sagged like a half-filled sack about his middle. His black trousers and shirt were crumpled and his jacket, I noticed, was threadbare round the cuff. I wondered whether there was a Mrs Dugdale – I suspected there was not.

Hector ushered him to a seat not far from mine. He sat down heavily and tucked the briefcase he was carrying between his shoes, which, like the rest of him, appeared shabby and poorly polished. Once seated, he fidgeted to retrieve a creased greying pocket square from his trousers, and proceeded to dab at his forehead, where minute beads of sweat glistened like dew drops.

Hector took charge of proceedings, but not before Madeleine had asked Maisie to bring in the tea things. The vicar looked relieved to see the tray being set down. He slurped at his cup of Earl Grey and, with great enthusiasm, received a large wedge of cherry cake which he demolished in a rather ungainly fashion. He was, I have to say, the most uncouth vicar I had ever encountered. This damning assessment did nothing for my confidence in his abilities.

'I think it might be best if we carry out the exorcism in the area where the presence is strongest,' he said when he had at last been sated with tea and cake. 'It seems to me the nursery would be the most obvious location.' He dabbed again at his brow and ran a finger along the inside of his dog collar. He sported a shaving cut in the stubble-speckled flesh above its rim. 'I think it is only right that I point out again, Mr Brightwell, that I can make no promises as to the outcome of this exorcism.' He paused. 'In short, I cannot guarantee it will work.'

'I have complete faith in you, Reverend,' Hector assured him. The problem, I observed to myself, was that the vicar did not share Hector's conviction.

The discussion dwindled, and it became apparent we could delay no longer. Reverend Dugdale opened his briefcase and withdrew his stole – white silk, richly embroidered with large garnet crosses at each end – which he draped about his neck. Next, he took out a rather battered leather-bound bible, its pages reassuringly dog-eared, and finally he extracted a small bottle. He spotted my interest and smiled.

'Holy water,' he explained, tucking it into his pocket. I suspected he would have preferred a flask of fortifying liquor.

'I think perhaps you should wait here,' Hector said to Madeleine.

'No, Hector, I want to come – I need to come.'

'Is that wise, darling? I'll stay here with you if you like,' I offered, though I longed to accompany the men upstairs.

She shook her head. 'No, Stella. I need to see this spirit laid to rest.' Her palm strayed to her belly.

We trooped from the room like condemned convicts being led to the gallows, with only Mr Sheers displaying any carefree enthusiasm for the whole escapade. We reached the hall to find Annie lurking in the corner, pretending to be cleaning. She ceased her activity as we began to ascend the staircase. I fell in last, after Mr Sheers, and was conscious of her scrutiny. As I reached the twist of the half-landing, I looked down upon her, a frustratingly closed book, and my courage wavered.

In nervous anticipation we gathered before the nursery. I just wanted it all to be over and I felt a surge of relief as Hector took the plunge and opened the door.

Cold air swept out to greet us, winding around our ankles as we shuffled forward to secure front row seats for the unfolding drama. I detected the unpleasant sweet mustiness that I had smelt previously in the room, but it was stronger than before. My stomach churned as I hovered on the threshold.

'Right. Well, shall we begin?'

There was a revealing tremor in the vicar's voice as the flimsy pages of his bible fluttered to the appropriate section. He coughed, a phlegmy hack, and tapped his jacket pocket to reassure himself of the holy water's presence. Madeleine slipped her hand into mine. Hector joined us, while Sheers rested against the wall with a practised air of nonchalance, but I could tell he was humming with excitement. Reverend Dugdale paused to dab again at his shining forehead, before speaking in a low, steady voice – rich in tone and surprisingly strong.

'We cast you out, every unclean spirit, every satanic power, every onslaught of the infernal adversary, every legion, every diabolical group and sect, in the name and by the power of our Lord, Jesus Christ. We command you begone . . .'

As he spoke, I felt the cool air in the room shift, and the tips of my fingers began to sting as if frozen by wintry gusts. The others gave no indication they were suffering similar discomfort, indeed Reverend Dugdale was perspiring heavily. I watched a large drop of sweat trickle from his temple and stream down his cheek like a misplaced tear. He dabbed at it with his hand-kerchief, his hand shaking, though his voice continued in its steady incantation. In a strange way I found it calming and for the first time, I felt a flicker of optimism that this extraordinary exercise might actually work.

But just as I allowed myself hope, the cracking began.

Chapter Twenty-Eight

Madeleine gripped my arm. I followed her terror-stricken gaze to the fireplace. The glass in the picture frame hanging above it fractured before our astonished eyes, dissecting the words of the sampler beneath – 'We Are All God's Children'. The vicar continued to recite his scripture with a look of dawning horror as the harsh sound split the frigid air. Withdrawing the bottle of holy water, he set his bible upon the smaller bed, and without breaking the steady pace of his delivery, he removed the cork.

'God the Father commands you. The Son of God commands you. God the Holy Ghost commands you . . .'

Madeleine cried out in alarm as something small flew through the air, smacking into the wall beside the vicar, before clattering to the floor. I watched, petrified, as it came rolling towards me – a glass marble. Hector flinched as he was struck on the arm, then Reverend Dugdale faltered as one hit him in the chest. A flurry of marbles whizzed through the air and we ducked to avoid them. They soon littered the floorboards like hailstones.

I was unable to decipher the expression on Mr Sheers' face, his arm elevated against the unnatural storm that continued to pelt us. Madeleine sobbed as she cowered against the door frame, but stubbornly refused to heed Hector's plea to leave. I wrapped my arm around her shoulders and pulled her against me. There was a hint of desperation in Reverend Dugdale's rising voice as he incited the spirit to depart, while he scattered his holy water about him.

Madeleine gasped, catching everyone's attention as she stiffened in my arms. Terrified, she stared down at her swollen belly, the colour draining from her cheeks.

'Dear God, Madeleine, what is it?' I cried.

'His hands! I can feel his hands on me.'

I have known no horror like the horror I felt in that moment. My whole chest contracted, and I could not breathe, as if the weight of fear itself was smothering me. I followed her gaze to the protrusion below her waist, innocuously covered by a pretty sprigged-cotton dress. I half-expected to see the fabric lift, plucked by invisible fingers.

'Hector! Stella! I can feel a child's hands spread across my belly!'

'For God's sake, do something!' Hector implored Dugdale.

'Begone, Satan, inventor and master of all deceit . . .' The vicar's voice hiked again in volume. The marbles that lay scattered across the floor began to roll, knocking into our feet, rebounding off furniture legs. 'Give place to Christ in Whom you have found none of your works . . .' he cried, louder, though with less confidence before. The sampler began to rock on its hook. 'Tremble and flee when we invoke the Holy . . .' It flew from the wall and smashed face down on the floor before the grate, causing even Mr Sheers to cry out in alarm, though when he turned to me, I was horrified to see thrilled wonder upon his face.

Madeleine was wailing for her baby now. Hector desperately batted the air about her in a futile attempt to dislodge the invisible palms. The sampler frame began to lift side to side, rocking, as if fuelled by Dugdale's words. I cried out as it flipped completely onto its back, splinters of glass tinkling onto the floorboards.

The reverend was also transfixed by its movement. He was stumbling now over his fruitless incantation, desperately shaking the bottle of holy water to elicit one more sacred drop. A shard of glass still caught by the frame began to lift and pivot, worked loose by an invisible force. My scream pierced the cacophony as it shot like an arrow towards him. He cried out in pain, his hand flying to his neck as he instinctively jerked aside, shrinking into a corner. Whimpering, he stared in horrified awe at the crimson blood staining his fingers.

I grabbed hold of Hector's arm, tugging him towards me, forcing him to listen.

'You must stop this. He's making it worse.'

'Yes . . . yes indeed.' Shaking, he stepped forward, the broken glass crunching beneath his feet. 'Enough!'

The reverend's holy words, now reduced to a pleading rasp, stumbled into silence. The marbles careered to a stop. The only sounds were our ragged breathing and faint bird calls from beyond the window panes.

I reeled around as Madeleine emitted a tiny cry. She was staring down at her belly, running her palms over the precious swell.

'They've gone,' she whispered, clutching Hector's jacket lapels as he pulled her into his arms.

'It worked – did it? I did it?' Reverend Dugdale looked utterly bewildered. A marble flew into the back of his head, and he yelped, his hand shooting up as if to swat away a mosquito.

'No, Reverend. You didn't.' I collapsed down on the nanny's bed, the springs squeaking in protest. I slipped my shaking hands under my thighs.

'That was fascinating,' Mr Sheers murmured as he bent down to pick up the broken sampler frame. He propped it up on the mantelpiece.

'Fascinating?' Madeleine cried out. 'How can you say that? It was horrible. Horrible!' Her shoulders doubled over as her whole body convulsed with sobs. Shamed, Sheers thrust his hands into his trouser pockets, and mumbled an apology.

'I – I – I did warn you there were no guarantees . . .' Reverend Dugdale stuttered. A trickle of blood ran down the length of his neck from where the shooting shard of glass had cut him. It soaked into his dog collar, a spreading spot of scarlet against the pristine white. The sight of the battle-bloodied vicar brought me to my feet.

'You're hurt,' I said, holding out my hand to guide him to the door. 'Please come, we must dress that wound.'

He came to me like a dazed child injured in an unprovoked playground brawl. His bottom lip wobbled as he tucked his empty bottle of water into his pocket, while keeping his bible clutched to his chest. I took his arm and led him to the door, Hector and Madeleine falling in, all of us eager to leave the horrors of the room. Mr Sheers followed behind. He paused to draw the door to.

Annie was still hovering in the hall, the tension in her features slackening with relief as she saw us all descend. I ordered her to bring salt water and a dressing to the drawing room, where I settled the reverend by the fire. He unclipped his dog collar, and held it before him, confounded by the stain of his own blood.

Mrs Henge arrived with the first aid box, while Annie followed with a tray of tea things. I cleaned the wound, the blossoming blood in the bowl of water reminding me of the ink prints Dr Mayhew's colleagues had presented for my interpretation. Once I had bandaged him up, I sat back on my heels and assured him his wound would soon heal. I fortified him with some sweet tea.

Madeleine had finally stopped crying, stifling any residual sobs with a handkerchief pressed against her lips. She and Hector sat together on the sofa, both deathly pale.

'I don't know what to make of it . . .' the vicar said. 'You have a very serious situation here, Mr Brightwell, very serious indeed. I shall have to seek counsel from my bishop if I have any hope of assisting you further.'

He was, understandably, eager to be gone. He shoved his stole back inside his briefcase with great urgency and little care. Hector got up to see him out, but I waved him back down, urging him to stay with Madeleine while I escorted the reverend to the door.

'I have never experienced anything like it,' he confided as Annie helped him into his coat in the hall before handing him his hat.

Once in the porch I pulled open the front door and shivered as I was assailed by a gust of wind. He pursed his lips and pressed his trilby to his head. He stepped out onto the first step.

Words of farewell were forming on my lips when without warning he lunged at me, catching hold of my arm. 'For God's sake, take care, Miss Marcham,' he hissed, his breath hot on my face as I tried to shy away. 'I fear the devil himself is in this house.'

Chapter Twenty-Nine

I flew back into the hall, my heart thrumming in my chest.

'Come with me. Now!' I ordered Annie Burrows as I smartly marched down the corridor to the lady's parlour where there was little danger of us being disturbed. I thrust open the door. Having no wish to be enclosed with me, she hesitated, but I wasn't giving her a choice. I shut the door, resting on it as I turned to face her, my breaths rapid, a dangerous concoction of anger and fear bubbling through my veins.

'Enough of your games, Annie! You must now see the consequences of your silence. You know there is something in this house, some unnatural force at work. You can see it, you can understand it. Be honest with me, *please*. Speak out and help me. I beg you, help Madeleine and me.'

She lowered her hands to her sides and squared up to me, running through her options, deciding which tack to take, which story to tell, which lie to fall back on. But in the rigid set of my jaw and the fierce glint in my eye, she must have seen my frayed patience and unwavering determination. A sullen pout crept onto her lips.

'What difference would it make? No one would believe me.'

'I'll believe you, Annie,' I said, stepping forward. She huffed and shook her head, her gaze sidling once again. I was surprised – encouraged even – to see a glaze of tears. 'Please, Annie. I don't know what else I can say to you. Since the night of the fire, I have nursed what I thought were absurd beliefs about your father, but since coming here, to this house – I am convinced my assumptions were right.' Her forehead creased; she bit her lips so tightly they blanched. I took a step closer. 'I believe you have a gift, the same gift as your father, one which he used for good – he used it to try and save a life.'

'And look what good it did him.'

Her words threw me. She was right. It was hardly a compelling example. I let out a ragged breath. 'Your father was a brave man. A selfless man . . . oh dear God, Annie – won't you show the same courage and help me save Madeleine now?'

'I can't.'

'You can, Annie. You must!' I could see my pleas were falling on deaf ears. 'I promise to help you.'

'You can't help me.' I flinched at the derision in her tone. 'Even if I did what you want, they'll just ridicule me, scorn me, just like always. They won't believe a word I say.'

'I'll make sure they do.'

'They won't believe you either, miss, not with your history, you know that.'

I was stunned into silence. She stared at her feet, aware she had been too forthright. I was reminded of the old adage 'truth hurts', and I found I could not chastise her for her apt rebuttal. Instead, I offered up a wry smile.

'You're right. How alike we are, you and I. We have both had to endure the unjust judgement of others. Both of us have been deemed in some way or other unstable or fanciful . . . dismissed as lunatics.' Wearied by battle, I sat down on the arm of a chair. 'We don't need anyone else's help to change things in this house, Annie. I think with your ability, and my doggedness, we can achieve something remarkable here by ourselves – just you and me. No more hiding, no more pretending, no more appeasing others. Let us work together.' Reinvigorated, I got to my feet. 'To hell with everyone else and what they think. Will you do it? Can you do it? Does Lucien Brightwell haunt this house, and can you send him away?'

She didn't respond immediately. I could see her weighing up the possibilities whilst calculating the costs, but my words had clearly struck a chord and at last, with a resigned sigh, she spoke.

'It is Lucien, but I can't make him go. He's waited too long, he won't stop. But perhaps . . . perhaps if we get him what he wants . . .'

'And what does he want? Make him come and tell us.'

My naivety elicited a sardonic smile. 'I'm not a conjurer, miss. I can't just summon them for my own purposes.'

Them.

'Are there more spirits around us?' She looked me straight in the eye. 'Can you see them all . . . all the time?'

'Not all, not all the time. Only if the conditions are favourable.'

'And are they favourable here?'

She shrugged. 'They seem to be.'

My hand flew to my mouth as I dared to pray that somehow, the stars might align for Gerald and me, and that through some alchemy, there might be a way for us to commune once again. But first, I had to think of Madeleine, and what could be done to make her safe in this house, not just for now, but for always. I lowered my hand.

'So, this boy, how do we find out what he wants? Is there any way you can ask him?'

She snorted. 'It doesn't work like that, miss. I can't just have a conversation with him like you and I might.'

'Then how does it work?'

'They show me things, each in their own way, so I understand what they've seen, what they've felt, what they've done – so that I get a sense of them, a sense of what's happened, a sense of what they need.'

'Need?'

'To satisfy them.'

The chilling detachment of her words sent a shiver of apprehension down my spine.

'And what will satisfy this boy?'

Her violet eyes locked with mine. 'Justice, miss. What he wants is justice.'

The ruckus of Lady Brightwell's return filtered into the room. I heard the faint call of my name. Annie fidgeted to be gone. My name was called again – it was Madeleine, her voice shrill and needy. I was torn between intrigue and duty.

'We must speak on this further. You have more to tell me, Annie,' I urged, fearful that in the interlude the girl would change her mind about helping me. Madeleine called again and I had little choice but to answer her insistent summons.

I met her in the hallway. Annie hurried past me to help Maisie who was struggling under coats and fur stoles and enormous feathered hats. Madeleine took my hand, leading me in the direction of the drawing room.

'Oh, you must come! Lady Brightwell has returned – she saw the vicar on the road. And Mr Sheers, well, Mr Sheers has drawn one of his stunning conclusions, even now.'

Sheers and Hector were stood by the mantel. Lady Brightwell

and Miss Scott were seated in their usual positions on the sofa as if they had never been away, listening, open-mouthed, to Hector's account of the day. As he concluded, he pushed back the fringe of hair from his forehead. 'However, it seems Mr Sheers has a theory to belie the nature of these events.'

'A theory?' I advanced into the room. 'Come, Mr Sheers, surely even you must now concede there is something extraordinary occurring here?'

'Something extraordinary is indeed occurring, just not what you think.'

Flummoxed, I sat on the edge of the armchair nearest to me, whilst Madeleine settled into its seat.

'Have you heard of telekinesis?' When Sheers had gauged we were all ignorant, he continued. 'We don't fully understand all facets of telekinesis yet,' he continued. 'But, in layman's terms, it's the power of the mind over objects. I am confident that what I witnessed earlier was a truly astounding display of this phenomenon.'

'Are you saying yet again that we made it all up?' I protested. 'You were there yourself! You saw it all, so how can you possibly deny—'

He quickly held up his hand to stop me. 'I'm not denying anything. It all happened – the breaking glass, the flying marbles. Absolutely. Quite astounding. What I am questioning is the cause of these extraordinary occurrences. You all have leapt to the conclusion they were the result of a malevolent spirit. With a more, dare I say, scientific view, I think they were the result of the amalgamated power of four intelligent minds.'

We all began to object, but he held up his hands to stop us, his expression indulgent.

'Everyone in that room was aware of the events that had

brought them there – the breaking glass, marbles moving by their own volition, the presence of a ghost child. Whilst you may not have consciously known what to expect from the exorcism, I suspect subconsciously, you all thought a recurrence of these phenomena a distinct possibility. The result? The combined power of your mental thoughts physically affected your environment to fulfil those shared expectations.'

He was met by a confounded silence as we all tried to process this staggering argument.

'But how did these things happen in the first instance?' Madeleine braved at last.

'Naturally, I'm sure,' he said. 'The photo frame probably was broken by accident; the marble set rolling by movement in the floorboards—'

'But the hands . . .' she said softly.

'Merely the power of your imagination.'

'I don't know, Sheers.' Hector rocked on his heels. 'I understand what you're saying, believe me I do, and I'd be lying if I didn't say a large part of me buys into it wholeheartedly – but however hard I try, I just can't get past what I experienced in the cellar, and then today . . .' He shook his head.

'I think you're wrong, Mr Sheers,' I piped up. 'I think it is you that is blinkered to the possibilities, not us. You have not presented a shred of evidence except your own say-so. I have to put greater faith in what I have seen with my own eyes.'

'But your own eyes are part of the problem, my dear.' Lady Brightwell's acidic interruption took me by surprise. Until now she had sat in silent attendance upon Sheers' lecture. 'I think Mr Sheers has presented a most fascinating and compelling argument. Telekinesis. Wonderful. I must say, Mr Sheers, once again you have managed to debunk these fanciful theories. Your keen mind is most impressive, young man. Most impressive indeed.'

'He hasn't proven anything!' I contradicted. 'I say again, Mr Sheers – where is your physical evidence? There must be something more tangible than theory that you can offer us?'

'In all fairness, Miss Marcham, I have not yet carried out a full investigation, but,' he addressed Hector here, 'if you give me the liberty to stay, I will happily set up some equipment and hopefully then provide some concrete elements to my argument.'

'Oh, I really don't think there's any need for that,' Lady Brightwell protested. 'I'm sure we have taken up enough of your valuable time as it is.'

'I'm not satisfied, Hector.' Madeleine's voice cut a swathe through our chatter. 'You want me to stay here, but how can I? How can I stay in this house after what has happened today? How can I ever live here again? I know this is your home, and I want so much for it to be my home too, but until this matter is resolved I shall never feel safe here. I'm sorry, Mr Sheers, I mean you no offence, but it will take more than your logical analysis to reassure me.' She turned back to Hector. 'I cannot remain in this house.'

'And I don't think you should,' he replied. 'I'm not prepared to take any chances, not with you and our child. I think you should return to Haverton for the time being. I can drop you and Stella back on my way to London. All right, Sheers. Stay, as long as you need to conduct a proper investigation, but I'll be expecting some hard and fast facts to explain what's been going on here.'

'Of course.'

'Then I would like to stay too,' I blurted out.

'For what possible purpose?' Lady Brightwell demanded.

I knew full well that Annie and I were Madeleine's only real hope. There was so much at stake, I could not allow us to be banished from the house now – not with Annie finally on side and certainly not with the prospect of contacting Gerald so tantalisingly within reach. I would not leave Greyswick, not for anyone. I drew myself up, ready to brandish my sword in whatever battle lay ahead. I was determined to be victorious.

'What if Mr Sheers is wrong? What if there is another force at work here?'

I did not dare to try and explain Annie's extraordinary ability, knowing it would serve against me. Instead, I chose to strike a blow at Hector's Achilles' heel.

'Hector, please. I think Madeleine would take comfort from my staying, and at the end of the day, if I don't experience anything, and if Mr Sheers manages to convince me there is nothing awry, then what greater reassurance could Madeleine have?'

Everything rested on the success of my appeal. Hector vacillated, but Madeleine came to my rescue once again.

'Oh, Hector, Stella is right. If I knew she considered it safe, I would have no reason to stay away.'

'Stuff and nonsense,' Lady Brightwell muttered.

'Very well.' Hector knew when he was defeated, and he surrendered with good grace given the circumstances. 'If you want to stay, Stella, then stay, but I don't want you causing mischief and I don't want you getting in Tristan's way.'

I resented being chastised like a school girl by a man barely older than myself, but I eschewed that fight and celebrated my victory instead: I was staying.

With a satisfactory plan of action decided, the party broke up. A very disgruntled Lady Brightwell announced she had caught a chill whilst walking to the Rolls, which, due to a war bonds rally, had been unable to collect her from outside the town hall. She was already sniffling into a camphor-soaked handkerchief. Miss Scott promised to see off any illness by keeping her wrapped up and comfortable, but Lady Brightwell was unconvinced.

'It is too late, Scottie! I am practically on my death bed already – I can feel the ague seeping in to my very bones as we speak. I shall be most ill by morning, mark my words.'

Aghast at the grim prophecy, Miss Scott wasted no time ushering her charge to bed. She returned a few minutes later, declaring that her Ladyship was indeed 'most unwell', before disappearing off to prepare a hot honey drink.

Mr Sheers requested permission to continue using the study and whilst Hector made no objection, he did warn the room had lain untouched since Sir Arthur's death and was not, as a result, in the best order. Assuring Hector it was quite satisfactory, Mr Sheers excused himself, as he needed to arrange a delivery of equipment, necessary for his investigation.

I myself was eager to pursue my consultation with Annie, and detecting that Madeleine and Hector wished to be alone, I returned to my bedroom. I summoned the maid with the bell-pull and paced the room while I waited for her knock. She closed the door behind her. I so wanted to discuss the prospect of contacting Gerald, but I knew I could not. There would be opportunity yet for that precious matter. For now, I had to prioritise Madeleine. I wasted no time.

'What did you mean, when you said that Lucien wanted justice?'

She stood before me, her clasped hands dimpling her white apron front, her head hung low.

'Have you not worked it out yet?'

'What?'

'I thought perhaps after what happened you might have realised the truth.'

'What truth?'

She looked up. She waited. Thoughts charged through my mind as I struggled to make the connections she so obviously expected of me. *They share experiences, or feelings . . .* And then I recalled those small hands shoving against my back. The blood thickened in my veins. The girl before me already knew what I had only just this moment understood.

'Dear God!'

Lucien Brightwell didn't fall to his death in a tragic accident. Lucien Brightwell was pushed.

Chapter Thirty

It seemed an age before my shock abated. Tendrils of implication choked my thoughts.

'Do you realise what you're saying?'

'Yes, miss.' The maid's youthful guise slipped away, revealing a life-worn sagacity that belied her age. 'He seeks justice for the wrong done to him,' she offered quietly, 'and maybe . . .'

I waited, eager for her to impart her terrible knowledge. A seismic shift had occurred between us, one that had pitched me into unfamiliar territory, a reversal of power that to my shame I almost resented. I needed her, this freckle-spattered slip of girl. I needed her to interpret things I had no hope of understanding alone.

'And maybe?' I prompted.

'Retribution.'

'But against whom? Who would push a child to his death?' The concept was repugnant; there could be no justification for such an unconscionable act. 'Are you sure it wasn't an accident?' I groped for a more innocuous if no less tragic explanation. Accidents with children happened so easily – they were fragile and foolish, irresponsible and impetuous. A silly stunt could easily result in an awful outcome.

'He knows what was done to him.'

I wanted so much in that moment to doubt her, ridicule her,

but I had come too far and acknowledged too much to deny her abilities now.

'Who did it? Who is responsible?' I managed at last.

'He either doesn't know or can't show me – but I sense it's someone who's still here.'

Faces danced before me – Lady Brightwell, Miss Scott, Hector, Mrs Henge. I closed my eyes as their swimming images blurred together. The prospect of being under the same roof as a murderer was distinctly unnerving.

'We have to get rid of him,' I whispered.

'Then we must give him what he wants.'

'And how are we supposed to do that?'

'By finding out who killed him.'

I knew we could not divulge this latest revelation to anyone. For one thing, I had little appetite for the ridicule that such a pronouncement was sure to bring, for another, I was in the vulnerable position of not knowing who was friend and who was foe.

Annie was soon summoned from me. Madeleine was keen to start packing and tasked Annie with helping Maisie lug the trunks down from the attic. The dull step-by-step thud as the cases bounced down the nursery stairs stirred up my turbid thoughts.

The reality of Madeleine's imminent departure left me feeling daunted and rather morose. I would be remaining in this strange house as an unwelcome guest with Annie Burrows as my only ally – a prospect that didn't inspire much confidence. I sought the solace of my sister's company, but she was embroiled in the chaos of packing and it soon became clear I was in the way.

Redundant, I retreated to my room, leaving my door ajar in case she should call for my assistance.

Having nothing else to occupy me, my thoughts turned to the mystery of Lucien. I tried to recall the titbits of information I had gleaned since my arrival, things I had dismissed as irrelevant at the time, but which now appeared potentially pertinent. It was like rummaging through a wastepaper basket, looking for a letter accidentally discarded, now lost amongst a muddle of scrunched-up notes and unwanted papers. I was determined to appreciate the significance of all I had learnt – the motherless boy, the dismissed nanny, the influenza outbreak. I would find a way to fit the pieces of this appalling puzzle together. I just didn't know where to start.

Feeling rather useless, and in need of comfort, I kicked off my shoes and sat on the bed, retrieving my copy of *The Woman in White* from the bedside table. My fingers caressed the brown leather cover. It was my last gift from Gerald, and I could recall the day he gave it to me in minute detail.

It was just after Madeleine's wedding. Our being able to attend together had made the celebration a blissful interlude from the relentless misery of the front, but his leave had drawn to a close, though I still had a few more days remaining of mine. I had insisted on travelling with him to Victoria station, where he would join his troop train for the south coast. We sat together in a first class carriage, our shoulders tightly pressed, his hand trapped in mine, determined not to let our mounting sadness ruin these last precious hours.

Victoria had been a swirl of choking steam, soot, sweat and cigarette smoke. Khaki-clad bodies milled across the platforms. I was jostled by shouldered kit bags, as Gerald led me through the clamouring crowd, screeching whistles piercing the muted sobs of farewell and the shouted jests of naive young men buoyed by the prospect of battle.

We had an hour to wait, and had taken tea at a kiosk, standing beside it with our white porcelain mugs. For some reason, the conversation had turned to books, and Gerald was horrified when I confessed I had never read any Wilkie Collins.

'Well, I'm sorry, that just won't do,' he said with mock disgust. I looked suitably chastised and laughed in bemusement as he threw back the dregs of his tea, and scooped up our mugs, handing them back into the stallholder, before returning to me. He clapped his hands together, the sound muted by his leather gloves.

'Right, you Philistine you, wait here.'

'Where are you off to?' I asked, alarmed. I snatched a glance at the station clock. Our time was running out.

With a lopsided grin, he gripped my arm and pressed his lips to my cheek. 'Never fear, I'm not abandoning you, not yet at least, but there is now something I have to do, in the name of Mr Collins.'

He winked before dashing off. I watched him weave his way through the crowd, saddened to be left alone when I prized every second with him, but when I saw him duck into the bookstall at the far side of the station, I couldn't help but laugh. He came jogging back a few minutes later, a book in his hand. He grinned as he presented it to me.

'Sorry I didn't have time to wrap it.'

I turned the book on its side to read the spine. The words *The Woman in White* were written in gold.

'Have you a pen to hand?' he asked.

'What?'

'Come on, you're a practical girl, I bet there's a pen or a pencil in that bag of yours.'

Chuckling at the absurdity of it all, I scrabbled amongst the contents of my handbag until, with a look of triumph, I produced a fountain pen.

'That's my girl!' he cried, taking it from me and reclaiming the book. He opened the cover and turned to rest it against the station wall, but he stopped, glancing back at me over his shoulder. 'Don't peek,' he instructed. Rolling my eyes, I obediently complied. 'There, all done,' he said at last, blowing the ink dry. He closed the book before returning it to me, our fingers brushing in the exchange. I went to open the cover, but he laid his palm upon it. 'Don't read it now,' he said, 'save it for later.'

He picked up his case and took my hand and together we walked towards the platform where his train was waiting, my legs growing heavier with each step, my chest tighter, and my tears more threatening.

There was a tremendous bustle, as soldiers of all ranks jostled their way through the open doors, those with loved ones seeing them off pausing for a final farewell until, God willing, they would see each other again. Gerald found his carriage and turned to me, a brave smile on his lips, a wistful sadness dulling his eyes.

'Well, this is it,' he said.

I couldn't speak. I threw my arms around his neck and held him close, not caring one jot for propriety or who might see, as I pressed my lips to his.

'Let's try and meet in France . . .' I pleaded. 'We can get leave . . .'

'It's against the rules, old girl,' he said softly.

'I don't care about the rules,' I declared with uncharacteristic defiance.

I jumped as the train whistle screamed, eliciting a sudden surge of activity as the last remaining soldiers shouldered their way on board, for fear of missing the boat.

'I have to go,' Gerald said, gripping my arms. 'But know this, Stella Marcham, I love you with every fibre of my body.'

Before I could answer the whistle sounded again, and swiftly kissing me, Gerald grabbed his case and leapt on board. The door clunked shut.

He pushed down the window and leant out. I hurried forward to take his hand.

'I'll write,' I promised, 'and I'll let you know when I'm back at the hospital.'

'Safe journey, my love,' he said, bringing my fingers to his lips.

The guard blew his whistle and dropped his flag. Slowly the train started to move. Maintaining a stubborn hold of Gerald's hand, I began to trot along the platform, keeping pace.

'Try and come and see me at the hospital,' I cried, swallowing back my tears. 'Try and get leave, even if it's just a day or two . . .' The train was picking up speed. 'Please try!' I begged.

Our hands fell apart, but I continued to run alongside.

'I'll try!' he called out above the chuntering wheels. 'I'll try!'

And then he vanished into a billowing cloud of steam as the train roared out of the station. I ran on for a few steps then came to a stuttering halt, my legs so like jelly I thought for a moment they might not hold me. My shoulders sagged, unable to resist the crushing misery weighing upon me. And then I remembered the book, still clasped in my hand, and I scrambled to the opening leaf. I devoured the precious sentiment captured in his wonderful words and I sobbed as if my heart would break.

It didn't break then, of course, though it would, later, when Gerald fulfilled my parting request in the worst possible way.

I was now reading that book for the third time. I knew the story off by heart, but that was neither here nor there. The book itself was another link to Gerald, and when I cradled it in my hands, I was holding something he had touched, and that was all that mattered. I had only read the inscription once. Those words would unhinge me if I allowed myself to see them. So, I did not. Instead, I treasured their memory in my wounded heart.

To my annoyance, subdued voices filtering through the gap in the doorway interrupted my recollections. As it seemed Madeleine was now unlikely to call for my help, I decided I might as well close my door and secure my peace and quiet. Setting the book down on the counterpane, I got up and padded across the room in my stockinged feet. As I drew nearer the doorway, I recognised the voices and my steps became stealthier.

'She's got you running up and down these stairs like a skivvy. You'll wear yourself out answering her beck and call.'

'Oh, Constance,' Miss Scott protested. 'She's not well.'

Mrs Henge made no attempt to conceal her derision. 'It's nothing more than a sniffle. She takes advantage of you.'

'I am here to see to her needs. Constance . . . what of this talk of Lucien?'

'Hysterical nonsense, just as that Mr Sheers said.'

'What if it isn't?'

'Ruth,' Mrs Henge chided. There was a rustle of skirts. The

edge of the door dug into my cheek. 'Pay no heed to it. Those girls are too highly strung.'

'But Hector—'

'The mind can play funny tricks, especially when encouraged to do so.'

'But—'

'That's enough, Ruth.' After a pause she sighed. 'Ruth . . .' It was such a gentle rendition of the companion's name. 'You must not dwell on it.'

I heard them part and waited until all was quiet before easing the door to, taking every care not to give myself away.

Chapter Thirty-One

Hector and Madeleine left early the next morning. It was a sombre leave-taking. Lady Brightwell, pale as a sheet and suffering, left her sick bed to see them off, kept upright by the inflexible steel core I was certain had replaced her soul. Miss Scott helped her descend the carved staircase, step by painful step. She steadied herself on the circular oak table, tilting her leathery cheek for Madeleine to kiss, like a queen demanding homage. She showed more tenderness towards Hector, patting his arm, her features softening with maternal fondness and more than a hint of pride. Miss Scott wrapped Madeleine in a warm embrace, entreating her to take good care of herself, and she was just as affectionate with her former charge, brushing invisible specks from the shoulder of his uniform before throwing her arms around him, imploring him to stay safe. No mention was made of the other Brightwell boy, still lingering in the corridors around us.

Mr Sheers also came to bid them farewell. He assured Madeleine he would strive to gather sufficient evidence to reassure her, before turning to shake hands with Hector. The two men huddled for a few minutes with much head-nodding and murmured agreement, before Sheers retreated to the study once again.

I followed Hector and Madeleine out to the car. Madeleine and I stood opposite each other, strangely bashful, the fur of her stole rippling in the soft breeze, tickling her jaw. The brim of her hat was ridiculously wide, and we laughed as I was forced to contort my way underneath it to deliver my farewell kiss. Her fingertips dug into my back as she embraced me.

'I've changed my mind – you shouldn't stay. Please come back with me.'

'You know I have to stay.'

'You don't have to, Stella. I'm frightened . . .'

I reached out and cupped her cheek in my palm, my heart blossoming. 'Don't be frightened, I'm not.' It was a transparent lie, one unable to withstand close examination. 'I couldn't have survived the loss of Gerald without your love – so let me do this for you.'

With a cry she flung her arms around me. Hector cleared his throat and reminded her they needed to hurry. She broke free, nodding, not trusting herself to speak as she gave me a final haunting look before ducking into the car. I flinched as Hector slammed the door shut.

'Be careful, Stella,' he said, his voice low. 'I trust Sheers is right, but . . .' He lightly touched my arm as his lips brushed my cheek.

I stepped back and hugged myself to protect against the persistent breeze. The car engine stuttered into life and I waved as it receded down the driveway, a slight ache in my heart as I saw Madeleine's face peering through the narrow rear window, her gloved hand pressed to the glass. When I could see her no more, I turned and mounted the stone steps back into the house.

Lady Brightwell was sitting on one of the hall chairs, attended by an agitated Miss Scott who was encouraging her to drink from the glass of water she was offering. The dowager looked awful and I felt a tug of concern as I enquired whether there was anything I could do.

'Oh, it was too much for her, coming down to see them off,' Miss Scott cried. 'I knew it would be. You are unwell, my lady, and you should have stayed in bed.' Lady Brightwell had taken faint once we 'youngsters' had gone outside. 'She fell into quite a swoon, it was all I could do to stop her from falling,' Miss Scott exclaimed, pushing her glasses up the bridge of her nose. 'I must summon the doctor, this just will not do.'

'You will do no such thing. A most unnecessary course of action,' Lady Brightwell wheezed, her protest precipitating a coughing fit.

Miss Scott insisted she return to her bed, and at last she met no opposition. I stepped forward to lend a hand, but I was swatted away. As Hector's mother rose unsteadily to her feet, her clawed fingers clamping Miss Scott's arm, she paused.

'So now it is only you and Mr Sheers who remain, Miss Marcham. I hope neither of you will find it necessary to do so for long.'

'I appreciate it's an inconvenience to you.' It was remarkable that ill as she was she could still be effortlessly caustic. 'I'm sure we all want this riddle of Greyswick to be solved as soon as possible.'

'It is a riddle of your own making, Miss Marcham. I very much hope common sense will prevail, so that the house may return to normal. It is about time.'

I watched them struggle up the mountainous staircase, simmering at the woman's audacity. Part of me wished I had gone with Madeleine, but instead I was trapped here and in danger of being stifled by the poisonous atmosphere that filtered through this house, suspended in the air like mustard gas.

I had to escape, if only for a short time. Snatching up my cardigan, I hurried through the glass doors of the orangery, out into the garden.

As I trotted down the steps of the terrace I noticed the comforting weight of a cigarette packet in my low-slung pocket. I turned my back to the stiffening breeze as I cupped the flaring match to light one. I drew in deeply, tossing back my head, savouring the sensation. Looking up, I saw the blank windows of Greyswick watching me with disapproval and its overpowering presence annoyed me. I decided the kitchen garden would afford me some privacy – somewhere peaceful to kick my heels while I summoned the stamina to return inside.

I ducked under its bricked archway and the breeze dropped away, kept at bay by the high walls. Only a fraction of the beds had been tended and within them, new life was unfolding over the cultivated ground, while the rest had become throttled with weeds. On the far wall, espaliered fruit trees sported delicate blooms of pale pink and white, and in one corner sunlight glinted off the panes of a large glass house.

Movement in the archway opposite caught my eye. Annie Burrows was talking to the same soldier I had seen before. I was surprised to find her fraternising with a young man and as if sensing my disapproval, she looked my way. The distance between us was too great for me to be able to discern her features, but she smartly stepped away from him. He disappeared through the doorway without acknowledging my presence.

I felt like a killjoy for having ended their tête-à-tête and I turned to leave, but I heard her soft tread behind me, and she called out to catch my attention.

'Sorry, I didn't mean to spy.' I angled my head to the side to blow out my smoke, holding the cigarette down by my thigh, the tip smouldering red. She looked at me quizzically. 'Your soldier,' I said.

'Oh.'

'On leave, is he?' I asked, tapping off the ash.

'I suppose . . .'

'Just be careful, Annie, soldiers have a habit of breaking your heart.' I felt a rush of embarrassment at giving unsolicited advice. 'Does he have a name?'

'Billy, miss. His name is Billy. He used to work here, before.'

'Did he now?' I raised an eyebrow as I brought the cigarette back to my lips.

She hesitated, and I wondered what lay at the root of her instinctive reticence, but whatever it was, in the next moment she had overcome it.

'He says we should talk to Cook, miss.'

It was the flare of excitement in her violet eyes that piqued my interest and evoked a twist of anticipation deep in my belly. Taking a final drag, I tossed my cigarette into the flowerbed and gestured for her to lead the way.

It would appear our search for the truth was about to begin.

Chapter Thirty-Two

Annie led me into the below-stairs domain via the back door. This was very much the dingy tradesman's entrance. It was dank and musty, and the walls that tunnelled before me were blighted by green-speckled patches that oozed upwards from the skirting.

She led me up the passageway, past recessed doorways set under arched lintels – boot room, dairy, larder, scullery, still room – there seemed no end of them. I glimpsed through one open door and saw a small brick-lined room with a tiny window set high towards the ceiling to catch the meagre light. It reminded me of a prison cell and all at once I felt claustrophobic, conscious of the weight of this great house bearing down upon us, crushing us to its will.

Soon the stone steps leading to the green baize door rose before us and I took some comfort from being able to orientate myself. Feeling more at ease, I followed Annie into the vast kitchen. Natural light flooded in from the row of broad windows that formed the outer wall, their arched tops almost brushing the ceiling.

Cook was working at the long pine table in the centre of the room, a mobcap hiding her hair, though a few grey curls, moist with sweat, clung to her gleaming forehead. She wore a white pinafore, drab with age, over a simple blue check dress, its cord double-wrapped around her thick waist. Her sleeves were rolled back above her elbows and her meaty fingers were at this moment kneading a large lump of dough.

'Miss Marcham! I'm so sorry, I wasn't expecting guests.'

She drew her forearm across her brow and wiped it on the side of her skirt as I asked whether we might take a moment of her time. She invited us to 'take a pew' and declared herself happy to help if she could. Chair legs scraped on the flagstone floor as Annie and I settled ourselves down opposite her.

'We've been advised to speak to you by someone who thought you might be able to help us.'

'Oh yes,' she said with a good-natured smile. 'Who might that be?'

It was Annie who answered her, before the boy's name even formed on my lips. Cook's head snapped up. She skewered the girl with a penetrating stare, the smile slipping from her lips – I could almost see the goodwill leaching out of her. She snorted and shook her head before focusing once again on the dough which she appeared to work with renewed vigour. I was rather disheartened by her reaction. It seemed clear to me there was no love lost between the cook and the soldier, and I wondered whether we were running a fool's errand. Annie, however, appeared unfazed by the older woman's reaction, and looking up from under her thick red lashes she spoke again.

'He also said you make the best apple pie in the whole of England – but if you added just a touch more cinnamon, then it would be the best in the whole wide world.'

The vigorous activity stopped. Cook leant into the dough, resting her weight on the table. Her features softened as her lips spread into her ruddy cheeks. She fixed her keen eye on

Annie. 'Did he now?' She laughed in spite of herself and shook her head. 'Well then . . .'

She scooped up the dough and dumped it into the large ceramic bowl on the table, then draped a clean tea towel over the top. She paused to take in Annie one more time, before crossing to the sink.

'Well, I suppose if Billy sent you to me . . .' she called out as she lathered her hands on a block of cracked green soap. She rinsed them, shaking them free of water before reaching for the towel hanging off the rail on the range that dominated the far wall. '. . . I'd better see what I can do for you.' With her fingers crisp, she neatly folded and replaced the towel. She rested her bottom against the range, folding her broad arms across her chest. 'I think I can guess what it is you want.'

She chuckled at my look of surprise. 'Oh, Miss Marcham, you don't live in a house like this and not know everything that's going on. Certainly not when you've got a loose-lipped little mischief like Maisie running around sucking up gossip like a sponge,' she grumbled. 'You think this house is haunted.' She bent forward. 'You want to know if I've got any ghost stories.'

I laughed, somewhat taken aback. 'Well, have you?'

Cook's demeanour changed, jest giving way to something more unsettling. I could see her hesitation and I invited her to sit with us, if only for a short while. With an air of uncertainty, she drew out a chair opposite, her broad thighs spilling over its hard edges as she sat down. She rested her forearms on the table, her large knuckles interlocked. I asked whether she had experienced anything strange in the house.

'You know, I thought I was being daft,' she said at last. 'It was only the once – it was late at night and I was dog tired. You know how it is, your mind plays tricks . . .'

After much prompting she shared her story, the words catching at times like fish bones in her throat. She had stayed up to finish some pastries. Everyone else had long been in bed, but in the stillness, she thought she heard soft running footsteps – so light she convinced herself she had imagined them, but even so, she still looked up expectantly at the doorway, wondering who might be burning the midnight oil with her – but no one appeared. It crossed her mind that someone was playing 'silly buggers' as she put it, so she brushed off her floured hands and went to look in the passage, but only the lamp by the stairs was lit, the rest was in darkness and she couldn't see a thing.

'So, I came back here to the table and I swear . . . I swear I heard a laugh – no,' she corrected herself, 'not a laugh – a giggle. It shook me, it did.'

She fell silent, and when I gently prodded her to explain further, she unclasped her hands, pressing them palm down on the table top.

'Because had I not known better, I would have sworn it sounded just like Master Lucien.' She banished the memory with a shake of her head, smiling at her own foolishness. 'Daft, isn't it, the tricks the mind plays on us at night?'

She dabbed at the beads of sweat clinging to her upper lip. 'Nanny would bring him down here, you see, if she knew I was baking that day – buns or biscuits – so he could have one while they were still warm, as a treat. He would know as soon as he reached the baize door what was what and he would run down those stairs, giggling his head off, eager to get in here and snaffle one.'

'What were you cooking that night?' I asked with a smile. I liked her. She was the type of woman who wore her heart on her sleeve, and it was a good one, pure and kind.

'Apple pastries, his favourite!' She laughed, but her burst of humour died abruptly. 'Here, you're never saying . . .' Her cheeks blanched. 'Well, it's all a bit rum if you ask me,' she muttered.

'How long have you been at Greyswick, Cook?'

She seemed to welcome the opportunity to veer away from the previous topic and some of her characteristic cheeriness returned as she began to regale us with the history of her employment. Like Mrs Henge, she had served Sir Arthur in London when he was plain Mr Brightwell, and throughout his first marriage. She spoke of the original Mrs Brightwell in glowing terms, expressing genuine sadness at her early demise. I asked her then about Lucien, and she grew wistful.

'Oh, he was such a sweet little thing. An angel to look at and a kind heart, just like his mother. He was no trouble, good as gold he was. And his father doted on him – when he was here,' she added.

'And how did Lady Brightwell take to him?'

Something passed across her face. She rubbed at her bulbous nose. 'Well, she was very young when she came here – she didn't know a lot about children.'

'He didn't take to her?'

'She didn't take to him!' she snapped. She settled back in her seat, her lardy features curdling with disapproval. 'She was soon too preoccupied with her own babe on the way to be bothered with him – didn't want him around. She just wanted peace and quiet, so she could *rest*. Nanny did her best to keep him occupied.'

'What was the nanny like? Was she good to Lucien?' I asked, inching forward in my seat.

'Oh, she adored him! With his father always away in town and a stepmother who couldn't bear the sight of him, Nanny was all he had, poor lamb.' She sighed, losing herself in the mid-distance of memory, easing back in her chair. 'Oh, she was beside herself over the accident. She'd only left for a minute – a minute! And the next thing you know . . .' She sniffed, her plump lips pleating. 'A tragedy, for everyone – and poor Nanny was blamed. Treated like a criminal, marched from the house by Mrs Henge before she had a chance to defend herself.' I winced as her chair legs scraped on the floor like fingernails down a blackboard. She heaved herself up, shunting the chair back under. 'Now, I'm sorry, miss, but I have a world of work to do and I'd best be getting on. I don't much like talking about the past.' Her face clouded. 'It's a painful place to dwell.'

Expressing my thanks and apologising for monopolising so much of her time, I got to my feet, Annie following suit.

'Just one more question, if I may, Cook. Did Nanny ever say anything about that day, about what happened?'

'No, she never did. I did try to ask about it when I first wrote, but she wanted to put it all behind her, so I let it lie and never mentioned it again.'

Sensing she had now had enough, I thanked her once more for her time. Annie and I returned to the hall via the baize door, and immediately ran into Mrs Henge.

'Miss Marcham, might I borrow Annie if you are done with her? Some boxes have arrived for Mr Sheers; I would be grateful if Annie could help Maisie bring them in.'

'Mr Sheers' investigative equipment, I presume?' I observed

with tempered enthusiasm. 'Well, I certainly wouldn't want to hinder him in any way. Perhaps when you are done, Annie, you might bring some tea to the orangery?'

Mrs Henge expressed her gratitude with a curt nod, sweeping past me to disappear below-stairs. Annie scurried outside. I stood for a moment, feeling whimsical and very alone, before pulling myself together and departing the hall at a sharp clip. I was mulling over Cook's evidence as I travelled down the corridor, and just as I entered the orangery I let out a cry. How stupid I'd been! Cook had referred to letters – correspondence required an address! As fresh possibilities dawned, I turned on my heel and retraced my steps.

I felt like an intruder as I crept through the baize door and made my way down the stone steps, aware that this was not my domain. I headed into the kitchen, but though a large copper pan now bubbled furiously upon the range, its lid lifting and clanging on the steam, the room was empty.

Convinced that Cook must be nearby, and given my eager impatience, I decided I would seek her out. I padded softly down the passage, peering in through the open doorways hoping to locate her. I had not gone far before I heard terse voices filtering out from a doorway on my left.

'This has been planned for weeks, Ruth.'

'Well, I'm sorry, Constance – it's quite impossible.'

'But I've waited so long to get an evening off so that we might go.'

'And it's unfortunate, I know.'

'But I have already purchased the tickets for the music hall.' I heard a drawer sliding open. 'Look, here. Just as we discussed.'

'She is too ill. I cannot leave her like this, especially with all that is going on.'

'Isn't it a shame she never showed you such loyalty when you needed it most?'

I couldn't prevent my sharp intake of breath. The housekeeper's words dripped with venom, and from the raw silence that followed it was clear that Miss Scott had been rendered speechless. When she recovered, she responded with gall and wormwood.

'I should never have relented and agreed to the trip in the first place. I cannot come with you, and I will not go with you again, and that is the end of it.'

Muffled sounds of movement spurred me into action. I darted into the still room to avoid the embarrassment of discovery. I pressed myself flat against the wall so Miss Scott could not see me, but after she had stormed past my doorway I peered round to spy on her departure – her steps sharp, her shoulders squared, her fists tight at her side.

I remained where I was, not wishing to expose my inadvertent eavesdropping. The damp wall chilled my back, but still I did not move. I heard a chair creak, and the sound of ripping paper, over, and over again. Still I waited, my eyes ranging over the array of bottles and jars lining the walls. I watched the minute hand on my wristwatch circle five times before I peeked again from the doorway, and seeing the coast was clear, I crept back to the stone staircase, silently slipping up the steps to the baize door. I pulled it open and let it swing shut, before retracing my steps back down, as carelessly as I could, to make my presence known. I hovered by the empty kitchen, before carrying on down the passageway. I made a brazen entrance through the doorway on my left.

The housekeeper's room was a decent size. The one wall was

almost entirely taken up by an expansive cupboard polished to the colour of malt vinegar, a row of panelled doors lining the top, while beneath, jutting out proud, were stacked drawers dressed with brass drop handles hung from golden backplates. A small grate, flanked by sash windows, occupied the rear of the wall, a pair of armchairs covered in striped cotton set before it, a small circular table with spindly legs nestled alongside one of them.

The writing table Mrs Henge sat behind cut into the middle of the room from the right-hand wall, serving almost as a barrier, as if she was guarding the cosy fireside arrangement behind. She looked up, startled by my unexpected appearance, but she rapidly collected herself, rising in a fluid motion.

'Miss Marcham?'

'I was looking for Cook but she's not in the kitchen.'

'I believe she went outside, I'm sure she'll be back directly. I can send her to you.'

But I assured her there was no need to trouble herself – I would seek Cook out.

As I turned to leave it was impossible to miss the tiny pieces of cerise ticket paper scattered across the table top like confetti, the enduring evidence of a wedding that had long since been over.

Chapter Thirty-Three

I found Cook sitting out in the yard. She stuffed the letter she had been reading back into its envelope, before lowering her face, to dry her eyes with furtive dabs of her apron.

'Oh, I'm so sorry . . . I didn't mean to . . .' I stuttered, mortified by my ill-timed intrusion, but she cut off my apology with a chubby hand.

'Oh, no matter, miss. I've been putting off reading it all day . . . I'd guessed what it was going to say.' She sniffed and stood up. 'My cousin's lad,' she explained. 'He's the third one she's lost to this blessed war, poor love.' She shook her head. 'Sometimes I wonder whether it's all worth it. I have my doubts.' She cleared her throat. 'Now, what can I do for you, miss?'

I could see she was putting on a brave front, and not wanting to make an imposition of myself, I briskly enquired whether I might trouble her for the nanny's address. Her reluctance to accommodate my request was clear, but I assured her I meant no mischief and in the end she agreed to pass it on via Annie, as she needed to consult her address book, which was upstairs in her room.

'She's a strange one – that girl of yours,' she said, watching for my reaction. I simply smiled and thanked her again for her help, before leaving her in peace.

On returning to the hall I encountered Mr Sheers surrounded

by a multitude of boxes. He righted himself when he saw me and offered a diffident smile. I commented on the amount of delivered equipment.

'Oh, it looks far more impressive than it is. Just a gramophone to record any suspicious sounds, a fancy thermometer, and my box brownie camera is around here somewhere, too.'

'I don't know how photogenic our ghost is, Mr Sheers.'

He laughed at that and carried on rifling through his boxes. 'I'm not expecting to capture a ghost on film, Miss Marcham. Photography is a useful tool to demonstrate that at times our eyes really can deceive us.' He shot me a wry grin when I responded with a derogatory snort. 'Well, I intend to do everything in my power to prove to you and your sister there is nothing here to be scared of. There truly is a rational explanation for everything.'

'Well, I'm afraid I'm going to need quite some convincing of that, Mr Sheers, but you're very welcome to try.'

He let the flap of the box fall from his hand. 'And how do you intend to solve this perceived mystery, Miss Marcham? I'm curious.'

'I have my own methods,' I said, and excused myself before he could press me further on the issue.

Greyswick felt different without Madeleine. Whereas before I had been a visiting member of the family, I now fulfilled the unpleasant role of interloper. The house shunned me, turning a cold shoulder of endless corridors and closed doors, offering me no warmth or comfort – indeed, I felt an absurd compulsion to apologise to the monolith for my continued occupancy. Madeleine had been my benefactor, but now I was friendless – without sponsor, without support. As Annie was occupied with chores, retreating to my room seemed my only option as I whiled away the long hours until dinner, when my presence would be expected – demanded, even. I passed Madeleine's room, abandoned now, the door ajar. I stopped abruptly. Recovering my steps, I thrust the door wide.

'What are you doing?'

Mrs Henge was hunched over Madeleine's bedside drawer. When she didn't respond, I demanded an answer. Slowly she straightened, her left arm bent before her, hidden from view. She squared her shoulders as she turned to face me. Cradled in her arm was the collection of toy soldiers.

'What are you doing with those?'

'Returning them to the nursery, where they belong.'

The black enamel on the figures blended into the jet of her clothing, whilst the bright scarlet stood out so starkly her shirt appeared speckled with blood. I nursed a niggling doubt as I thought back on the vicar's parting words – could there be more than one devil at work in this house?

'How did those figures end up in my sister's room?'

'Don't you think you ought to ask Mrs Brightwell that?'

'I have. And now I'm asking you.'

'I wouldn't know, miss.'

'Did you put them there?'

'I don't have time for silly nonsense like that, miss.'

She closed the drawer and came around the bottom of the bed, her skirts swinging back and forth with each confident stride, the keys chinking at her waist. She brushed so close to me that I had to recoil to avoid her as she swept through the doorway.

I don't know what induced me to follow her. I had no

stomach for further confrontation, but there was something intriguing about the housekeeper and I was caught up in her irresistible current. She mounted the end stairs, but as I reached the bottom, she stopped, and instinctively I followed suit, my skin tingling with alertness. A sound drifted down from the nursery: a rhythmic wooden creak.

Neither of us moved.

'Dear God,' I whispered. 'What is it?'

'It is nothing.' She stared up at the landing, steely eyed. 'It can be nothing,' she reiterated with more conviction, and before I could respond, she took off up the remaining stairs.

My pulse skittered as I followed her. The closer we got to the nursery, the louder the creaking became, predictable in its steady rhythm. She didn't hesitate on the landing but strode towards the open doorway, apparently oblivious to the icy cold air that wrapped around us. I began to shiver as it bit into my ankles and curled round my throat, kissing my cheeks and sliding down my spine, pulling me ever closer towards the open door. Dear God, did she not feel it?

The housekeeper halted on the nursery threshold; I felt compelled to join her.

The cradle was rocking.

It listed from side to side, to and fro, to and fro, like a boat bobbing on the waves – and beside it, her back to us, stood Annie Burrows.

She appeared unaware of our presence. Mrs Henge bristled, but before she could reprimand the girl, I laid a restraining hand on her arm and softly called Annie's name.

The cradle stopped.

My heart in my mouth, I called the young girl's name again.

I sensed the housekeeper's resentment at my interference, but I merely increased the pressure on her arm. Annie's head tilted up. Awakening from a daze, she turned to face us. Her cheeks ran with tears.

'The baby's dead.'

'Baby? What baby, Annie?'

'The baby in the cradle . . . the baby in the cradle is dead.'

I stared at the wooden crib, ominously restful. With a tightening chest, I forced my leaden feet forward, leaving a stunned and silent Mrs Henge behind me. Blood roared through my ears as I approached. It took all my courage to look inside. I saw only bare slats.

'I see no baby, Annie . . .'

Her eyes shimmered with tears as they locked with mine.

'I do . . .' she whispered. 'And it's blue.'

'Liar!'

The toy soldiers cradled in Mrs Henge's arm clattered to the floor as she swooped upon Annie, grabbing the maid's wrist, her face screwed tight with rage.

'You set the cradle rocking yourself, you mischief-making witch!'

Annie cried out in pain as the housekeeper wrung her wrist until the pale skin blushed with blood. 'I didn't! I swear! I heard the cradle rocking . . . I came in to see . . .'

'You are a *liar*!'

'I swear it's true – I heard the noise and came to see!' Annie sobbed.

Unmoved, Mrs Henge dragged her from the room, ignoring my angry protests as she pushed past me, hauling Annie onto the landing.

'Let her go!'

I reached forward to physically intercede, but the older woman was incandescent. All reason was lost to her as she manhandled the girl towards the top of the staircase, chanting 'witch' over and over again, dragging her down step by stumbling step, Annie sobbing uncontrollably, each utterance of the epithet a brutal blow.

'What in God's name is going on?'

Sheers came limping up the hallway. Mrs Henge growled with irritation as she pulled herself up to her full, stately height.

'This girl has been meddling in the nursery, trying to cause mischief. I intend to deal with her.'

'You will not.' The words tumbled from me on shuddering breaths. 'I will remind you Annie is my maid, she is no concern of yours. You will unhand her this instant.'

I took hold of Annie's free arm and yanked her towards me. For a terrible moment, I thought the housekeeper would maintain her grip, and the poor hysterical girl would be reduced to a rag doll in a tug of war, torn apart rather than surrendered. But the housekeeper's professionalism reasserted itself. She released her grip and let her hand fall, regaining her dignity as she regarded me with chilling indifference. Annie shuffled to my side, battling to regain her composure.

'Miss Marcham, the evidence was there for all to see.' It was taking an extraordinary effort for the housekeeper to regain her equilibrium. 'The girl had no business being in the nursery. She set the cradle rocking herself – and then to say what she did! Well, I would not be at all surprised if her malevolent interference wasn't behind all that has happened here of late.'

'How can that be when my sister experienced things before Annie even set foot in this house?'

'I think—'

'Mrs Henge, I am not interested in what you think!'

'What on earth is all the noise? It's woken Lady Brightwell from her sleep and you must know she needs her rest.'

Miss Scott came hurrying up the corridor towards us. She looked first to the housekeeper and then to me for an explanation, letting out a cry of alarm at the sight of Annie weeping.

'What's happened?'

'The cradle was rocking in the nursery.' I had intended to stop there, but Annie's words had conjured a hideous image in my mind's eye, and I could not mute its horror. 'Annie saw a dead baby in it.'

Miss Scott flinched. 'What? I don't understand. What do you mean "saw"?'

I gaped for a moment, conscious of revealing too much. 'Like a vision,' I said at last.

'Malicious nonsense,' Mrs Henge hissed, her cold eyes drilling into me, driven by utter contempt.

I refused to be intimidated by the housekeeper and I resented Mr Sheers' exasperated exhalation. I knew Annie hadn't started the cradle rocking, I *knew* it – a conviction formed in the very marrow of my bones – and I might be struggling to comprehend her macabre discovery, just as I was struggling to fathom her extraordinary abilities, but instinct told me it was significant. I was dependent on Miss Scott to quench my thirst for knowledge.

'Well? Has there ever been a dead baby in that cradle?'

'How can you ask such a thing?' The companion glared at me, repulsed and flabbergasted in equal measure. Protesting, she hotly chastised me for the insult and wondered at my credence of Annie's claims, who she declared 'depraved' for such gruesome and offensive fabrication. But the ferocity of her denial was so out of character that I felt encouraged to persist.

'I want to know – has there ever been a dead baby in this house? Well, has there?'

'No, Miss Marcham.' The voice that answered me was flimsy in strength yet flinty in nature, like hammered steel. 'My son is the only baby that has ever been in this house – dead or alive.'

We all turned to witness the entrance of Lady Brightwell as she shuffled up the corridor, her frilled dressing gown floating around her like surf on a breaking wave. One gnarled hand rested on the flocked crimson wallpaper as she made her painful progress. A miasma of illness surrounded her, draining her of all vitality. She stopped just short of us, exhausted, her breaths laboured. Miss Scott hastened to her side, slipping an arm round her waist and reproving her for such wanton recklessness. Lady Brightwell dryly observed that rest had been impossible with all the carry-on.

'Lady Brightwell,' I persevered, 'are you absolutely sure?'

'Miss Marcham—' Batting away Miss Scott's fussing hands, Lady Brightwell took a further step. The muscles about her eyes twitched as she regarded me with ill-concealed contempt. 'Have I not already explained this to you? Very well, let me make it clear, one final time. That cradle was commissioned especially for Hector, and he is the only baby who has ever lain in it. I was blessed but once, Miss Marcham, and that one time robbed me of the possibility of another. In short, I have never carried, nor borne any other child, living or dead. Do I make myself very clear?'

'But Annie—'

'Why do you credit that girl?' She shook her head, reaching

out for Miss Scott's arm. 'She is a mere scrap of a maid. No doubt all the nonsense created by you and your sister has intrigued her mind and perverted her imagination.'

'No, no, she saw—'

'Nothing, Miss Marcham, the girl saw nothing.' She had no intention of brooking any discussion. 'Mrs Henge is completely correct – she should be disciplined, regardless of whether her actions were borne of malicious intent or simple foolishness.' She fought to catch her breath, looking aged and frail, the effort of confrontation taking its toll. 'Now perhaps if you will all be so kind, I would like to return to my room and rest – without any further disturbances.'

Miss Scott, though the older of the two, made a spritely contrast to Lady Brightwell as she assisted her slow return up the corridor. Mrs Henge held back until they were out of hearing.

'Well, Miss Marcham?'

'That will be all, Mrs Henge.'

'Lady Brightwell—'

'As I have already stated, Annie is my responsibility and I will take care of this. You may go,' I added for good measure.

The housekeeper sparked with animosity. 'She should be punished for such wickedness,' she spat, her eyes narrowing, her mouth hard and unforgiving, but seeing she would gain no quarter from me, she raised her chin and strode away.

'Do you see now? Do you see what it is you ask of me?' Annie demanded, wiping her nose with the back of her hand, gulping back her misery. Before I could answer, a fresh sob caught in her throat, and with no propriety whatsoever, she fled up the nursery stairs. I started after her, but my progress was prevented by the hand that caught my arm.

'Let me go, Mr Sheers.'

He released me at once. 'Leave her, Miss Marcham.'

'No, I must speak to her.'

'Later, perhaps.'

'No, Mr Sheers, now,' I snapped. I had a sense of something precious slipping from my grasp and I had to act.

I ran after her, paying no heed to the open nursery door as I plunged through to the servants' quarters. I drew up short, out of breath from my rapid ascent and thwarted by my unfamiliar surroundings. I called out – Annie's name pierced the uninhabited corridor before me. When I received no reply, I hurried forward, grabbing at door handles one by one, to see if they would relent. After four frustrating failures I called her name again as I passed the servants' staircase leading down to the lower levels of the house. I stopped – I had come far enough. A door just in front of me was ajar.

My emotions collided as I hesitantly advanced – embarrassment, frustration, guilt and regret. I pressed it open with the palm of my hand. It squeaked on its hinges as it eased inwards, revealing a small room lit by a single window, with two beds pushed against opposing walls. On the left sat Annie Burrows.

She had curled herself into a hedgehog ball, her shoulders rounded, her face hidden behind the tuck of her knees. Perhaps she hoped to conceal herself – disappear, even – if only she could become as small as physically possible.

I hovered at the end of the bed. She made no attempt to acknowledge me and seeing her reduced into this terrified huddle humbled me. After an age, I gingerly sat down.

'Do you see why now?' Her body muffled her words, and

I had to strain to make them out. 'Why I didn't want to help? And now they'll all wonder about me.'

There was resentment in her voice, and I couldn't blame her for it. I had persuaded her to lower her defences. I had encouraged her trust, induced her to help me without consideration for what it might cost her – I had thought only of Madeleine, what happened to Annie Burrows had been of no consequence. I felt ashamed of my selfishness.

She slowly unwound, her shoulders rolling back, her head lifting. 'Do you know what it's like to be called "witch"?'

Like a lightning flash illuminating the night, I had a sudden insight into her life. A little girl distinct from everyone else, a little girl with a remarkable gift – but not one that marked her as special, but as different, and in this cruel world of ours, different was not a good thing to be. To survive she had learnt to hide in plain sight, but I could only imagine the painful lessons she had suffered along the way.

'I'm sorry.' The apology was woefully inadequate – a piece of cotton to moor an ocean liner. Awkwardly, I reached forward and rested my hand on the arm that belted her legs, but soon withdrew it to my lap. 'She had no right to say that.'

'They all say it,' she said with such heartbreaking resignation, I wondered if she might consider the spiteful slur deserved.

'Well, they are wrong to do so. It isn't true, for starters. What you can do is remarkable – *you* are remarkable, Annie Burrows. You have a precious gift, you should not be ashamed of it.'

'It is a curse, not a gift.'

'It is whichever you choose it to be.' My agitated fingers toyed with a fold in the blanket beneath me as I tried to formulate my tumbling thoughts. 'I cannot claim to understand what it is you do, Annie, or how you see the things you do, but I find myself unable to dismiss you, as others might. I believe you, Annie.' I shrugged lightly in the face of her sceptical scrutiny. 'I don't know what else to say, I can't even explain my conviction to myself, just that it is clear and plain to me, even when it should be anything but. I believe in you.'

The first fragile buds of rapport unfurled through the congenial silence that followed – an exchange of shy smiles, a softening of defences, the onset of spring.

'What do you think it meant, what you saw?' I asked.

'I saw a dead baby.' She drew her knees tighter against her narrow chest.

'Who was it, Annie? Whose baby?'

'I don't know.' She lifted her head higher, unwinding a smidgeon more, growing bolder in the thaw. 'I can only see what he shows me. He shows me what he has seen, just as he has seen it. I know no more than that.'

I nodded, my inept mind struggling to understand. 'It is all connected – it must be,' I mused. 'The question is how? What can it all mean? Dear God,' I whispered, the monstrous horror sinking in anew. 'What happened in this house?'

An apologetic knock startled us both. I spun round, surprised to see Cook hovering in the doorway, clutching something to her waist.

'I'm so sorry, perhaps now's not a good time, but I happened to pop up and I heard voices . . .' Flustered, she thrust out her hand, and I saw now what was caught in her thick fingers – a fold of paper. 'Well, I said you could have it and I happened to be up here, and . . . well, anyway, here it is.' I accepted her offering with some confusion. 'Why, it's what you wanted!' she said, eager to please. 'Edith's details.'

'Edith?' I echoed stupidly, unfolding the sheet.

'Why, Edith Jenkins: the nanny.' She beamed as the penny finally dropped. 'That there's Nanny's address.'

Chapter Thirty-Four

The address revealed that Edith Jenkins – Nanny – had not travelled far to assume her next post, and this discovery presented an exciting new possibility: a face to face meeting. I was convinced she held the key to discovering what had happened all those years ago.

With mounting excitement, I shared my plan with Annie, pacing her draughty room, the wind pushing against the tiny window with its paltry view of roof tiles and a hint of sky. When I stopped, bright-eyed and enthused, I looked at the dejected figure hunched on the bed and felt an overwhelming sense of guilt. She had been a queer but contented creature until I had wedged my knife under the lip of her shell and prised it open, determined to find the pearl hidden within. Now she sat there exposed, hollowed out and alone – haunted by the dead and shunned by the living – and it was all my doing.

'You should come with me,' I blurted out. The dried trails of her tears caught the light as she turned her face to me. She looked so lost, so fragile. I knew what it was to conceal one's true self, how difficult and isolating it could be. I was in a unique position to help Annie Burrows – my company could be a haven where she could finally be herself.

'Yes, yes, you should come. There can be no truth without you, Annie – I need your help.' Again, her instinctive wariness flared, that innate caution that had served her well. 'We are all alone in this house, Annie, you and I. We must stick together.' I touched her shoulder. 'Come, help me dress for dinner. And tomorrow – tomorrow we will visit Nanny Jenkins.'

Dinner was a strange affair. Lady Brightwell was bedridden and unable to join us, but Miss Scott lent us her company, though she made it clear from the start she did not intend to tarry long, as she was keen to return to her ladyship. She confided that recent events had taken a profound toll on her mistress. All the talk of Lucien had reopened a distinctly unpleasant chapter in her life, and there was only regret and self-recrimination to be found within its pages.

Intrigued, I encouraged Miss Scott to elucidate. She huffed and faffed as was her manner, but eventually she admitted Lady Brightwell held herself partly responsible for the boy's death.

'She always felt guilty for not taking to him, I think,' Miss Scott explained, toying with her egg mousse. '"Scottie," she would say to me, "it's so terribly hard having to see your pre-decessor's progeny every day, and worse to be expected to have affection for him."'

'She was jealous of him?' I was unable to mask the disgust in my voice.

'Oh! Don't judge her too harshly, Miss Marcham. She was so young, and Sir Arthur had so adored his first wife, you see, and Lucien was her spitting image. Lady Brightwell couldn't help feeling second best. After the accident, I think she felt in some way she had made it happen, by wishing the boy didn't exist. Once she was expecting herself, you see, she just wanted a fairy tale ending – a palace, her husband, a son.' She lowered her gaze. 'She got what she wanted . . . but at a most dreadful cost.'

'She wanted Lucien gone?'

'Oh she never wished harm on the boy!' Miss Scott was quick to assure me. 'She just wished everything had been different – that Sir Arthur had never been married before, that he had not had any other children. It all tarnished it for her, you see, his history.'

'She knew what she was getting into when she married him.'

'Oh, Miss Marcham, you think it is all so easy . . .' a sad smile hovered on her lips, 'but back then, one had to do as one was told, not what one necessarily wanted.' She set down her cutlery, the egg mousse barely touched. 'It was considered an advantageous match.'

'Were you here, Miss Scott, when the tragedy occurred?' Sheers chipped in.

'I was. I had not long come back – I had been away, looking after my parents who had succumbed to influenza, which was terrible that year.' She paused as Maisie collected her plate. 'So, I just missed Hector's birth – poor Lady Brightwell had such a time of it.'

'And she was still confined to her bed?' I asked.

'Oh no, she was just beginning to get about again – she had been bedbound for days after the birth, and quite unable to care for Hector. If only I could have been here to help her, but my parents, you see. Hector was cared for by the nanny, but after her carelessness with poor Lucien – well, she couldn't be trusted, not with Hector.'

'And so, you became Hector's nanny?'

A blissful smile illuminated her face, and again, the beauty she must have enjoyed in her youth radiated through the faded exterior. 'Yes! She said, "Scottie, I cannot trust anyone but you." So, I looked after him. He has been my joy.'

271

The conversation was steered to happier topics for the remainder of the meal, and as soon as pudding was cleared, Miss Scott excused herself. I assured Mr Sheers that I would be quite content with my own company if he wished to partake in brandy and cigars, but he elected instead to escort me back to the drawing room where Maisie had set out the coffee.

'How is your maid?' he asked once I'd poured for us both.

I brushed off the incident. He watched me as I sipped my drink, before asking if I truly believed the cradle had been rocking prior to Annie's entry to the nursery. In no uncertain terms, I told him that I did. I refrained from going into detail, but I made it very clear I had good reason to believe Annie Burrows.

'What is it about this girl that evokes such trust in you?' he asked, smiling in wonderment. 'She makes the frankly extraordinary claim of having seen a dead baby and you don't bat an eyelid! I find it quite astounding that you don't question her, not for one moment, and yet common sense and the evidence would support Mrs Henge's theory rather than your own.'

I bristled at the mention of Mrs Henge and tartly observed I would favour my maid over Greyswick's housekeeper any day. He was still not satisfied though and pressed me again about Annie. He leapt at my hesitation.

'There you are! You've done that before.' He dispensed with his coffee to better study me, determined to discover what lay beneath my veneer. 'I ask you about that girl and you clam up, as if you're tempted to tell me something but think better of it.'

'When have I done that before?'

'When I interviewed you.' He laughed and apologised for the rather grandiose description of what had taken place in the study. 'You seemed reluctant to be drawn on her then as well. I'm curious.'

My guard went up. There was something about Mr Sheers that made me wary, I realised. He had a disarming charm about him that created the impression he was harmless, yet I couldn't shake the feeling that behind that façade lay a cunning mind, deft and dangerous.

'She's shared your experiences in this house, I know, but there's more to it than that, I'm sure. She demonstrated the same reluctance. Why?'

I turned my face to the fire and closed my eyes. The heat prickled against my eyelids, and all I could perceive was a solid wall of gold. The overwhelming sense of loneliness that had enveloped me since Madeleine left shouldered its way to the fore and subconsciously my fingers clasped my locket.

'Tell me about Annie Burrows. Please, Miss Marcham. I would so like to help if I can.'

I hadn't expected to want to confide in him, but there was something so kind, so encouraging – so *beguiling* – in his sincerity. In that quiet moment, when the only other sounds in the room were the soothing crackling of the fire and the rhythmic tick of the ormolu clock, I wanted him to hear my story and believe me. So, gripping my locket and gazing into the hypnotic flames to avoid the gentle mockery in his eyes, I told him everything – from the night of the fire, to Jim Burrows, to the hideous incidents at Greyswick, and Annie's conviction that Lucien was seeking justice for his death – his fall by foul play.

'You can say it. That I'm a fool.'

'I don't think you're a fool, Miss Marcham.'

'But still, you don't believe me.'

'Would you like a drink? A proper drink?' He pushed himself up from his chair and made his way to the decanters on the sideboard. He poured generous measures of whisky into two tumblers and made his way back to me, his uneven gait a constant reminder of the sacrifice he had made for his country. When I had taken my glass, he held his aloft.

'To the fallen,' he said without sentiment and took a hearty swig.

I echoed his words, my fingertips alighting on my locket again. After a few sips, I held up my tumbler, the light refracting in its carved pattern.

'There, Mr Sheers, I'm suitably fortified. Let's hear it. Belittle me if you wish, I'm ready for you.'

He chuckled. 'I have no wish to denigrate you in any way, Miss Marcham.'

'But you think I'm mad.'

'No, no I don't. I've learnt not to think that at all. I appreciate you taking me into your confidence. Your revelations are . . . eye opening. You want my thoughts on the matter?'

I assured him I was most eager to hear his analysis. Indeed, I reiterated, I would be fascinated to hear it. He met the irony in my voice with a wry smile before delivering his theory. He believed I had misconstrued what I had witnessed on the night of the fire.

'In the light of this lingering fantasy, I think the transference of "supernatural" power to Burrows' daughter is perfectly understandable. However, I do think that for her – an insignificant young girl who is never likely to amount to much – having someone like you, a lady, her mistress, bestow such abilities upon her and then believe the stories she makes up to promote the idea . . . well, I'm sure she must find it intoxicating.'

It was a neat if erroneous theory, and I told him so. He didn't look disappointed by my rebuttal, more resigned. He asked who *I* thought had set the cradle rocking that afternoon. Before I could answer, he asked me to give careful consideration to the evidence: that Annie was alone in the room when I found her.

'You see, Miss Marcham, all of this, this terrible tale of Lucien Brightwell pushed to his death and now a dead baby, we must ask ourselves where it all comes from and there is but one source. Your maid has created an imaginative work of fiction.'

'But Madeleine was aware of things in this house before Annie even arrived.'

'I am convinced I can supply rational explanations for everything Mrs Brightwell has experienced. The situation, however, has been skilfully escalated and manipulated by the ingenuity of your young maid, filling in the blanks with mischief and mayhem – and now to top it all off, we have a dead baby.'

I lost myself once again in the flames and continued to sip my whisky, only vaguely aware of Sheers' continued efforts to win me round. My thoughts turned to Gerald, and I wondered what he would say if he were sitting opposite me now. Would he have joined in the chorus of disapproval, or would he have understood the profound realisation I had come to that terrible night at Haverton? A knowledge that had lain dormant all these years, to be awoken by Greyswick.

I became aware of Mr Sheers' voice again, piercing the carapace of my thoughts.

'Tell me, Miss Marcham, how long will you persist in believing everything that comes out of that young girl's mouth?'

I found the answer to his question in the flickering flames of the fire.

Chapter Thirty-Five

Annie Burrows and I rendezvoused in the hall after breakfast, ready for the day's adventure. I had asked Maisie to send for the car, and news of our imminent departure must have reached Mrs Henge for she swooped through the baize door, her features drawn, enquiring where we were going and for how long we would require the services of the chauffeur. I offered a chilly smile and informed her we only needed to be taken to the station. It was clear she itched to know what we were up to. I had no intention of telling her.

It only took an hour to reach Swindon by train, and from there we secured a taxi to take us the rest of the way, to a village that lay just beyond the chalk downs. I must confess my stomach knotted with nerves the closer we came. I had no plan of action – the whole trip was spontaneous and ill-conceived – but I knew I had to come and speak to Edith Jenkins myself.

We soon entered the quaint village, its rambling streets formed of attractive dwellings the colour of marzipan, topped with clay-tiled roofs. The taxi stopped before an impressive property that reminded me of the doll's house Madeleine and I had as children. I paid off the driver and we stood before the picket gate. After a minute or two, Annie asked me what we were going to do and I had no answer for her. It was now very apparent to me that I couldn't simply pitch up at the front door and ask to speak to the nanny – it was hardly the done thing, and the poor woman had no idea who we were. I cursed my impetuosity.

I suggested we walked while I tried to formulate a plan. After the wet and windy weather that had plagued us recently, it was a pleasant change to have the pale-yellow beams of a low spring sun lighting our way. The village was quiet – only a butcher's boy passed us, the wicker basket on the front of his bicycle laden with paper-wrapped parcels. A pretty church with a stunted square tower stood at a junction of lanes and, somewhat at a loss, we decided to dally within its grounds.

The sexton, who was tending to a flowerbed that ran the length of the graveyard wall, paused in his weeding as we slipped through the lychgate. He doffed his cap as he cast us a quizzical look, before taking to his task again, his metal hoe chinking against the stones as he worked the earth. Every now and then he bent to pull a weed, shaking the excess soil from its stringy roots before tossing it into his wheelbarrow.

We drifted aimlessly. I was most frustrated that a feasible plan was proving so elusive and was about to call time on the whole idea when Annie touched my arm. We could just see the house, and my heart leapt as an old woman with a snowdrift of hair, dressed in a half-caped navy coat, exited the front gate, escorting a girl of about five. They began to walk down the lane towards us, the girl gambolling by the woman's side, talking nineteen to the dozen, her blonde ringlets bouncing about her shoulders from underneath her tam o'shanter. Though smartly turned out, the old woman didn't look sufficiently well-heeled to be the child's grandmother. I shot a triumphant look at Annie – we had just found Edith Jenkins.

As they approached the church, they veered off along one of the lanes. Fearful of losing them, we hurried from the graveyard, earning a bemused look from the sexton as we scurried past him.

We were just in time to see them disappear between two cottages. We soon found ourselves in a narrow walkway trimmed with nettles, but at the end of the dwellings the path opened into a meadow. The nanny and her charge were taking a scythed path towards a large pond that stretched out from under the shade of an ancient oak tree.

I called out in greeting, but when the nanny failed to acknowledge me, I quickened my pace and called to her again, this time by name. She stopped, glancing over her shoulder, surprise etched on her worn grey features. The little girl twisted round to look at me, her sapphire eyes inquisitive within her china doll face.

'Edith Jenkins?'

When she cautiously confirmed she was, I introduced Annie and myself, explaining my connection via Madeleine to Greyswick. Her grip tightened on the girl's hand at the mention of her old home, and her manner turned distinctly cool. A hint of hostility came into play when I asked whether we might trouble her for a few minutes of her time.

'We're going to feed the ducks,' the girl chirped up, brandishing a brown paper bag.

'How lovely! Would it be all right if we came too?'

She was most insistent we should. Nanny Jenkins scowled with disapproval, but I renewed my appeal and promised we wouldn't take long, assuring her the nature of our visit was of the greatest importance. In the end curiosity got the better of her.

When we were approaching the sloping bank of the pond, Nanny Jenkins released the girl's hand and allowed her to go forward on her own, warning her not to get too close to the edge. A plain park bench had been placed under the great oak, and when she sat down upon it, I joined her. Annie hovered near the girl, keeping a watchful eye as she tore up the heel of a loaf she had been given. She tossed pieces onto the water, scolding the ducks for their greed as they swarmed, quacking and splashing, batting their wings and pecking at rivals, to gobble up the floating pellets.

Never taking her eyes off the idyllic scene, Nanny asked how I had found her and I explained about Cook.

'I don't see how I can help you. Greyswick was a long time ago and I've put it all behind me. I really don't have anything to say.'

She sat stiff-backed, her palms spread over her knees, her swollen ankles tucked to the side, just visible under the hem of her coat. Her discomfort was clear to see, but gradually I coaxed her into telling me about her time in service to Sir Arthur. Her eyes filled with tears as she recalled the first Mrs Brightwell, who had chosen Edith Jenkins during the last weeks of her confinement, and how a young inexperienced doctor had managed to save the child at the cost of the mother. She had raised Lucien from that tragic day, and it was clear to me she had doted on the boy.

Her responses grew terse and disapproving as I brought up the subject of the new Mrs Brightwell, who she dismissed as vain and conceited. Sir Arthur himself fared as poorly in her cutting assessment. The light dimmed in her face as I guided her to the critical part of the story, the part I so desperately wanted to hear.

'Perhaps it would have all been different if not for the influenza,' she said, fiddling with a button on her coat. 'He brought it in, Sir Arthur. He'd picked it up in London, they thought, then came down for the weekend bringing the contagion with him. It went through the house like wildfire – Lord, you wouldn't believe how it spread.'

She glanced at me, before returning her attention to her young charge. The bread had all gone now, and the ducks had glided away, rippling the surface of the pond, no longer interested in the girl who pouted with disappointment. Under Annie's guidance, she retreated into the shadow of the oak tree and began scanning the ground. With a shout of delight the girl crouched down then held aloft an acorn. Annie congratulated her and encouraged the scavenging to continue. The nanny nodded in satisfaction before taking up her story.

'First Lady Brightwell got it, then the maids, then Lucien, then me – we were all laid out flat in no time. And then of course the mistress goes into labour at last – overdue she was, the illness must have finally brought it on. Oh, the chaos! There was me, sick as a dog, having to get the nursery ready for a baby. I said to Mrs Henge, the baby should be kept separate, but she was insistent it would be all right up in the nursery where it belonged. Sir Arthur had recovered and gone back to London by that time, not that it would have made any difference, he always deferred to Mrs Henge, and Lady Brightwell was too ill to even be aware of what was happening.'

She was painting a pitiful picture. I was surprised that Mrs Henge hadn't caught the 'flu, but when I said as much Nanny blew a derogatory gust of air through her teeth. 'Nothing would dare infect her. She was right as rain. She said she would take over from me in the nursery, if needs be, but she was adamant the baby would go in there as planned.'

'So, Hector was put in the nursery as soon as he was born?'

'That's right. I didn't know how I was going to cope with him and Lucien – who was still poorly – feeling the way I was. I managed for a few days, battling on, but then I got very bad. I think I had pushed through when Lucien was so ill, but once I could see him improving, my reserves just left me. I couldn't even lift my head off the pillow. So, Mrs Henge moved me into one of the servants' bedrooms and she stepped in to look after the children.'

'So, Mrs Henge took over the nursery?' I was astonished. I couldn't imagine a less appropriate role for the dour house-keeper than nanny to a young boy and a new born.

'I know what you are thinking, Miss Marcham. It was hardly a natural fit, but you must appreciate, the place was in chaos, with almost every member of the household staff stricken to some degree or other. And in all fairness to the woman, she did well. I was bedridden for days, but when I returned, Lucien was much improved, and baby Hector, well, he was bonnier than ever.'

She went on to recount how her return to the nursery seemed to coincide with a watershed in the illness. Lady Brightwell began to rally, and even made brief visits to her new son, supported by Miss Scott who had just returned from nursing her parents. Sir Arthur stayed in London, satisfied to have an heir and a spare safe in the nursery. Life at Greyswick, it seemed, was beginning to return to normal.

'Nanny, may we go now? I've fed the ducks all the bread I had.' The little girl came running through the long grass towards us. One of her white stockings bore a muddy mark. Annie came up behind her, throwing me an apologetic look.

'She's getting bored, miss,' she said.

Nanny Jenkins was already on her feet, her hand outstretched. 'Of course, Miss Alice. It's nearly lunchtime, after all.' She started to lead her charge away.

I sprang up. 'Oh please, I just have a few more questions.'

'You want to ask me about that day, the day he died. Why else would you have come all this way?' She looked pained and weary. 'But I don't want to talk about it, don't you see? It haunts me. I think about that lovely sweet boy, *every day*. I made one mistake and I will never be able to forgive myself. I don't want to rake it all up – it hurts too much.' She started to walk away. I darted forward.

'Nanny Jenkins, please. I need to know what happened that day.'

'Whatever for? What's it to you?'

'Oh please, it's terribly important.' She went to move around me. 'I think something happened that day, Nanny, something other than an accident.'

I hadn't meant to blurt it out, but the thought of losing her cooperation now, when I felt we were inching closer to uncovering the truth, made me throw caution aside. She stopped. Her broad shoulders sank in shock as the girl continued to swing impatiently from her hand.

'What would make you think that?'

'Please cast your mind back, was there anything else, anything that day that might suggest . . .' I trailed off hopelessly. The girl was whining now, bored and fractious. Nanny Jenkins snapped at her to stop pulling. Chastised, Alice stood still, her pert mouth downturned in displeasure.

'No . . . no . . .' The cumulus of hair quaked as she refuted the suggestion. 'It was an accident,' she reiterated, but I thought behind her eyes I could see something stirring, some long-suppressed memory, and it seemed to unsettle her.

'Please, can't you stay, just a bit longer?'

'I can't. I have to get Alice back for her lunch.'

Alice stomped crossly on the spot and tugged again on her nanny's hand, loudly protesting her hunger. The china doll face was less appealing when petulant.

'All right, I'm coming now, mind your manners.'

I felt a crushing sense of disappointment as the two of them began to walk away, but they hadn't gone far before Nanny Jenkins faltered.

'Alice has a nap after lunch, about two o'clock. If you come to the back door, I'll meet with you then.'

Chapter Thirty-Six

Annie and I had lunch at the village pub and waited until five past two before we trooped up the drive to the back of the doll's house. Edith Jenkins opened the door as we approached. She led us through an uneven-floored scullery and down a narrow passageway into a small sitting room. It was simply furnished with a square dining table that seated four, and two chairs placed on a threadbare rug set before a stone fireplace, blackened with soot.

'No one will bother us in here,' she said, offering me a chair, while Annie elected to take the footstool beside it. A tray of tea things had been set upon the table alongside an old shoe box. Nanny Jenkins poured and held out the sugar bowl.

'I dug out some things, after I saw you,' she said by way of explanation, as she lifted the lid from the box. I got up to join her, Annie shadowing me, hovering by my shoulder. The box was filled with keepsakes, which she spread across the table for our perusal: a tiny pair of socks; a bundle of photographs capturing Lucien at various stages of his short life. I caught my breath as she brought out a single toy soldier, but the next item stilled my heart. It was a coiled lock of blond hair, tied at one end with a thin blue ribbon. A cry escaped me as I reached to touch it – it was silky soft. The horror of what was unfolding struck me afresh. A little innocent, murdered.

'They're just odd things no one wanted,' Nanny said in her

defence, as if somehow it was wrong for her to have stolen away with the sentimental treasures. I smiled to reassure her I was not passing judgement.

The final thing she removed was a piece of white paper, folded neatly in half, which she opened before me. It was a child's drawing depicting a boy I took to be Lucien, holding a baby wrapped in a colourful blue and gold blanket, carefully drawn and utterly charming. I smiled.

'He was quite an artist. Look at the detail.'

She glowed with pride at the compliment. 'Aye he was, sharp-eyed and accurate. It was a complicated pattern on that blanket, yet he's coloured it in perfectly.' She picked up the drawing to study it. She smiled, her voice softly lost in the past. 'Yes, he has, it was just like that,' she said, folding the picture up again. She tucked it back into the box and replaced the other poignant mementoes she had kept with her for nearly thirty years. 'I just thought you might be interested to see those,' she muttered, embarrassed now to have troubled us with them.

We re-took our seats. The room stretched with awkward silence as we sipped our lukewarm teas. I mustered my courage and asked her to tell me about the day Lucien died. Straight away she quizzed me on my suspicions, but I managed to defer her interrogation, explaining my need to understand every nuance of that day before I could draw conclusions. Somewhere down the hallway a grandfather clock chimed the half hour and air whined in a pipe as the kitchen tap was turned on and off again. Still Nanny Jenkins made no move to speak, fumbling in her pocket instead for a pressed cotton handkerchief which she shook open and used to wipe her nose. We waited.

She placed her cup and saucer on the table and rose with

a sigh, anxious lines drawing her brow as she drifted to the window, where she stood looking out upon the well-stocked garden. When the words came they were faint and incredulous, as if even now she struggled to comprehend how an innocent flow of events had led to such tragic consequences.

It was her first day back in the nursery, she told us. Mrs Henge had assured her there was no need to rush, but she felt better – the fever had subsided and the ache in her bones was gone. She even managed a few spoonfuls of porridge for breakfast.

'Perhaps if I hadn't eaten . . .' She turned back to face us, her eyes full of misery. 'I missed him so, you see. I wanted to be with him, and I thought I was well enough, I really did. He was so pleased to see me.' Her eyes swam as a smile lifted her doughy cheeks. 'He clung to me, begging me not to leave him ever again and I promised him I wouldn't. I promised.'

She brought the handkerchief to her eyes. I gently encouraged her to continue.

'Nothing out of the ordinary happened that morning. We stayed in the nursery – I thought that would be best. We played some card games and I read to him. I had the baby, of course, so I was seeing to Hector too.'

She sighed as she sat back down on her chair. 'I asked Lucien if he wanted to hold him – usually he doted on the little chap, but he didn't want to that day, he was just being cross and moody, bless him. He must have been feeling more poorly than he let on.' She paused, her head sinking towards her chest. 'And then I felt the wave of nausea. That's how it had taken me, the 'flu. Amongst other things, my stomach hadn't been right. I'd felt fine until then, and suddenly I knew I was going to be sick, and I couldn't be sick in that room, not with those two littl'uns in it. So, I made a dash for the servants' bathroom – it was only through the door on the landing, not far. I told him to stay put and watch his brother and I just ran, before it was too late.'

'And when you got back . . .' She didn't need to answer my rhetorical question. We both knew the heartbreaking conclusion to the story.

'It all happened so quick,' she whispered, wiping her eyes with the handkerchief, the horror raw again. 'I was gone moments, *moments*, Miss Marcham – but it was still too long.' Distress drove her to her feet once more, and she busied herself collecting our teacups, the china tinkling in her shaking hands. She returned them to the tray on the table and paused, her back still to us. 'If he had just stayed put,' she said. 'If he had just stayed in the nursery as I told him.'

'Was there anyone else about?' I asked.

'Oh well, there must have been people about, it's a great house.' She stopped, trawling her memories with extra care, searching for tiny details dusty from neglect. 'I heard a door open on the lower landing, so that must have been Lady Brightwell's room and, of course, I saw Mrs Henge.'

'Mrs Henge?'

'Yes, yes that's right – she was coming up the servants' staircase as I dashed past it to the bathroom.'

'And was it you who found Lucien?'

She shook her head. 'No. No, I heard the commotion from the bathroom – shouting, a scream. I knew then. My heart just fell out of me – a sixth sense, I suppose. I started running back to the nursery, but it was too late. They were already gathered around him, at the bottom of the stairs.'

'Who, Nanny Jenkins, who was already there?'

'All of them. They had heard the fall, and all come running: Miss Scott, Mrs Henge – even Lady Brightwell. They were all crowded round him – Lady Brightwell calling for a doctor to be summoned, Miss Scott crying, Mrs Henge saying it was too late. And it was – it was too late.'

Nanny Jenkins sniffled into her handkerchief before fussing again with the tray, but her actions were a sham, her busyness a thin veil to mask the misery that tore at her soul. Chilled by her story, I wrapped my arms around me, images of Lucien circling before me like a zoetrope, animating him in my mind's eye.

What had really happened on that nursery landing, all those years ago?

'There was one thing that stuck in my mind,' Nanny offered. 'It struck me as odd at the time, but – well, I didn't really think about it after. I suppose I was too grief-stricken, and then there was all the added unpleasantness that followed . . .' She didn't finish. I knew she was alluding to her dismissal, done with such cruelty and abruptness. I could only imagine how she must have suffered.

'What was it?' I noticed Annie lift her head, and I became aware of her quiet aura.

'The last thing I said to him as I ran from the room was "Keep an eye on your brother", but as I reached the landing I heard him call after me. I didn't stop – I had to get to the bathroom – and I put it down to sulkiness, from him still being under the weather.'

'What did he say?' I asked, every nerve in my body tingling with expectation.

'The most curious thing, so out of character, but I heard it clear as day.'

'What was it? What did Lucien say?'

'He said, "He's not my brother."'

Chapter Thirty-Seven

Our journey back was subdued. Hearing Lucien's last hours recalled in such detail had lent a corporeal quality to the whole episode and it left me feeling bereft, as if I had known the boy personally. The strange occurrences at Greyswick were so terrifying it was easy to think they were fired by a malevolent intent, but Nanny Jenkins' fond conjuring now threw doubt on that conviction. I raised this with Annie on the train home and she admitted that the motivations of the dead could easily be misinterpreted by the living.

And then there was the conundrum of Lucien's last living message – *He's not my brother*. Were those the words of a tired, petulant boy? Had he resented the responsibility of watching the baby, perhaps jealous now the novelty had worn off? Or did something far more sinister lurk behind the declaration? And what of Annie's dead baby? Nanny Jenkins had looked at me in blank bewilderment when I questioned her on the subject and Annie herself seemed unable throw any light on the matter – indeed, she was now as confused as I was. I could hear Mr Sheers' droll voice echoing 'How convenient' in my ear, but I dismissed him. I still had faith in Annie Burrows. There was a mystery here, but not of her making and I was convinced I would be unable to solve it without her unique insight.

It was late afternoon by the time we arrived back at

Greyswick. I was in the process of unbuttoning my overcoat as we moved through the vestibule into the hall, when I came to an abrupt halt – Mrs Henge stood by the oak table, her hands clenched by her sides.

'I trust your visit with Nanny Jenkins proved satisfactory?'

Cook, it appeared, had been unable to keep our secret and now Mrs Henge knew. Mrs Henge who had been coming up the servants' staircase. Mrs Henge who had declared Lucien Brightwell beyond saving.

'Is that where we've been?' I said, tilting my head to extract my hat pin.

She came forward, the accompanying jangle of keys muted by the folds of fabric that rippled with every step.

'Edith Jenkins was dismissed from this house following an unforgiveable dereliction of duty. I need hardly say, therefore, that whatever the woman has told you should not be trusted.'

I handed my hat and pin to Annie. 'I will make my own mind up about Nanny Jenkins, if that is indeed where I've been.' I began to walk past, but I stopped as I drew abreast of her.

'Did you see Lucien on the landing? You were coming up the servants' staircase – you must have used the nursery stairs to join Lady Brightwell and Miss Scott by his body.'

'He had already fallen when I reached the landing. It was too late to do anything by then.' She whipped round to Annie. 'You'd best hurry up and put those things away. Cook needs your help with dinner.'

And casting me a final glance, as if daring me to challenge her order, she spun on her heel and strode away, disappearing behind the green baize door.

*

The evening passed uneventfully. Lady Brightwell managed to join us for dinner but sat at the table like a wraith, devoid of her usual vim. She even meekly submitted to Miss Scott's demand that she absent herself from the following morning's Sunday service. Indeed, such was her listlessness, none of us were surprised by her decision to retire as soon as the meal was over. We wished her goodnight as she left, aided by her inexhaustible companion.

Mr Sheers and I took our coffee in the drawing room. I was so preoccupied with the day's revelations that his polite attempts at conversation went largely unnoticed, and in the end I excused myself, apologising for my distracted behaviour. I retreated to the quiet confines of my room where, alone with my thoughts, I could work further on the puzzle before me.

I woke early the following morning. Knowing Lady Brightwell would herself be absent, I had already decided to miss church, so I promptly rolled over and went back to sleep. I came to a good deal later, hauling myself out of an unpleasant dream. Though I was unable recall the details, it left me with a residual feeling of fear.

The fire was crackling in the grate. I stretched underneath the covers to dispel any remnants of tension, then lay listening to the spluttering flames and the chirping of birdsong beyond the window panes.

Throwing back the covers, I reached for the bell-pull before hurrying to the bathroom to answer a rather pressing call of nature. I heard a faint tap and my bedroom door swish open. I flushed the water closet and washed my hands, calling out to Annie that I would be with her in a minute. I finished my ablutions and went to join her in the bedroom – but the room was empty, and the door was shut.

A light knock interrupted my puzzlement and Annie bobbed into the room.

'Did you come in earlier? When I was in the bathroom?'

'No, miss.' Her colour was up, and she was breathing hard, as if she had been running. 'I'm sorry I'm late answering the bell, but, well, there was a bit of an incident in the kitchen that I had to clear up.'

I assured her I wasn't inconvenienced. Directing her to take out a black skirt and a lavender shirtwaister from the wardrobe, I slipped on my undergarments. When I was ready, she helped me into my things, her chapped fingers fumbling over the skirt's petite buttons. Once attired, I sat down at the dressing table and applied some scent while she brushed through my hair, scooping it up and pinning it in place. She dressed it in a different style, but I thought it quite becoming and told her so. Her cheeks glowed with pleasure at the unexpected praise. Abashed by her reaction, she busied herself tidying away my night things and straightening the bed. I lifted the lid on my jewellery box and selected a cameo brooch which I pinned to my high, frilled collar. That done, I reached for my locket.

It was not there.

I frowned. I had taken to hanging it from the hinge of the triptych mirror that stood upon my dressing table. Bemused, I looked again, at both the left and right set of hinges. I stood up and peered behind the mirrors, thinking it had perhaps slipped round, out of sight, but it was still nowhere to be seen. I felt the first inkling of concern, but batted it away. I had been sleepy and distracted when I went to bed – perhaps the chain had missed the hinge and the locket had fallen to the floor instead. I pushed back my stool and peered underneath. No gold locket.

My hands were beginning to shake as I scrabbled through the contents of the jewel box, but still it was not to be found. I asked Annie whether she had put my locket away the previous night.

'No, miss. Didn't you hang it up?'

'I thought I had . . .' I spun back to the dressing table, pressing my palms flat on the polished surface to steady myself, as a wave of pure panic surged over me. 'I was definitely wearing it last night, wasn't I? To dinner?' I tried to picture myself. I didn't always wear it with my evening dress after all, sometimes I wore my pearls. The nights all blurred into one as I tried to focus on events not more than twelve hours old. I was sure I had worn it. I could picture myself at the mirror, taking it off. And that *was* last night – wasn't it? My mind was playing tricks on me.

'Miss?'

Annie had detected my rising angst, bubbling up inside me like lava, threatening to overflow. I whirled round to her. I tried to mock my foolishness, but the laugh that escaped me was brittle and fraught.

'I can't seem to find my locket. I'm sure it must be here right in front of me – I just can't see it.'

I was pathetically grateful that she grasped the gravity of the situation right away. She hurried over to the dressing table, searching about its top and drawers, while I stood helpless. She dropped to her knees, sweeping her hands flat across the carpet in case it had merged with the pattern, before diving them underneath the base of the dressing table.

After what seemed an age, she confirmed my worst fears.

'It has to be here somewhere,' I declared. 'We must look for it, we must look everywhere for it.'

With rising dread, I began pulling out drawers, searching through their contents, even those I knew I hadn't touched for days. It had to be in the room somewhere, it just had to be! Tears pricked at my eyes as my frustration grew, every search proving futile. With Annie's help I began removing my clothes from the wardrobe in the vain hope it had somehow got snagged on a dress, a hanger, put in a pocket – anything, anything had become a possibility, though in the back of my mind I knew I was clutching at straws. Fear knotted in my stomach. I couldn't lose that locket. It was all I had left.

'Perhaps the clasp broke and it dropped off without you realising it,' Annie suggested. 'Try and think back to the last time you remember having it.'

I crumpled down on the end of the bed trying hard not to cry. I cast my mind back, raking through the events of yesterday, scene by scene, but it was so hard to remember. The locket was my constant companion. Even on the rare occasions I didn't wear it, I still felt its weight against my chest, in the same way that Gerald was forever in my thoughts – even when other things distracted me, he was always there, milling in the background.

'After dinner!' I looked up, my eyes shining. 'I remember fiddling with it during coffee with Mr Sheers in the drawing room.' I beamed at her as if this memory was the key. A pernicious voice in my head warned me it wasn't.

But it was a start. Annie suggested we retrace my steps from that point, she was sure we would then find it. There was something comforting about her confidence. She understood how important it was that the locket was found, an importance that had nothing to do with its monetary worth. Its value was far more profound than that.

We raced downstairs and burst into the drawing room. Lady Brightwell, looking vastly improved, was engaged in a sedate game of cards with Miss Scott. She expressed her surprise at our explosive entrance, and her surprise again as I dropped to my knees and began reaching under the armchairs.

'My locket, I've lost my locket, have you seen it?' I gabbled, praying one of them would declare it had already been discovered and set aside for safekeeping.

'Oh no! Not your precious one?' Miss Scott cried.

Precious. The word summed it up perfectly. The terrifying thought that it might be gone for ever insinuated its way into my mind. I sat back on my heels and pressed my hand against my forehead as I fought back the tears. I nodded, not trusting myself to speak.

'Oh, my dear, I'll help you look.' Miss Scott lay down her cards and got up. Lady Brightwell huffed at the abandonment of the game, but even she possessed sufficient sensitivity to appreciate my distress.

'It must be here somewhere. When did you last have it? It couldn't have been lost outside, could it?' Miss Scott said, coming to my aid.

Annie had been ferreting around the room while we were talking. She caught my eye. My heart sank as she shook her head. Miss Scott, with forced positivity, declared it must be in the house somewhere. Learning that after coffee I had returned to my room, she charged Annie with searching the corridor and the hall, while she marched me back upstairs.

Mr Sheers was embroiled in setting up his gramophone on the landing. He must have detected my anxiety for he stopped what he was doing and asked whether everything was all right.

'Poor Miss Marcham has lost her locket. It's so terribly important to her. I don't suppose you have seen it, by any chance?'

'The gold one you were wearing last night?' I was surprised he had noticed such a trifling detail. 'I was trying to entertain you with a mildly humorous tale from my university days, but you were clearly miles away, clasping your locket as if it were a talisman.'

'Oh dear, we really must find it, poor girl,' Miss Scott cooed. 'We must search your room again.'

'I stopped into Madeleine's room first!' New hope lifted my heart at the recollection. 'I borrowed a nightgown – I had been too hot in mine. Perhaps it fell off in her room.' Buoyed, I ran to Madeleine's door. When Miss Scott failed to move, I urged her to join me.

As soon as I entered I began to search. Miss Scott hovered just through the doorway, gawping about as if she were visiting an exhibit.

'Goodness, I haven't been in this room for so many years.' She drifted towards the bed, her fingers alighting on the carved bed post. 'This was Lady Brightwell's room when we first arrived. They were still drawing up the plans for the new wing where her suite is now, so she had this room.'

'I can't see it on the floor anywhere, can you? Will you help me search the dressing room?'

Miss Scott blinked as my appeal pulled her from the past. She looked beyond me to the white panelled door that separated the two rooms. She bit her lip, distracted.

Muttering under my breath I pushed open the door and began to search the floor near the armoire where I'd found the nightgown. Miss Scott made it as far as the doorway but came no further. She looked pale and out of sorts as she fiddled with the length of pearls that swung low on her chest. 'You search in here, Miss Marcham,' she said at last, backing away, 'while I check the bedroom once again, just in case . . .'

Ten minutes later my stomach roiled. There was no sign of my locket – I was running out of places to look.

'Any luck?' Mr Sheers called as we closed the door behind us.

Too upset to speak, I shook my head and hurried to search my own room once again. This time I was ruthless in my endeavour – flinging things from drawers, pulling the coverings from my bed, upending trinket boxes – but still nothing. I sank down into the tumbled mass of bedding and covered my face with my hands as tears began to slide down my cheeks. I thought of Gerald, of how I had betrayed him with my negligence, and my heart ached.

'Miss Marcham . . .' Sheers' voice was soft, and kind and I couldn't bear it. I wondered how long he had been stood in my doorway, silently watching my grief. There was a bustle of activity and Miss Scott materialised at my side, her fingers resting on my shoulder.

'Oh, my dear. Still no joy?'

Sniffling, I wiped my hands across my face. I was surprised to see that Mrs Henge now stood beside Mr Sheers.

'I think, miss, if your search of the house has proven to no avail, we must think of alternative possibilities.'

'What do you mean?' I asked her.

'I think, given the circumstances, we should search the servants' quarters.'

'But I haven't been in the servants' quarters.'

'I think Mrs Henge is suggesting the locket may have found other ways of ending up there,' Sheers said.

Perplexed, I stared at him, until at last the meaning of his carefully chosen words dawned on me. 'Are you suggesting that someone might have *stolen* my locket?'

Miss Scott emitted a sad sigh of resignation, but it was Mrs Henge who answered me. 'I believe the locket to be valuable, miss.'

'To me, in sentimental terms, of course,' I snapped. My tears had initiated a headache that was beginning to drill through my temples.

'But to others there might be a more monetary value,' Mr Sheers explained.

'I just want my locket.' I couldn't keep the catch from my voice.

'I know, my dear, but sadly Mrs Henge might be right. We ought to consider all possibilities,' Miss Scott said as she sat down beside me, spreading a comforting arm around my shoulder. The unexpected tenderness almost undid me.

Mrs Henge crossed my room like an ominous cloud, to exert three tugs on my bell-pull. A short time later, Annie, Maisie and even Cook appeared at my door.

'Miss Marcham's locket appears to be missing. So that no stone is left unturned, I will be performing a search of your rooms. You may accompany me upstairs now.'

She swept out. The servants exchanged anxious glances before meekly following her. Miss Scott, Mr Sheers and I fell in behind.

We processed up the nursery staircase and across the landing. Mrs Henge whipped open the half-glazed door and led the way into the bland servants' corridor beyond. She instructed the three servants to stand beside their rooms. As if part of a protocol I didn't understand, the three assumed their positions, without question or objection. The two younger girls seemed calm if unassured – only Cook appeared agitated, wringing her pudgy hands on her apron. She muttered something about cakes and I realised her anxiety arose from abandoned baking rather than the unfolding events.

Mrs Henge didn't so much as glance at Maisie as she glided past her. Like voyeurs, Miss Scott and myself crowded around the door, Mr Sheers hovering behind us, as we watched the housekeeper carry out a cold, almost callous, systematic search of the room. No nook was left untouched. Mrs Henge brushed the blanket straight over the bed as she finished.

She went into Annie's room next, us ghoulish followers drawn after her, like metal filings to a magnet. She yanked open the top drawer of the tallboy, the only furniture beside the two beds, and rifled through the contents – a single cotton nightdress, three smalls, and to all our embarrassments, some sanitary napkins. Once she had satisfied herself with the drawers, Mrs Henge turned her attention to the beds. She hoisted up the mattress on what appeared to be the spare, peering underneath at the ledges in the frame. She cast the pillow onto the floor before smoothing her hands over the bed linen for any tell-tale lumps. She replaced the pillow when she was done and turned her attention to the second bed, which, judging by the nightdress neatly folded at its end, was the bed Annie was sleeping in.

Mrs Henge tossed the pillow aside before lifting the mattress.

She never finished her search. As the pillow hit the wooden floorboards, we all heard it: a distinct metallic clatter.

Chapter Thirty-Eight

We all froze, all, that is, except Annie Burrows, whose head snapped round in shock and confusion. Playing to her audience, Mrs Henge slowly bent down to pick up the pillow. Revelling in the drama, she slid her hand into the case, raking between the thin cotton and the feather-filled pillow inside. She stilled. There was a quiver of satisfaction about her. She withdrew her hand, my precious locket entwined in her fingers.

A spontaneous cry leapt from my throat as I rushed forward to snatch it from her grasp, clutching it to my chest, trying very hard to stay on my feet though my legs were trembling, so great was my relief. I had my locket, and in that moment, I didn't care about anything else. But it appeared others did.

'Annie Burrows – would you care to explain?'

Mrs Henge waited like a hanging judge for my maid's defence. It was blurted out without hesitation.

'I don't know, I never put it there.'

'You took the locket.'

'I did not.'

There was shuffling as the others withdrew from her, fearful of the criminal class. Annie focused on me alone.

'I did not take your locket, miss. I never would.'

A snort exploded from the housekeeper. 'So, it grew legs and walked here by itself, did it?' She tossed the pillow upon the

301

bed, and in two powerful strides, she reached the young girl, seizing her wrist in the tight manacle of her fist. 'Thievery is instant dismissal. Pack your things and leave this house at once.'

Annie fought against the housekeeper's iron grip as she continued to protest her innocence with rising panic and unshackled emotion. Miss Scott, her sweet features screwed with disappointment, murmured, 'Oh dear, oh dear.' Mr Sheers rested on the doorpost, his arms crossed, his expression indecipherable, the ever-silent observer of others' pain.

Something reasserted itself within me, as if the locket had grounded me once again. Sheers was right – it was my talisman. With it, I remained infused with Gerald's gentle guidance, strength, morality and perception. As I watched the housekeeper tower over Annie, I realised I was looking at a distorted image – a photograph where the subjects had moved too soon, blurring reality and obscuring the truth.

'Let her go, Mrs Henge.'

My commanding tone caught the housekeeper off guard.

'The girl has been caught red-handed, Miss Marcham.'

'I am her employer. It is up to me how she is dealt with – if indeed she is found guilty of any crime.'

'The locket was discovered in her room.'

Her irritation and anger assaulted me in waves, but I bore the brunt of each wash. I studied Annie's face. I saw bewilderment, fear, resentment and a profound sense of injustice, but I saw no guilt.

'Just because the locket was found in her room does not make her responsible for its theft.'

'Oh, my dear.' I felt the pressure of Miss Scott's slender fingers on my arm. 'I am sorry to say, I do think that in this case Mrs Henge is right. The evidence seems rather damning.' She drew close, her confidential words warm on my ear. 'And when Lady Brightwell hears of this, she will not want the girl in the house.'

'I didn't do it, miss.'

It came down to a simple question: who within Greyswick did I trust? The convenience of the allegation did not escape me: Annie Burrows reveals a dead baby and lo and behold she's caught in an uncharacteristic display of theft – the penalty for which had to be her dismissal, leaving me further isolated and alone. How long would I be brave enough to remain once I had lost my final ally? The whole thing struck me as akin to Mr Sheers' theories on telekinesis and suggestion – too neat to be true. But for those with secrets to hide, it was the perfect way to dispose of a perceived threat. I refused to be so easily beguiled.

'I know Annie better than any of you, and I also know that at times things are not what they seem.' I clutched my locket. I fancied I could almost feel it radiating the warmth of Gerald's approval. I rebuffed the flurry of attempts to convince me of Annie's guilt as I brought her to my side.

'I am very grateful to all of you for your assistance this morning. I cannot tell you what it means to have my locket back, but I am not one to take things at face value, and something here sits ill with me. I know very well how it looks, but I am also very aware looks can be deceiving. Now if you'll excuse me, I would like to speak to my maid alone.'

Sheers moved to the side, freeing me to leave. I maintained my hold on Annie, though my fingers slackened as I bustled her out of the servants' quarters. Our steps rang off the polished treads of the nursery staircase as I ushered her towards my room. Once safely inside, I closed the door and braced myself against it, as if my extra weight might help resist the unpleasantness outside, pressing to get in.

Annie wasted no time in pouring out her profuse denials, her outrage simmering just below the surface. Her vent was clearly cathartic, and when I sensed it had served its purpose, I waved her into silence.

'I know it wasn't you.'

I pushed myself from the door and crossed to the window, shunting up the sash. I flattened my hands on the broad sill. 'Why would you take it? You and I both know the diamond earrings I brought with me have a far greater monetary value than the locket and were less likely to be missed. It is all too convenient, Annie; I never trust convenience. Someone has gone to great trouble to incriminate you,' I concluded.

'But why, miss?'

Nature's breath whispered into the room, cooling my angry cheeks, as I contemplated Annie's question, but I already suspected the answer.

'Because you saw a dead baby in the cradle. You saw a dead baby where there shouldn't have been one – a dead baby that doesn't exist.' I folded my arms to keep the pervading chill at bay, as my mind's eye conjured the horrible image. 'Something has happened in this house, something that has led to terrible consequences. I think that's what Lucien has been trying to tell us. And there's someone still here who never wants it revealed – and whoever that person is intends to stop us, by whatever means they can.'

'So, who took your locket?'

I remembered my surprise earlier when I found my room

empty. I was so certain I had heard the door swish softly on the carpet, felt the charge of another's presence in the air. Could I have been right? Could someone have slipped in and out while I was still in the bathroom?

'What happened to delay you attending my bell this morning?'

'Lady Brightwell's tray got knocked from the table,' Annie recalled. 'Maisie had asked for my help in preparing it because she was running behind and Miss Scott was waiting to take it up. So, I was dashing about getting everything together when the whole thing went flying. Mrs Henge blamed me for being careless – she said I'd caught the edge of the tray.'

'So, Mrs Henge and Miss Scott were both in the kitchen?'

She nodded. Suppositions raced through my mind as I tried to establish the possible intrigues behind my locket's disappearance, but before long I felt like a puppeteer trying to work a marionette with broken strings – without connections to the limbs, I was unable to bring the puppet to life.

'We need to be careful, Annie. We are not wanted in this house – there are those who wish to conspire against us.' Her features donned a look of utmost seriousness and my heart swelled with unexpected affection.

I needed some fresh air and time to think. I asked Annie to bring my outdoor things to the orangery in the hope that a therapeutic walk might help me conquer this fragmented puzzle, whose picture stubbornly eluded me.

I had no desire to amble under the watchful eye of Greyswick. I was now, more than ever, suspicious of figures – living and dead – who might observe me from its windows, obscured from view. And yet, it seemed no matter what direction I took, no matter how far I walked, Greyswick was ever present, its monstrous form obstructing the horizon whenever I turned about. In the end the only way to escape it was to plunge into the beechwoods beyond the arboretum. Only then, when tracks of rotten mulch muffled my steps and trees concealed the hideous house from my view, did I feel myself relax.

The wooded hill stretched up before me and I began to pant as I took on the incline, enjoying the cleansing quality of the exercise. Troubling thoughts of Lucien receded as I found myself immersed in nature's glory, for bluebells carpeted the woodland around me in breathtaking sweeps of sapphire, their sweet scent intoxicating. Flies and midges zig-zagged before me, playing in the strains of sunlight that penetrated the verdant canopy – itself alive with bird calls, whistles, trills and tweets – to prettily dapple the path.

I soon reached the top, reinvigorated and almost carefree – if only for a short time. I decided to continue along the ridge before turning back towards the house – anything to buy me a few more precious moments of peace – and spotting a suitable route, I began to make my way. Ground elder choked the wood here, tangling with mounds of brambles and spurting holly bushes. A squirrel scampered across the path in front of me, springing up the smooth trunk of the nearest beech, causing me to start; a crow cawed from the interlaced branches, amused by my skittishness, but the innocuous incident had shattered my tranquillity.

I broke off from the ridgeline to follow a narrow path downwards. The descent was steep and more overgrown than the other tracks, and I found myself ducking under low branches and pushing aside overhanging brambles. Gnarled tree roots protruded through the dirt and I had to take care not to trip as I gingerly continued down. The pungent smell of decomposition hung in the air.

As I got nearer the bottom, movement, some distance away through the trees, brought me to a standstill. Caught in a shaft of sunlight in a glade below me were two women, familiar figures, the one easily recognisable in her black ensemble, the other dressed in a rich burgundy coat with a high cowl collar. They stood close together, angled in, the tension in their bodies revealing the urgency of the words I could not hope to hear. Intrigued, I sneaked forward.

A crack split the air. I felt the twig give beneath my careless foot, but it was too late to prevent it. I froze with the horrifying guilt of a peeping Tom. Two heads snatched my way. They must have seen me poised between the trees, for they instantly drew apart. Miss Scott, distinct in her burgundy coat, darted away through the wood, back towards the house. Mrs Henge waited. She was staring straight at me. A menacing moment later, she stalked away, leaving me once again plagued by troubled thoughts and burdened by dangerous suspicions.

Chapter Thirty-Nine

Mrs Henge was waiting for me when I returned from my walk. I had deposited my things in the orangery and was proceeding down the corridor to the hall when she stepped from the gloom. Somewhat startled, I thought she intended to offer me some explanation for her meeting in the woods, but instead she informed me Lady Brightwell had requested an interview in the drawing room. She turned and walked before me, like a warder leading her prisoner to the cells, sweeping open the drawing-room door before stepping aside, allowing me to pass.

Lady Brightwell – still looking peaky but with a glimmer in her eye – sat beside the roaring fire which had been banked perilously high. Miss Scott fussed about her, tucking a fringed tartan blanket around her knees. She flushed when she saw me, but soon returned her attention to Lady Brightwell, plumping a cushion to position behind her back.

'Is there anything I can bring you, my lady?' Mrs Henge asked, impassive as she watched the companion's careful ministrations, which were being rather unfairly rewarded with barbed criticisms by the patient.

'I think some Bovril would do you the world of good,' Miss Scott declared, either deaf or immune to Lady Brightwell's complaints. 'It would be just the thing to build you up, don't you think? Yes, indeed, Mrs Henge, do bring up a nice strong cup of Bovril for her ladyship.'

I saw the muscles twitch in the housekeeper's jaw as she took her orders, but she dipped her head in silent compliance and withdrew, closing the door behind her.

I knew of course why Lady Brightwell wanted to see me, and after Miss Scott had entreated me to take a seat, she launched into a diatribe against Annie. Her illness had in no way weakened her opinionated vigour, and whilst at one point she was forced to see out a coughing fit, she made it quite clear she was not happy with Annie's continued presence under her roof, as if she expected the girl to start pilfering the family silver at the first opportunity.

When her litany of accusations and complaints had come to an end, I made it very clear I did not hold Annie responsible for my locket's disappearance, though I declined to answer when Lady Brightwell demanded to know whether I had another culprit in mind. Displeased by my 'stupidity and stubbornness' she dismissed me with short shrift, warning me any further incidents would result in Annie and me both being asked to leave, a threat I accepted with equanimity.

I was relieved to escape the enervating encounter. I was beginning to find the company in the house unbearable, and I wondered how long I could endure it alone. But any wobble was quickly dismissed as I thought of Madeleine and how desperately she needed my help. I felt ashamed then of my weakness, when she had proven herself such a pillar of strength in my time of need, all the while stoically bearing her own devastating loss. My difficulties paled in comparison and I resolved to fulfil my commitment, come what may.

I decided to retreat to the sanctum of my room. Mr Sheers was sitting on the bottom step of the nursery staircase, making notes in a large leather-bound book. I slowed my pace to observe him and sensing my propinquity, he glanced up. Duly caught, I offered him a rueful smile.

'You are keeping yourself very busy.'

'I'm just trying to be as thorough as I can,' he said, his focus slipping past my shoulder. 'Ah, Maisie, did you get it?'

The young maid, radiating excitement, came running up behind me, a large paper bag in her hand. On closer inspection, I noticed it was a brand of flour.

'Goodness, you are a man of many talents. Don't tell me you're planning on doing a spot of baking while you're here?'

He laughed, a deep spontaneous rumble. 'I don't think Cook would appreciate my efforts. Maisie, perhaps you could help me, you're nimbler than I am.'

Maisie was more than happy to oblige. Sheers directed her up the stairs to the half-glazed door on the landing. He then instructed her to retrace her steps backwards, all the while scattering the flour before her, until the landing and each step was completely covered. She looked aghast at the prospect of such wanton mess but set about the task anyway.

'Does Lady Brightwell know you intend to cover her house in baking products, Mr Sheers?' I asked.

'Lady Brightwell is happy for me to do whatever is necessary to disprove the fanciful notions flying about,' Mr Sheers assured me, watching the girl spread the flour with a broad sweep of her hand. 'Don't leave any gaps now, Maisie,' he called up, resting on the newel post.

'I confess, I'm intrigued, Mr Sheers. What is the purpose of all this?'

'Ghosts don't leave footprints, Miss Marcham, mischievous maids do. I have a feeling this flour might have a restful influence on Greyswick's marauding spirit.' He had the audacity to wink as he listed my way. 'I suspect we will all sleep soundly tonight.'

He was wrong.

The sound, all too familiar now, ripped me from my sleep. I stiffened. There it was again – weeping. I flung back the sheets, my drowsiness banished as I scrambled from my bed. Pulling down my rucked-up nightdress, I hurried across the room, gathering up my wrapper on the way.

The thrill of vindication was not enough to keep my trepidation at bay as I stepped out onto the dimly lit landing. I heard it again: crying – snuffling, whimpering, crying. With trembling hands, I pulled on my gown, yanking the satin sash tight about my waist. My heart beat so strongly I was certain the vibration must be visible through the flimsy material.

Mr Sheers stood, still fully dressed, at the bottom of the nursery staircase, its flour dressing a blanket of grimy snow in the wan moonlight. He shot me a look as I approached. The night's dark growth of stubble contrasted starkly with his drained cheeks.

'You hear it?' I asked.

'I do.'

'Is it your imagination, Mr Sheers?'

'I've switched on the gramophone, so we'll know soon enough.'

I looked down at the wheeling disc on the contraption at my feet. 'You don't need that to tell you the truth.'

'Suggestion is a powerful thing, Miss Marcham.'

He opened his mouth to continue, but a new sound punctuated those heartbreaking sobs, staunching his words. Familiar creaking now cleaved the frigid air with its grim repetitive rhythm.

'Stay here,' Sheers instructed.

He grabbed the newel post and swung himself up onto the first step, causing the flour to drift. I had no intention of letting him investigate alone. I wanted to see things for myself, not be subject to his biased reporting, but when I announced my intention he told me in no uncertain terms to stay where I was. With an air of defiance, I took the first step, silently daring him to stop me. He muttered an expletive under his breath.

'Mind the bloody flour then,' he cursed as he hauled himself onto the next tread.

My palm was slick on the banister. I was careful to tread only in the brown lakes left by his shoes as they disturbed the flour. The comforting moonlight from the arched window below dissipated with each upward step, until we were enveloped in darkness on the galleried landing. The nursery stood before us.

The sobbing drifting out from under the closed door began to quieten, but the rocking cradle maintained the slow, hypnotic tempo of a metronome keeping time. The soft hairs on the back of my arms had risen like hackles, and I was sure Sheers could hear my heart thudding against my chest – I fancied I could hear his.

I stifled a shriek as the servants' door began to rattle. I recognised the outline caught in the golden smear behind the frosted glass.

'It's Annie, she can't get out.'

'The door's been locked,' Sheers hissed, 'to minimise activity.'

'Unlock it.'

He looked at me in disbelief. The sobbing had ceased now, but the creaking persisted. The air was harsh with rimy chill, and I was beginning to shiver, my bare feet, dusted with flour, aching from the icy boards. My growing discomfort fired my irritation.

'For God's sake, Mr Sheers, look at your precious flour. Except for our footsteps it's untouched. Unless Annie can levitate, she can't have interfered with anything up here. Let her out!'

Airing his frustration with a few choice words, he stalked over to the glazed door, pulling a key from his trouser pocket. He struggled to find the lock in the gloom, but the key eventually slid home and Annie slipped past him, bright ginger hair trailing down her back in a corrugated sheet. She frowned as she noticed the powdery carpet, but there were more extraordinary events for her to worry about, and she wisely passed no comment.

We clustered in heightened expectation. Gentle crying began again. Only our laboured breaths and the insidious sounds seeping from behind the nursery door pierced the frigid air. Sheers gripped the doorknob. He hesitated for a beat, then twisted it round.

The crying stopped as the door gaped open. A shaft of silver moonlight pierced the centre of the room, streaking in through the dormer window, spilling about the wooden cradle like a theatre spot. The cradle itself rocked gently, side to side, creaking with each list.

Sheers muttered another expletive, his muscles as strained as guy ropes pulling taut in a storm. Even Annie, always the epitome of tranquillity, appeared unnerved.

The cradle stopped.

Nobody moved. None of us spoke. The air became thick.

Annie jerked by my side. Her eyes flared with panic, her mouth opening and closing in a futile attempt to speak. I called out her name in horror as guttural noises escaped her throat, her hands struggling about her face, wiping, pushing and clawing as she fought against an unseen foe.

'Dear God, Annie! What is it? What can I do?' I lurched to catch her as she collapsed to her knees, the blood draining from her cheeks, her eyes sliding frantically, her narrow chest heaving in desperation. 'For God's sake, help me!' I implored Sheers who stood beside me, ashen but alert. 'Do something!' But he shook his head. In that split second I identified the flint in his expression: suspicion.

I grabbed her shoulders as her eyes rolled backwards, the bags underneath them so devoid of colour I could distinguish the tiny thread veins laced within them, turning purple as I watched. Her hands slowed their struggle and dropped to her sides, folding against the floor.

'Lay her down,' Sheers instructed, urgent now and courting a degree of concern.

Annie's lifeless body flopped back onto the floorboards. Her eyes rolled again. She wheezed for air. I had seen seizures in France, but I knew whatever was happening to Annie had no medical explanation. As I looked on in horror at her blue tinged features, an unwelcome thought forced its way into my mind: she looked as if she was being suffocated.

They show me things, each in their own way, so I can under-stand what they've seen . . .

I thought of her hands swiping about her face, desperate to free herself of something. The rocking cradle that rocked no more. The dead baby – *it's blue*. The dead baby in the cradle. Hands pushing. Straining. Unable to breathe. Clarity shot through me like an electric charge: smothered.

For a moment I was paralysed. I gaped, shocked by the gruesomeness of it all, my mind labouring to process such inconceivable evil.

'No . . . it can't be true . . .' The hoarse plea fell from dry lips, but as I looked down on Annie's starved face, every vein in her cheeks now a streak of fading blue, I knew I was right – and it was my only hope to save her.

'I understand.' The words emerged as a faint croak. 'I under-stand,' I said with more force, addressing the charged air around me. 'Let her go.'

Nothing happened. Annie's chest was still. She was giving up the fight, surrendering to the terrifying force dominating the room. I swallowed back my mounting terror and tried once more.

'The baby was smothered – I understand. Please let her go!'

Annie's body arched upwards with such violence I was thrown back. An excruciating wheeze raked her lungs. She coughed and gasped, her eyes dark and bulging, her hands scrabbling at her sides, her fingernails raking the floorboards, scuffing at the varnish, until at last the blood vessels in her cheeks began to recede and a pink flush coloured her stricken features. She lay on the floor, panting, weak as a new-born kitten.

'Say it's not true . . .' I begged as I cradled her head in my lap, stroking her hair, eager for her to deny it all – yearning for her to do so. Solemn eyes met mine; her very silence tore at my soul.

The door slammed shut. I started – and so, I noticed, did Sheers, but I was too preoccupied with the shocking truth to find any dry humour in his skittishness. I twisted round to look up at him, anger flaring in my chest.

'Well? Are you satisfied yet?'

He didn't answer. He limped to the door and flicked a switch. Moonlight and shadows were swallowed by the luminescence of the single bulb strung above us.

'It was quite a show,' he said.

'A *show*? My God, you saw her, she nearly died.'

He folded his arms across his broad chest. 'I have seen mediums collapse to the floor convulsing, appearing to spew up ectoplasm – mere parlour tricks designed to fool the gullible with little more than spittle and cheesecloth.' He shrugged his shoulders and pulled a dismissive moue. 'She held her breath very convincingly, I'll give her that, and you managed to draw some very creative conclusions, but yes, a show all the same.'

'This is ridiculous.' I helped Annie to her feet. She wobbled, and I slipped a supportive arm around her back before confronting him. 'What of the rocking cradle?' I demanded. 'What of the crying? Really, Mr Sheers, what exactly will it take to convince you?'

He grinned, a spontaneous boyish grin that vanished with such speed I might have imagined it. He crossed to the cradle and began bouncing on the floorboards. The cradle did not move.

'I'm sure there is a logical reason for all of it, Miss Marcham.

I will have to see whether the crying recorded. In answer to your question, that might be enough evidence to satisfy me.' He stopped testing the floor. 'But so far, I remain unconvinced.' He crossed the room, clearly intending to leave. He addressed me for a final time. 'If you want my honest opinion and some free advice, get rid of that light-fingered little actress and I think you'll find this nonsense will soon come to an end.'

He pulled the door wide open and stopped dead.

'Mr Sheers?'

When he failed to respond, Annie and I drew forward, until the three of us crowded the doorway, looking out onto the landing.

There, muddled amongst the tracks and scuffs of our own feet, were the perfectly preserved footprints of a small child.

Chapter Forty

I cleared my throat. 'I think Annie will accept that apology whenever you are ready, Mr Sheers.'

'What the hell . . .?'

I didn't attempt to answer him. I squatted down and touched the first imprint. It was perfect – the scoop of the heel, the bend of the foot, the tiny toes.

'Where's your camera?' I asked.

'I left it on the landing. I'll go down and get it, take some pictures while these are still fresh.' He couldn't hide his bewilderment. Like a blind man who could suddenly see, the world around him took on new meaning, as he was blessed with a clarity he had never dreamt of.

'I'll fetch it for you,' I offered, the thought of his torturous journey down and back again too much to bear.

He nodded his thanks, distracted as he struggled to comprehend the enormity of those small footprints.

'This can't be. There must be a child – a live child – in this house.'

'There isn't, Mr Sheers.'

'Ghosts don't leave footprints!' He immediately regretted his raised voice, his loss of self-control. His eyes darted about, desperate to avoid the terrifying proof, but in the end, they were drawn downwards, unable to resist the evidence before them. 'Are you trying to tell me it's all real? The crying? The cradle?'

'Well, it would appear so.'

'Then why does no one else in this house experience anything?'

I started down the stairs, taking care with each step, so as to leave the precious prints intact.

'Annie has a theory – that Lucien doesn't choose to make himself known to them.' I kept my voice light, not wanting to wake the slumbering household.

I could have done of course, and part of me wanted to – to hammer on their doors and demand they look upon the evidence of the little life lost but lingering. But tonight's revelations had exposed a new dreadful twist in the tale, and I needed time to contemplate its significance.

Sheers apologised to Annie as I made my descent. I appreciated his humility – it was only right, after all. I found the camera waiting on the landing, already primed, the flash powder ready. I made quick work of my return, eager for the irrefutable evidence to be captured for posterity. Annie and I huddled in the nursery until he had finished. Agreeing no more could be done for the time being, we separated for what remained of the night.

Sheers and I, both of us stifling yawns, made our careful descent. Adrenalin was ebbing from my body now, and as the first rays of dawn tinged the sky a heathery pink, I realised how exhausted I was. Sheers must have been dead on his feet, for he'd been on watch the whole night. As I reached my room, I advised him to get some sleep.

'Miss Marcham, is there anything else I should know? Anything you haven't told me?'

'I think you know everything I do, Mr Sheers, the question is surely how you choose to interpret it.'

'But what you said in the nursery – do you realise the implications?'

'Can you honestly ask me that? Don't you think I know? This house is full of terrible secrets, Mr Sheers, secrets the dead are no longer content to let lie.'

A tortured breath escaped him as he rubbed at his temple. 'So, we're saying there is no doubt? This house is haunted?'

'After tonight, after those inexplicable footprints, how can there be any denying it? This house is haunted, Mr Sheers. Now we must find out why.'

Despite being deprived of sleep, I woke at my usual time. I was keen to get on, so I washed and dressed without summoning Annie; I had looked after myself in France after all – the more I thought about it the more it struck me as absurd that I did not do so now.

I met Mr Sheers on the stairs, coming up as I was descending for breakfast. I knew at once something was very wrong. His dark eyes blazed, and his mouth formed a thin angry line within his freshly shaven face.

'Have you seen the staircase? They've gone. Everything's gone.'

'I'm sorry, Mr Sheers, you've lost me.'

'The footprints.' He hobbled up a step, close enough for me to detect the woody notes of his aftershave. 'Mrs Henge swept them all away this morning.'

'What? Why?'

'She claims the flour was getting traipsed into the landing carpet and presuming it had served its purpose she cleared it away.'

'But she must have seen Lucien's prints.'

'Apparently not.'

'And she cleaned it up herself? Not one of the girls?'

'Herself, she said.'

'Now tell me that doesn't strike you as suspicious,' I retorted, appalled by the news. 'But you still have the photographs?'

'I do – if they come out. The conditions last night were hardly ideal. I've converted one of the storerooms downstairs into a darkroom – I was just on my way now to collect the film.'

'And what of the recording?'

'I've yet to listen to it.'

'Well then, we must hope you have captured some evidence, one way or another.'

Mr Sheers promised to find me as soon as he had more news. I carried on to the dining room, deflated by the loss of the footprints. I had been reluctant to share them in the night, but in the cold light of day, I longed for the vindication they would have afforded. Instead I now found myself dwelling on Mrs Henge's suspicious actions. The dining-room door was ajar as I reached it, and my hand was on the panel to push it open, when a hissed conversation stopped me in my tracks.

I held my breath and angled my ear closer to the draughty gap. I snatched a quick glance up and down the corridor to ensure that I was quite alone and in no danger of being discovered, but the corridor was empty; the woman who inhabited its shadows was ensconced within the dining room – and she was not alone.

'What was I supposed to do? They belonged to a child.'

'Dear God . . . How is that possible? What devilry is this, Constance? What can it mean?'

'I don't know. I can make no sense of it, Ruth. We should have left this place a long time ago.'

'I can never leave this house – you made sure of that.'

'Would you have preferred the alternative? What I did was done for the best.'

'Whose best?' Wounding spite dripped from the companion's tongue; even from behind my wooden shield I sensed the housekeeper's flinch.

'All of it comes back to her!' Mrs Henge retaliated. 'If she had just acted all those years ago—'

'I will not see her punished for her part in it all, not by you nor by anyone else.'

Miss Scott's vehemence pushed me from the fissure. Fearing detection, I backed away and retreated along the corridor on soft fleeting steps, having no desire to be caught listening at doors, once again learning secrets I did not have the where-withal to understand.

Chapter Forty-One

I was deeply troubled by what I had heard, and I churned the conversation over in my mind. Of one thing I was becoming increasingly convinced: behind the crass grandeur and tasteless opulence, the walls of Greyswick were infused with so many secrets and lies that the very fabric of the building breathed deceit. Last night's revelation had stunned me. There seemed no end to the horrors that had occurred within the auspices of this awful house, and I was more determined than ever to uncover the truth.

But how could I possibly hope for success when the crimes had been committed over a generation ago? I was faced by an overwhelming task, but I took some comfort from the fact that within this raging torrent that engulfed me there were nuggets of gold, occasionally catching the light through the swirling waters above. I felt certain that if I panned through enough grit and dirt, they would be left, gleaming, ready to reward me for my industry. And of course, I did have a very particular asset – I had Annie Burrows.

I rang for her in the afternoon and insisted she sit with me for a while, to escape the multitude of menial chores Mrs Henge was punishing her with. She rested, diffident, on one of the chairs flanking the bedroom grate, while I took the other. I wasted no time in relaying the curious information I had gleaned from my morning's unintentional eavesdropping. Her snub nose wrinkled in concentration and when I was done, she sat back, her self-consciousness easing as she chewed over my account.

Miss Scott, it turned out, was an infrequent visitor below-stairs, but Annie had noticed when she did appear Mrs Henge was most attentive, though a discord clearly existed between the two. Miss Scott's integral sweetness soured in the housekeeper's company, while her visits always left Mrs Henge looking disappointed, as if a tempting piece of cake had failed to live up to expectation.

Annie's observations, added to my own, drew me to the conclusion there was a long and complicated history between the two women, and I was beginning to suspect their present breach had its roots firmly in the past. For the time being we appeared unable to make any greater in-roads into the whole mystery. Annie expressed a hope that her new friend, Billy, might be able to assist us further on the matter and I encouraged her to speak to him as soon as an opportunity afforded itself.

I paced my room after she left me, navigating its edges, crossing its width, like a caged tiger. I was too preoccupied to remain confined. I decided to make the most of the dipping light and headed outside for a snatched cigarette before it leached away completely.

The restorative solitude of the parkland to the front of the house beckoned me as I heaved open the front door. Dusk was settling in, and I wouldn't have long before the ink of night swallowed me, so buttoning up my cardigan, I scuffed down the broad stone steps, my eyes set on the horizon.

I was surprised to hear my name called, and I turned to see Mr Sheers propped against the porch wall, a smouldering pipe in his hand, the collar of his tweed jacket turned up against the bite of the evening air. He righted himself and crunched across the gravel towards me. He gestured with the pipe, admitting he too had needed something to settle his discomposed nerves – it had not, he informed me, been a good day. It turned out that the gramophone had not captured the crying. When he listened back to the shellac disc that had spun so promisingly, he had heard only the harsh crackle of static.

When I enquired about the photographs, his expression flattened with disappointment once again. The film, developed in the newly established darkroom, had merely revealed over-exposed images.

'So, we have nothing?' I cried. I hadn't intended for there to be any criticism in my voice, but he winced as if I blamed him personally for the failure.

'We will have to try again – if we get the opportunity.'

I couldn't hide my frustration. I would have relished being able to confront Lady Brightwell and the others with some tangible evidence, but we were chasing little more than will-o'-the-wisps, what had I expected? Angst churned in my stomach.

'There is a story here, and we must get to the bottom of it. We must decipher these clues. Madeleine will never be able to return if we don't.'

'You are very worried about your sister.'

'I promised I wouldn't leave until it was safe for her to return.'

'Miss Marcham, it may simply prove impossible to unveil the truth.'

I refused to shoulder his negativity. 'No, Mr Sheers, I will not rest until I have discovered what happened. I must – I owe Madeleine that. You couldn't possibly understand but without her . . .'

'I think perhaps I understand more than you might appreciate.' He paused before proceeding with caution. 'Hector did his best to explain your sense of debt.'

My flare of embarrassment was damning and instant. I nudged the toe of my shoe into the gravel, unable to bear the compassion I saw drawn across his aquiline features. He cleared his throat, realising he had crossed some invisible line and was now regretting his blunder.

'I suspect we are both tortured souls, Miss Marcham.'

A harsh bark escaped me, a strange chimera, half-laugh half-sob, which, to my relief, I managed to quell. 'I'm sure we both have our stories to tell, Mr Sheers.'

He reached to the side, and for a bizarre moment I thought he was going to put his arm around me, but instead he tapped his pipe against the pillar of the porch beside me, knocking the spent tobacco to the ground.

'Well, if you will tell me your story, Miss Marcham, I will gladly tell you mine. We can be tortured souls together, for once.'

He was not smiling, and whilst his words had been delivered with some levity, shimmering under the surface was something else – a willingness to share experiences, an offer of understanding. The invitation to unburden myself to someone who had been there, been to hell and seen the death and devastation first-hand, was overwhelmingly attractive.

Had I ever attempted to properly tell my story before?

Perhaps, half-heartedly, but each time I had tried – with my parents, with Madeleine, with Dr Mayhew and his cronies, even – I could see the lack of comprehension – *appreciation* – in their eyes. They were incapable of recreating the scenes I described, those scenes that haunted my every waking hour. How could they? I was glad they had never endured the experiences I had been forced to endure. So when I spoke, I always halted, hesitated, edited and redacted – in short, I sanitised my story for their benefit, allowing them to continue life in blissful ignorance, free from nightmares and atrocious images that no man, woman or child should ever have to see.

But before me now stood someone who did understand, who had seen such things, and who was offering to hear it all, to take from me my burden of death, blood and pitiless war. His mind's eye would be able to conjure the images seared into mine. He would appreciate the horror of the film that played incessantly before me. Dear God, he would *understand*.

'It's chilly standing here, will you walk with me?' He held out the crook of his arm, and I took it. He folded it against him, drawing me in to his side. I took warm comfort from the smell of his pipe tobacco – so redolent of Gerald's – the wool of his tweed jacket, his sandalwood cologne. He offered a solidity that was irresistible.

He tugged on me with each ungainly step, but neither of us mentioned it as we walked out into the twilight, away from the golden glow cast from the windows. We walked the length of the house in silence, then broke away from the building to take a path that led towards the arboretum. Somewhere, from across the park, a nightjar's churring song pierced the fading light and a fox bark echoed from the woods in the distance.

He did not encourage me to talk, but when I felt moved to do so, I began – stutteringly at first, then with increasing courage. I told him of Gerald and of our courtship. I told him how excited we had both been to give our services to our country – our naive enthusiasm for war. I told him of my various postings, the thrill of growing independence and self-determination, and how I had inched closer and closer to the action, seduced by the perceived drama of the front. I told him of the exhilaration, the exhaustion, the camaraderie, the humour – for there is always humour to be found in a theatre of war, a dark-souled humour that facilitates survival.

And finally, I told him of that day, the day my nightmares were created.

A big push was on the way and we were warned to prepare for casualties. We cleared the wards as best we could, then we waited, listening to the distant rumble of exploding shells, the prelude for what was to come.

The convoys began to arrive early in the morning. A wave of wounded men, caked in mud and blown to bits, surged into the hospital, filling it with their agonised groans, calls for water and pleas for anything to take away the pain. We were soon overwhelmed, dashing from patient to patient, as exhausted orderlies left men on stretchers because there were no beds to be found. And yet still the convoys kept coming. Operating theatres became conveyor belts of hacking, filleting and drilling, as limbs were amputated, spilt intestines reinserted, and skulls bored with drills. All effort was made to alleviate suffering, though in most cases it was futile. Too many of the poor devils were heading west.

Sister called my name and hurried me to a side room of gravely wounded men.

'The MO has had a quick look, but he doesn't hold out much hope for any of them. Do what you can. He'll come back when he gets a chance,' she promised, racing away.

The three of them at least had beds, I thought, as I took a deep breath and approached the first pitiful soul. Shrapnel had ripped away his side and from the smell that hit me I knew infection had already set in. I cleaned him, applied fresh dressings to his wounds and whispered some words of comfort before moving on – there was nothing else I could do. Brutal experience told me he would be gone before the hour was out.

The next fellow was already dead when I got to him, so I covered him with a sheet and moved on to the third man, heaped on the bed by the far wall.

He was mumbling to himself as I approached. Two field dressings had been crudely applied, one positioned to the side of his head, the other over his forehead and eyes. His uniform was stiff with mud and splattered with blood. Soil embedded the pits of his skin and his fingernails were black. I saw straight away from his shoulder straps that he was an officer.

'Right, Lieutenant, let's get you cleaned up, shall we? We'll have you right as rain in no time.'

I ran my scissors along the length of his uniform, snipping it away, trying not to recoil at the sight of lice crawling all over it. When I had cast off the filthy clothing, I began to wash him. I drew the sheet over his cleansed body as I finished.

'I'm sorry . . . It's a dirty business, this war . . .' The words scratched from his throat.

'Are you thirsty? I can get you a glass of water when I've done.'

He attempted to lick his lips, already dry and cracking. He thanked me as I began to gently clean his face below the bandages, washing away the rusty blood and dirt.

'My fiancée's a nurse, you know. When you spoke . . . your voice . . . I thought . . .'

And that was the moment I realised.

My heart ceased to beat, and I began to quiver. I felt the blood drain from my face and there was a strange buzzing in my ears, as I stared at the bottom half of the officer's face. My lips parted but I couldn't speak, my throat too narrow.

'I'm going to remove the dressing from your eyes,' I managed at last.

I was all fingers and thumbs. I steeled myself as I lifted the grubby lint away. It was sticky with blood and gore. The right eye had been shot through. What remained was a mushy mess all mixed into the eyelashes. The left eye though was perfect. My hand flew to smother my whimper.

'Stella.'

His exhaled breath carried my name. I began to shake, tears blurring my vision.

'Gerald . . .'

My fingertips tentatively touched his cheek, wiping away the tear that ran from his eye.

'I'm so sorry . . .' he said.

'No, no, no, my love . . . please don't . . .' I tried to pull myself together. 'It's going to be all right . . . I promise . . . it's going to be all right.'

I forced myself to focus. I needed to see the extent of his

damage. I set to on the second field dressing. I drew back. The bullet that pierced his eye had left the skull just beyond his right ear. From the ominous hole oozed bloodied matter and creamy fragments of skull. I gasped, snatching up a fresh dressing. I applied it the best I could, impeded by my trembling hands.

'I can't believe you're here . . .' Gerald whispered.

I leant down to him, gripping his shoulders. 'I am here, my darling, I am here. It's going to be all right . . . it is . . .' I choked.

'Oh, Stella . . .' His eye closed and I froze. For an awful moment I thought he was dead, but the dark lashes retreated once again. 'I love you . . .'

'I'm going to get the doctor,' I said, righting myself and dashing away the tears from my cheeks. 'I'll be right back . . . don't . . .' But I couldn't finish the sentence. There wasn't a second to lose as I ran from the room.

The corridor was heaving. Walking wounded propped themselves against the walls; sisters hurried past carrying steel kidney bowls, their contents hidden by cloths; and harassed VADs scurried to their next task, smears of blood on their tunics. I ran past all of them, glancing into the side wards until I found an MO, a young Scottish doctor who I knew and liked.

'You must come now!'

Taken aback, he hurried after me as I retraced my steps, my heart pounding, fear the like of which I had never experienced heightening my senses, as foolish hope bloomed.

He looked at me in surprise as we entered the room, as if he could already see death waiting patiently in the corner. Detecting his change of heart, I seized his arm.

'*Please.*'

'I've already . . .'

'You hardly looked at them.'

He frowned. Against his better judgement, he allowed me to lead him to Gerald's bedside.

The doctor spoke kindly to him. Gerald, his voice weaker than before, struggled to reply. The doctor lifted the dressings and examined his wounds, his expression grim as he replaced them. He patted Gerald on the arm and throwing me a look, withdrew through the doorway. I joined him in the corridor outside.

He shook his head. 'I'm sorry, nurse, but . . .'

'He's my fiancé!'

'Then for God's sake, tell him you love him,' he said gently, 'and stay with him . . . he's not long for this world.' He laid his hand on my arm. 'Be with him while you can.' He looked so terribly careworn as he walked away.

My knees crumpled, but I reached for the wall just in time and steadied myself. I managed to stand, still reeling from the unreality of it all. I would not believe him. I could not. There would be a miracle. My Gerald would show them all. I was sure of it.

'Are you there, Stella?' he asked as I hastened back to him, his voice so faint I could hardly hear it.

'Yes, yes, Gerald, I'm here.' I clasped his hand in mine and perched on the side of his bed.

'I'm glad . . . I got to see you . . . one last time.'

'You're not . . . you're not dying, Gerald,' I insisted, though my tears belied the statement. The bandage at the side of his head was already soaked with blood and fluid.

'Live . . .' he sighed.

'Yes! Yes! My darling!' I gasped, leaning forward. 'You are going to live!'

His eyelid slipped shut again as a sad smile pulled at his lips. 'No . . .'

Every word, every breath was becoming an effort, I could see that. I urged him to save his strength, but his eyelashes fluttered open again.

'*You* must live . . . Stella . . .' A breath rattled in his throat. I could hear the tackiness in his mouth as he fought to form the words he was so desperate to speak. 'I must go . . . but you must stay . . . and *live your life* . . .'

A sob escaped me. How could I do that? I could not live – not without him.

'Are you still there, Stella?'

I gripped his hand tighter, closing the gap between us until my face hovered above his.

'I am here, Gerald. I am still here.'

He frowned, staring blankly at my face. 'I can't see . . .'

I stroked his cheek and murmured his name, my tears dripping onto his skin.

His chest lifted. I heard a slight breath slip in his throat. He was still. His eye darkened.

I had lost him.

And I hadn't said 'I love you', when it mattered most of all.

Chapter Forty-Two

Mr Sheers offered me no banal words of comfort. He just
listened as I went on to tell him about the days after Gerald's
death: my disgraceful return home and the overwhelming grief
that followed. I even confessed my desire to die, now the life
I had planned and dreamed of had been taken from me by a
single German bullet.

When I finished, he looked ahead into the encroaching
darkness, his breathing rhythmic. I thought I felt an almost
imperceptible tightening of his arm on mine, but then again,
I might have imagined it. When we had drunk in the silence,
he spoke.

'I'm sorry.'

So devastatingly simple, but so heartfelt, his words brought
tears to my eyes. I was grateful for the low light.

'And you, Mr Sheers? What's your story? How did you end
up with that burdensome leg of yours?'

My delivery was deliberately brusque and insensitive, and I
saw from the grin that exploded across his face that he appreciated it.

'Shrapnel. Amiens, last year.'

I waited. He snorted, amused I was not going to let him
get away with such a brief summation after my lengthy essay.

'It was an early morning advance. We'd been waiting for

days, and finally the order came. The ladders went up and the whistles went off. I remember feeling relief when I blew mine, glad to be doing something, rather than just sitting around, waiting for death in the mud. I was sick of the trench, sick of the squalor, sick of the rats, the lice, the stench. I was even sick of the men – sick of being surrounded by them, never alone. I just wanted to get on with it, get it all over and done with, no more hanging about. I'd given a rousing speech, sent round the rum . . .'

He stopped. Apologising, he uncoupled me from his arm, as if he didn't want me to absorb his misery through some sort of osmosis. He took a couple of steps away, settling his focus on the band of trees in the distance, though a sharp plunge of his eyebrows suggested he was seeing a different landscape outlined before him, one where the only singing in the air was the whistle of descending shells and the zing of bullets.

'I'd been over maybe ten minutes when I got hit. One of the men, a chap from Durham called Burns, was a few feet ahead of me. The resistance we were encountering was greater than expected, but then, it always was.' The murky light shadowed him. 'Anyway, Burns took one in the shoulder, the force of it jerked him round. He looked straight at me, grinned, swore, and turned back to carry on walking. Then he just disappeared, vanished, in a cloud of smoke, dirt spraying in all directions. I felt something slap into me, but I thought it was just, you know – clods, stones. My knees buckled, and I fell. I couldn't hear a thing – my ears were just ringing – and the smoke was choking me. Then I felt the pain and I looked down and saw my leg, cut to pieces, just an ugly mess of flesh and bone, strips of torn cloth and blood – lots of blood. Are you sure you want to hear all this? It's terribly dull, you know.'

My voice had deserted me, so I just nodded.

'It's getting quite dark. Perhaps we ought to turn around. I hope we're not going to be late for dinner, her ladyship rather terrifies the life out of me.'

He came back but made no attempt to offer me his arm this time. He kept his hands in his pockets and we walked side by side.

'Anyway,' he continued after we'd retraced our steps a short way, 'I dragged myself into the crater and was soon joined by some other poor sod who'd had his ear shot off. He managed to tourniquet my leg, which was a good job because I was getting rather woozy by then. We waited there until nightfall. When the Hun had finally stopped shooting and bombing, and all we could hear was the wounded moaning, he dragged me to the top of the crater. He threw me over his shoulder and carried me all the way to our trench. Bloody hero. Saved my life, no doubt about that.' He fleetingly glanced my way. 'The rest, as they say, well, the rest is history. Doctors took one look and lopped off my leg. Sent home. Nice prosthetic care of King and country' – here he tapped the wood that lay beneath his trouser leg – 'and, well, months of learning to walk again. That's my story. That's the end,' he finished, shooting me another grin.

What could I say? I'm sorry? I'm sorry you lost your leg, I'm sorry you're crippled, I'm sorry you saw your friend obliterated before your eyes? In the end I said nothing, but let the silence convey all that I felt, all that I wished. Instead, I asked him how he came to be doing what he was doing now – investigating the paranormal.

'I had a brother, Will.'

Here my sympathy was instinctive, but he waved away my condolences, and I realised this was territory he was less callous about. This was not the bearable loss of a leg, it was far worse than a sacrificed limb – this was a brother, a friend, a cohort in the misdeeds of youth. I thought of Lydia, and I shared his pain.

'He was younger than me – and in case you're wondering, by far the better man.' A hank of hair slipped down over his forehead and he pushed it back. 'My father swears that Will appeared to him when he died.'

I didn't bother to try and conceal my astonishment. He was obviously quite used to the reaction and held up his hands by way of tempering my shock as he continued to explain. 'My father was reading in the garden and looked up from his book to see Will standing by the gate. He was in full dress uniform and my father thought he must have got some leave. So, he jumped up, all excited, and called for my mother through the back door, but by the time he'd turned around Will was gone.' He paused, a sorrowful breath easing from him. 'They received a telegram two days later saying he'd died of wounds sustained.'

I reached out to touch his arm in sympathy, but he stepped away, leaving my hand to fall.

'My father became obsessed with similar tales of boys appearing to loved ones at the moment of death. He took comfort from them, believing them to prove that life continues in some way, but I've seen life ebb away from enough young men to know there is nothing beyond. When I came home, it was difficult – to see them carry such hope, such absurd belief. We fought.'

'And so, this work of yours . . .'

'Actually, my father encouraged it. It was his challenge to me. I think he thought if I immersed myself in enough enquiries I would start to see the truth. Instead, I made it my absolute goal to debunk as many money-grabbing mediums as I could and provide logical explanations for these so-called manifestations – and I've been very good at it.'

'Until now.'

He grabbed my hand, his fingers biting into mine. 'I don't want to believe, Miss Marcham. I want things to be straightforward, simple: death is death. I can't stand the thought of the men I stood beside – the good men I saw fall – wandering hopelessly, miserably, in some never-never land existence. I need to know they are gone and gone for good, that they truly feel no more pain, feel no more fear. What's happened here has jeopardised the only comfort I've been able to take – that there is an end, a solid, unfeeling, nothingness end.'

I cupped our joined hands. 'But you can't deny what you have encountered here?'

He tore himself free of my grasp, spinning away from me. He ran his hand through his hair in abject despair.

'No, I can't. And it terrifies me.' I almost missed his confession, the words stealing into the cool night air, but as if to make sure I had absorbed their significance, appreciated his torment, he whirled back to face me. 'It absolutely bloody terrifies me,' he clarified for good measure.

We had reached the porch now, and bearing the weight of his confession between us, we mounted the steps to the door, the oily black paint glistening in the flickering light of the braziers that burned either side of it.

I hesitated, my hand on the large brass handle, eager to say something to ease his anguish.

'I am determined to fathom all of this out, Mr Sheers. And maybe then, I will be able to offer you an answer to your quest.'

'Tristan.'

I blinked. 'I'm sorry?'

'My name is Tristan. You don't have to keep on calling me Mr Sheers. It makes me feel terribly old and quite frankly I feel old enough.'

'Oh.' I blinked again. 'Then you should call me Stella.'

'Stella.'

He seemed to savour the sound of it on his tongue, before turning to face down the darkening night as it drew ever closer, holding it at bay while I entered the dubious protection of Greyswick, alone.

Chapter Forty-Three

The atmosphere at dinner was somewhat taut. Lady Brightwell, now returning to form, pithily bemoaned our continued presence, leaving us in no doubt that we were most unwelcome houseguests. She refused to temper her opinions and Miss Scott was left to mop up the spillages of her foul temper and frustration. It was a relief to have Tristan as an ally. He took her ladyship's comments with remarkable good humour – indeed his gentle jousting was so successful that in one unguarded moment Lady Brightwell chuckled at his riposte. I nearly choked on my wine.

After dinner, he kindly forewent his cigar and brandy to offer me support in the drawing room. Placing himself beside me, he enquired after the title of my book and on hearing the answer, took it from my hands, extolling the virtues of the author as he flicked through its pages. He was about to return it when he spotted the handwriting on the inside leaf. Only after he had read the inscription did he close the book and pass it back to me; I found I was unable to meet his eye.

We did not tarry long after dinner. Miss Scott chivvied Lady Brightwell to bed as soon as she saw her head begin to droop, and Mr Sheers and I were happy to follow. We parted company on the landing, with Miss Scott escorting Lady Brightwell to her rooms in the new wing, whilst Mr Sheers and I retreated into the older part of the house.

'Will you be keeping a vigil again tonight?' I asked as I hovered outside my door.

'I think I ought to, though there's no telling whether it will bear fruit. I can't stay here for ever; I think Lady Brightwell's patience is beginning to wear thin, but I would like to discover something definite before I go.'

'I fear my time is running out as well,' I admitted. 'I'm no detective, Tristan' – his name felt unfamiliar to me, and my tongue seemed to tease it out – 'I'm not sure I know where to begin, but I must – for Madeleine's sake. I must somehow find a way to the truth.' And with that I bid him goodnight and good hunting and let myself into my room.

I am dreaming of Gerald, and whilst I ache with awareness that it is just that, simply a dream and as such unsustainable, my heart is tumid with happiness. Gerald's face, perfectly conjured in intimate detail, leans towards me, his lips slightly apart beneath the dense hairs of his moustache, as he presses them to my cheek . . .

I woke with a gasp, my fingers brushing the icy impression that scalded the soft flesh just above my jawline. I scrabbled to sit up, fighting to free myself from the tangle of sheets sticking to my damp body. It was then that I saw it: my open door. In my heart of hearts, I knew it was not Gerald who had visited me.

Ignoring the flutter of unease, I forced myself out of bed, thinking only of Lucien and what I might learn, rather than the fear his unnatural abilities provoked. Even so, my fingers trembled as I tightened the belt of my wrapper and stepped into the shard of light that cut across my carpet, my feet shunting forwards.

Sheers stood just beyond my room, coiled for action.

'Your door opened of its own accord not five minutes ago,' he said by way of greeting.

'Lucien,' I whispered. A thread of excitement stitched through me. We both reacted when we heard a door creak open on the nursery landing, and I emitted a small mew of relief as I saw Annie scampering down the stairs, her bare feet tugging from the treads.

'My door opened.'

'As did mine,' I informed her. She nodded, keen yet wary.

'What now?' Sheers asked.

The wall lights began to flicker and dance. Glacial air swept around us. My spine tingled as I recalled the touch of those icy lips on my cheek.

'He must be here,' I gasped.

'He is.' Annie glided between us, her focus fixed before her.

'Dear God, you can see him?' Tristan demanded, but she did not respond.

The wall lights began to buzz, as if agitated wasps were thrumming against the etched glass of their shades. They dipped and flared the length of the landing. The bulb nearest me popped and died, with the next one down following in quick succession. Pooling darkness replaced pulsing radiance.

'What the . . .' But Sheers' question died as the next light blew, then the next, and the next, until only silver moonlight lit our end of the corridor. Annie drifted forwards, drawn to the artificial golden glow that remained, but as she drew abreast of the next wall sconce, it too fizzled and died. Entranced, she moved on.

'Breadcrumbs!' Tristan exclaimed. 'She's following the blown lights. He's leading her somewhere.'

With mounting excitement, he snatched up his camera and thrust it into my hands, before heaving the gramophone up into his arms, his muscles strained by its cumbersome width and weight. Wincing with effort he limped towards me, urging me to pursue Annie, who was now disappearing down the main staircase. I felt a niggling concern over how he would manage the contraption on the stairs with his leg, so I slowed my descent until he safely reached the bottom.

We were just in time to see Annie disappear from the hall into the new wing.

'After her,' Tristan hissed through gritted teeth, sweat beading his brow.

The marble tiles were blisteringly cold against the bare soles of my feet, incentive enough to fly across them, leaving Sheers in my wake, his laboured breaths echoing in the darkness. Annie stopped before the smoking room, her hands hanging at her sides. The door creaked inwards.

'Did you see that?' My heart was in my throat as Sheers wheezed to a standstill beside me, as stunned as I was by what we had just witnessed. The brass horn knocked his chin as he shifted the weight of the gramophone. Shoulder to shoulder, we advanced.

Annie stood in the centre of the room. I called her name, and she swung to face me. The moonlight spilling through the blank windows threw into relief the confusion scrawled across her features.

'Is Lucien here?' I asked, half-expecting a spectral figure to materialise before me – almost longing one would – but she shook her head.

Behind me, Tristan set down the gramophone. A couple of

seconds later, the chandelier burst into light, causing me to cry out, but he sheepishly admitted responsibility – he had spotted the light switch by the door.

I put the box brownie upon a chair and took a moment to absorb my surroundings. It was the first time I had ever set foot in the smoking room, having only previously managed a glimpse from the doorway as Madeleine whisked me around that first day. It had the feel of an exclusive gentlemen's club, with its oak-panelled walls, its leather wingback chairs and chesterfield sofas. A grey-veined marble fireplace dominated the far end of it, the two picks crossed like sabres above its mantel, testimony to Sir Arthur's mining fortune. Heavy brocade curtains were swept back from the windows by ropes of cord as thick as my arm, revealing the black beyond, while the vast Abyssinian rug spread over the floorboards reeked of wealth.

The room left me with an indelible impression of raw masculinity – bawdy jokes, cigar fumes and the sour taint of intoxicating spirits. As a woman, its ambience made my skin crawl, and the musty vapours of disuse compounded its lack of appeal.

'Why are we here?' I asked Annie.

As if in answer to my question, the chandelier began to flicker and fade, before beaming again. There was a curious charge in the room and the air around us began to agitate in a most peculiar manner. My heart quickened as the chandelier stuttered and dipped again, only to explode into light a second later. Behind me, Tristan switched on the gramophone, and the shellac disc began to rotate slowly on the deck.

'Do you see anything, Annie?' he asked, his voice low. Annie shook her head, her crinkled red hair fizzing around her shoulders. Her eyes narrowed, as she watched the chandelier pulse above us.

'But he's trying to tell us something,' she said.

'What? What's so important about this room?' I whispered.

The chandelier hummed as it once again regained its glow, dazzling us with its brilliance.

'Miss Marcham?'

I spun round, startled by the unexpected interruption. Mrs Henge stood in the doorway, her face pinched, her mouth puckered like a drawstring purse, her eyes scanning the room, certain we were up to no good.

'What are you doing here?' I gasped, my cheeks bearing the flush of a naughty child caught red-handed.

'I heard Annie leave her room. When she failed to return I decided it might be best to see what she was up to.' She scowled at the maid, who cast her eyes to the floor. 'I didn't want her getting into any mischief.' She inserted a droll note into her voice, but the smile she summoned was malicious. 'May I ask what you're doing in here?'

Tristan came to my rescue.

'It's part of my investigation,' he said, returning to the gramophone, the disc still spinning slowly on its top. 'But I think we're done now.'

'It is very late to be running around the house,' she replied, her brows beetling as Tristan pressed a switch to stop the record's movement. 'I wouldn't want her ladyship to be disturbed. She is still recovering, after all – it is essential she gets her rest.'

Sheers hoisted the device up into his arms, tipping it against him. 'Quite.' His eyes slid my way as he headed for the door. Mrs Henge stepped aside to let him pass.

I went to retrieve the box brownie, but the housekeeper beat me to it, striding into the room, the knotted cord of her dressing gown swinging from her waist like a hangman's noose. She picked the camera up, turning it in her hands before passing it to me.

'You shouldn't meddle with things you don't understand, Miss Marcham.'

'Lucien Brightwell means us to find the truth, Mrs Henge.'

'Lucien Brightwell is dead. Should you not leave him be?'

'He will not leave us be.'

It was Annie that answered her. To my surprise, the housekeeper's austerity wavered for a second, as if she saw something in the young girl's face that inspired fear.

'I have served this family for most of my adult life. I will not have their peace disturbed, and I will do whatever necessary to ensure their best interests are met – as I have always done.'

There was no disguising the implicit threat. I held her steady gaze until, with a smirk, she broke away to wait by the door, her finger resting on the light switch, a grey eyebrow hiked. I brought my palm to the small of Annie's back and guided her from the room.

The two of us didn't speak as we hurried down the corridor, our feet tacky on the harsh marble. As we crossed underneath the arch into the hall I looked back. Through the folds of shadow, I saw Mrs Henge close the smoking-room door. With a furtive glance our way, she extracted her ring of keys from the pocket of her dressing gown. Selecting one, she twisted it in the lock and turned to walk away.

Chapter Forty-Four

As much as I tried, I couldn't get back to sleep. I rose when the first rays of dawn filtered through the tramlines of my curtains. I washed and dressed myself before peeking outside. Unperturbed by the striking red sky that greeted me, I slipped on a fitted tweed jacket, having decided a brisk walk and some restorative fresh air might help untangle my thoughts.

The heels of my shoes clicked lightly on the marble flags as I crossed the hall floor into the vestibule. The great bolts on the front door grated loudly in protest as I pulled them back, bemoaning their early start. I headed out through the porch, down the steps and onto the drive, pausing only to debate which route to take.

The density of the mist rising from the dank parkland discouraged my initial plan to stroll out into the wilds. I decided instead to cut through the cobbled courtyard to the side of the house and head to the rear garden, its gravelled paths being far more practical than the dew-laden meadows. As I reached the courtyard's brick archway I saw Maisie at the back door, already dressed in her black and white uniform, accepting the contents of a basket from an older woman, who wore sensible sturdy shoes and a rather shabby overcoat, with a small but neat hat on her head.

It was obvious from their stark similarities and their clear familiarity that the woman was Maisie's mother. Not wishing to interrupt them by barging through, I hung back, resting against the cold stone as I afforded them some time, mulling over the ever-present conundrum of the dead baby and Lucien. As I did so, a thought sprang to mind, and fired by a burst of inspiration, I ducked into the courtyard – only to find it empty. The back door was now closed and there was no sign of Maisie's mother. I was just cursing my luck when I realised she must have left via the path to the stables, and sure enough, I saw her departing on that very route at a fair pace, already some distance away. Determined not to lose this unexpected opportunity, I set off in hot pursuit.

I was forced to run to catch up, and in the end, fearful she would outstrip me, I called her name. Her rapid steps stuttered as she looked around in surprise. Seeing me, she obligingly came to a stop.

'Can I help you?' she called as I approached, panting from my exertion.

I laughed at my own disgraceful lack of fitness, planting my hands on my hips as I struggled to catch my breath. 'My goodness! You do walk fast!' I laughed. 'Stella Marcham, how do you do?' I held out my gloved hand, a broad smile splitting my puce cheeks. 'I'm Mrs Brightwell's sister.'

She hesitated before transferring the basket so she could shake my hand. Her grip was firm, and the no-nonsense set of her mouth and the intelligence in her eyes warned me this was not a woman to be trifled with.

'Hannah Probert.'

'You're Maisie's mother?'

'I am.' Threads of red burst through the weathered skin on the swell of her cheekbones.

'I wonder whether I might walk with you for a moment?'

Her brows dipped into the cleft above the long narrow nose that rather dominated her features. 'If you wish,' she said.

We did not make easy companions as we started down the drive. She was clearly bemused by my presence and made no effort to engage with me as I played with the cuff of my glove, uncertain where to begin.

'I understand you used to work at the house,' I said at last, gesturing back over my shoulder, where the sun's early rays were attempting to cheer the grim grey brick of Brightwell's fantasy.

'That's right. Long time ago now,' she said, keeping up her unrelenting pace.

'Maisie told me you were a maid too?'

'I was.'

We entered the shade cast by the avenue of trees that lined the drive, their leaves whispering above us, sharing secrets of their own. I expressed my interest in the good old days that Maisie had alluded to, but Mrs Probert didn't take the bait. Instead she offered me a curt smile, no doubt hoping I would scamper back to the house if given no encouragement, but I was not so easily deterred.

We were passing the stable block now, which was set back from the main drive. A young lad with his cap tipped back emerged from under its stone archway leading out a towering Shire horse, bedecked in a leather harness decorated with brasses that jangled as it shook its blinkered head. The shoes on its huge feathered hooves rang out as they clipped the stone and we stopped to let them pass. Spotting Mrs Probert, the lad's forefinger touched the tip of his cap and she gave him a pursed smile and a sharp nod. The horse's thick tail switched round its broad undulating rear, chasing away a lethargic bluebottle warming up for the day. As soon as they were clear, Mrs Probert resumed her departure. Rolling my eyes, I hurried to catch her.

'I am intrigued, Mrs Probert, by the advice you gave to Maisie when she came to work here.'

'What's the foolish girl been tittle-tattling about now?'

'Maisie said you warned her to avoid Sir Arthur – I'm curious as to why?'

The end of the drive was in sight, and she seemed to be calculating her chances of escape.

'I don't like to speak ill of the dead, Miss Marcham,' she said at last.

'Well, I won't tell if you don't.' It was a flippant response on my part, but I hoped an attempt at humour might reverse her uncommunicative stance, and it appeared my gamble had paid off. A wry glint lit her eye. A moment later she shook her head, and a begrudging smile loosened her tightly drawn mouth.

'Very well . . .' The tone she adopted was that of a weary mother capitulating to her nagging child. 'Sir Arthur was a typical man, I suppose. He had a roaming eye and a tendency for roaming hands too. So, having experienced them myself once or twice, I thought it only right to warn my girl what to expect – I doubted age had changed him.'

'Did he ever harass Maisie?'

'No, thank God!' she exclaimed. 'My Bill wouldn't have stood for that if he'd caught wind of it.' She shrugged her shoulders, broadened by labour. 'I don't know, maybe he had mellowed with age. Maybe he knew who my girl was and thought best to steer clear.'

'But when you worked here, as a young woman yourself,

you were aware he . . .' I chose my next words carefully, '. . . acted inappropriately. . . with some of the girls?'

She twisted to face me, distrust narrowing her features and hardening the line of her jaw. 'You're asking a lot of strange questions, if you don't mind me saying. Why should you care what Sir Arthur got up to? The man's been in his grave a good few years, what use is it hanging out his dirty laundry now?'

'Mrs Probert, forgive me, but I have very good reason to ask you this.' My nerves were mounting for I was acutely aware of the sensitivity of my next question. 'Did Sir Arthur . . . is it possible that Sir Arthur might have got one of the maids into trouble – in the family way?'

I held my breath as I awaited her answer, but I saw it before she spoke – a flicker of unwanted knowledge that crossed her face in the split second before she schooled her features to match her blank denial.

'No.'

I took a step closer.

'Mrs Probert, please – to your knowledge, has there ever been another baby – a baby other than Hector Brightwell – at Greyswick? It's so terribly important, please.'

The colour ebbed from the ruddy network scrawled across her cheeks. 'No,' she reiterated coldly, her hostility tangible as she backed away from me.

'Mrs Probert—'

'Forgive me, Miss Marcham, I don't know what your game is, or why you find it necessary to ask such questions, but I can't help you. Now if you don't mind, I need to get back. I've got pigs to feed.'

And before I could say another word, she took off, her basket banging against her thigh with each long stride as she passed through the gates to disappear down the lane. I watched her go, curiosity twisting inside me as I turned to retrace my steps. She had tried to hide it, but I had seen it in her face. Maisie's mother knew something.

I had just reached the carriage sweep when the front door was flung open and Sheers came hobbling down the steps to meet me. There was an urgency about his movement that pricked my attention and hurried me towards him. His handsome features split into a broad smile.

'My God, where have you been? I've been looking for you everywhere!' His bubbling excitement was infectious. As soon as he was close enough he grabbed my hand and practically dragged me to the open door. 'You won't believe it. Dear God, I can scarcely believe it myself.'

'What?' I laughed, stumbling up the steps after him.

'And it's not just me,' he grinned. 'Annie can hear it too.'

'What are you talking about?'

The dull hallway was chilly after the gentle warmth of the early morning sun. He led me through to the study, where Annie stood beside the gramophone, which had been set upon a table. The same wondrous excitement illuminated her own freckled face.

'Come, come,' he urged, closing the door behind me. 'We don't want anyone sneaking up on us.'

'Miss, it's amazing.'

'Will one of you please tell me what on earth is going on?' I said, as Tristan escorted me across the room.

'This is what we recorded last night,' he said as he pressed a button on the machine, setting the turntable in motion. The engraved disc upon it began to rotate beneath the stylus. There was a constant rhythmic rasp of static before clumping noises reminiscent of some sort of kerfuffle. 'Don't worry about this bit, this is when I had it upstairs on the landing,' Tristan explained. I went to speak but he held up his hand to stop me. 'Now hang on, yes, this is where it gets turned off and I lug it downstairs. Starting up again now, in the smoking room . . .' He reduced to a whisper as he drew his commentary to a close. He held his finger to his lips to deter any further questions, his head cocked to one side. Annie, too, inched closer. I listened to the resumption of static, deafeningly loud and rather unpleasant – and then I heard it.

My heart staggered as my jaw quite literally dropped on its hinge. Mystified, I looked first to Tristan, then to Annie, and back to Tristan for confirmation, but the eruptive euphoria on both their faces told me all I needed to know.

Amongst the harsh static I had heard a voice – a soft, high-pitched child's voice, an expelled breath cutting through the din. It had uttered a single word:

Here

Chapter Forty-Five

Light-headed I reached for the table to steady myself.

'Are you all right?' Tristan's euphoria was replaced with concern as he switched off the machine.

I assured him I wasn't unwell, I was quite simply mystified. Captured in a groove on a shellac-coated disc was the voice of a boy who had been dead for over twenty years. My dull brain was struggling to fathom how that could even be possible.

'Is this what you hear?' I asked Annie.

'Yes, but, no . . . not like this. When *I* hear their voices, they're trapped in my head. To hear a voice like *this* . . .' She shook her head in wonderment.

'So what does it mean?' I asked, perplexed. 'What's "here"?'

'Whatever he's trying to tell us, the smoking room holds the key,' Annie said.

'Mrs Henge holds the key,' I retorted. I met their confused stares. 'I saw her lock the door last night. I doubt she'll be keen to unlock it again any time soon.'

'Well, we have to get back in there, one way or another,' Tristan declared. 'For whatever reason it's significant to Lucien.'

I told them of my conversation with Mrs Probert, and my absolute conviction that she knew more than she was willing to let on. We also discussed whether we should share the existence of the recording with the others, but after the incident with the footprints we decided the record needed to be safeguarded, and the best way to do that was keeping its content secret for the time being.

I was keen to persevere with Mrs Probert and proposed to visit her that afternoon. I suggested that Annie accompany me, in the hope a joint appeal might prove more successful. Tristan, meanwhile, intended to revisit the architectural plans, now fearing he had missed something of significance during his initial inspection. So decided, we parted, all of us more determined than ever to decipher the clues that Lucien Brightwell was laying out before us.

Using a little flimflammery, Annie and I managed to glean Mrs Probert's address from Maisie and were readying ourselves to depart when Lady Brightwell and Miss Scott came down the stairs, themselves dressed for an outing.

I hailed Lady Brightwell's apparent return to full fettle and enquired whether they were off somewhere nice, deciding some bonhomie might go a long way, given the circumstances. Diplomatically ignoring Lady Brightwell's ill-tempered scowls, Miss Scott informed me they were visiting the vicar to discuss the flower rota.

'The displays have been somewhat meagre lately,' she confided, 'which has quite distressed Lady Brightwell.'

'I don't care if there is a war on,' her ladyship barked, her voice displaying no detrimental effects of her recent illness, 'there is no excuse for letting standards slip.'

The vestibule door rattled open and Mrs Henge swept in, like a carrion crow fresh upon a carcass. She eyed Annie and me with distaste before attending Lady Brightwell, informing her that the car was waiting out front. Seeing we too were preparing to go out, she waspishly offered to have the dog-cart sent for. I thanked her for her most generous offer but assured her such luxury was not required as we wanted to stretch our legs and enjoy some fresh air.

'Are you going anywhere in particular? Perhaps we could drop you somewhere if you are heading towards the village? There are some lovely walks from the churchyard,' Miss Scott suggested, only belatedly thinking to seek Lady Brightwell's approval for the plan. Her ladyship did not look best pleased. I explained we wouldn't be going as far as the village.

'Well then, where are you intending to go?' Lady Brightwell demanded. I dodged the question, not wishing to reveal our actual destination. 'Well, there is plenty of fresh air to be had in the grounds. You may have noticed they are quite extensive.' She tapped her cane on the marble floor. 'Why, before my stroke I would walk for miles every day and never have need to leave the estate.'

But those days were over. The enduring effects of her afflic-tion were blatantly clear as we followed her from the house. She was now reliant upon her stick and Miss Scott stayed in close attendance in case further help was required. Mrs Henge oversaw our departures from her perch on the top step of the porch. I could almost feel her hooded stare boring into my back.

The promising brightness of the morning had taken on a threatening yellow hue as Annie and I started down the drive, the air close and heavy, compounded by the fug of exhaust fumes and spewed-up dust, gifts from the departing car. A bank of leaden storm clouds moved in from the west, and as the wind picked up a parliament of rooks took off from a cluster of oaks in the park, cawing raucously.

The entrance gates creaked as we passed through them, buffeted by the mounting breeze. We took the lane leading to the village until we reached the stile that broke the hawthorn hedge on the left. Following Maisie's instructions, we climbed over to find ourselves in a field of brown and white cows, peaceably chewing the cud. Avoiding sloppy pats colonised by marauding metallic-green flies, we made our way across, letting ourselves out through a wooden gate into the rutted lane beyond. The bulbous heads of sprawling mayweed thrashed against our boots as we strode towards the low-slung farmhouse that stood before us, smoke winding from its chimney.

A lichen-spattered stone wall adorned with cascades of mauve flowers separated the front garden from a farmyard bordered with ramshackle buildings. I battled with a sticky latch on the picket gate. It pitched alarmingly when I finally managed to release it, giving us access to the flagged path leading to the front door. A rambling rose had been trained around the lintel, and it already boasted a few peach blooms, heady with scent. I raised the brass knocker and rapped it heavily against the wood, my stomach churning with nervous anticipation.

We heard approaching footsteps. There was a screech of dormant bolts being yanked from their beds. A key turned with difficulty in the lock. I smiled as Mrs Probert regarded me with a flash of astonishment that soon morphed into hardened wariness. Her simple dress, its sleeves rolled to the elbows, was covered by a pinafore bearing an unpleasant red stain, and her feet were adorned with threadbare slippers.

'Miss Marcham, well, this is unexpected. What can I do for you?'

'Mrs Probert, I do apologise for calling on you unannounced

like this. I was wondering whether my maid Annie and I might perhaps come in for a brief word?'

'What about?'

'I was very much hoping to continue our conversation from this morning.'

'I've said all I have to say.' She began to close the door.

'Please, Mrs Probert, it's very important.' I pressed my hand against the paint-peeled wood. 'You're one of the very few people who can help us.'

'Help you with what? I'm sorry, Miss Marcham, but I don't know why you're wanting to ask all these strange questions – the past is the past, God knows we've got enough going on in the present to keep us occupied. I suggest you go and do something useful rather than dredge up what has been.'

This elusive reference was all I needed to reinvigorate my campaign. I left my palm against the door, prepared to battle my way over the threshold if necessary. I was determined to wrangle from her what she knew, one way or another.

'Mrs Probert . . .'

'You should let us in, Mrs Probert.' The gentle timbre of Annie's voice was so at odds with the mounting acrimony that it stopped both Mrs Probert and myself in our tracks. Her eyes were feverish, yet otherwise she appeared placid. 'There is an older woman with you – she thinks it would be for the best. She knows all about the lost souls of children – but your two are safe, she has them with her. And you should get some new slippers – wearing those . . .' she gestured to the ones on Mrs Probert's feet, 'won't bring her back.'

The sturdy farmer's wife blanched. Her whole body began to quake.

'What did you say?'

'Please, Mrs Probert, may we come in?'

I wasn't sure she had heard me – I wasn't even sure she was listening. Annie's strange message had taken a profound toll on the woman before me. The wind whipped a handful of dead leaves into the house, and at this she gathered herself. She pulled the door wide open and we stepped into the narrow grey-flagged hallway. Closing the door, she shuffled around us to lead the way, past shut-up rooms, to the gaping doorway at the end of the hall.

We came out into a large kitchen. Dried posies of herbs hung from the fierce-looking hooks that studded the beams above our heads. A black range occupied the inglenook fireplace and before the window was a deep ceramic sink with a sturdy copper tap.

In the middle of the room stood a pine table. At one end, bundled together, lay four dead chickens, their thin necks stretched, the heads with their black sightless eyes lolled to the side, their sharp beaks open in silent protest. The kitchen window above the sink was slightly ajar and a cool breeze ruffled the birds' ruddy-brown feathers. There was a bucket at the foot of the table containing blue coils of intestine and glistening lumps of maroon-coloured organs and I realised that the putrid smell hanging in the air was that of discarded innards mixed with a hint of turps. The hessian sack next to the bucket was filled with feathers, and on the table above it was the stipple-skinned carcass of the chicken she must have been plucking before our arrival.

'Sorry, it's a bit of a bad time,' she mumbled, picking up a large kettle from the range. She began to fill it under the gushing tap. 'I'll make some tea.'

The stench was making me queasy and the prospect of lingering by the corpse-covered table was decidedly unappealing, so I assured her that neither Annie nor myself required a drink.

'Oh . . . are you sure?' She still seemed somewhat dazed. 'Oh, right then.' She abandoned the kettle on the drainer and looked at the table, as if seeing it for the first time. 'Well, we can't stay here. You'd best come through.'

Much to my relief, she ushered us into one of the closed-off rooms we had passed earlier – a sitting room which appeared to be kept for best, its stuffiness suggesting it hadn't been aired in a while. The furniture was of good quality. The sofa and chairs were protected with antimacassars, the dresser gleamed with polish and a bow-fronted display cabinet was crammed with china and trinkets. Mrs Probert took a wooden armchair next to the grate and indicated for us to take the sofa.

'What is you want then?' She directed the question to me, but her wary eyes were fixed on Annie.

'Mrs Probert – how do I begin?' I apologised for ambushing her earlier and admitted my abrupt questioning wasn't perhaps the most appropriate way of broaching such a difficult subject.

I paused, pondering how much detail to give away, how many secrets to reveal. I had no reason to suspect her of being a gossip, but what I had come to discuss was highly sensitive and I had a fear of idle chatter finding its way to the village. I was handling explosives, and I needed to proceed with utmost care to avoid a tragedy.

'Some curious things have been coming to light recently, up at the big house, and – well, we're just trying to get to the bottom of it all, for everyone's sake. I can't go into full detail

– I'm sure you'll understand why – but all I can impress upon you is how important it all is.'

She may have been listening to me, but Annie remained the subject of her intent focus. As I stopped speaking she seemed to remember her manners, and, with some reluctance, favoured me with her attention.

'Mrs Probert, we are trying to establish the identity of a baby we believe to have been born at Greyswick. Not Hector Brightwell, of course, but another baby, perhaps one not every-one is aware of – perhaps one that ought not to have been there at all.' I hardly dared ask my next question. 'Would you know anything about that?'

Outside the window the branches of a silver birch were flailing in the increasing wind, its pale green leaves sparkling as they fluttered. The attractive image caught Mrs Probert's eye, and she watched it for some time, her fingers playing with the hem of her apron.

'There was another baby,' she admitted at last.

'Below-stairs?'

'If you like.'

'Was it . . . had Sir Arthur fathered the child?'

It didn't take an expert to decipher the dilemma written all over her face. The woman before me knew something, some secret, a secret she had nursed for over twenty years, a kernel of truth she had stifled within her for all that time.

'It's really not my story to tell.'

'Mrs Probert, please, please help us.' Suddenly I had a hor-rible thought, and aghast I blurted out, 'Oh Mrs Probert! It wasn't your baby?'

Her head jerked up. 'Good God no! It wasn't mine – but

it's not right for me to talk about it. You should be asking her yourself.'

'Who Mrs Probert, who should we be asking?'

'Why, the babe's mother, of course.'

The wind was howling down the chimney now. Annie and I exchanged glances while Mrs Probert focused on her fidgeting fingers. I took a deep breath.

'Who is the baby's mother, Mrs Probert?'

'Miss Scott. Miss Scott was the baby's mother.'

Chapter Forty-Six

'Miss Scott?' I echoed in shock.

Mrs Probert nodded just once.

'Dear God.' A bewildering array of evidence lay scattered before me, tantalising fragments which when assembled would form an intricate mosaic of the truth, but vital parts were still missing. I had to find them. 'Mrs Probert, you must tell us what you know, it's imperative.'

'I don't even know with absolute certainty that I'm right.' Perhaps regretting her indiscretion, she attempted to back-pedal, but it was too late. She had lifted the lid on Pandora's box, and there was no replacing it now. 'I hate gossip,' she said, throwing herself back against the chair. She gripped the curved ends of its polished arms. 'I've always told my Maisie to watch that wagging tongue of hers, and here you are asking me to tittle-tattle, and I don't even know you from Adam – I don't even know that I've got the baby you're after!' she declared with a hint of defiance now. 'Miss Scott's baby was never actually at Greyswick.'

'What do you mean?'

I didn't mean to be sharp, but the last few days had shredded my patience and set my nerves on edge and this convoluted dance with Mrs Probert was not helping my humour any. I disliked talking in tongues at the best of times – I just wanted her to be frank. I decided to adopt a more direct approach.

'Look, Mrs Probert, the cat's out of the bag so to speak, so why don't you just tell us what you know and then we can decide whether we're talking at cross purposes. I promise you now, whatever you tell us will be treated with the utmost confidence.'

I was in no position to make this last pledge, but I offered it up as an inducement. It appeared to be ample balm for her conscience and she let out a sigh of defeat.

'Well, it looks like it's the only way I'm going to get rid of you, short of throwing you out!' She scowled. 'All right then, but this is just between us. Like I say, some of it is me putting two and two together and maybe I've made five, I don't know.'

The wind gusted now against the walls of the house, rattling the windows in their frames. Beyond, the branches of the birch tossed wildly. Mrs Probert sighed again as she collected her thoughts, opening her album of memories, lifting the tissue sheets that protected each precious glimpse of the past from the destructive effects of time.

'I was an upstairs maid responsible for, amongst other things, Lady Brightwell's room. I'll tell you now, there isn't much a servant doesn't know in a big house like Greyswick. I must have been one of the first to realise she was expecting. I was responsible for collecting her napkins, you see, and I noticed there weren't any one month. I spoke to Miss Scott about it because I didn't want to have missed anything, but she confirmed what I already suspected. The mistress had just fallen, but it was far too early to be presumptuous and I certainly didn't want to tempt fate. Miss Scott asked me to keep it quiet and I was most happy to do so.'

She sat forward, crossing and uncrossing her ankles,

uncomfortable with the whole torrid affair. Annie and I stayed quiet, while she fidgeted herself back into a place of calm from which to continue. The room was growing darker and darker as the threatening clouds continued to mask the sky, shielding the sun.

'It wasn't long after that conversation when one night I bumped into Miss Scott in the servants' corridor upstairs. I'd popped up to get something from my room, and when I came out she was just standing there in a complete state, crying and shaking. I asked her what on earth was wrong, but she couldn't control herself long enough to tell me. Well, I didn't know what to do. I took her into my room and sat her down, but I couldn't seem to do anything to comfort her.' The colour drained from her cheeks. 'It was awful.' It was a hushed admittance, delivered in the deferential tones one talks of death. 'I'd never seen a girl so upset before.'

We all jumped as rain struck the window, clattering as the heavens opened. Distracted by the ferocity of the storm, we paused to watch in wonder as it lashed down in thick sheets, blown diagonally by the same vicious wind whipping the trees. Mrs Probert made a shocked observation on the severity of it all before continuing.

'She managed to ask me to get Mrs Henge. I ran downstairs and found her in her office and told her Miss Scott was in a terrible state and that she ought to come. Well, she went deathly pale and hurried upstairs. I trailed after her because I didn't know what else to do – and Miss Scott was in my room after all.'

Her cheeks took on a guilty hue, afraid we would think ill of her for inveigling her way into another woman's misery. I didn't care – I was just glad she had.

'Mrs Henge was shocked to see Miss Scott like that. She went straight over and put her arms around her. I don't think they realised I was there, to be honest – I just stayed in the doorway. I knew they had a . . . special . . . friendship.'

Ill at ease, she rose from her chair and busied herself repositioning the shepherdess figurine that graced the mantelpiece.

'Miss Scott said that Sir Arthur had, he'd . . . he'd forced himself upon her.' She turned back to observe our horrified reactions. 'Mrs Henge realised I was still there at that point. She pushed me from the room and told me in no uncertain terms that if I wanted to keep my job I'd best keep my mouth shut. Well, you don't disobey Mrs Henge and I certainly had no intention of losing my position, so I did as she bade me: kept quiet and got on with my duties.'

The rain continued to slap against the window. My heart ached as I thought of poor Miss Scott and the unforgiveable violation she had been subjected to. But I thought too of Mrs Henge, flying to her side, and the closeness that Mrs Probert had alluded to. I wondered why it had waned over the subsequent years.

'How awful.' It was a feeble and inadequate summation, but I didn't know what else to say – how did one even attempt to capture the horror, the violence of it all? 'But why do you think there was a baby?'

'Oh, there was a baby all right.' Done at the mantelpiece, she returned to her chair. Perching on its edge she pitched forward to confide further secrets. 'Perhaps others wouldn't have noticed, because, well, for one thing, they didn't know what I knew – and you have to remember Miss Scott was a slender thing, even more so than she is now. Women like that, they can go full term and hardly show. Me, I was the size of a house by the time I was four months gone!' She permitted herself a wry chuckle.

Fragments of soot, dislodged by the rain, clattered down the chimney. One pinged across the tiled hearth and Mrs Probert tossed it back into the blackened confines of the grate.

'I noticed, though. Some mornings Mrs Henge would send me up to tend to Lady Brightwell because Miss Scott was feeling "unwell". And I noticed other changes – it's inevitable things alter when you're in that state. Oh, she hid it well and she had everyone fooled, I'm sure, but not me. And then the next thing you know she's given leave to look after her parents, conveniently ill. That Russian 'flu proved most timely,' she added.

She picked a piece of lint off her skirt. 'She'd been sent away to have the baby.' She paused, deciding whether to elucidate further, but I could see she was in the thick of it now and had a misplaced pride in her powers of deduction. She couldn't resist showing us just how clever she was. She pitched forward again. 'I thought back on it then, you see, worked it all out. She would have been about seven months, and the mistress no more than eight. And then a couple of months later, back she comes, looking healthy and well.'

'But she can't have brought the baby with her,' I said.

'Of course not. I dare say she had it adopted by some couple or other. That's how these things are usually done, isn't it? But this is what I'm saying – that baby was never at Greyswick, so how can it be the baby you're after?'

It was a conundrum, to be sure. I had come hoping for answers and yet I found I was floundering in a mire of confusion.

But there was one more topic I hoped the former maid might be able to assist me with. Her loaded comment about Mrs Henge had not escaped me, and it gave new meaning to the other piece of advice she had given to her daughter, which only now echoed through my memory: *'be sure not to catch Mrs Henge's eye'*. I didn't need to say much for the farmer's wife to grasp my inference. She harrumphed as she settled herself back in the chair.

'She could be as bad as him, if she took a fancy to you.' There was clearly no love lost between her and the housekeeper and she showed none of her earlier reticence. 'But it's different with a woman. The contest is a bit more equal than with a man, isn't it? A few sharp words and she'd soon back off. She and him were as thick as thieves, of course. I suppose she'd served Sir Arthur for so long she knew all his proclivities and he all of hers – they accepted them, pandered to them. I think she made a point of taking on girls who would appeal to him, but when Miss Scott appeared, well . . .'

She tapered off. I had learnt by now to wait, and sure enough, in due course, she continued. 'She was like a lovesick girl around her.' Her lips quirked but there was no humour in the expression, only sour disapproval. 'She would fawn and flatter, it was almost embarrassing. I'm not saying it was anything more than an affectionate friendship. To be quite honest with you, I was never completely sure whether Miss Scott was driven by the same *inclinations* or whether she was just flattered. But one thing's for sure, that night she just wanted Mrs Henge, and I have no doubt it was Mrs Henge who made all the arrangements for her when the time came. She would have looked after her that way.'

She stood up, signalling our time in the past had come to an end, that the album of memories contained no more snapshots – at least none she was willing to share.

'Now that really is all I can tell you. I don't mean to be rude, but I have work that needs to be done.'

Annie and I stood, thanking her for taking us into her confidence, though we remained dazed by what we had learnt. Mrs Probert led the way through the array of furniture to the door. I spotted a photograph of a young man in uniform and I stopped, lifting it from the dresser.

'Is this your boy?' I asked.

She nodded. 'Vic. He went last year, silly bugger. Didn't need to go, could've stayed here on the farm and done his bit feeding the country rather than fighting for it, but he wouldn't hear of it.' I didn't have to listen too closely to hear the pain in her voice. 'It can't go on for much longer, can it?' I couldn't meet her eye – the desperate appeal was too much for me to confront with any sort of honesty. I placed the frame back where I found it.

'No, no I'm sure it can't.' I hoped there was sufficient conviction in my voice to give her some degree of comfort. 'Have you just him and Maisie?'

'I had twins.' She turned her focus to Annie who was waiting patiently by the door. 'I lost them both to mumps when they were eight months old.'

I understood now why Annie's words had defused the woman's hostility and gained us access to her recollections. I followed her gaze to the self-conscious maid who, feeling the weight of our wonder, slunk closer to the wall as if willing to melt into it, out of sight.

The rain had subsided by the time we left the farmhouse, but great puddles from the shock storm pocked the yard. We decided to return via the farm lane rather than crossing the sodden field.

'Back there . . .' I said at last, curiosity getting the better of me. 'How did you . . . What did you do?'

'Not much. She was already there when Mrs Probert opened the door,' Annie said, keeping her eyes on the path before us. 'She hasn't been gone long – she's been hanging on, not wanting to cross over . . .'

'Cross over?'

She glanced up at me. 'That's what the dead need to do. They move on . . . unless something stops them.'

'Like Lucien.'

She nodded, brushing a stray strand of hair from her face. 'They have to be at peace to go.'

'And why isn't Mrs Probert's mother at peace?'

Annie shrugged. 'She's not ready yet. She's worried about her daughter . . . about her grandson. She wants to wait until it's all settled and he's safe . . . one way or another.'

There was something chilling but also achingly sad about her explanation. I thought, of course, of Gerald and I wondered whether he had chosen to wait – and I wondered whether it was selfish of me to hope he had.

'And where do they move on to?' I persisted. 'Is there a heaven? A hell?'

The corner of her mouth curled into her cheek, as her eyes danced with mischief. 'I don't know, miss. I've never had one come back to tell me.'

A car was approaching as we reached the road and we waited

by the verge for it to pass. The silver Rolls that was by now a familiar sight flew by us. I saw Miss Scott squirm round in her seat to peer through the rear window.

Noting our dry clothes her expression transformed from recognition to fear, no doubt wondering what we might have learnt whilst sheltering from the storm.

Chapter Forty-Seven

We had nearly reached the house when we spied a familiar figure loitering by the arch to the servants' courtyard. Annie's young soldier was leaning against the brick, his back hunched against us, a cigarette burning between his lips. He made no indication that he had seen us, and it would have been possible to pass by without his knowing, but like a greyhound eagerly snapping at the gate, I could tell Annie wanted to go to him. I was happy to indulge her – though I still nursed doubts about the wisdom of this budding romance. She promised she wouldn't dally long and as she scampered away it struck me again how young she was, and how foolish I had been at the same tender age.

I did not dwell on the topic for long. I was intent on devoting my powers of analysis, such as they were, to the material provided by Mrs Probert. I had been left shaken to the core by the defiling of poor Miss Scott. I now understood why Mrs Henge had spat on Sir Arthur's grave, and I had a powerful urge to do the same thing. I hoped he was rotting in hell somewhere, and I was glad no flowers adorned his tomb – a man like that did not deserve to be remembered. I could only imagine the torment the poor woman must have endured realising the assault had left her with child. But, as Mrs Probert had gone to great pains to point out, that child had never been to Greyswick – so how could it possibly be the dead baby in the cradle?

It made no sense to me whatsoever and raised a daunting question – had there been a further baby at the house that we weren't aware of? Or – and here I heard Mr Sheers' words, whispering harpies, in my ear – perhaps Annie had made a mistake. How I longed to make sense of it all!

Maisie greeted me as I entered the hall. She was obviously intrigued by my visit to her mother and gabbled away trying to elicit the reason for the call – once again I marvelled at the disparity between the two of them. I side-stepped her avid enquiries, mildly amused by her ill-concealed frustration, but it couldn't be helped – she would just have to sulk. Mr Sheers, she informed me when I asked, was to be found in the study. Handing over my coat, I went to find him.

He had certainly made himself at home since my last visit, rearranging the furniture to the edge of the room so he could spread upon the floor great tracts of architectural drawings – intricately produced line diagrams on mushroom-coloured paper – held down at the corners by ornaments purloined from around the room.

He had been trying to work out the possible significance of the smoking room, but from what he could see, there was nothing to differentiate it from the rest of the house: it utilised the same materials and had the same cavity wall structure. It appeared there was no benefit to this line of investigation.

I then brought him up to date with my own disappointing discoveries. I shared my discomforting intelligence with awkward embarrassment, and he received it in similar fashion. I found his muttered choice comments about Sir Arthur rather heartening.

'So, we're no further along then?' he concluded.

'It would appear not. Miss Scott deserves our absolute sympathy, but she had the baby away from here. I just don't see how it can be the same one that Annie saw.'

'And you're sure Annie . . . well, you're sure there can be no mistake?'

'I knew you'd say that.'

'But we do only have her say-so that there even was a dead baby.'

'Scandalous things have happened under this roof.'

'I'm not calling that into doubt. I'm questioning the detail.'

'Well, don't. I can't profess to understand it all either, but I do know that I have utter trust in Annie.' My hands flew up. 'Ugh! This is all so bizarre. How can we ever hope to make sense of it all, when we're dealing with the ghost of a child and his perceptions of past events?'

'Well, if not Annie, maybe Lucien himself made a mistake.' He barked with laughter. 'Good God, listen to me! Oh, the credulity I have come to.'

I smiled at that and experienced a tweak of curiosity as to what he may have been like before France, before the war. What would his life be now if an Austrian duke hadn't been shot and an antiquated arrangement of alliances hadn't dragged us all into years of mindless bloodshed? One thing was for sure, he wouldn't have been sitting in this awful house with me investigating the spirit activities of a dead child. It was absurd. Perhaps the only way to survive it all was to laugh. If I started crying, I feared I would never be able to stop.

We were interrupted by a knock at the door and Annie burst into the room bright with excitement, pleading for something to write on. Tristan, somewhat bemused, hurried behind the desk and after a short search discovered a carbon copy writing pad in a drawer. He tossed it onto the leather-inlaid surface sending the loose sheaf of blue carbon paper floating to the floor.

Annie gratefully accepted the pen he found, and I joined them at the desk as she wrote out an address. What struck me as odd was her writing. I can't say I had much experience of Annie's handcraft, but I had on occasion surveyed the laundry book at home, which she was responsible for. I was baffled to see the neat writing I had encountered in the lists of linens and clothing replaced by the untidy hand now scrawled across the ivory notepaper. I had little time to ruminate, however, for I was soon too distracted by the words themselves: Ivy House, Silver Road, Hackney.

'What on earth has that got to do with anything?' I asked her, as she set down the fountain pen.

'It's an address,' Mr Sheers observed – I thought somewhat unnecessarily.

'But how is it relevant?'

Annie shifted her weight and chewed at her bottom lip, trying to make sense of it herself. In the end she admitted she wasn't sure what it meant, just that Billy seemed to think it was of possible importance – it was an address he knew to be linked to Miss Scott.

'Doesn't he know any more than that?' I was rather irritated he had given us such a paltry piece of information and I couldn't see how it played into the mystery that was unfolding. I wondered whether there was something of greater value to be gleaned from the young man and suggested to Annie that it might be best if I spoke to him directly. She blushed and mumbled that Billy had already left, apologising for failing to get anything further from him. I made a poor show of hiding my frustration.

'Look, it's not the end of the world.' Tristan ripped the address from the pad. 'I've got to travel to London tomorrow anyway. I should be able to fit in a trip to Hackney while I'm there. Why don't I go and see what I can discover?' He shot me a broad grin. 'It'll be an adventure.'

'What are you doing in London?' I asked, disheartened by the prospect of his unexpected departure. It was not that I had come to rely on Mr Sheers' support, but I couldn't deny I drew some comfort knowing Annie and I were no longer alone in our pursuit of the truth.

Perhaps picking up my alarm, he reassured me with a gentle smile that he would be back at Greyswick by the evening. He had a medical appointment – with his 'leg quack' – which he could not miss. He already intended to pick up some more camera film from his supplier in Clerkenwell, so a diversion to Hackney, though unexpected, was not completely out of his way. He would still be back and ready for action should Lucien indulge in any further midnight mayhem.

I felt his gaze rest upon me as he concluded his speech, though I chose not to meet it – instead I busied myself picking up the dropped sheet of blue carbon paper.

As I opened the pad to reinsert it, I discovered a brief missive, its faint blue writing revealing it to be a copy of a letter written by Sir Arthur himself, unfiled and forgotten.

I might have once deemed it inappropriate to read a dead man's correspondence, but the name of the addressee caught my attention and I knew I could not afford this letter any privacy.

My eyes flew over the lines, my chest tightening with each

astounding word, until, quite breathless from shock, I reached the final flourish of his signature. My hand began to shake as I cast my eye back to the date at the top. The transformation in my demeanour had not gone unnoticed; Tristan asked me what was wrong.

'This is a dismissal letter written by Sir Arthur.'

'Dismissal of whom?'

'Miss Scott. And if I'm not mistaken, it was written the day before he died.'

Chapter Forty-Eight

I was in time to take breakfast with Mr Sheers the next morning. We were huddled at the far end of the table when Lady Brightwell and Miss Scott joined us. I tried so very hard not to look at the fluttery companion any differently as she fussed about her ladyship, but it was difficult not to think of her as she would have been all those years ago – a pretty, young maid encountering a lecherous master. Nearly thirty years later that same master would draw up an insouciant dismissal without consideration for what she'd suffered, let alone the lifetime of service she had dedicated to his wife.

It seemed safe to presume the letter had been presented the very day it was written – the author and addressee had both been under the same roof after all. But Sir Arthur was never able to enforce his decision – he was dead almost before the ink had dried, trapped in the mangled wreckage of his motorcar. Had it simply been overlooked? Had Miss Scott kept its contents secret? Had Lady Brightwell simply chosen to prolong her trusted servant's employment – which begged the question why had the letter been written in the first place?

Its discovery had thrown up so many questions. The gentle servant with her bird-like stature and quirky idiosyncrasies was a far more complex creature than any of us appreciated. How could she have remained under this roof after what had happened, bowing and scraping to the perpetrator of the heinous crime? Perhaps it was the threat of being dismissed without references, and the associated fear of impaired prospects that forced her to stay and suffer in silence. The very thought of it all made me feel quite ill, and as I watched her now, my heart went out to her.

She seemed out of sorts this morning, more distracted than usual, proving a butterfingers with the serving spoons, spilling food onto Lady Brightwell's plate and sloshing tea into her saucer.

On any other day, such carelessness would have provoked the old lady to caustic comment, but today she too was subdued, as if she had absorbed the unhappiness radiated by the servant who had become her friend. She had no harsh words, no bitter complaints or exasperated chastisements. Instead she induced her 'not to worry' and that there was 'no harm done' though later she eyed me with blatant distaste, as if she held me to blame for the poor woman's discord. And perhaps I was.

Tristan finished his breakfast and begged us to excuse him, so he might catch his train. The prospect of his imminent departure at last brought a spark to Lady Brightwell, but it was quickly extinguished by the assurance he would return in time for dinner. She entreated him not to rush back on her account.

Miss Scott ate very little and spoke even less. She nibbled half-heartedly at a slice of toast but soon abandoned it and instead, looking most dejected, supped a single cup of tea while Lady Brightwell finished her breakfast. In the end she whispered into her mistress's ear, who nodded in agreement. Casting me a scant glance, Miss Scott rose from the table, explaining she was plagued by a headache and was off to take some powders to alleviate it. I expressed my sympathies and wished her a speedy recovery.

'She is unhappy today,' Lady Brightwell said when she was gone, pinning me with an accusatory stare that had me wondering whether she might be privy to her companion's secrets.

'I'm sorry to hear that.'

'This insistence of yours – stirring up the past – it does no good, Miss Marcham. I am at a loss to understand exactly what it is you hope to achieve.'

'The truth, Lady Brightwell. Isn't that all any of us can hope to strive for?'

'Ahhh, but whose truth, Miss Marcham?'

'This house has become a repository of secrets and lies, Lady Brightwell.'

She leant forward, the tiny muscles about her eyes pinching. 'I thought you were here to chase ghosts?'

'Perhaps they are all the same – ghosts, secrets, lies. Just the residue of long-forgotten crimes.'

'Pah!' She pushed herself to her feet, snatching up her stick. She glared at me with utter contempt as she made her way to the door, her cane stabbing the rug, a precursor to each shuffling step.

'There are no phantoms in this house, Miss Marcham, only the ones you brought with you.' She stopped at the door. 'How many people must you upset before you realise you are doing no good here? I will not tolerate this upheaval within my household for much longer, no matter what my son, or your sister, might say. This is my home and always will be. Your malicious intrigues are not welcome. Your time here, my dear, is drawing to a rapid close.'

She slammed the door behind her, leaving me to choke on the vaporous hostility she so effortlessly expelled.

I was determined not to be beaten. I was in a steely mood by the time I left the dining room. I stood in the hall waiting for Annie to bring me my coat and hat, determined to be industrious, determined to leave no stone unturned, and there was one stone that I could investigate on my own.

Abandoning Annie to her plethora of chores, I struck out down the drive at a smart pace. Fired by irritation, I made short work of the walk to the village. I wasted no time turning the twisted ring of the lychgate, letting myself into the churchyard. I found my way back to Sir Arthur's weather-worn tomb, and I walked around it until I found the carved words I sought. Just to make sure there was no mistake I scrubbed away the green algae that had colonised the stone facing until the inscription was distinct and the implication unmissable.

A sturdy breeze ruffled the long grass about my feet, lifting the branches of the holly tree by the graveyard wall. I was right. The letter that should have turned Miss Scott out into the street, banishing her from Greyswick for ever, had been written the day before its author, the man who had raped her and fathered her child, had died in a terrible accident.

An unpleasant taste of bile stuck in my craw. Coincidence, perhaps.

But I had stopped believing in coincidences a long time ago.

I could not bring myself to return to Greyswick immediately. The possible implications of all I had learnt were bearing down on me, an unshakable burden, and I needed time to think. So I walked, without direction, across the fields, and into the woods, deliberating over all I knew. I could not avoid returning to the house indefinitely though, and as the morning slipped seamlessly into the afternoon, I found myself tracking back into the estate, past the now familiar meadows, until Greyswick itself reared before me, beckoning me back into its corridors of shame.

It was Maisie who dashed into the hall to greet me, relieved that I had returned in the nick of time, because Mr Sheers was on the telephone. I had an inkling he had made a discovery – otherwise I could see no reason for him to call, not when he was due back in a few hours' time. She trotted after me as I headed to the study. I thrust my coat and hat into her waiting arms and closed the door behind me.

The receiver was lying on the desk. I slid into Sir Arthur's swivel chair and lifted it to my ear, drawing the ebony body of the candlestick telephone towards me. I positioned myself before the mouthpiece.

'Stella, is that you?' Tristan's words spilled from him with quick-fire rapidity. 'I had to telephone, I couldn't wait until I got back to tell you.'

His excitement, palpable even over the hiss of the telephone line, was infectious, and an irrepressible thrill bubbled inside me as I asked him what had happened.

'I went to the address in Hackney. Stella, it's a Salvation Army home for unmarried mothers.'

It made perfect sense. Mrs Probert was convinced Mrs Henge would have made the necessary arrangements and her options would have been limited. The home in Hackney would have been the best idea – care for Miss Scott at the end of her confinement, access to medical attention during the birth, and no doubt a grateful couple waiting to adopt at the end.

'But, Stella, there's more. I managed to charm the matron – a financial incentive goes a long way these days – and she checked the records for me.'

'And?' Desperate to hear the rest, I almost wished I could somehow transport myself through the network of lines so that I could hear it all face to face.

'She found a Miss Ruth Scott in the records. The dates are a match. She delivered a healthy baby . . .'

There was a tantalising pause. I pulled the telephone closer to me, pressing the receiver tighter to my ear, fearful that whatever Tristan was about to impart would become garbled by the static and lost.

'The adoption of the baby had been arranged, but Stella – it never took place.' Tristan's voice dropped. 'Stella, Miss Scott left . . . and she took the baby with her.' There was another pregnant pause. I could almost picture him in my mind's eye, summoning the courage to tell me the rest, wetting his lips to speak the words. 'Stella . . . she had a son. Miss Scott gave birth to a baby boy.'

The line rasped and clicked as we lapsed into a loaded silence. Two babies. Two boys. Two Brightwell baby boys. My mind raced back over what I had been told – Lady Brightwell's son delivered late, while Miss Scott's son had presumably been delivered on time. Two births, almost coinciding.

'What did she do with him? What did she do with her baby?'

'Don't you see, Stella?'

I could tell from the pleading note in his voice that he didn't want to say it out loud, he wanted me to spare him that, to spare him the horror of putting into words exactly what had happened in this house all those years ago. But I wouldn't say it, I couldn't. It was too horrible to contemplate, the ramifications – ramifications which would have a profound effect on the one person I loved above all other living souls – were too far-reaching. But the teasing fragments of information, those colourful shards of gossip, supposition and deduction, were beginning to settle themselves into position, creating a telling picture. I closed my eyes. I would not be the one to say it.

Sensing my reluctance, Tristan's voice came once again through the line, the realisation formed in his mind slipping unbidden into my ear, worming its way into my brain.

'What if she brought him with her, Stella, back to Greyswick . . .'

His words tapered off, his courage failing him. In that split second, we had the chance to remain in blissful ignorance, to ignore the facts and walk away, leaving the pieces of the puzzle scattered behind us, an unformed truth. But he did not hold his tongue, he would not keep his own counsel.

'What if she brought her son back . . . and hid him in plain sight?'

I clung to the edge of the desk. Dear God, could he be right?

'Stella, Stella, are you still there?'

I assured him I was – still present but reeling.

'We need to talk more on this,' he said. 'I'm going to catch the next train. I'll be back in a couple of hours at most. Are you all right?' he added, the concern evident in his voice.

I lied when I told him I was quite well. There was a resonant click on the line as he terminated the call. I replaced the receiver on its hook and pushed the telephone back into its correct position at the corner of the desk. My following immobility contradicted my racing thoughts. I was a duck on the pond – so peaceful above the surface, but all frantic movement beneath, as I propelled myself through the horror augured by this latest intelligence. After a while I couldn't bear to contemplate it any longer, and I rose, steeling myself as I headed for the door.

Maisie was loitering in the corridor, waiting for me. She dipped a shifty curtsy and I wondered whether she might have been eavesdropping. She informed me Lady Brightwell wished to see me in the drawing room. I pressed my fingertips to my aching temples.

My surroundings seemed unbearably oppressive now, knowing what I did, and as I trailed after Maisie, I was more aware than ever of the coffin-like quality to the airless corridors, the density of the shadows clinging to the walls, and the burden of secrets that depressed this monstrous confection.

Maisie opened the drawing-room door and pulled it to as soon as I had crossed the threshold. I had the perturbing sensation of a prison door clanging shut.

Lady Brightwell and Miss Scott were seated on their usual sofa beside the fire, facing me, but I was surprised to see they were not alone. Sitting opposite them with his back to me was a broad-shouldered gentleman, a few ribbons of grey hair stretched across his liver-spotted pate.

I was alerted by a familiar rustle of skirts. A shifting shadow caught the corner of my eye and I snatched round to see Mrs Henge move to bar the door. My instinctive alarm bells, honed from months of bitter experience, began to clamour their frantic warning.

'Ah, Miss Marcham, here you are at last.' Lady Brightwell's

jewelled hand tapped the arm of the sofa in satisfaction as she fixed me with a rapacious smile, her beady eyes gleaming with satisfaction. 'We've been waiting for you. Miss Scott and I have had the pleasure of enjoying the company of an old family friend of yours . . .'

With a gusty puff of breath, the gentleman before me set down his teacup and stood, turning to face me. He smiled, though the expression failed to alleviate the arctic qualities of his frozen eyes.

Dread flooded through me.

'Dr Mayhew,' I whispered in horror.

Chapter Forty-Nine

'Hello, Stella, my dear, how are you?'

He seemed so harmless standing there in a tweed jacket buttoned over a plum waistcoat, a complementary paisley cravat tied at his throat, his puffed-out cheeks mottled red. He looked like a genial uncle come to visit, but I took his presence as a portend of things to come. This was no chance encounter – he had been sent here, and there could be only one possible reason for that: he had come to take me back.

I fought to maintain my indifferent exterior, clutching my hands before me in a crenulation of knuckles to hide any tell-tale tremor. I offered him a spurious smile and bade him welcome, hoping I alone could detect the potency of my insincerity. It was all I could do to squeeze the platitudes out – my throat felt like a tied off vessel and I could feel the pressure building up behind the stricture; I doubted my ability to contain it. If I ended up screaming at the man like a banshee all would be lost. It would be everything he desired – it would be my undoing.

I managed to clear my throat and I expressed my surprise at seeing him at Greyswick.

'Your mother asked me to come, Stella. Ever since receiving Lady Brightwell's letter she's been very concerned about you.'

'Lady Brightwell's letter?' I blurted out, staring at the woman in disbelief. She shivered with triumph over her skilful coup de grâce.

'She was rather taken aback by Madeleine returning unexpectedly, but the fact that she did so alone – leaving you here – struck her as very odd indeed, especially with Madeleine unable to offer any sensible explanation as to why. She was quite beside herself when she received Lady Brightwell's note and so, contacted me. I managed to wheedle out of Madeleine the details of recent events. Your mother,' he continued, tucking his hands behind his back in a most officious manner, 'wants me to bring you back to Haverton.'

'Oh, dear Miss Marcham,' Miss Scott shuffled forward on the sofa, 'we had no idea you had been so unwell – you poor child! Some rest at home will be just the thing. You've had so many crosses to bear, you must look after yourself now, my dear.'

'But I can't go home, not yet.' This multifaceted attack put me on the defensive, and not in a way that could be construed as beneficial. Even to me my rebuttal sounded petulant. 'There's no reason for me to go home just yet, Dr Mayhew.'

'I think there is, Stella. Madeleine is no longer here – there is therefore no need for you to stay, and I understand that your continued presence has become rather *unsettling* to the rest of the household.'

I couldn't help but respond to the irony of it all, and the laughter that erupted from me had a tinge of mania to it – how could it not, knowing all I did? They found *my* presence unsettling!

'Dr Mayhew,' I informed him at last, 'they are unsettled by what I have uncovered.'

There was a palpable frisson in the air. Lady Brightwell's talon-like fingers contracted, anchoring her to the sofa. Beside her Miss Scott paled, bearing the startled look of a hare caught in a lamper's beam.

It was Dr Mayhew who spoke, though I had expected a rejoinder from one of the women present. He scratched at his head.

'Ah yes, Stella. Lady Brightwell has been telling me about your unhappy obsession with her late stepson.'

'I might point out, Dr Mayhew, that Madeleine has also—'

He didn't allow me to finish. A flare of irritation crossed his face and he held up his hand which, to my shame, brought me to a faltering stop. 'Stella, Madeleine herself has told me the sad tale of the boy, and your shared conviction he haunts this house.' The wet tutting that punctuated the statement indicated his exasperation. 'Miss Scott was so kind as to show me the portrait of the boy. Don't you see it, Stella? I saw it straight away. I understand why the child's unfortunate history should have such a profound effect on you and your sister.'

His comment threw me off kilter. He waited for my confusion to embed before continuing.

'He was the same age as Lydia when he died – the same golden locks, an angelic face, a tragic end . . .' He swung back to Lady Brightwell. 'The loss of their sister when they were all at such a tender age has had a long-lasting impact on these girls, Lady Brightwell. I fear we are still seeing its unfortunate repercussions.'

'He's not Lydia,' I cried out, catching hold of the chair before me. 'It's not because of her—'

'You have been unable to save the ones you love, Stella

– trying to find some mystery that doesn't exist to explain this young boy's death won't help you save him either. Don't you see this pursuit of yours is as firmly entrenched in the present as it is the past? It is all intricately bound to the loss of Gerald – you must realise that?'

'No, you are wrong, Dr Mayhew. Madeleine heard him too – and Hector and—'

'Madeleine has her own reasons for being susceptible to this sad, sad story, Stella, you know that. And as for the rest, well, Lady Brightwell has been explaining this Mr Sheers' theory for it all and I have to say, it seems the most likely explanation.'

'But he doesn't believe that any more!' I was growing desperate. The walls were closing in on me. 'Tristan has also experienced things now which have made him revise his first impressions—'

'And where is Mr Sheers?'

'He's not here – he's on his way back from London.'

The snatched look Dr Mayhew exchanged with Lady Brightwell did not escape my notice.

'Stella, I've already asked for your things to be packed. You and Annie will be returning with me this afternoon.'

Annie. 'I won't come,' I announced, tightening my grip on the chair. 'I'm not coming home yet, Dr Mayhew, no matter how much you might try and make me. We're so close, you see, so close to discovering the truth, and we owe that to Lucien. The truth is what he wants, and he won't rest until he has it. And until he rests, Madeleine will never have any peace in this house.'

'Stella, Stella, Stella . . . Have you stopped to listen to your-self?'

The good doctor had undergone a marked transformation. Gone was the kindly cajoling; there was an underlying malice to his temper now. I had tested his patience, it seemed, and worn it thin. Too thin.

'All this talk of ghosts and ghouls – can't you see the absurdity of it all?'

It was a test. The answer to the question could clear or condemn. It was so tempting to acquiesce, but I would be betraying myself and all that I believed in. One of the characteristics Gerald had always cherished in me was my forthright self-belief, my unwavering convictions, and I wouldn't waver now. Annie, Tristan and I were on the brink of discovery. It would be treachery to turn my back, to selfishly save my own skin.

'I would have been the first to agree with you when I arrived at Greyswick, Dr Mayhew,' I told him in as mild a manner as I could muster. I did not want confrontation for confrontation's sake. I knew I had to do my best to appear rational and controlled – *reasonable*. 'But since then I have experienced things that are inexplicable – and I have learnt things which are unforgiveable.' I paused. 'Have you not wondered why everyone is so keen to see the back of me?'

'From what I've heard of your behaviour – and am now witnessing myself – I don't think I need to ask,' Dr Mayhew retorted, earning a 'harrumph' of approval from her ladyship.

'Perhaps your energies would be better spent contemplating the behaviour of others within this house, Dr Mayhew.' A thought occurred to me. 'You're a magistrate, aren't you? Don't you have a duty to justice? Or is that only when it suits you?'

'Careful, Stella, you are in danger of overstepping the mark.'

'How is trying to seek justice for a little boy pushed to

391

his death "overstepping the mark", Dr Mayhew?' I left the allegation to ricochet around the room.

'Stella, that is a fanciful, malicious – good God, a libellous – thing to say,' he blustered, outraged at my audacity.

'It is merely one of several scandals I have uncovered since my arrival, Doctor.'

'Enough, Stella! I will not hear any more of this fanciful nonsense.'

'It is not fanciful nonsense, Dr Mayhew. You can ask Mr Sheers when he returns, you can ask Annie now—'

'Ask Annie Burrows?' He spluttered her name with utter contempt, the thread veins in his cheek flaming with indignation. 'Good God, why would I believe a word that came out of that miscreant's mouth?'

'She is hardly a miscreant.'

'She is a malevolent troublemaker and has been since she was a child. Honestly, Stella, you surprise me. Are you telling me you lend credence to that girl? I know your parents feel some misplaced debt to her family, but if you have been gullible enough to swallow the stuff and nonsense that girl so wilfully fabricates—'

'You malign her for no reason, Dr Mayhew.'

'I have known Annie Burrows long enough to know what type of girl she is, Stella. I must confess I am most disappointed in you. All I can think is she has exerted some poisonous influence over you, taken advantage of your weakened state—'

'My weakened state?' I laughed at that. Here was the real absurdity: the doctor's inability to see things as they were, to empathise with me in any way, shape or form. 'Annie Burrows has not taken advantage of anyone, Dr Mayhew. She has never asked for anything—'

'Stella, I hear from Lady Brightwell that the wretched girl stole from you and yet you refused to punish her.'

'She didn't steal from me, the theft was a frame-up – another attempt to get rid of us, this time because of what she'd seen – a dead baby in the cradle.'

'Dear God, Stella.' He rubbed his forehead with caricatured weariness, before chuckling, a charming twinkle in his eye. 'Are we really up to two murdered children now? Dear me, Lady Brightwell, I do wonder what kind of house you're running here.'

Miss Scott had the good grace to look uncomfortable. From her rictus smile and rigid posture, it was clear that my comments had struck a raw nerve in her at least, but Lady Brightwell was unmoved, and in an uncharacteristic display of humour, chortled with the doctor.

The jarring ridicule resonated through my skull until my head throbbed. I closed my eyes, trying to quell my broiling anger and resentment. But I could not.

'Enough!' The word shot from me like a single round. 'I will not return home with you, Dr Mayhew, and nothing you can say or do will induce me to change my mind – not until my work here is done. Madeleine must be able to return to this house without any fear, so, yes . . . I must lay ghosts to rest. I apologise for your wasted trip. I will contact my mother directly to assure her I'm quite well, but Hector has given me leave to stay, and stay I shall.'

I pivoted round only to find Mrs Henge blocking my way. In no uncertain terms, I asked her to step aside.

'I am not at liberty to do that, miss.'

I went to move round her, but she side-stepped to block

me. Her eyes flared as she dared me to try and outwit her. I have not hated many people in my life but in that moment, I hated the housekeeper with vehemence. Animus flowed like scorching lava through my veins, and before I knew it, I thrust my snarling face towards her and demanded to know her part in the whole sordid affair.

Like peering into a mirror, the strength of that contempt reflected straight back at me, her pupils onyx gateways into the abyss of her soul. I shuddered and pulled back in alarm, shocked by the innate nefariousness I saw.

'Come, Miss Marcham. The doctor wishes you to go with him.'

'I will not go,' I reiterated, backing away from her. I spun around to face Dr Mayhew. 'I will not go with you. You cannot make me.'

I twisted between the two of them, aware they were both advancing upon me. I had to get out! I made to dart around Mrs Henge, but she was too fast for me. With speed that denied her age, she sprang sideways to block my path, her face alive with the thrill of it all.

'Come, come, Miss Marcham, you should do as the good doctor asks, no one wants any fuss.'

'Who are you to tell me what to do, Mrs Henge?' I hissed. I was a trapped creature, preparing to fight for its survival. It was an ambush, I realised that now. I was never intended to walk out of this room except under duress. I wondered where Annie could be and whether she would come if I screamed her name. But then what could she, a mere maid, do in the face of Dr Mayhew, Lady Brightwell, even Mrs Henge? Tristan might have added some authority to my cause, but he wasn't here. I realised the extent of my vulnerability.

'You're getting worked up, Stella, you need to calm yourself.' Agitated, I whirled back to face Dr Mayhew who was moving closer now.

'I am not.' But my breaths were frantic. 'You don't understand all the facts, Dr Mayhew. What I'm saying is true, what Annie saw in that cradle – it's all true. There was another baby in this house, another Brightwell boy—'

'I think things have gone far enough, Doctor,' Mrs Henge interjected. I spun back to glare at her. 'Poor Miss Marcham is clearly unwell, it is for her own good.'

Before I could retort I felt a stinging pain, as something sharp plunged into the soft flesh at the back of my neck, penetrating deep into the tissue. I cried out in alarm, slapping at the site of the puncture wound, turning my head in time to see the good doctor push the contents of his syringe into me.

My head began to swim, my vision narrowing, drawing me into a tunnel edged with darkness. Mrs Henge's stern features blurred before me, as Dr Mayhew's voice became a distorted echo in my ear. I tried to speak, but my tongue, thick and cumbersome, was unable to form the words that oozed drunkenly around my brain. I couldn't feel my legs.

Strong arms supported me as I sank to the ground. My head was lifted and something soft placed under it, while the rest of my bones butted against the floorboards. I wanted to call out for help – I knew I needed to, I *must* – but my voice was as paralysed as my useless body.

'I have arranged for a private ambulance to transport us back to Haverton.' Dr Mayhew's words seeped through my befuddlement. 'I asked them to be here at five, that's only an hour. This should keep her quiet until then. Is the maid around, do you know? I'll take her with me, of course. Lady Brightwell, I can only apologise on behalf of the family for what you've endured. I put it down to losing her young chap – it hit her terribly hard, you know – that and the pernicious influence of the Burrows girl. She's a "bad 'un" as they say – a troublemaker to the core. I did advise Mrs Marcham against her employ, but there is a history there, you see . . .'

I was vaguely aware of the conversation continuing as Mrs Henge's polished boots crisscrossed before my eyes. I drifted in my mind as they discussed what to do with me, where to put me until the ambulance arrived. The lady's parlour was agreed upon – out of the way and lockable, should it prove necessary.

I saw the bottom edge of the door loom towards me, and I watched Mrs Henge's black boots retreat through it. Dr Mayhew's brown brogues, sheened to perfection, passed before me. I noticed a thread from the turn-up of his trouser trailing down, floating in the air as he moved. He and Lady Brightwell launched into an amiable discussion on the weather, while I lay draped across the floor like an animal pelt. A solitary tear toppled over the rim of my eye and trailed down my cheek.

A pair of stubby legs ran up to me through the open doorway, stopping just short of my face. I could see buckled black-patent shoes, and long white socks topped at the knee by the buttoned cuff of blue knickerbockers. My heart, sluggish until that moment, surged into life. I managed to move my lips to form a name, though I had no voice to utter it.

Lucien

I watched as those same sturdy legs turned and ran back through the doorway.

Lucien

I hung on for precious seconds then, defeated, I let go . . . sinking into oblivion.

Chapter Fifty

I am drowning, sinking down and down into the cold swirling waters, waiting for Gerald to escort me from this world to the next.

But then I am buoyed up, towards a pool of light shimmering on the rippling surface. An obscured face peers through the undulating skin of my watery grave.

It calls me back.

My chest exploded with a wrenching gasp as I jerked awake. Pinpricks of colour exploded and died before my eyes like dissipating fireworks, fading from the night sky. I blinked, trying to orientate myself. I wanted to move, but my head was a leaden weight and my limbs refused my will. Annie's familiar freckled face hovered above me, her lips moving, and gradually I began to interpret the sound.

'Miss? Are you all right, miss?'

I was lying on a chaise longue. I had no feeling below my neck and my mouth had an unpleasant metallic taste. I wet my lips.

'Dr Mayhew . . .'

'I know.'

My eyes blurred with unexpected tears. Though my body had been deadened and defeated by whatever immobilising drug he had shot into my veins, my emotional heart remained strong and vibrant, pumping raw fear.

'Don't let him take me.'

'I won't.' Annie took my hand. 'But you can't stay here – an ambulance is on its way. We must hide you. Can you move?'

I thought I detected a twinge of life in my legs, but after an age of trying I was still lying motionless on the chaise, my head spinning, darkness swooping from the edge of my vision like a flock of crows. Terrified, I shook my head.

She patted my shoulder in a gesture meant to reassure, but the comfort was undone by her look of sheer panic.

'No matter,' she whispered. With a rustle, she got to her feet and crossed to where I could no longer see her.

'Can you help her?'

Whoever was with us in the room was beyond my limited range of vision. I tried to raise my head, but I hadn't the strength. My eyelids slid shut like a bank teller's blinds, closing me off from the world. My breaths were shallow, and I knew I was fading again – it was easier to succumb than to try and forge against it.

I was roused by two strong arms shuffling under me, hefting me up. I landed against a khaki uniform jacket, redolent of tobacco.

'Gerald,' I whispered.

'No, miss,' Annie said. 'It's Billy, Billy's here to help.'

Of course. How foolish of me. Gerald was dead – even in my drug-befuddled state I knew that, for that phantom pain was untouched. I was too weary to express any apology for the confusion. I surrendered to Billy's arms and as oblivion repeated its insistent summons, I closed my eyes and offered it no resistance.

When I finally came to, the rich golden beams stretching into
the room suggested evening was approaching. I groaned as I
tried to move. My muscles ached as if they had been wrung out
like a dish cloth, and darts of pain flew up my calves and thighs.
With considerable effort, I hauled myself upright. I grabbed the
edge of the sofa as a whirlpool of nausea swirled in my stomach.

'You're awake.'

Annie squatted at my feet, her white pinafore scooping
between her knees, her keen eyes searching for residual signs of
Dr Mayhew's doping. I assured her I was much improved and
pushed myself to my feet. I wobbled alarmingly. She steadied
me, holding me firm until my sense of balance awoke from its
drug-induced dormancy. Her suggestion that I perhaps sit down
and rest a while longer seemed sensible and was delivered just
as my knees gave way. I crashed back down upon the leather
sofa. Gradually my equilibrium returned, and I ceased to feel
like a bobbing pony on a speeding merry-go-round.

'Goodness . . .' I rubbed my eyes and tried to place myself
– the fixtures of the room all vaguely familiar yet not quite
within my grasp. And then I knew. 'We're in the smoking room,'
I declared, with a mix of horror and grim fascination.

'I didn't know where else to take you. They'd put you in the
lady's parlour. This was the nearest room.'

'But Mrs Henge locked it up.'

'There are many ways to open a locked door, miss.'

Annie moved over to the window, holding back the heavy
swag of brocaded curtain to peek out. I remembered Madeleine
saying this room afforded the best view of the driveway, and I

realised with a shudder that Annie was on the look-out for the ambulance. The perilousness of my situation struck me anew.

I was living on borrowed time. I couldn't hide for ever, and Dr Mayhew was a determined man. Whatever Lady Brightwell had written to my parents – whatever Madeleine had revealed – had placed me in terrific jeopardy. For months I had managed to resist his single-minded campaign to have my recovery facilitated by an institution, but now my ill-advised dalliance in a ghost story had provided fuel for his fire. My parents would no longer be swayed by Madeleine – not now she had revealed her own convictions. I was on my own. Alone – save for Annie Burrows.

My liberty now depended on the two of us finding a way out of this hopeless situation. The only escape route I could envisage was to reveal what had really happened in this house all those years ago. That truth and evidence of my sanity were now inextricably linked – the exposure of one would confirm the other. I had to prove I was not mad and securing justice for Lucien was the only way to do it.

Annie called for my attention at the sound of crunching gravel and the drone of an engine. I waited for her report with bated breath.

Her taut shoulders eased. 'It's only a taxi, miss.' The dull 'thuck' of a closing door penetrated the room. 'It's Mr Sheers back, miss!'

I couldn't contain my relief for here, at last, came reinforcements! Tristan would argue the case with Dr Mayhew, I knew he would, and an ex-officer would be harder to ignore than a perceived hysteric like myself. On weak legs, I staggered to the window.

Tristan placed his trilby before pushing back the side panel of his trench coat to delve into his trouser pocket for change. He counted the fare into the driver's hand through the open window, before the cabbie wound up the glass and steered the taxi away.

'He won't know what's happened,' I said.

Annie began to sharply rap her knuckles against the glass. When Tristan failed to respond, I joined her, trying to get his attention, but he must have been too far away or otherwise distracted. He picked up his battered briefcase and began to limp towards the front door. He disappeared up the porch steps.

'What do we do now?'

We couldn't risk leaving the smoking room – no one knew we were here, and whilst I wanted nothing more than to run from Dr Mayhew, I knew I couldn't leave the mystery of Greyswick unsolved. And where would I run to? I couldn't run home, and I couldn't run for ever. While my sanity was in question, I would never be safe from the good doctor's ministrations or my parents' misgivings. I had to quite literally lay this ghost to rest, to vindicate myself once and for all.

I longed to speak to Tristan. I needed to discuss with him the implications of his discovery. I was just debating how I might get to him without being caught when fate intervened.

Familiar voices leaked into the room, and from their rapid modulation, it was evident an argument was unfolding. Annie and I hurried to the locked door, straining to hear the growing dispute between Tristan and Dr Mayhew, brusquely interrupted by Lady Brightwell.

The voices clashed in anger, their words indistinguishable, muffled by the thick oak door, but as they got louder and nearer, the words became clear. Tristan demanded to know where I was, only to be rebuffed by Mrs Henge, whose strict tones had been added to the fray. His temper heightened, and I froze with dismay as Dr Mayhew informed him I was unwell and would be leaving shortly. He was adamant I could not be disturbed.

'She was perfectly well when I spoke to her on the telephone but a short while ago.'

'Sadly, there has been a rapid deterioration in her condition, Mr Sheers. I do think it would be wise for you to concede to my medical experience in this instance. Poor Miss Marcham has been unwell since her return from France. We had hoped with sufficient rest she might make a full recovery, but it seems her time here has proved an intolerable strain. It's just all been too much.'

'I, for one, have seen no such evidence, Dr Mayhew. I would very much like to speak to Stella myself.'

'I'm afraid that won't be possible.'

'What the devil have you done with her?' There was a plaintive note in Tristan's voice, and I pressed my palm against the door, willing him to come closer, to sense my presence. Lady Brightwell waded into the argument.

'Mr Sheers, really, it is most advisable that you leave Dr Mayhew to his work. He has far more knowledge than anyone else in these matters. Miss Marcham has fooled us all with a show of stability but sadly that is all it is – a show. Her parents are deeply concerned for her well-being, Dr Mayhew would not be here otherwise.'

'No.' The single word was stubborn and bullish. 'There is nothing wrong with Stella. I will see her – I demand to see her.'

'My dear boy, it is beyond your authority to do so,' Dr Mayhew informed him.

I wouldn't – couldn't – wait a minute longer.

'Open the door!' I urged Annie.

'I can't. I haven't got the key.'

'But you got in here!'

Without waiting for her answer, I hammered on the wood to summon Tristan's attention. It worked. He shouted my name. Hurried footfalls and conflicting voices indicated a flurry of activity drawing towards us.

'Stella?'

He was just beyond the thick barrier of oak. The handle rattled, twisting round but to no effect. He demanded the door was opened, but Mrs Henge denied his request. The wood shuddered as he landed his shoulder against it.

'Open this door, I tell you!'

'She is not in there, Mr Sheers. She cannot be.'

To refute the housekeeper's statement, I banged again, calling Tristan's name.

'Open it, I tell you.' The door bucked in its frame.

Clearly astonished, Mrs Henge was most vociferous in her assertion I had been left in the lady's parlour.

'I don't care where you think you put her, Mrs Henge, she is clearly here now, and you'd best open this door without further delay or so help me I will break it down.'

To make his point, he slammed against it one more time. Lady Brightwell, alarmed now at the potential damage to be wrought, ordered Mrs Henge to unlock the door.

Annie and I stumbled back as the key clattered into the lock, and with a click, the door was thrust open. Tristan wasted no time barging past the housekeeper-cum-gaoler to reach me. He grabbed me by the arms, but the roughness of his action was countered by the sincerity of his concern, as he asked whether I was quite well and if I had been hurt in anyway.

'Don't let him take me,' I whispered. With an almost imperceptible shake of his head, he relinquished his hold, but remained by me. Lady Brightwell and Miss Scott stood either side of Dr Mayhew, while Mrs Henge began to stalk around us, as if intending to outflank our position.

'I see nothing wrong with Miss Marcham,' Tristan said, 'and I see no reason why she should be removed from this house against her will.'

'Mr Sheers, I'm sure you nurse a belief these actions of yours are somewhat gallant but believe me when I say your gentlemanly intervention is unwarranted and unnecessary.' Lady Brightwell punctuated her points with the tip of her cane which she tapped against the floorboards. 'The girl's parents want her back and Dr Mayhew here is to escort her home.'

'I don't believe for a moment home is where you will take me, Doctor.' My voice was tight, and I hated the vulnerability that crept into it against my will.

'You are unwell, Stella,' he purred, like a hypnotist using suggestion to exert his will over a subject. 'Now, all of this nonsense has to stop . . .'

He had inadvertently awakened the kraken.

The knocking started so faintly I almost missed it. While Dr Mayhew and Lady Brightwell continued to discuss the benefits of my removal, Annie caught my eye and tipped her head towards the soft sound emanating from the wood panelling by the fireplace. Tristan mirrored my confusion as he too detected the light telegraphic tapping. It was like a shy child tugging on a sleeve, begging for attention. My pulse skipped as I realised it was quite possibly just that. It grew louder and more insistent.

'What is causing that noise?' Lady Brightwell demanded at last.

'I assure you it's not water in the pipes,' Tristan murmured.

'It's here . . .' There was a pensive quality to Annie's speech as she stepped forward, eerily transfixed on a particular panel, a slight smile playing at the edges of her mouth. 'He's found it.' She turned to face us. 'He's found what he's looking for.'

Lady Brightwell's creped skin drained to the colour of weathered bone. Her grip tightened on her cane. 'Who are you talking of, girl?'

Annie blinked in surprise. 'Why, Lucien, of course. He knew it was here somewhere. Now he knows where.'

Miss Scott darted a look at Mrs Henge, and in that unguarded moment I saw something pass between them: a shared frisson of shock.

What sounded like a hammer blow resounded off the two-foot square of oak. 'This is your malevolence at play,' Dr Mayhew blustered, rounding on Annie. 'Whatever witchcraft you're engaging, I demand you stop at once.'

'This is not witchcraft, Dr Mayhew,' I assured him, invigorated by the strange energy in the room. 'This is not Annie Burrows' doing. This is Lucien Brightwell.'

Before the good doctor could protest further, a second blow sounded off the very same spot.

'It's there,' Annie whispered. 'We must look there.'

Wasting no time, Tristan crossed to the fireplace and lifted down one of the picks. I held his grim gaze. Taking an awkward step back, he swung the pick, hesitating for only a second before he brought it to bear. Its spiked head splintered through the wood, ringing against the brick beyond.

Lady Brightwell cried out in dismay, but Tristan paid her no heed. Instead he looked to Annie. She nodded. Dr Mayhew called out for him to stop, but Tristan either didn't hear or didn't care, for the pick crashed into the wall again. He grabbed hold of the fractured wood and yanked it clear, fragments of plaster clattering onto the floorboards. Hell-bent, he lifted the pick one more time.

There was an avalanche of masonry and a cloud of dust as the exposed brick shattered under the pick's blow. Coughing, Tristan batted his hand to clear the air, before bending down to tug away at the loose debris until a decent-sized hole had formed, a miniature gateway to the crevice beyond. His shoulders stiffened as he peered into the darkness. With some difficulty, he plunged his hands into the cavity, and with utmost care, he withdrew his treasure.

It was a small bundle, a dust-encrusted lozenge, thickly draped in drab cobwebs with clearly little weight to it. The room was silent, the rest of us reduced to alabaster statues.

'What is it?' I whispered at last, making a guarded advance.

With extreme caution, he peeled back the top layer of fabric.

As the grimy exterior fell away, it revealed a brilliant array of blues and gold. My heart stopped.

I knew that blanket.

I had seen it once before, meticulously reproduced in a cherished drawing. Lucien Brightwell's drawing.

Taking infinite care, Tristan unwound a further layer. With a ragged intake of breath, he laid the parcel upon the chesterfield and recoiled. My hand flew to my mouth, but too late to contain my moan of abject horror.

There, jutting up through the final fold, was a tiny, perfectly preserved, skeletal hand.

Chapter Fifty-One

'Well? You're a doctor, aren't you? What's your professional opinion on that?'

Tristan's voice was laced with bitterness. His question woke the rest of us from our horrified stupor. Dr Mayhew cleared his throat and with great reluctance advanced on the pathetic parcel. The atmosphere in the smoking room was so taut with expectation that it threatened to snap at any moment; we could only guess what the consequences would be.

I realised with a shudder that, deep down, I had expected this discovery. With it, all the tantalising clues fell into place. A bizarre calm spread over me, and when I looked at Annie, she too bore a serene expression, as if everything was unfolding exactly as she hoped. Except, of course, none of us had hoped to find a dead baby buried in the wall.

Dr Mayhew hovered over the sofa, building his professional courage before drawing back the remaining curtain of blanket, his pudgy fingers making light work of the leaden task. The fabric fell away, and the tiny skeletal figure lay fully exposed, tattered remnants of greyed clothing draping the pale bones. Lady Brightwell wheezed, while Miss Scott began to sob quietly beside her. Only Mrs Henge remained unmoved.

To my shame, I stared at the poor creature with morbid fascination, unable to look away. There was no mistaking it was a human baby – the swell of its tiny ribcage, its little legs and arms, its skull too big for the rest of its fragile body. Holding my breath, my heart slamming against my chest, I peered closer.

'Its head . . .' I murmured, '. . . it looks funny – misshapen, almost.' It was perhaps a wretched observation to make, but the distortion was there for all to see, distinct and even to my inexperienced eye, unusual.

Mayhew tugged his crumpled handkerchief from his trouser pocket and wiped his mouth before answering. 'It's a very young baby who no doubt suffered a difficult birth . . .' He paused in his explanation as he shoved the pocket square back. A thick finger gestured to the sides of the skull. 'The indentations you see there would be consistent with the use of forceps. The pressure that is exerted pushes the skull out of shape but of course, a baby's bones aren't hard like ours, they're somewhat malleable. Over time – usually a few months – the bones settle themselves back into a normal appearance.' He let out a sigh, punctuated with a pitying shake of his head. 'Sadly, this baby didn't live long enough for that to happen.' Reaching forward, he replaced the blanket over the skeleton, restoring some dignity.

'So, there was another baby,' Tristan said. The corrosive suspicion we shared was eating away at him. I could see it in his haunted expression, an expression I knew mirrored my own.

'My baby was born with forceps.'

Lady Brightwell spoke with shocking timidity. She shrank away as we all turned to her, cowering in the spotlight of our attention. Her imperiousness had been replaced by dawning terror.

'It was a most difficult birth. I couldn't . . . the doctor had to pull him out, my boy, he pulled him out with forceps . . .'

She rallied, her shoulders squaring, the weak chin lifting with innate pride. 'But lots of babies are born with forceps,' she said almost with defiance, though the furrows remained in her brow and the quiver in her voice. 'And this couldn't be my baby because Hector is my baby and he is alive and well.' The laugh she meted out was tinny, lacking in substance. 'Hector is my baby.' The words trembled.

I will never forget the fearful sound Miss Scott made at that moment. It was borne deep within her, in the very bowels of her soul, and it came scuttling up her insides, forcing its way through the ventricles of her heart, to burst from her as a mortifying wail of misery mired with guilt.

'I'm sorry, my lady, I'm so, so, sorry.'

Tristan closed his eyes and I longed to do the same. We stood on the brink of catastrophe and I had no desire to witness it. Annie's fingers brushed mine as they hung, splayed, at my side – in sympathy, in unity, in vindication? I didn't know which, but I took comfort from the light touch and the reassurance that I was not alone.

Lady Brightwell was quaking as she turned to her long-serving maid. Miss Scott had slumped against a chair and its sturdy arm was all that propped her up, as her body folded with wrenching sobs. Mrs Henge's stolid demeanour at last showed signs of cracking. She started towards her, her hands raised in comfort but was stopped by the harsh 'No' that cut from the companion when she got too close. The housekeeper jerked back as though physically slapped.

'Ruth – you don't have to do this.'

'Yes, I do, dear God I do!' Miss Scott sobbed. 'I can bear it no longer.'

'Bear what, Scottie?'

'Hector is my son.'

Under the insurmountable pressure of nearly thirty years' labour – the daily propagation of a terrible lie – the dam of deceits finally gave way, and the emotional confession poured from Miss Scott as we watched on in astonished silence.

'You must have known he left me with child,' Miss Scott sobbed. 'That was the real reason I went away.'

'No, you . . . you went to look after your parents.' Lady Brightwell delivered the line with the aplomb of a well-practised lie. Perhaps once, all those years ago, she had suspected – perhaps even known – the true reason for her maid's absence, but she had recited the concocted story so many times she had convinced herself of its veracity. But now Miss Scott, her face swollen and blotched by the disease of guilt, decided to disabuse her of her convenient fantasy.

'No, my lady, you know – deep down, I know you do. I went away to have his child and I would have done the right thing, I promise I would. I was all ready to give him up, even though I had come to love him so fiercely. I would have given him up if there had been no other way—'

'Ruth—' Mrs Henge's warning went unheeded.

'But my lady, your baby . . .' Miss Scott's words raced away from her and she had to gulp to recapture them. She adopted a steadier pace, ensuring their gravity would not be lost, nor the empathy and compassion she so eagerly wished to convey. 'Oh, my lady – your baby, your precious boy, I'm so sorry – but he passed away.'

The rhythmic ticking of the mantel clock was the only sound that pierced the deadened silence. Lady Brightwell's lips moved as she silently repeated Miss Scott's words to herself, as if in her own inner voice she might be able to grasp their meaning. As she did so, her bewildered gaze slid towards the blanketed bundle lying on the sofa.

'My baby passed away?'

'Oh, my lady . . .' Miss Scott took a step forward. Her instinct was to fly to her mistress, but unsure of her reception her courage failed, and she ended up hovering where she stood. 'You were so ill, and no one knew except Mrs Henge. And I loved my boy so much . . . and suddenly, I didn't have to give him up, and you didn't have to grieve.' Her tone softened, as she attempted to cajole understanding. 'And it was still his son – his flesh and blood, his heir . . .'

And here was the warped logic, I realised. She had convinced herself of the righteousness of her actions for all these years. She saw the placing of a cuckoo in the nest as a kindness. There would be no need to experience the terrible loss of a child if another was substituted in its place, for the parent to love and raise and cherish as their own. But just like the cuckoo, the placing of an imposter came at a murderous cost – something Miss Scott chose to overlook in order to perpetuate her own sense of justification, but I could not. Lucien would not permit it.

'But Lady Brightwell's baby didn't die of natural causes.' I had hoped there would be a forcefulness to my voice, but so awful was the revelation, the words crept from me, as if hoping to go unnoticed, but that was not to be the case. Released from the confines of my thoughts, they were now exposed with nowhere for them to hide, and I was glad of it. Annie nodded her approval, shimmering with fervour. Encouraged by her support, my voice rang out like a striking sword. 'Lady Brightwell's baby was smothered to make room for yours.'

'Stella!' Dr Mayhew blustered, but I ignored him. Miss Scott was shaking her head in sheer disbelief, darting frantic glances between us as she spouted her defence.

'That's not true, it's simply not true. What an awful thing to say.' Her long fingers pressed against her cheeks, nudging her glasses askew. 'Why would you say such a thing? Lady Brightwell's baby died a natural death, as so many poor mites do.'

'Is that what Mrs Henge told you, when she wrote to you at the home in Silver Street?' Tristan demanded. 'She must have urged a quick return to Greyswick – you absconded, stealing a child already promised to another.'

'It was *my* child.' Her voice was low and defiant as she met the accusation head on, unrepentant. 'How could I *steal* my own child?' She lowered her hands. 'What would you have done if fortune had smiled on you and allowed you to keep your baby?'

'Fortune didn't smile on you, Miss Scott – Mrs Henge did.' I whirled round to face the housekeeper. Only her balled fists gave any indication that her composure was slipping. 'A baby for a baby, who would know? Was that your thinking?'

Her apparent complacency fuelled the fire of indignation smouldering in my chest, as I thought of Lady Brightwell's ill-fated babe and brave Lucien refusing to be complicit. I would hold my tongue no more. The intricate fragments had coalesced, the mosaic was staggering. I took a deep breath and like an Old Bailey barrister summing up, I laid out my case before the jury.

'Everyone was stricken with the Russian influenza – who then would notice the swap? Lady Brightwell, struck down by malaise, was still confined to her bed and had barely laid eyes on the child; Sir Arthur was already back in London and I imagine in no hurry to return; and Nanny, poor devoted Nanny, succumbed at last to the illness when she saw Lucien on the road to recovery – allowing you to insinuate yourself into the nursery and put into effect your plan. You would have revenge on the master you had come to detest, while at the same time securing the eternal gratitude of the woman you loved, by enabling her to care for the child she longed to keep, however terrible its conception.'

I looked at the stricken faces before me. 'The awful reality was both boys – though begotten in very different ways – had the same father. So, who would be able to tell, in the long run? There were bound to be sufficient physical similarities to make his paternity beyond question – who would look at him and wonder about his mother? Only Mrs Probert knew about the assault and suspected the results' – I turned to Mrs Henge, my hatred bubbling – 'but you had threatened her well enough to ensure her silence. It was a perfect solution. Was that what you told yourself as you held the pillow over that poor pathetic creature? Tell me, Mrs Henge, did you feel him struggle?'

Tears pricked at my eyes, but I swallowed hard and steeled myself for the rest. 'But Lucien Brightwell witnessed your crime, and he wasn't prepared to let you get away with it, was he? That brave little boy who declared the imposter in the cradle was not his brother – even though he was, truth be told. But you couldn't take the risk, could you? And when the opportunity afforded itself, you struck again – pushing him down the nursery stairs to his death, achieving the perfect fait accompli.'

My allegations reverberated around the smoking room.

I was shocked to see silver trails scarring Lady Brightwell's withered cheeks as she struggled to compute the full meaning of what she had heard. This grief, the grief of a lost baby, was a new emotion to her, and utterly confusing, for the child she had raised and loved lived on. She now nursed this unfamiliar burden, allowing it to grow into something comprehensible. She may not have known the child she lost, but it was still part of her and precious, and it deserved so much more than the paltry hand it had received.

She was not the only one crying. There was a different grief in the room: Miss Scott was grieving her own lost innocence. She looked at me in blank disbelief, her thin lips twitching denials, yet something whispered to her, convincing her my words were true. The pleasant veil she had drawn over the intricacies of it all had been yanked aside to reveal the twisted abomination beneath.

'This cannot be . . . Her baby wasn't killed, he just died . . . And Lucien? Lucien fell – poor, poor boy. An accident.' A sob caught in her throat as she turned to Mrs Henge. 'Dear God, Constance, tell them what happened. Disavow them of these terrible lies – let them know the truth.'

A stale smile spread across the housekeeper's face. 'The truth? But you know the truth, my dear. The truth is simple: everything I have ever done, I have done in the best interests of this family. What you call murder, Miss Marcham, I prefer to think of as an example of Mr Darwin's natural selection: I acted to ensure the best of a generation went forth into the next.'

Chapter Fifty-Two

'Natural selection?' Tristan echoed in disbelief. 'You took the lives of two children.'

'It was in the best interests of this family,' she reiterated, animated by the manic conviction of a travelling evangelist as she swept towards him. 'What chance did that baby have pooling the character of those two? It was already a mewling brat – with his arrogance and her conceit, what would that child have become? A curse on the Brightwell name. But Ruth's child . . .' she spun about, her whole face easing as if caressed by a lover's breath, '. . . at least it shared her goodness, her kindness, her beauty—'

We faded away as she gazed, enthralled, at the companion, delivering a love letter of sorts – one that bore the bloody prints of the hand that wrote it.

'He would be legitimised, take his rightful place, rather than be cast out like a piece of rubbish, labouring under the badge of bastard all his life – when it hadn't been his fault, when it hadn't been of Ruth's doing.'

She pressed the heel of her hand against her forehead as she tried to control her mounting fervour and a second later her feverishness abated, and her characteristic aloofness was restored. She continued in a chilling prosaic tone that captivated us all. 'I hadn't intended to harm Lucien. I didn't know he'd seen me – I hadn't realised he was well enough to understand – but when he began with his careless comments, I had no choice. And besides, it meant Ruth's boy would become the sole heir, and after what had happened, there was poetry in that.'

There was no regret, no remorse, just an unwavering sense of her own vindication as she stood proudly before us, daring us to challenge the twisted logic of her appalling actions.

'Oh, Constance – how could you?'

Miss Scott's whisper tore the silence. Mrs Henge regarded her with genuine confusion.

'I did it for you, Ruth.'

'No, no, don't say that, never say that! I want no part in this. I told you before – I want no part in murder, but you didn't listen. You didn't listen – and now you make me carry the guilt of two murdered babes as well? No, don't say you did this for me.' She covered her face with her hands, blotting out the horror.

'What do you mean, you'd told her "before"?' Tristan asked, but Miss Scott shook her head, still refusing to look, wallowing in denial. 'What else has she done?'

'You killed Sir Arthur Brightwell,' I gasped, looking at the defiant housekeeper. It had been no coincidence after all – I had just cast the wrong woman in the role of murderess.

Miss Scott began to sob. From the corner of my eye, I noticed Lady Brightwell steady herself, one gnarled hand tightening on her silver-topped cane, the other gripping the nearest armchair. My heart contracted – how many revelations could the poor woman take?

'Sir Arthur died in a motor accident.' It was Dr Mayhew who protested, albeit half-heartedly. He tugged at the edge of his tweed jacket, hopeful yet of restoring some order to the chaotic proceedings. 'I remember it well, it was reported in *The Times*. He collided with a tree – he was dead by the time they found him.'

'I'm willing to bet Mrs Henge played a part in that crash,' I said. The housekeeper's mouth tweaked in approval, as if pleasantly surprised by my aptitude. 'It seems too much of a coincidence that his "accident" occurred mere hours after he'd written Miss Scott's dismissal letter.'

She stared into space, deliberating whether to grant me the full story. In the end, she saw no reason to hold back. Perhaps she was revelling in the attention – or perhaps she expected gratitude for services rendered.

'He was going to get rid of her – discard her, just like that, after all those years of service, and after what he'd done. I wasn't going to let him treat her like that – treat *me* like that. I knew what he was. I always made sure I hired girls who would titillate his fancy – and he knew what I was. But when you arrived . . .' She paused, casting a desperate glance at Miss Scott, but she turned her tear-streaked face away, refusing to even meet the housekeeper's eye.

Mrs Henge could see she was losing her, second by second. Any hope she had fostered of their relationship being restored was turning to dust, and the raw pain of this realisation was a pitiful sight. But I felt no pity, for I could not forget, nor could I forgive the misguided acts of love that had brought this misery upon her. My heart refused to be affected by her lovelorn words.

'You were everything I had ever wanted, and he knew that. I tolerated his crudeness, his ribald jokes – I let them roll over me like water off a duck's back. But when he did what he did to you . . . I knew I'd have revenge. It might take a lifetime, but I was determined to have it.'

Through her sobs, Miss Scott begged her to stop. Mrs Henge reached for her in silent appeal, eager to draw her into a comforting embrace, but Miss Scott now felt only revulsion for her former friend. Seeing all was lost, the housekeeper's arms fell to her sides, her shoulders bunching with defeat as her chest lifted and fell on great gasps of mounting despair.

Passing clouds drained the early evening light from the room, casting us in macabre shadows as we stood, inert, all of us struggling to process the lurid events that had taken place in this monstrosity.

I wondered then whether Greyswick had always been like this – dark and inhospitable – or whether over time, corrupted by these evil events, it had come to reflect the hatred and unhappiness trapped within its walls, gradually infecting all those that occupied it.

I certainly had been contaminated during my time here. I had longed to be cleansed by the truth but now, doused in it, I felt more sullied than ever. But details eluded me still and so I swallowed down my abhorrence and pressed on.

'What did you do to Sir Arthur?'

Miss Scott's rejection had left a rancid taste in the housekeeper's mouth. Her lips contorted into a cruel smile.

'Oh, it was easy. He took his racing car out on the same route around the estate every day at the same hour, driving as fast as he could for the pure thrill of it. He was like a child with a toy! I chose my spot and lay in wait, readying myself for his approach. I knew it was risky, but I was careful about the timing. I stepped out just at the right moment. He was so startled, he yanked the wheel to avoid hitting me, and slammed into the tree instead. He had it coming to him.' She paused, revelling in the recollection, closing her eyes to savour the destruction she had wrought, the life she had taken. 'Well, someone had to do something,' she said, then quick as lightning, she rounded on Lady Brightwell. 'Because we all knew you would do nothing, just as you did nothing that night! You were in the adjoining room, listening to her screams and yet you didn't even get your sorry soul out of bed to stop it.'

Lady Brightwell buckled under the verbal assault. Her cane slipped from her fingers and clattered to the floor as she tottered against a chair, wretchedly lamenting her guilt.

'She might have forgiven you for your despicable cowardice that night, but know this, your ladyship, I never shall.' Shoulders hitched, her fists clenched, her face hardened with hatred, Mrs Henge advanced on her crumpled mistress. 'You deserve all the misery I have cast upon you and more besides.'

Tristan moved to intercede, but the housekeeper stopped of her own volition. The tension in her shoulders eased as she smoothed her hands down the front of her ebony skirts, her ring of keys tinkling as she did so. She wore a blank expression as she turned to face the door.

'It is not about what has passed, for the past is lost,' she said, a surprising musicality to her voice. 'It is the future we must play for now.'

And before any of us could decipher her unsettling pronouncement, she strode from the room.

'Good God,' Mayhew spluttered. 'Is all that true?'

'I'm afraid so,' Tristan replied.

'But the woman's quite clearly deranged.'

'That's your favourite prognosis, Doctor.' There was acid in my observation, but I didn't care. There had been a sizeable shift in the room, and Dr Mayhew's pre-eminence had faded with the dying sun. 'For once you might be right.'

'Lady Brightwell, are you quite well, ma'am?'

It was Annie who noticed her ladyship's decline, her deathly hue, her glassy eyes, dull and sightless. She darted forward, falling to her knees to support the old woman as she slid to the floor. Lady Brightwell's white lashes fluttered against the charcoaled skin beneath her eyes. Every crease in her face accentuated her age and her frailty, each one less flatteringly drawn than ever before. With infinite care and kindness, Annie cradled her head, her fingers fumbling to undo the tiny pearl buttons on the high neck of her blouse.

Alarmed, Miss Scott pushed aside her own distress and moved to attend her mistress but Tristan blocked her way.

'Don't you think you've done enough already?'

The companion raised herself up, defiant and determined.

'I didn't know what she'd done – not with the children, at least. I believed her when she wrote about Lady Brightwell's baby, and I won't lie – her suggestion that I replace the dead boy with my own son filled my soul with joy. I hope you never have to face the prospect of surrendering a child, Mr Sheers – you cannot begin to imagine the pain and the agony. So yes, when she offered me an alternative – an alternative where I might see him grow, spend time with him, love him – I seized it, and I thanked God for it. But I swear to you I didn't know she had taken a life to make way for my boy. And I didn't know about Lucien. I truly thought it was a tragic accident and nothing more. I had no reason to suspect otherwise.'

'But Sir Arthur, you knew about that,' I said.

She faced me. 'She found the letter on his desk. She came

straight to me and told me I was to be dismissed. I was heartbroken, of course I was. I was to lose my job, my security, my lady . . .' Her expression plummeted as she glanced down at the stupefied woman, but steeling herself, she reasserted her dignified composure, though she was unable to keep the emotion from her voice. 'But most of all I was going to lose my son – but from the beginning I had known I was taking that risk and I had come to accept it. Constance told me she was going to kill Sir Arthur – God forgive me, I didn't believe her, not until it was too late.'

'All these years, all those lies,' Tristan muttered.

'How could I tell my lady the truth? For my part, a benefit of the deception was to save her pain. She didn't have to be broken by the death of her child, and not just any child, the only child she would ever be able to bear. What do you think that would have done to her? So, I let her cherish my child. It was my gift to her. I have been by her side since she was seventeen years old and, other than Hector, I have loved her more than anyone else in my life.'

And to make her point – defying us to stop her – she lowered herself to the floor and in a tender display none of us could refute, she took one of her mistress's gnarled hands and rubbed it, as she spoke soothing words of comfort to the woman she had betrayed – and who perhaps had betrayed her.

Lady Brightwell stirred, her lashes parting, the tears caught amongst them glinting in the waning light. She whispered Miss Scott's name and seeing she was with her she relaxed, reassured by her companion's consoling presence.

Tristan and Dr Mayhew helped her onto the sofa. She lay there waxen, her breathing laboured, but she rested easier with Miss Scott nudged alongside.

'What happens now?' Tristan murmured as came to me.

My response lodged in my throat as Mrs Henge reappeared in the doorway. She bore an eerie expression of peace, but that was not what had caught my attention. Clutched in her right hand, nestled against the black folds of her skirts, was a Webley revolver.

'Dear God, what the hell do you think you're doing with that?' Dr Mayhew spluttered.

In answer, she raised the gun and shot him.

Chapter Fifty-Three

Someone screamed – I realised with horror it was me. I watched in shocked disbelief as Dr Mayhew whipped backwards and toppled to the floor like a sack of spilt potatoes.

'Dear God, what have you done?' Tristan cried, as Mrs Henge lowered the pistol.

'There, Miss Marcham,' she said, 'my gift to you for providing me with the way out of this annoying inconvenience. You've wanted him dead for a long time, I saw it in your eyes when you walked in and found him.'

Annie scrabbled over to Mayhew's prostrate body. She tugged loose the bow of her apron and lifted it clear of her head, balling it up to press against the hole in his shoulder that was belching blood. The doctor made no sound.

It was Miss Scott who found the courage to face the house-keeper. She rose from the sofa, her knees clicking as she did so. She straightened her glasses on the bridge of her nose.

'What are you doing, Constance?'

'It is not too late, Ruth. I have it all worked out. Everything will be all right.'

'What are you talking about?' Despite her best efforts, a tell-tale tremble crept into the companion's voice; she was no longer dealing with the sane woman she had known all these years, but the scorned shadow of that persona, a shadow that was growing darker as the evening sun dipped in the room.

'Nothing needs to change,' Miss Henge reassured her. 'It's all thanks to Miss Marcham. It would have been more difficult without her contribution, but with her, it's all doable.'

My stomach lurched. 'What do you mean?'

'It will be a tragic tale.' She turned to me. 'We none of us realised you were so unwell, so unstable – the loss of a sweetheart can do that to you.' She said it with such sincere sorrow I realised she was speaking from her own experience. 'When you see Dr Mayhew – come to take you away – you quite lose your reasoning. We all think you've gone to collect your things, but in fact you've sought out Sir Arthur's pistol. Then you track down Dr Mayhew – and you shoot him.'

'This is madness,' Tristan said, walking towards her.

'Dr Mayhew is only the first, Mr Sheers,' Mrs Henge told him with that awful pragmatism that presaged disaster. She raised the gun to halt his limping advance. 'For this to work, more deaths will be necessary. Miss Marcham, you see, is quite deranged by grief, and sadly, she turns her hatred on anyone who tries to stop her. Including you.'

'And what about me then?' I forced my bottled voice to spill from my lips. 'If I shoot everyone in your little scenario, what happens to me?'

'Why, my dear, riddled with guilt, you realise what you've done, and you turn the gun on yourself.'

'Dear God, Constance, listen to what you're saying,' Miss Scott whispered. 'Are you going to kill us all?'

'I'm not going to hurt you, Ruth. All of this is for you.' Mrs Henge looked perplexed, disappointed by Miss Scott's lack of faith. 'With them gone, it can just be you and me here, and Hector will return to run the family estate, and the next generation will be born. We can all be happy, together, without the past interfering, casting cloud on our joy. Wouldn't you like that, Ruth? Wouldn't that be the perfect ending after all that's happened? Just as it should be. Your boy, heir to all of this, and you, always safe, always cherished.'

Tristan had used this distraction to make a surreptitious advance on Mrs Henge's position. He was forced to stop as the housekeeper finished her evocation of the golden age that awaited Greyswick.

I had to help him. Mrs Henge had lost all reason – our only way out was to force the gun from her hands.

'But she'll never be safe, will she? Not now – not from you.'

The housekeeper whirled towards me. 'I would never hurt Ruth! I love Ruth!'

'But look at the burden you've made her carry. You've killed three . . .' I glanced at Dr Mayhew's inert body and my stomach roiled. '. . . *four* people for her. How is her conscience supposed to live with that? Knowing that her happiness has been bought in blood – happiness that she never anticipated and never asked for.'

She shrugged, callous and disinterested. 'That will all be forgotten when it is just us here, with Hector.'

'You paint a rosy picture, Mrs Henge, but you have over-looked one small fact,' I said, fanning my sole ember of bravery; as it flared alive, it felt good to be so bold. 'You are rather taking it for granted that Miss Scott still feels the same way about you – but I am not so sure. It appears, to me at least, her unwavering affection is dedicated to another woman – the mistress she gave her son to.'

It was immediately apparent I had put my finger upon the canker that had been growing inside Mrs Henge. She had tried to deny its existence, but there it was, and its malignancy threatened to destroy her. Seeing Tristan inch closer, I pressed my advantage.

'I think when you revealed your true colours – when you killed Sir Arthur Brightwell – she realised what you were, and she found you abhorrent.'

'No—'

'A poor excuse for a human being – and you've just confirmed that now, here in this room.'

With a look of pure loathing, she levelled the gun at me. I looked down its threatening barrel, but I was not afraid. I had nothing to live for – death had long since ceased to hold any fear for me. I realised I was afraid only for those around me.

'Constance, no!' Miss Scott cried out, and the finger that twitched against the trigger hesitated. 'She's right – I might have cared for you once, but no more. Your decisions, your actions, have kept me here as your prisoner. I don't think you did it for me, Constance, I think you did it all for you.' The charge escaped her as a broken whisper bordered with contempt. 'You know I would have left, all those years ago. I would have put it all behind me and rebuilt my life, never forgetting my son, but accepting a life without him – perhaps I might have gone on to have a proper family with children I could raise as my own. But by keeping my son in this house, you made sure I stayed, condemning me to a bittersweet existence, able to love him yet suffering the pain of seeing him call another "mother". Your selfish actions have denied me any chance of true happiness – and I hate you for it.'

The loathing that spurted from the companion was lethal and effective. With an animalistic keen that was part-pain, part-fury, Mrs Henge swung away from me, the pistol barrel slicing through the air until it settled on the woman who had become her obsession. Tristan took his chance, launching himself at the housekeeper, grabbing her arm and forcing it upwards. Mrs Henge roared, clawing at his face with her free hand as he wrestled against her, trying to prise the Webley from her iron grip. Almost matching him in height, she proved difficult to overpower, but in a final ferocious tussle, he staggered back, the gun in his hand.

'It's over,' Tristan told her.

She glared at him, her chest heaving, incandescent. 'I don't believe so.' And before any of us could react, she spun about and sprinted through the door.

'We have to stop her,' Annie said.

The three of us dashed from the room, but Tristan, hampered by his prosthetic, soon fell behind. I hesitated, reluctant to leave him in the gloaming corridor, but he instructed us not to wait. He held out the gun to me. It was a deadly gift and one I wanted no part of. Instead I snatched up Annie's hand. Exchanging a look of profound understanding, we ran.

We charged into the hall and stopped, peering through shadows searching for the housekeeper. Annie's gasp alerted me to the staircase, and I looked up just in time to see a fleeting flash of jet skirts as they disappeared onto the landing.

We took the broad steps in heroic strides, two at a time. When we reached the top, my thighs ached and my lungs burnt, seared with effort. We paused to catch our breath, and this time, I saw her first. She stood, silhouetted against the arch window at the bottom of the nursery staircase, the cut of her old-fashioned dress forming a distinct outline against the twilight sky behind her.

Spurred on, we broke into a run again, side by side, pounding down the carpeted corridor, our heavy treads muffled, like footfalls in snow. We got to the bottom of the staircase just as Mrs Henge reached the landing above. I called her name, but for some reason I couldn't bring myself to pursue her, not up those glinting wooden treads. She spun round, peering down on me through the gloom, cawing when she saw my fear, ridiculing my halted progress.

'Still afraid of ghosts, Miss Marcham?' she mocked, a dry cackle scraping up her throat.

And then I felt Annie's cool fingers slip into mine.

'Lucien.'

His name escaped her as a euphoric breath and in an epiphany I realised: as it had all started, so it would all end.

Alarm exploded over Mrs Henge's mocking features. Her torso jerked forwards as her boots skittered over the polished precipice of the top step. Annie and I stumbled back as she plunged head first towards us, her black skirts buffeted by the icy breeze gusting from the nursery landing. Her shoulder hit a step with a sickening crack and her body tumbled over and over and over, until finally she came to rest in a lifeless heap just before our feet.

Chapter Fifty-Four

Dr Mayhew had not been killed, it turned out, and for that I was greatly relieved – I don't think my conscience could have borne a different outcome. Mrs Henge's rash aim had sent the bullet through his clavicle, neatly missing anything of great importance.

Ever the stalwart, Lady Brightwell improved under the devoted attention of Miss Scott, and by the time Annie and I returned, having gathered up Tristan en route, she was propped upright in one of the leather chairs, overseeing Miss Scott's care of the poor doctor. She looked up as the three of us entered. When I muttered that Mrs Henge was dead, she nodded and looked away.

The room fell silent. The blue and gold blanketed bundle still lay on the chesterfield, though none of us allowed our eyes to stray towards it. In the end Annie gently scooped it up in her arms, cradling it against her chest, conscious, I think, that Lady Brightwell's eyes were fixed upon her, an unimaginable strain dulling their lustre. She carried the bundle from the room when we heard the ambulance crunching over the gravel.

'Where are you taking him?' Lady Brightwell blurted out, raising her hand to touch it, but then, at the last moment, losing courage.

'To the nursery. I'll put him in the cradle for now – where

he belongs.' The girl smiled, such a sweet, kind smile that my heart burst at the sight of it. 'You can decide on a proper resting place for him later, when all this is done.'

Lady Brightwell nodded and watched her go.

It was decided that Dr Mayhew's well-being should take priority over dealing with Mrs Henge. I shuddered to think of her dead body sprawled on the landing, the sightless eyes dilated with shock, blood pooling beneath her, but the living had to take precedence over the dead.

I was duplicitous as I hurried the orderlies to the smoking room, explaining a dreadful accident had led to a change of patient. I kept the details vague, until the evident urgency of the situation made my ramblings redundant. All the while, I could feel the bulk of Mrs Henge pressing down from the floor above.

Once Dr Mayhew had been despatched, we remaining con-spirators withdrew to the drawing room to plan. We were most fortunate that Maisie and Cook were absent – they had gone grocery shopping not long after my return and so would know nothing of the catastrophic events that had taken place. We all agreed it would be best if Mrs Henge's death was ascribed to a tragic accident. Tristan was eager to know what had taken place on the staircase, but Annie and I were both reluctant to explain. In the end it was Miss Scott who filled in the blanks: she leant forward and whispered a single name.

Then the practicalities of it all had taken over, the cold necessities of death. The local funeral director was called, and it was his poor men who heaved Mrs Henge's leaden body into a crude coffin and carried it from the house. Miss Scott joined me to see them out. As the door echoed shut she said softly, 'Perhaps we might all find some peace now.'

Later that night, Tristan, Annie and I gathered before the fire in my room, sipping whisky purloined from the dining room. None of us were feeling particularly effusive and we sat in silence for the most part, forever bonded by the extraordinary events we had witnessed over the last few days.

I asked Annie whether Lucien was still with us, but she shook her head.

'But you saw him on the landing?' Tristan pressed.

'Yes, he was there. It was him . . .' There was no need for her to spell it out, we knew what she meant. Lucien had exacted his revenge. 'But he's gone now.'

'Will he be back?' I asked.

She shook her head, her red hair glowing in the golden firelight. 'No, miss. He got what he wanted and now he's passed over – to a better place.'

I stared into the flickering flames, surprised by an unexpected flare of emotion. I sipped at my whisky and frowned.

'You knew all along, didn't you, that he didn't mean to hurt us?' I was perhaps a little irked by her subterfuge, but any lingering ill-feeling was soon diffused by her apologetic smile.

'I wasn't sure in the beginning, but once I did know . . . I needed your help, miss, and I knew nothing would rally you like a threat to your sister. I knew you'd do anything for her.' The smile dwindled on her lips. 'But I must confess I was afraid for myself. I didn't want to get involved – with any of it – because I knew, if I did, I'd have to reveal who I am, what I can do. I'm sorry if I misled you, miss, or caused you any grief. I must be braver and accept my ability, even if I don't like it.'

'You are remarkable, Annie,' Tristan informed her, his voice gentle, as he studied the amber liquid in his glass. He met her shy gaze. 'You shouldn't be afraid – you have a gift. Don't squander it.'

She flushed with embarrassment, but I could see her pride.

Glancing at the clock, Tristan tossed back the dregs of his whisky. Setting his glass down on the grate, he pushed himself up, explaining he had an early train to catch in the morning.

'It has been an eye-opening pleasure, Annie Burrows,' he said, smiling as he shook her hand. 'I feel I must apologise for my rather appalling behaviour when we first met, and for ever having doubted your talents. You are a very special individual, don't forget that. Perhaps I might call upon your services again in the future, if I have need?'

'I would like that, Mr Sheers,' she said.

I escorted him to the door, holding out my hand as he opened it.

'If you're leaving early in the morning, Mr Sheers,' I said, teasing him with formality, 'I might not see you, so I'll proffer my goodbyes now.' His hand dwarfed mine in its warm grasp. 'I hope you've found some resolution and maybe something to draw a little comfort from.'

A sad smile lifted his lips. 'And I hope you might find some peace, too, Miss Marcham.'

I closed the door behind him feeling oddly bereft, but I shrugged off the unsettling feeling, putting it down to the maudlin whisky, and padded back to my seat beside the fire and Annie Burrows. The silence between us grew awkward and I knew it was of my doing, because I hadn't found peace and I wouldn't – couldn't – until I had voiced the question I longed to ask. I took a fortifying swig of spirits.

'Annie, that day you fished me out of the lake, you said something to me, just before they took us inside. You said that it "wasn't my time", that "*he*" wanted me to know that.' I tried to calm my pounding heart. 'Who, Annie?' I couldn't manage more than a whisper. 'Who wanted you tell me that? Was it Gerald?'

My heart sank as soon as I saw the compassion in those odd eyes.

'No, miss. I'm so sorry – it wasn't him.'

The lump in my throat stoppered the moan that bubbled up within me. I bit my lips, willing myself to some sort of composure.

'Then who?'

Her lashes rested against her cheek for a moment, and she let out a deep, resigned sigh, before they fluttered open again.

'Your grandfather, miss. It was your grandfather that came to me that day. That's how I knew where you were and what you'd done. He wanted me to save you.' She hesitated. 'He had failed to save your grandmother and your sister – he didn't want to fail again. You see, it was him who came for my father the night of the fire. He guided him through the flames to Miss Lydia – they were just too late.'

The fire crackled between us. Annie placed her untouched glass next to Tristan's.

'I know you loved Master Gerald, but he's gone.'

'You've never . . .' But my words died on my lips. She shook her head in quiet understanding.

'He's never been back, miss, and that's a good thing – it

434

means he's at peace. Your grandfather knew it wasn't your time, he knew you had more life to live yet. You will discover peace in this world, miss, before you find it in the next.'

Tears streamed down my cheeks as the young girl, blessed with such profound understanding, rose from her chair. Smoothing her pinafore, she dipped a curtsy and wished me goodnight, before closing the door behind her.

I watched Tristan leave the next morning. It was early, but I was already up and dressed, having suffered a broken night, one plagued by too many thoughts. I cracked the curtain and peered out through the grey light of the early morn, watching as he slid inside the waiting cab. He hesitated, glancing up at Greyswick for a final time. Then the door slammed, and he was gone.

I had already decided that I would leave as soon as possible. My work was done and I was certain Lady Brightwell would not want me to loiter, an unpleasant reminder of things best forgotten. The house was silent as I descended to the hall, but somehow less daunting, and after a moment's deliberation, I plunged through the green baize door to find Annie.

My shoes clipped against the stone steps. I didn't allow myself to dwell on Mrs Henge's empty room waiting down the corridor, but instead went directly to the kitchen.

'Miss Marcham! I'm sorry, I wasn't expecting anyone.'

Cook stood up from the table, her chair legs screeching against the flags. She brushed at her cheeks and cleared her throat. I saw she was wearing a black dress under her apron. Annie, she informed me, was attending to Lady Brightwell and Miss Scott in the dining room.

'Seems everyone's up early this morning,' she said, her voice low, turning her attention to the tray of rolls on the table, glazing them with beaten egg. 'Mind you, I'm not surprised, after the shock of yesterday and poor Mrs Henge, God rest her soul. I doubt any of us slept a wink last night.'

Part of me longed to disillusion her about the housekeeper, but what would be the purpose? It would be vindictive on my part – and I was done with recriminations. I had turned to leave, when a thought crossed my mind – there was one person who deserved my thanks.

'Cook, might you be able to tell me where I could find Billy?'

'I'm sorry?'

'He's proven most helpful over the last few days and I owe him quite a debt of gratitude. I would so like to speak to him before I go.'

She lifted the tray of rolls from the table and gave me a hard look before turning away to carry them to the range. She slid the tray into the oven and clanked the door shut.

'When your girl told me what he'd said about my apple pie' – her voice was hushed, her back still to me – 'it was like he was right here in this kitchen with me, and I thought to myself, I hope he appreciates my flowers each week. And I thought too about all the things I never told him, the love I felt for him, and how I wished I'd had the courage to speak out before he left to fight the Boer.'

She turned and held my gaze. 'I don't know who's been helping you, miss, but it can't have been Billy. My Billy died in Natal, defending Ladysmith, seventeen years ago.'

Chapter Fifty-Five

I was still shaking as I opened the dining-room door. The smell of kippers flipped my stomach and I went straight to the tea urn, the cup and saucer dancing in my unsteady hand as I pulled down the handle.

'Good morning, Miss Marcham.'

I jumped with surprise. Lady Brightwell sat alone at the end of the table.

'Lady Brightwell. Good morning.'

'I hope you're not thinking of dashing off. I've been waiting for you.' She gestured for me to take a seat. 'Well, we've had quite a time of it, haven't we?'

I offered her a strained smile. 'We certainly have.'

She turned her face to the window. She looked ill and I wondered how much sleep – if any – she'd managed, and what state her heart must be in this morning. As if she sensed my musings she spoke, her tone wistful.

'I always thought Hector was too good to be mine. He is so sweet, so generous, so even-tempered. I liked to think he was my greatest achievement. As it is, he wasn't my achievement at all.'

My fingertips rested on the rim of the saucer. 'He might not be yours by birth, Lady Brightwell, but you helped form Hector – you shouldn't underestimate the impact you have had upon him. He is the man he is because of you, as much as anyone else.'

'That's very kind of you, Miss Marcham, but I don't deserve your kindness.' She looked at me. 'I don't deserve anyone's kindness.'

With great effort she stood up from the table, taking up her walking stick. She relied on it heavily as she crossed to the window.

'I love this time of year – when the rhododendrons are out, and the trees are in blossom. You must come back in the summer, Miss Marcham, the gardens really come into their own, even without an army of gardeners. Nature will have its way and still put on a display we don't deserve. It is one of the things I have missed the most, since . . .' She held up her cane. 'I used to be able to walk for miles in the estate. I'm rather restricted to the formal gardens now. It's a shame.'

She observed, more to herself than to me, the shoots of this, and the appearance of that, and how the roses should have been pruned. I began to wonder whether I should discreetly withdraw.

'Everything she said was right, you know. I was a despicable coward that night.'

She continued to study the world beyond the glass, yearning to be out there rather than trapped inside. Perhaps once she had been a wild rose, but now she was reduced to a hothouse flower, smothered by her forced environment.

'He was not a nice man, my husband. I hadn't realised that, of course, until it was too late, although it wouldn't have mattered either way – my parents were set on the match. So beneficial for all concerned.' She tapped the silver head of the cane against the glass. 'I managed to fend him off that night, citing the baby. He was not best pleased. I saw the look in his eye when he heard Scottie in the dressing room. I knew then what he would do, and when he closed the door behind him . . .' She lost the courage to carry on with her confession, a confession I found unpalatable.

She forced herself to face me. 'Mrs Henge was right – I did nothing to stop it, to my eternal shame. I must for ever bear the cross of my cowardice. I think Miss Scott believed she had spared me some indignity that night – just as nine months later she believed she was sparing me the grief of losing the only child I would ever be able to carry. I don't think I deserved another, after what I'd done – I certainly don't deserve her loyalty or her friendship.' Abashed, she glanced away. 'I must admit, I always found Miss Scott to be rather ambiguous – about *feelings*.' She gave me a pointed look. 'I was, however, very aware of Mrs Henge's predilections, and that Miss Scott was the unwavering focus of her affections – which leads me to my next confession.'

Lady Brightwell was either unaware or uncaring of my discomfort. She moved away from the window and lowered herself back down upon her chair. She rested her cane against the edge of the table.

'I was quite taken aback yesterday, my dear, by your unerring accuracy. You have clearly been busy rifling through our dirty laundry, and the discovery in the smoking room . . . well, I'm sorry now that I wasn't more credulous in the beginning, but it all seemed so fanciful to me. Poor Lucien. I hope he can be at rest now.'

'Annie believes he has gone.'

'Good. Good. Poor little fellow. I can't profess that the role

439

of stepmother came naturally to me. I was young and foolish and self-obsessed. I would have been better, given time.'

Silence stretched between us, while a ticking clock and birdsong played in the background. I waited. She had taken on a faraway look, her mind in some other place, or at least some other time. Gradually, she came back, little by little, until at last she fixed me with a cool stare.

'You aimed well when you accused Mrs Henge of killing my baby, Miss Marcham, and of killing Lucien, but I'm afraid one of your arrows missed its mark.'

My heart skipped a beat. There was only one arrow left, and I was pretty sure Mrs Henge had declared it a bull's eye. Lady Brightwell saw my confusion and she smiled, a glint in her eye.

'Mrs Henge did not kill my husband, Miss Marcham, though not for the want of trying. That dubious honour is mine, and mine alone.'

Her admission crackled through the air between us, its static electricity lifting the roots of my hair and tingling the skin along my arms. My astonishment appeared to amuse her in some macabre way – perhaps there was a perverse pleasure to be gained when one reached her age at being able to shock the young.

'But Mrs Henge—'

'Was my patsy. Well – perhaps that's not quite right. I suppose in the end, I just finished what she had started.' She tilted her teacup and pulled a face, pushing it across the table towards me. 'Would you mind? All this confessing is dry work.'

The tea was stewed now and only lukewarm, but she didn't complain. She added a dash of milk and a cube of sugar and stirred well. I was quite hypnotised by the circular motion of the silver teaspoon as it swirled round and round. Once satisfied, she set it upon the saucer.

'He summoned me to his study, quite out of the blue, and told me that he intended to dismiss Miss Scott – the letter was already written, lying on the desktop.' She levelled her gaze upon me. '*Economising* he put it down to – ridiculous, of course.' Her upper lip curled in contempt. 'It was nothing to do with economy – he did it to punish me. I had made a sly comment at a dinner party the night before about his ridiculous new fancy – some fat opera singer I wasn't supposed to know about – and he'd felt humiliated. So, to punish me he intended to take away the one friend I had. It was an act of spite. I wasn't going to let him get away with it.'

Even after all these years, her resentment was so pronounced it was not difficult to imagine the unpleasant encounter. I wondered whether Sir Arthur had ever considered his vindictive act might lead to an untimely death.

'He practically pushed me from the room and took off for his daily drive in that ridiculous car he bought when he became too corpulent for a horse. I didn't know what to do, how to stop him – and then I saw Mrs Henge crossing the hall, and it dawned on me that maybe *I* didn't have to do anything after all.'

She stopped to sip her tea, her grimace confirming it was too cold to be pleasant, but it would wet her whistle and that was all she wanted. She stared at the patch of wall between the windows as if visualising the unfolding events of that fateful day.

'I called Mrs Henge over and explained I had left my spectacles in the study and asked her to be so kind as to bring them to me in the morning room. I had done no such thing, of course, but that was beside the point. She would see the letter. That was all I wanted.'

She drew herself up in her chair, shuffling her weight, her ancient joints stiff and protesting.

'I wasn't sure what she'd do, or how long I'd have to wait, but when Sir Arthur left with his driving goggles the next day, I saw her disappear down the end of the garden at quite a pace. I knew then the time had come.'

She pitched forward, her eyes glowing with excitement, revelling in the drama she was free to reveal at last. I should have been repulsed by her eagerness, and yet I felt as enthused as she was, hanging on her every word, impatient to reach the denouement.

'I followed her. I had to admire her bravery – it was a foolhardy thing to do, but still, she did it. She ran off afterwards, satisfied her work was done. I wasn't so careless.'

Lost in thought, she stared at the table before her, her hand banging a steady rhythm on the rosewood, reminding me of a drummer beating time before the condemned man snaps against the noose. Her hand stilled.

'He had been knocked unconscious. By the time I got to the wreckage he was coming to. Dazed initially – and then furious and derogatory and pompous as ever. He tried to get out, but he couldn't, the metal had twisted and crumpled – he was quite trapped. He called me gormless and shouted at me for just standing there, then he ordered me to fetch the tyre iron from the back so I could try and prise the door open. I still remember the weight of it in my hand. He couldn't believe his eyes when I raised it above my head. I smashed his skull clean open.

'I felt . . .' she frowned as she searched for the right word, 'thrilled,' she said at last, her voice light, 'liberated, and when it became apparent I was going to get away with it – very smug indeed.'

'And all these years,' I said, when I found my voice, 'you've never let on? Not even to Miss Scott?'

'My dear, when one becomes loose-lipped about things like that, one invites disaster. No, no, I didn't tell a soul.' She pushed her cup and saucer away and paused to collate her thoughts. 'It would seem we are in the business of truth, Miss Marcham. It is too late to perpetuate lies, it seems there is nothing to be gained from them any more.'

Her features morphed into a startling image of vulnerability. 'But there is much to be lost, by revealing the truth to everyone. Miss Scott and I, we have made our peace with each other – we both needed forgiveness, I think we both deserved it. She is my oldest friend, and certainly my dearest companion. I don't hold her accountable for any of this. She has given me the greatest of gifts, one I truly didn't deserve. You have in your hands the power to take that away from me. I hope you can understand what drove me to act as I did, and I hope that empathy might spare me the punishment of revealing my secrets to my son – to Hector.'

The blood coursing through my veins chilled, cooling my skin, the fine hairs on my arms rising as they attempted to catch my escaping heat. I thought of Hector, heavy-handed at times, but I knew his heart was in the right place. And I thought of Madeleine, darling Madeleine, so kind and sweet and blissfully happy with that precious life growing within her. And then I thought of Greyswick, and the home it might become – now the secrets and lies had been purged, with Lucien avenged and justice done, and Lady Brightwell and Miss Scott clinging to enduring friendship above all else.

I pushed back my chair and stood, smoothing my skirt. I looked at the woman watching me with stark desperation.

'I see no benefit in telling anyone the truth of what happened here. Mrs Henge was right about one thing – the past is lost, but the future is still to play for.'

Her eyelids lowered in relief, and when she raised them tears clung to her lashes. She got to her feet. Picking up her cane, she began to move round the table.

'Thank you, Miss Marcham. I suspect you will be leaving us now that your work here is done. I do so hope you will come and see us again. Perhaps when the baby's born – if not before.'

A smile, almost childlike in its unaffected simplicity, played upon her lips. She patted my arm – dare I say with fondness – and shuffled from the room.

I slumped as the door clicked behind her. I flattened my palms on the table and leant against them, my head lolling. I felt exhausted, yet also relieved – even strangely euphoric. At last – at long last – all was done, all was settled.

I spent a few moments embracing my solitude. Finally, I shook my head clear of my thoughts, locking away the revelations of the past few hours. I resolved to calm myself by doing something utterly normal, if only for a few minutes, before I left to find Annie.

I sat back down and reached for Lady Brightwell's copy of *The Times*. I spread it before me and leafed through, skipping over disheartening articles about the war, choosing instead more mundane stories, those considered sufficiently newsworthy to fill a couple of inches on the inside pages.

In the end, feeling somewhat restored, I closed the paper and stood. I was just pushing back my chair when the date at the top struck me: Thursday 31st May. I drew in a sharp breath, my fingers flying to my locket, as guilt scalded my cheeks.

It was Gerald's birthday – and I had forgotten.

Epilogue

I congratulated myself on how well I managed to fudge the truth. Annie and I returned home later that day, having bid an emotional farewell to Lady Brightwell and Miss Scott, who stood side by side on the top step of the porch, waving us off until we were out of sight. Before I climbed into the car, Miss Scott had pulled me into a surprise embrace, and pressed her lips to my ear. She confided they intended to bury the precious bundle under the cedar tree in the park, without fuss, and sadly without ceremony, but at least they could always look upon it and know that he was there.

I treated Annie to a first class ticket on the way back. My purpose was two-fold: I had become very used to her quiet company, but I also had some unsettled business. We were an hour into our journey before we finally had the compartment to ourselves. As soon as the door slid shut behind a rather harassed mother and her two demanding young children, I threw myself forward.

'I know about Billy.'

I didn't need to say anything further. She flushed with guilt – as well she should.

'I was surprised you could see him.'

'Did you not think to mention—'

'I thought it best not to.'

I leant back in my seat and marshalled my thoughts.

'He picked me up.'

She shrugged and smiled. 'He saved you.'

'And what of the address, the baby home – how did he know that?'

'Mrs Henge charged him with taking an urgent letter to Miss Scott, in London. She gave him the fare, so he could take the train up without delay. He didn't know its significance – the address meant nothing to him – it was just a big house as far as he could see.'

'He told you this?' I asked, still unsure how her strange power worked.

'He showed me glimpses – the envelope, the train, the house. But I didn't know what it all meant, not then.' She shuffled forward in her deep seat to speak in confidence. 'What I don't understand, miss, is how the baby ended up in the wall the way it did.'

'Well, there I can help.'

After my extraordinary encounter with Lady Brightwell – and disconsolate for having allowed events to distract me from the significance of the day – I had gone for a walk in the grounds where I chanced upon Miss Scott. It had been a very awkward meeting at first, but having had time to ponder, I now trusted she had acted in all innocence with regards to swapping in her baby and I did not hesitate to tell her so.

She was, of course, very grateful and most relieved that she could finally divest herself of the secrets that tormented her. She had received an urgent letter from Mrs Henge, telling her the awful news that the Brightwell baby had sickened and died. The housekeeper had begged Miss Scott to return as quickly as she

447

could with her son, suggesting they make an exchange – Mrs Henge, now in charge of the nursery, could conceal the death until Miss Scott's arrival. No harm would be done, she had persuaded her friend, and nobody need ever know.

Beguiled by the prospect of keeping her beloved new-born son, Miss Scott had returned with great haste, and under careful arrangement, slipped back into Greyswick in the early hours of the morning, Mrs Henge giving her entry while the household slept.

The question then was what on earth to do with the poor dead mite. In a broken voice, Miss Scott told me of their awful descent from the nursery carrying the tiny corpse, with no clue of how to dispose of it, terrified someone would catch them at any moment.

'We had so little time,' she explained, wiping her dripping nose with a laced handkerchief. 'Constance suggested the building site of the new wing and it seemed perfect. So, we crept out onto the foundations, and chose a wall that was already half-built. We lowered the baby inside the cavity, throwing in some powdered cement to conceal him the best we could. The following morning, I returned to take up my position as lady's maid as if nothing had happened. We lived on our nerves for days, expecting the body to be discovered at any time, imagining the uproar that would follow, but it never happened. The wall got higher and higher, and then they added the first floor, and he just got lost in it all. Until yesterday.'

She grabbed my arm. 'I never forgot him, Miss Marcham, I want you to know that. I loved my boy, but I never forgot hers. You must believe me.'

And I did.

My mother was relieved to see me home, though she seemed a little dubious when I told her that Dr Mayhew had declared me quite well. I naturally thought it best not to go into great detail about the unfortunate accident that had delayed his own return.

She took my chattiness and heightened spirits as a good sign, and accepted that I might indeed be making small but significant steps to recovery – if not to my former self, then to a new self, different perhaps, but more adept at dealing with the world around her – and in these uncertain times, that could only be a good thing.

When I squirrelled myself away with Madeleine a little later, things took on a very different tone. I explained the edited highlights of what had occurred, omitting all reference to Lady Brightwell's baby on the very sensible grounds that nothing could be gained but a lot of hearts could needlessly be broken. I assured her that Lucien had passed into eternal peace and there were no more ghosts at Greyswick – except perhaps Billy, but I thought it wise not to mention him either. For the first time in weeks, she looked truly happy.

'You look different too, Stella,' she said with a smile as I went to leave.

'Do I?' I laughed. 'I can't think why.'

'You look brighter about the eyes and there's a levity to you I haven't seen for a while. And you're wearing pink,' she declared. 'Pink always suits your complexion – you look very pretty in it.'

I rolled my eyes but blushed at the compliment all the same.

I bumped into Annie Burrows in the corridor, her arms full of freshly pressed sheets. She beamed at me.

'Pleased to be home, Annie?'

'Oh, very much so, miss. I'm grateful for the peace and quiet,' she called, heading for the linen cupboard.

I smiled and went into my bedroom, closing the door behind me. My steps slowed as I approached the dressing table. I studied the reflection of my gold locket in the mirror and felt a wave of unsullied – but not indulgent – sadness wash over me. I reached behind and undid the clasp, savouring the feel of the pendant in my hand, before separating its two halves. I looked for a moment at the young woman I once was but would never be again, and I felt no regret. Life moves on, and we have little choice but to move with it. My eyes slid to the other cherished image, my fingertip tracing the square jaw, angled from the camera.

'Oh, Gerald. I love you, I always will, but the time has come for me to let you go. You were right. I must *live* . . . just as you wanted me to.' I pressed my lips to the silken surface, then snapped the locket shut. I returned it to its velvet case, before tucking it away for good in the drawer of my dressing table.

I took a deep breath to contain my swell of emotion. I had anticipated it – forewarned is always forearmed – and I let it surge over me, until eventually it ebbed away, and I felt better for its cleansing. Then I checked my wristwatch and headed from my room. The timing would be perfect.

I tapped lightly on the door of my father's study. Smiling with satisfaction at the returning silence, I let myself in. It was empty, just as I had anticipated – at this time of day he would be dressing for dinner. I gazed up at the life-sized portrait hung behind his desk – my grandfather.

He had a kind face, I had always thought that. The artist

had captured it well – the crow's feet creases hinting at jollity, the humorous quirk about the mouth – but there was sadness too, a wistfulness caught in the eyes for what might have been. I studied those familiar features again, warmth building in my chest.

'Thank you, Grandfather,' I whispered. 'I know you tried, with Grandmama and Lydia. You didn't manage to save them – but you sent me Annie Burrows, and I rather think, between the two of you, you have succeeded in saving me.'

In a spontaneous gesture, I reached up and touched the glistening toe of his shoe. 'Thank you,' I whispered again.

And as I turned away, though there could be no possible explanation for it, I swear my nose twitched at the scent of pipe tobacco, lingering in the air like a sweet memory of a warm summer's day.

Acknowledgements

The Lost Ones would not exist without my dear friend Rebecca Netley, to whom this book is dedicated. It was only through her cajoling and encouragement that I found the courage to put pen to paper and pursue my dream. I never, in a million years, imagined this would be the outcome. Rebecca, thank you for everything.

I also need to thank my lovely agent David Headley, for having such faith in me from the outset, and for ensuring that *The Lost Ones* found its perfect home with the fabulous Kate Mills at HQ Stories, who has demonstrated such patience, understanding and good judgement. I have been overwhelmed by the enthusiasm shown by the entire publishing team but, in particular, I would like to thank Victoria Moynes and Joe Thomas for all their hard work behind the scenes.

I am very blessed to be surrounded by a wonderful group of friends who have cared for and supported me in so many ways over the years. I would especially like to thank Rachael Staines, Anita Matthews and Kate Fox, who have been with me throughout this journey, as well as my oldest friends Emma Redfern and Paul Turner, for always being there, even though I'm rubbish at staying in touch!

Writing can be a very solitary exercise, but I've learnt that writers are an incredibly friendly and supportive bunch in both the real and the virtual world. It is my good fortune to belong to the brilliant VWG – virtual friends and talented writers all – who keep me constantly entertained with humorous conversations and extraordinary gifs. Their unfailing support has been amazing. You guys are the best! I would also like to thank Helen Boyce and the members of TBC for their generous help and kind words.

Finally, I would like to thank my family. My dad for patiently answering my questions on crop growth and shooting seasons, my mother for never refusing to buy me a book when I was younger and for always encouraging me to read, and my brother Charles for being on hand whenever I have computer issues!

My wonderful husband Rod has lent me his editor's eye without complaint and has been a constant tower of strength throughout the years. My gorgeous girls Isabel and Molly, of whom I am so proud, have listened patiently to me expound story ideas when I'm sure there's something far more interesting they'd rather be doing, and Jack, my treasured boy, you are a joy to me. I love you all so much. I couldn't have done any of this without you, and I wouldn't have wanted to.

ONE PLACE. MANY STORIES

Bold, innovative and
empowering publishing.

FOLLOW US ON:

@HQStories